SARA JUST ISN'T HERSELF TODAY

It's a dream, she assured herself. *You're having a dream—*

She pressed fingers to her aching temples and felt unfamiliar, thick tendrils of hair falling on either side of her face. With a sharp shriek she sprang to her feet, frightened that her short dark hair had turned into a medusa's nest of snakes.

She pinched herself, hoping she'd wake up. But all the action did was draw her attention to her slender arm and the sleeve of a faded blue blouse. She recognized neither the sleeve nor the arm wearing it.

Also by Susan Sizemore

Wings of the Storm
My First Duchess

Available from HarperPaperbacks

My Own True Love

✒ SUSAN SIZEMORE ✒

HarperPaperbacks
A Division of HarperCollinsPublishers

HarperPaperbacks *A Division of* HarperCollins*Publishers*
10 East 53rd Street, New York, N.Y. 10022

Copyright © 1994 by Susan Sizemore
All rights reserved. No part of this book may be used or
reproduced in any manner whatsoever without written
permission of the publisher, except in the case of brief
quotations embodied in critical articles and reviews. For
information address HarperCollins*Publishers,*
10 East 53rd Street, New York, N.Y. 10022.

Cover illustration by Doreen Minuto

First printing: February 1994

Printed in the United States of America

HarperPaperbacks, HarperMonogram, and colophon are
trademarks of HarperCollins*Publishers*

❖ 10 9 8 7 6 5 4 3 2 1

For William Fawcett, KCTJ—because when I asked you what Napoleon was doing in 1811 you asked, "What day?"

And to Marilyn Pulley—who keeps me supplied with Electric Gypsies and Hollywood Vampires.

My Own True Love

1

*Some things are harder to accept than others,
magic rings, for example.*

"*The mail never comes* this early," Sara said as she met the mailman at her door.

He just smiled and nodded and handed her a tattered padded envelope covered in foreign stamps. She took it inside and ripped it open in her front hallway. The package held a letter written on stiff paper, and a small box.

Sara opened the box. Inside was a small silver ring set with a cabochon-cut citrine stone. It was a pretty thing. The yellow-orange stone glowed in the sunlight as she held it up in front of her hall window. The intricate silver knotwork pattern was delicate and graceful. She recognized it, of course. It was a replica of the legendary Bartholomew Ring.

The early morning air was stifling even for an

August heat wave, but the ring was cool to the touch. It seemed to vibrate. Sara could almost imagine it giving off waves of energy. What she was imagining, she knew, were all the wondrous tales of the ring she'd heard as a child. The Bartholomew Ring was an important part of Bororavian folklore.

She slipped on the ring—it was a perfect fit—and picked up the letter. The handwriting was familiar, rather like her own, but still hard to read. It didn't help that the language was Bororavian.

It wasn't that she didn't know the language. Sort of. She hadn't been the best of students. Bororavian was a combination of Romany and Lithuanian. It was a difficult bastard language at best, and it also didn't help that the first person actually to study it had been a Chinese linguist. Unfortunately Sara spoke it more often than she read it, and she didn't speak it all that often. She squinted at the writing and did her best to decipher it.

"This has to be a joke," she said aloud after she'd worked her way through the first improbable sentence. The sentence had stated that she'd sent the ring to herself. "Either my translation's way off, or we're dealing with a practical joke here. Probably Dad's idea of a practical joke," she concluded, and went on to finish reading the letter.

By the time she was finished she had eyestrain, and was convinced her father's sense of humor was the only possible explanation. The head of the family, was, after all, on vacation in the old country. There were Bororavian stamps all over the envelope.

He'd probably found a replica of the Bartholomew

Ring in a museum gift shop, she decided. Then he had someone write this letter about a legacy from her to herself that must be delivered on August twenty-fourth or dire consequences for all Bororavia would follow. "'Use it wisely and no harm will befall the souls of the Heroes of the Revolution!' Whatever that means. You're putting me on, right, Dad?"

Sara rubbed a hand through her short black hair. She didn't know what was wrong with her. It was just a harmless joke.

"Honestly. Grandpa never should have let you run away and join a circus—even if it was as an accountant, and it was Grandpa's circus. You've got odd ideas about what's humorous, Dad. Thanks for the present, though," she added with a fond glance toward his photo. A trick of sunlight made her think for a moment that her father's bright blue eyes twinkled at her in response.

Outside a long blast of car horn sounded. The noise startled her, but brought her back to the real world. The real world had a holiday in it today, she remembered happily. She'd been looking forward to the Renaissance Faire all summer. Checking her watch she saw that Nancy was actually on time.

"Talk about strange occurrences."

The ring was still firmly settled on her right ring finger when she hurried out to the car.

August twenty-fourth. Sara was unable to get her mind off the letter. What was important about August twenty-fourth? Which was today. She checked her watch. Two P.M., August twenty-fourth, to be exact. Funny the ring should arrive on the day the letter said was all-important. Her translation was probably completely wrong.

All day she felt strange, out of synch with the world. She tried to ignore it, tried to enjoy the fair, but the feeling wouldn't go away.

The crowd was thick. The staff and performers, dressed in Elizabethan finery, were far outnumbered by the casually dressed tourists swarming through the lanes lined with trees and gaudily decorated booths. Delicious aromas from the food stalls mixed with heated dust in the still air. The noise of the crowd, the calls and jests of the entertainers reached her ears with a faraway, muffled quality. Everything was dulled by the heat.

The sun was a mean yellow dot in the cloudless blue sky. The foliage hung beaten and limp all over the wooded fair site. The humans weren't faring any better, except that they had sunblock, while the trees just had to stand around and take it. It had grown from a stifling morning to a roasting afternoon, and every inch of available shade was crowded with hot fairgoers. Sara's sense of time was totally distorted. She knew she'd been at the fair for hours, but she kept catching herself glancing in surprise at her watch. It was always earlier or later than she thought.

Sara squeezed her way through the crowd, emerging in a grassy circular field at the very center of the fair. She was supposed to meet Nancy here, underneath the twenty-foot-high wooden statue of a dragon in the middle of the field. She was early, and Nancy, having last been spotted as she disappeared into a lane of clothes shops, wasn't likely to be on time. Sara looked around the crowded circle, not a spot of shade to be found anywhere. As she swiped sweat-soaked bangs off her forehead she concluded that roasting here for half an hour wasn't worth it. She headed up one of the paths that radiated away from the field like the spokes of a wheel.

She made her way uphill against the flow of foot traffic, then down a gentle slope to a tree-bordered glade. A row of gaily painted gypsy wagons formed a half-circle at one end. Music from a guitarist and drummer in Middle Eastern costumes filled the hot air with exotic music. A trio of belly dancers gyrated on the stage, layered skirts flying, coin-heavy belts jingling with their sensuous movements. The sweating audience was clapping and shouting in appreciation.

Several colorful tents stood to one side of the gypsy camp, their canvas walls painted with mystical symbols. The tents were shaded by a pair of imposing oaks. Sara made for the shade of the trees, leaned back against the rough bark of one of the oaks, closed her eyes, and listened to the music. She ignored the heat, her own indescribable feelings, the dust, and the thousands of people around her. She let herself be carried away by the music. Guitar music, the most beautiful sound in the world.

She didn't come to the gypsy camp looking for gypsies; there weren't any. If she wanted gypsies she had the majority of the Twin Cities Bororavian Rom population written down in her address book. She was related to most of them.

She came to the camp year after year for the music. The Renaissance Faire drew some of the best musicians in the Midwest to play at the camp. Despite years of dedicated practice Sara didn't consider herself a musician. She was too shy about her playing to perform in public. She was a pretty good accountant, if not exactly in love with the work. What she really wanted to be when she grew up was a guitar hero. Maybe in her next life, she sometimes told herself. This time around she would just concentrate on her lessons and enjoy other people's performances.

As she happily listened her callused fingers flexed surreptitiously. She played air folk guitar along with the dancers' accompanist, working out the chord changes by ear.

Too bad I'll never be able to make the transition to playing in public, she thought wistfully.

"Why not?"

'Cause I'm not good enough.

"I find your lack of self-confidence hard to believe."

She hadn't thought she'd spoken aloud. In the midday heat a cold shiver crept over Sara's flesh.

She swung her head around sharply.

"Who said that? Who's there?"

She was alone. She couldn't see anyone close enough to overhear anything she might have said out loud, especially with all the noise going on around her.

Must be someone in the tent, she concluded. She wasn't hearing voices, she tried to reassure herself. Not disembodied voices, anyway. Maybe she had heatstroke.

Just remember, she reminded herself, there's always a logical explanation.

"I quite agree."

She didn't know where the voice was coming from but she thought it was best just to ignore it. Maybe the best thing would be for her to get away from the tents where the joker was lurking. She'd already had enough jokes today. The music was ending anyway, in time to meet Nancy. She checked her watch. Her hand felt heavy as she lifted her arm, as though the ring had taken on weight. It had to be the heat. Maybe she needed some salt tablets.

She turned to head back up the hill, but the crowd leaving the gypsy camp blocked the path. Cut off from making quick progress, she sidled her way around the edge of the throng to pass between the tents. She wasn't watching where she was going. As she stepped around the front of a tent she ran smack into a thick pole, bumping her nose and forehead. The impact was hard enough to set the wooden signboard at the top of the pole swinging.

"Ow!"

Sara nearly screamed as the shadow of a large hand crossed in front of her face. She looked up quickly, heart racing, only to discover that the hand was a painted plywood cutout, a signboard announcing Sybil's Palmistry in elegant gothic script.

A woman in flounced skirts and a paisley headscarf emerged from the tent just as Sara mumbled, "*Gajo* nonsense."

The fake gypsy's head came up sharply. Her hand snaked out to grasp Sara's arm as she turned away.

"What did you say? Who are you calling a *gajo?*" she asked in indignant Romany.

Sara swung back around, and in a brief fit of dizziness said, "Excuse me, I—Mala Rajko?!" she exclaimed as she recognized the exotically dressed fortune teller; she was used to seeing her in suits. "What's a real Rom doing in the gypsy camp?"

The high school math teacher and pillar of the Twin Cities Bororavian community gave an elegant shrug. Then she adjusted her off-the-shoulder blouse to compensate for considerable slippage over her large bosom.

"A joke on the *gajos,* eh?" she asked. In English, but with a thick accent she must have borrowed from an old movie. "I've got kids in college," she went on in her normal voice. "My grandma taught me palmistry when I was little. So I decided the skill could help me earn some extra income. Come in," she invited. "I've got iced tea in the cooler."

Mala threw a sour look over the fairgrounds. Sara's glance followed the fortune teller's. Everything was obscured as dust and heat radiated up off the ground in shimmering waves. Sara wiped the back of her hand across her burning eyes. The dust and dense air was really getting to her.

"Business is slow today," Mala added, disappearing inside, holding the flap open for Sara to enter.

It looked cool in the tent. Pain was shooting from the spot where her forehead had hit the wood. She still felt a little dizzy. The crowd noise was scraping against her nerves. The thought of a place to sit and a cold drink sounded wonderful. Besides, she hadn't seen anyone from the old neighborhood for several months. She looked at her hand, and got the odd impression the little orange stone was preening in the bright sunlight. She dived in after Mala.

The tent held a foot-high round table covered in a brown-and-red paisley cloth, piles of velvet and tapestry pillows spread on a fake Persian rug, and a cooler covered by a patchwork quilt. Mala took out two cans of iced tea and handed one to Sara.

"I've got a problem," Sara announced as she settled onto a pile of pillows across the little table from Mala. No, she didn't, she corrected herself, she had a crazy father. "This ring arriv—"

"Show me your palm."

"It's my crazy dad."

"He's not crazy, he's a history nut. No one knows more about the history of Bororavia and the Heroes of the Revolution than your father," Mala reminded her. "Your hand."

"Tell me about it. He went and named me after one of them. Not that there's that much to know, really, other than names and a few scraps of evidence. And legends, lots of legends."

"All of which your father knows and has passed on to you."

"So?" Sara held one palm out for Mala to study. The other she pressed to the lump forming on her forehead. "I've got such a headache. Heroes of the Revolution, indeed," she added sarcastically. "I wonder what Sara and Lewis Morgan were really like?"

"Heroes."

"Of the Revolution," Sara added automatically.

"But I wonder what they really did to become heroes? All we really know is that they existed. The stories say the lady I was named after saved the Borava tribe and freed the nation from the mad duke."

Mala looked up briefly. "That's not all she did."

"No," Sara agreed. "She also wrote economics treatises and invented rock and roll. If the stories are to be believed."

"Don't you believe them?"

"I've lived with them all my life, but I'd like some documentation."

"Then why don't you research it yourself?" Mala questioned. "Your father would like that. Hmm. Interesting."

Sara considered Mala's suggestion. Her father was probably digging through dusty Bororavian archives even as they spoke, but Dad wasn't likely to bring any objectivity to the search. He wasn't going to like anything that contradicted his long-held beliefs. Now, if she took a crack at documenting the Heroes of the Revolution she might bring some unbiased insight to the records. Or at least turn up enough scandalous material for a steamy television movie. She chuckled. Dad wouldn't like that at all, but turning up a bit of scandal might be a fair exchange for his practical joke.

"You know," she said to Mala, "I wish I could. I wish I had six months free to do the research about what really happened back in 1811. I'd start in London and go all the way to Bororavia. Follow their trail and find out what really happened. What's interesting?" she added, finally reacting to the palm reader's last comment.

Mala whistled meaningfully, then cleared her throat. "Interesting," she repeated.

"Mala, why are you looking like that?"

Mala perused the lines of Sara's palm some more. Her hand felt like a talon around Sara's wrist. Finally she said, "You're about to go on a long journey." She looked up quickly to intercept Sara's skeptical look. "No, really," she insisted. "Adventure, romance, long life, many children. I've never seen anything like it."

Sara took her hand back and looked critically at her palm. The lines seemed blurred to her. "Maybe it just needs ironing."

Mala chuckled, the sound faintly nervous. "Or an expensive hand cream. Nice ring," she added.

Sara held it up so the fortune-telling math teacher could get a better view. "Look familiar?" A tickling sensation ran up her arm from her ring finger. It felt as if the ring were purring. She gritted her teeth.

"Looks like *the* ring. I've seen pictures of the Bartholomew Ring from the museum."

"The letter that came with it claims it *is* the Bartholomew Ring. I think my dad—"

"That's it?" Mala's voice was full of believing reverence.

"I don't think—"

"It's magical, you know."

"I know, but—"

"A wish ring. You must make a wish," Mala announced.

"Must I?"

"Yes." It was a definitive statement.

Sara felt as if she were back in algebra class where

Mrs. Rajko was not one to be argued with. "What do I wish for?"

"Whatever you most want," was her emphatic answer.

What did she want? Sara wondered. What did people wish for? She used to want a little sister, but Mom wouldn't go for that at this point in her life. Other than lack of siblings she had almost everything she desired. A home, a wonderful family, a nice butt. She was employed and doing just fine. She supposed she could wish to be the greatest guitarist in the world, but somehow that seemed like cheating. Did she really believe this stuff? No. But there was no harm in wishing.

"Start with something traditional," Mala suggested.

"Wish for what?" Sara questioned. "To find my own true love?"

As the words were spoken the voice she'd heard earlier insinuated itself into her mind, sounding bored and sarcastic. "I knew that would be next."

"What?"

"What?" Mala echoed.

The word rang in Sara's head as the pain from the bump suddenly became sharply intense. She heard a voice, whispering just on the edge of hearing, yet insistent enough to drown out the sounds outside the little tent. She saw faces looming up out of nowhere; a black cat, a blue-eyed fox, a stunningly attractive man. The images blended until the human one filled her mind. She could clearly make out a triangle of sharp chin and high cheekbones below a wing of night-black hair held out of his eyes by a wide red headband. Eyes. Brilliant, intelligent blue eyes, sooty lidded, uptilted, framed by heavy black lashes. He sought—soft-footed as a cat, wily as a fox—something, someone. Her. Huh? What?

Why on earth was the tent spinning at about warp ten? Who was calling her? Why did it sound so far away?

Someone nearby said, "Stay here. I'll get the medics."

Stay here. She couldn't move. She'd hit her head. She'd just hit her head. Dizzy. It felt as if someone were sucking on her toes. She liked it. Felt as if gravity were getting very fresh with her. Pulling her . . .

Where was she going?

The citrine twinkled. She could *feel* it twinkle. "How about," it suggested stonily, "1811?"

2

The world smelled bad; worse than bad. The world smelled horrible. The noise outside the tent was louder, more rude and raucous somehow. Sara didn't feel right. She didn't feel ill, but she definitely felt different.

When she opened her eyes she found the world was a darker place than she remembered. Maybe the blow on her forehead had affected her eyes. And her nose? Phew! What was that smell? Sort of like dead fish and sulfur and horse dung and—her stomach gave a dangerous warning lurch—and Sara decided to give up cataloguing scents.

"Just breathe through your mouth and try not to think about it," the familiar, unnatural voice advised. "You'll get used to it in time."

I'm still hallucinating, Sara thought, reaching up to rub her temples.

Unlike Mala's colorful, lightweight tent, this one was made of heavy canvas. The shape and size were different as well. Was this the first-aid tent? Who had moved her? How long had she been out?

She was covered by an old quilt. She threw it off and got shakily to her feet.

"Where'd these clothes come from?"

The words hadn't come from the disembodied, hallucinatory voice this time, but from her. She'd spoken, but the voice was not hers. This voice was lighter, younger, with a distinct accent.

Sara put a hand on her throat. "What is the matter with me?"

"You're about six inches shorter, for one thing."

Sara dropped with shock, landing on the bunched-up quilt. She looked around. This was not a first-aid tent, it looked like someone's untidy, crowded home. The quilt was part of a bedroll. There were clothes hung on a central tent pole. A battered wooden chest took up much of the tent's small space.

It's a dream, she assured herself. *You're having a dream—*

"You're not."

Calm down. Ignore the voice. It's part of the dream. The worst part. Like being haunted. I don't believe in ghosts. Has a ghost started to believe in me?

She pressed fingers to her aching temples and felt thick tendrils of hair falling on either side of her face. With a sharp shriek she sprang back to her feet, frightened that her short dark hair had turned into a medusa's nest of snakes.

"I don't want to know," she said, her stranger's voice no more than a dry whisper.

"There's a mirror in the chest. You might as well get on with it."

She pinched herself, hoping she'd wake up. But all the action did was draw her attention to her slender arm and the sleeve of a faded blue blouse. She recognized neither the sleeve nor the arm wearing it.

Rather than think about having a new body, a new voice, and being in a strange place, Sara gingerly fingered the material of the blouse. It didn't hold her attention for long. Curiosity inexorably drew her to look at her hand instead. It was the sort of hand she'd always wanted. The palm was narrow, the fingers exceptionally long. She found herself holding her hands up in front of her face. She flexed them cautiously, then rubbed her thumbs across her palms and fingertips.

"Beautiful," she said with awed wonder. "A guitarist's hands."

"Pickpocket's hands," the intruding voice chimed in.

Sara jumped. She would have dropped the hands if they hadn't been attached to her. All her confusion shifted into anger.

"Who are you?" she demanded. "Where are you?"

"Not a who, a what. I was right in front of your face a moment ago. Got any more wishes?" the voice added sarcastically.

In front of her face? She held her hands back up. She saw the citrine-and-silver ring. The ring. Sara's ring. The Bartholomew Ring. It was the real thing after all. She glared at the narrow silver band, her anger so heated she hoped to melt the delicate knot-work design.

"What did I wish for? To go crazy?"

And why was she yelling at a piece of jewelry? she wondered. Because a part of her was still trying to deny this odd situation. She'd gotten a bump on her head, maybe heatstroke. If she was lucky this was just a hallucination.

"If you hurry, you'll be able to catch your own true love's next performance."

"What?"

"You did wish to meet your own true love."

Sara gestured wildly around the unfamiliar surroundings. "But I didn't mean it!"

"Is that my fault?" the ring questioned.

Sara sputtered indignantly, then subsided into silence, unable to believe she was carrying on a conversation with a magic ring. She felt so, so ridiculous. No. She felt . . . brand new. Not out of her mind, out of herself. Which made no—

"You should hurry."

Sara ignored the voice. She scurried across the tent to the wooden chest. The lid lifted with a brassy creak. A smell of dried herbs and wool assailed her nostrils. Her newly long fingers fumbled through layers of old clothes until she came across a dingy square of silvered glass. She lifted the mirror gingerly, not trusting her own grasp. She was afraid of what she'd see, but she had to know. She took a deep breath, and held the glass up before her face.

The eyes she looked at herself with were blacker than night. So was the curling mass of hair framing the exotically featured oval face. The small but full-lipped mouth was open in surprise. The eyes were the wrong shape and color, much larger than her own eyes, but Sara saw herself looking out of them. She also knew the lovely stranger's face. She wasn't a stranger; she was a legend. This girl looked just like the official portrait of Sara Morgan in the Bororavian National Museum.

"Sara? The real, uh, first Sara?"

"Just so."

"But . . . how . . . I don't understand. I . . . She . . ."

"Stole me. I let her. Right off my wearer's hand. Not everyone can see me, you know. Not unless I want them to. The girl had such a light touch and my wearer didn't appreciate what he'd inherited from his ancestors. He came from a long line of wizards, but he's no more than a jumped-up city merchant in love with wealth. The bloodline's gone downhill from Merlin, I can tell you. Imagine, he was thinking of using me as a watch fob. Is it any wonder I let the gypsy girl steal me? Such pretty fingers. I've got a weakness for attractive hands. Cleverest fingers I've ever seen. I look handsome on them, don't you think? Pity about her heart."

Great. Not only did she get a magic ring, she got a talkative one. The ring rambled on, without Sara paying much attention. She tried pulling it off, but it was stuck on her finger. She wondered if there was any soap in the chest she could use to lubricate—

"No, there isn't. I'm staying right where I am. And no one can see me but you unless I want them to. So don't try getting any help pulling me off. Bedlam still exists, you know. I wouldn't want you to end up in a madhouse."

A mind-reading magical ring.

Okay, she decided abruptly. She was crazy. Even the ring thought so. She'd just pretend this was really happening until she woke up somewhere nice and safe and padded, she decided. Meanwhile, she'd just cope, go along with the delusion.

She nodded decisively and spoke to the ring. "What am I doing here? What happened to Sara? The other Sara?" Her new voice still sounded strange to her ears.

The ring remained silent. She'd never experienced a hallucination before, and wasn't sure how to deal with a reluctant one.

"Where is she?" she insisted.

"Right here."

"What do you mean, 'right here'? I'm right here. Where is she?"

"It's complicated. I don't know if you'll grasp the metaphysical—"

"Try me."

"Reincarnation. A sort of retrograde variety. She died, you see. She was quite ill when she stole me. As her spirit left her body she wished for it to come back. I granted her wish. It just took me a long time to find her spirit."

"Me?"

"You. Sara's soul reborn in the twentieth century. Then I had to wait for you to make the proper wish for yourself so I could then make hers come true as well. It would have been much easier if she'd wished to live instead of—"

"She died of heart trouble?" Sara wasn't sure what

to make of the ring's tale of granting a dying girl's last wish. She was suddenly worried she might be dying any moment herself if this body had a bad heart. "If she died from a weak heart, isn't the heart still weak?"

"No. I fixed it. We're leaving now."

"You what? Wait a minute—"

Her body gave a violent lurch as she was pulled forward, hand first, toward the tent flap. She fought the pressure, but the force was inexorable. She was propelled outside, and there was no way for her to stop. Before she could protest she was standing out in the open, too shocked by her new surroundings to make a sound.

The difference between this place and the Renaissance Faire was obvious, complete, and altogether unnerving. Sensory overload hit her like a slap in the face. Inside the tent it had all been muffled; outside it was another world. The noise was alien to her ears. Her nostrils and lungs reacted badly to the stinking air. Her eyes noted the subtle difference in the daylight from a bright August afternoon in Minnesota. Her mind had begun to believe she was in 1811; now the rest of her senses accepted the truth as well.

The ring didn't give her time to stare numbly at her surroundings, or dive back inside the tent. The force controlling her gave her only a moment to take in the area. There was a horse paddock to one side, gypsy wagons on the other. The tent was one of several set up behind a row of ramshackle, unpainted shacks. The sky overhead was a smoky yellow-gray—worse than Los Angeles during a smog alert. She had the vaguest impression, like a Turner watercolor, of ship masts and buildings in the distance.

The overriding impression wasn't of sight but of sound, raucous, riotous, tumultuous—a carnival of sound. The air was full of noise, all of it coming from somewhere beyond the line of buildings. Even without the ring's unstoppable tug she would have been drawn toward the sound. Curiosity pulled her toward the fairgrounds as much as magic.

"But where are we going?" she demanded as she rounded the last low building and the crowds came into sight.

The ring remained adamantly silent; it just moved her onward. She was marched inexorably through a sea of humanity milling around booths and tents and stages. This was not the fair she'd come to hours before. The August heat still burned down on the sweating crowds, but it shone on a different world. There was no psuedo-Elizabethan pageantry here, no T-shirts or jeans or sunglasses or anything at all like she'd left behind. There were food vendors and booths full of wares; jugglers and musicians strolled through the throng. She was taken past many stages where loud and bawdy shows were being performed. She caught sight of puppet shows, and a dancing pig, in passing.

Everyone here was dressed in period clothing. Some were in rags, some in silk, but every last man, woman, and child pushing and shoving and staring at the entertainments was wearing costumes from a bygone era.

"Looks like a set for *Pride and Prejudice*," she

muttered. She sighed with relief, glad she at least recognized the style of the fashions worn by the more prosperous fairgoers. "Regency period. I can deal with the Regency."

The women were in simple, high-waisted gowns. Their hair was mostly short and curled, bound with ribbons; a few wore pretty hats. Those few who noticed her staring at them looked haughtily away. Men's dress was more extreme than the women's. Everything about masculine attire was designed to enhance their masculinity. The light-colored, skin-tight pants, especially, left nothing to the imagination. Sara blushed and looked away every time her gaze strayed below waist level on the passing men. And she a veteran of many a hard-rock concert.

"Now I know why they called trousers inexpressables," she said as she was pulled by the invisible force to the foot of one of the larger stages.

"Here we are," the ring announced. "Just in time."

"Just in time for what?" Sara demanded while people pressed in behind her.

"You have an appointment with destiny. Or have you forgotten that you wished to meet your own true love?"

"Yeah, but I didn't ask to be transported through time to do it," she complained. "I'd have preferred meeting him at a Bon Jovi concert. Where are we, anyway?"

"London. We're at St. Bartholomew's Fair—where you will meet your own true love. All wishes cheerfully granted." There was a metallic sigh. "Some just take more work than others."

Sara wanted to scream. She wanted to yell in frustration, to tear the ring off and stomp on it. But furious and frightened as she was, she was able to remember she'd been talking out loud to a magic ring in the middle of a crowd in the early years of the nineteenth century. She'd seen documentaries on how crazy people were treated in olden times. It wasn't easy, but she made herself remain silent to keep from drawing attention to herself. She counted to a high number and studied the stage while trying to regain her temper and her coherence.

The stage held juggling clubs and a chair and hoops and balls. Three sharp-looking daggers hung from a stand at the back of the stage. A rope was strung about ten feet in the air over a long metal basin. The stage was still empty, but from the size and enthusiasm of the gathering she assumed they were waiting for a popular performance.

When she felt calm enough to carry on a reasonable conversation, she tried thinking, very loudly, at the ring.

I appreciate the effort, she began. *But this reincarnation thing wasn't exactly what I had in mind.*

"I did the best I could with what I had to work with."

The ring sounded so wistfully affronted she didn't know how to answer. She was saved from any immediate reply when a wizened little man in a patchwork vest jumped up on the stage. The audience roared, and Sara was completely distracted as a rush of anticipation caught hold of her.

The impatient crowd shifted and shoved forward

as the man came to the edge of the stage. Sara could see the cracked leather of his boots as he stopped inches away from her nose.

She craned her neck to look up at him as he waved his arms dramatically and pronounced, "Defying death and the flames of hell! Toma the Magnificent!"

Behind her the crowd shouted and clapped and cheered as a slender figure in red tights jumped up on the stage behind the announcer. Sara was aware of a great deal of feminine sighing going on. She assumed it had something to do with the tights.

As the announcer stepped aside she got her first good look at the lithely muscular performer as he took an elegant bow in the center of the stage. It wasn't just the tights, she decided, it was the man's whole compactly built body. He wasn't tall or conventionally handsome but he definitely had his share of self-confident sex appeal.

His darkly furred chest was bare and sun bronzed. His hair was blue-black, thick, and straight. It fell past his shoulders, held out of his face by a wide silver-and-red striped headband. His face was triangular with wide cheekbones that narrowed down to a sharp chin. Even from a distance she could tell that his eyes, narrowed against bright sunlight, were intensely blue. The clinging material of his tights molded his well-shaped thighs and calves and emphasized the bulge at his groin in a way that made the trousers she'd noticed earlier seem baggy and completely forgettable.

Sara swallowed hard. She was very warm. Tingling. Very . . . She tried to drag her eyes away from the young man so confidently accepting the audience's cheers and applause. She couldn't seem to do it, though.

"Well? What do you think?"

What?

"Do you like him?"

Who?

"Don't be obtuse. Toma. Your own true love."

My own—

Toma had turned from the audience, and was ascending a rope ladder up to the tightrope. She watched his backside as he did so. It was a very firm, flat backside. The smooth ripple of wiry muscles in his back and thighs fascinated her. On the stage the announcer set a torch to the contents of the metal tub. People in the crowd shrieked and surged eagerly forward. Sara was momentarily distracted as she fought to keep from being pressed against the stage supports. When she had secure enough footing to look at Toma again he was on the tightrope platform cheerfully juggling a trio of knives.

While standing on one foot.

Sara considered the ring's announcement, and found herself mentally measuring this Toma, handsome though he was, against her private criteria for romantic interest.

"I don't know," she said, trying to remain skeptical. "Isn't he a little short for an own true love?"

3

MY OWN TRUE LOVE

"Own true loves come in all sizes," the ring answered testily. "I don't know what you're complaining about. You're only five feet tall."

No. This body is only five feet tall.

The ring ignored her thought. "Besides," it went on, "the man's an acrobat. They don't have to come in a Viking-god model to be fine athletes."

She knew that. She was from a circus family even if she'd never had anything to do with the circus herself. She couldn't help but be impressed with his talent as she watched Toma the Magnificent. She could feel the heat from the flames licking up from the metal trough. They created a wavering haze in the already smoggy air. Toma was oblivious to the heat. He danced forward on the rope strung across the fire pit, nonchalantly continuing to juggle while the flames licked and crackled below.

Sara gaped, as mesmerized as anyone in the audience. She wasn't just impressed by his skill. Like many another woman in the crowd, she also appreciated his sheer physical beauty.

All right, she thought with a wry smile. *He's not a Viking god, but he's . . . nice.*

"He's very flexible, too," the ring assured her. "You'll like that."

She didn't bother trying to think an answer. She just lifted her head haughtily, and tried not to breathe too heavily as Toma tossed away the knives with a seemingly careless, fluid motion. He then began to dance a slow and sensuous ballet across the narrow strand of rope. Sara watched the graceful play of muscle, the flowing gestures and teasing pauses for audience appreciation with a growing sense of awed hunger. It was only the knowledge that she was just one of several hundred women he was playing to that kept her from licking her lips in hungry anticipation.

Perspective, she told herself. *You have got to keep your sense of perspective. He's perfect, but . . .*

The citrine ring on her finger acknowledged this concession with a smug tingle.

But, she thought, *I don't really want anything to do with the man. Thank you for bringing me here,* she added.

Toma paused, then did a backflip that turned into a handstand on the swaying rope. Sara screamed and applauded with everyone else while her interior conversation with the ring went on.

It's nice to know there's an own true love somewhere for me. It's just that I'd rather be in my own century, she explained. *I'm sure there's someone there, somewhere, who—*

Something tugged on her hand.

"You don't have to get physical," she complained aloud.

"Sara?"

She raised her hand to look at the ring, but a hand tugging forcefully on her skirt made her look back down immediately. She saw a dirty-faced little girl with the biggest, greenest eyes she'd ever seen.

"'Allo," said the little girl. "Wat're you doing 'ere?"

"Uh—" Sara began uncertainly.

"You're supposed to be round back," the child went on. "You promised 'im, remember?"

"Uh. No," Sara replied honestly. "I don't."

The girl's expression twisted into a disgusted grimace. "You sick again? If you ain't sick lately," the child went on, "you're sneakin' around with *'im.*" The girl tugged forcefully on Sara's skirt. "Come on, then," she insisted. "'E promised me a penny to remind you."

"You'd better go with her," the ring suggested.

"Come on, it's almost over," the girl said, grabbing Sara by the sleeve.

The heat and press of bodies near the stage was stifling. Oily smoke from the fire made the already thick air even worse. Sara gave one last, lingering glance at Toma the Magnificent and let the girl lead her away from the stage. She didn't want to admit to the pang of loss at leaving the show without having actually met Toma. Own true loves, even impossible ones, didn't come along every day. However, she knew it was also for the best if she got out of here without making any actual contact with the man.

And, she told herself firmly, *he really isn't my own true—*

"Her name is Beth," the ring interrupted her thought. "She's ten, an orphan, and your apprentice."

She's not my apprentice, Sara corrected. *I'm not Sara. I'm Sara. I mean . . .* Her thoughts trailed off in a confused mental stutter. Both she and the ring remained silent as Beth led the way through the jostling audience. Sara noticed that Beth seemed to bump into people a bit more than was necessary, and that her childish smile seemed just a touch too innocent.

Apprentice what? she thought suspiciously.

"Pickpocket."

Is she . . . picking? Right now?

"With a great deal of skill and enthusiasm."

She ought to be ashamed.

"Orphans need to eat, Sara."

Sara didn't know how to respond, or what to do. She did know that drawing attention to the child's activities wouldn't do either of them any good. She was very glad when they at last emerged from the crowd. Beth turned them away from the fairgrounds and led the way down an alley. Sara soon found herself in an enclosed area behind the stage. A quick look around showed her a bedroll and a leather-bound trunk placed under a wooden awning. A water barrel was set to one side of the enclosure.

Toma's announcer stood in the center of the narrow space. He drained the contents of a tin cup and put it down before he turned toward them. He gave Sara a disapproving look, then sidled past her to the alley. Sara nearly coughed at the distinct aroma of gin his passing left hanging in the still August air. The man smelled as if he'd been pickled in the stuff.

"Who's he?" she asked after he'd gone.

"Sandor, of course," Beth answered. "Dizziness gotten to your brain, gypsy?" the girl asked sarcastically as she sat down on the dusty ground. She settled back against the bare wooden wall. "Show's over. I can 'ear 'em clappin' for more. "'E won't give 'em more, though. Got better things on 'is mind." She cocked her head to one side, continuing to look Sara over critically. "You ain't blushin'. Why ain't you blushin', gypsy girl? You been red as roses before."

"Before what?"

"Before."

Beth looked at her as if she thought Sara was an idiot. Sara thought that maybe she was, and turned away from the green-eyed girl's stare. She knew she was missing something significant. Something about the activities of the Sara she wasn't.

Listen, she complained to the ring. *I'm living somebody else's life here, and I don't like it. I mean—*

She heard a soft tread behind her. There was an aroma of soot and scented oil and masculine sweat. Strong hands came around her waist, and turned her. As she faced the man who held her a flash of details rose out of her memory. A fox face. Sharp blue cat's eyes. Raven black hair. Memory mixed with vision as her gaze met Toma the Magnificent's. She reached up, tracing a finger unthinkingly along the angle of one wide-set cheekbone, down to the tip of his sharply pointed chin. His flesh was warm, smooth, flushed with exertion.

He was smiling, bright blue eyes full of laughter and triumph. "Sara. I knew you'd be here."

She knew him!

In her dreams she'd always known him.

A hand tangled in her hair, drawing her closer. His mouth covered hers and thought was swiftly lost to sensation. His lips and tongue filled her with heat while his hand moved over her back and hips with distracting skill. The tips of her breasts grew hard against his bare chest as she found herself pressed close against him. Her bare toes curled in the warm dust of the enclosure and her arms came around him. Her hands slid up the slick length of his back, tracing the wiry, corded muscles of his shoulders and arms. Silky hair caressed her cheek. The scent of smoke and spice filled her nostrils. Her tongue twined playfully with his and she could feel his surprise as she answered his demanding skill with her own.

He pulled away from kissing her. "Sara?"

"Hmmm?" she responded as she slowly opened her eyes. Her body was flooded with the heady rush of sensation. Her body. Yes, definitely her body. Never mind what she'd said about this body belonging to somebody else; this arousal belonged to her.

He was still holding her tightly around the waist. She looked up into Toma's bright blue eyes. Eyes full of concern, and sensual promises. Maybe this was her own true love after all.

She was almost ready to thank the ring when her attention was distracted by the sound of giggling. Childish giggling. Oh, right. Beth. She eased herself away from Toma and turned to look at the girl.

"Is this who I was supposed to meet?" she questioned needlessly.

She looked back at Toma, who gently ran a finger across her lips. Lips still sensitized by the intensity of their kiss. She felt an odd clutching at her heart and recognized it as jealousy because he'd been kissing a Sara who wasn't her.

Toma's glance moved past her, to the still-laughing Beth. "What are you doing here, mud lark?" he asked the girl.

Beth rubbed her fingers together suggestively. "I'm a proper chaperon . . . until I get paid."

"You're a rascal and a thief," he told her.

"I should 'ope so," the girl answered back. She bounced to her feet. She gave a sly smile that Sara found totally unsuited to her young face. "For another coin I'll stand lookout for Beng."

"Beng?" Sara asked. "Who's Beng?"

Toma looked at her strangely.

"She's dizzy again," Beth explained. "Found her out front during the show."

"I saw you," he said to Sara. "You looked as if you were going to eat me, little one," he added with a slow smile.

A pair of small coins appeared in his hand. He tossed them to Beth while Sara wondered just where in his tights there could possibly be room for pockets. Beth caught the coins and quickly ducked out into the alley.

Now that she was alone with Toma, Sara wasn't sure what to do next. She knew what she was tempted to do. She wanted to start by kissing him again. He certainly didn't look as if he'd mind. He stepped away from her, and she put her hands firmly behind her back as he went over to the water barrel. She knew what she should do. Was going to do. She was going to make the ring take her home. It was best to leave it at just one memorable kiss.

She couldn't take her eyes off him, even as she sternly reminded herself she didn't really know this man. He thought she was someone else. He picked up the cup and doused his chest and head a few times.

"I smell like a pig," he said as he grabbed a dry cloth and began scrubbing his chest and hair. "I'd like a bath, but I'd better hurry up and change. Beng's bound to show up. No use making more trouble by having him find me half-naked with his daughter," he added. He gave her another warm look. "Or completely naked." He took a step toward her. "It's very tempting. I didn't realize you knew how to kiss. Here I was trying to take you by surprise and—"

"You've never kissed her before?" The words escaped before Sara could stop them. She hadn't liked the thought of Toma and the other Sara being lovers. It wasn't jealousy, she told herself. It would just be more weirdness than she could handle, that was all.

Puzzlement crossed his sharp-featured face. "Kissed who?"

"Her. I mean me. You've never kissed me before?"

Toma smirked. "If I had you'd remember. And don't worry about getting your words mixed up," he added kindly. "I did too when I was the gypsy half-breed at the charity school. You speak the *gajos'* language better all the time. I'm a better teacher than Beth," he added in Romany. "Better at lots of things."

"I bet," she mumbled in reply, her hand covering her mouth to keep the words from reaching him.

He went to the chest and took out a white shirt. He pulled it on, belted it, and added a dark blue vest. His hair was drying quickly in the hot sunlight. He shook out the dark, silky locks and tied a blue headband around his forehead. Sara found the effect piratical, and perfect for him. She hadn't failed to notice the bone-handled knife sheathed on his belt, either. The weapon helped remind her that she really wasn't in the twentieth century. Toma, she told herself, was probably a dangerous young man. She wished she didn't find the idea intriguing; it spoiled her own civilized image of herself.

"Have you talked to Beng yet?" he asked as he finished dressing.

She'd gotten the idea Beng was the other Sara's father. She wondered what she was supposed to talk to him about.

"No," she answered truthfully. "What should I say?"

She hoped the leading question would give her some clue to what was going on. She could ask the ring, but it had been quiet since Beth had led her to Toma. She rather liked it that way. She couldn't spend too much more time with Toma. Better to give him her full attention than to be distracted by the ring's asinine comments.

Beth came racing in before Toma could answer. "Sandor brought 'im!" she exclaimed. She grabbed

Sara's hand and pulled. "Sara, 'ide! "E'll beat you for sure this time. 'E said 'e would!"

The little girl looked panic-stricken. So Sara did the first thing that came to mind: she hugged her.

"It's okay," she soothed the girl. "No one's going to hurt anybody. Calm down, sweetheart."

Beth struggled in her embrace. Sara and Toma's glances met over the little girl's dirty head. A gleam of warm affection showed briefly in Toma's eyes before he turned swiftly at the sound of a roar.

"Sara!" a deep masculine voice shouted from the entrance.

Sara pushed Beth behind her and turned to confront whoever it was.

"Dad?" she questioned in confusion when she saw the angry figure framed in the gap in the flimsy wooden wall. The man was a bit shorter than the twentieth-century version of her father, the shoulders were wider, the eyes were brown instead of blue. But the face was the same. The stance was the same. The paternal outrage was similar to that time after the senior prom when he'd caught her and Joe Malkos . . .

"Dad?" she repeated as the spitting image of her father strode furiously toward her, large hand raised to strike her. Beth cowered behind her. She saw Toma reaching for his knife.

She planted her hands on her hips and shouted, "What do you think you're doing?"

He responded to her tone if not her words. He dropped his hand to his side. "What are you doing here?" he demanded. He pointed at Toma. "Haven't I told you to stay away from this Calderash filth?"

Before she could respond Toma stepped between her and the angry Rom father.

"She's here because I asked her here. We are chaperoned," he added.

Beth sidled around Sara and spoke up. "I wouldn't let 'im touch Sara, Beng."

"A *gajo* girl is no chaperon," Beng told Toma. "You leave my girl alone. No decent man will want her if you're seen with her."

"A decent man already wants her," Toma answered.

Beng bristled. "Sara, we're going. There's work for you," he added. He jerked a thumb toward the opening. "You're wanted."

There were two large men waiting in the alley, their hulking forms just visible beyond the gap in the wall. Waiting for her?

Sara didn't know what to do. Beth grabbed her hand and began her insistent tugging again. "You're wanted. Can't keep 'em waitin'."

"I . . ." Sara began.

Toma said, "Stay." He didn't take his eyes off Beng.

"We're going with the *gajo*," Beng told her.

"Not until we're through," Toma said.

"She doesn't listen to a half-breed Calderash."

Toma took a step closer to Beng. He was more lightly built than the broad-shouldered man, but Sara had no doubt about which of the two was the more dangerous.

"Don't push him, Beng," she suggested. She definitely didn't want these two fighting over her, or whoever it was they were fighting over.

Toma put his hands on his narrow hips and said calmly, "I have no family here, no mother to make arrangements. I have no one but myself who can speak, and Sara has no mother, so it must be between you and me."

"I do not hear you," Beng countered, his jaw set stubbornly. "Sara will leave now."

Sara stayed where she was, between Toma and Beng, and the strangers beyond the wall. She didn't know what was going on as she watched their confrontation, but she didn't like it. Beth continued to tug on her skirts, trying to get her to obey Beng. She ignored the girl. She didn't know who wanted to see her, but she wasn't going anywhere.

Toma shot her a quick, reassuring smile before addressing Beng once more. "I know Sara's value, and am more than willing to pay it. I ask for her hand in marriage, as the *gajos* say."

Beng went red with outrage; then he spat on the ground at Toma's feet. "You don't get her hand. You don't get nothing, Calderash."

"Marriage?" Sara asked, going hot and cold with pleasure and stunned disbelief. She gaped at the men. Both of them were staring at her. Hope and encouragement shone in Toma's eyes.

"Marriage," she repeated hoarsely. "Wait a minute." She spoke to the ring more than to the watching men. "Own true loves are one thing, but who said anything about marriage?"

4

Sara shook her hand. "Are you broken? Are you listening to me?" Beth was still tugging on her arm. One of the hulks appeared in the doorway and crooked a commanding finger at her. Beng was herding her toward the exit. She could feel Toma's beseeching gaze on her.

"Hurry up," Beng ordered.

"Marry me," Toma repeated.

Sara moved toward the menacing figure blocking the doorway. She was afraid that if she didn't, the anxious Beng was going to start nipping at her heels like an exasperated border collie.

"Sara," Toma called, but she didn't look back at him. She could still taste his kiss; the memory of it was almost more disturbing than the unknown menace waiting by the wall. It wasn't her he wanted to marry, she firmly reminded herself. He wanted the other girl. The ring may have misplaced her in time, but that was as far as her own involvement went.

"Who are these guys?" she asked as she was urged forward. Nobody answered. Most annoyingly, the ring didn't answer. Hell of a time for its batteries to go dead, she thought as she reached the gate.

The big man standing there turned an evil grin on her. "'Allow, Sara. The missus says you're shy but she wants to 'ave a little talk. So me and Billy come to fetch you personal."

"How kind," Sara said, "but I don't think—"

The big man looked past Sara to Beth. "The gypsies must be feeding you, girl. You look like you've grown tall enough to set yourself up on the game. Tall don't matter none if you're lying down, does it?"

He laughed at his own wit while Beth disappeared behind Sara's skirts. Sara felt the girl's hands clutching tensely at the worn fabric as she hid behind her. Having watched a great deal of British television on PBS Sara recalled that "on the game" was slang for prostitution. What the man had just suggested was disgusting.

To divert the man's attention from the frightened child, Sara gently pushed Beth away and said, "Let's go."

He nodded. "Come on, then. She don't need no company," the man added when Beng would have joined them. "She's just going to see me missus."

"Women's business," Beng agreed reluctantly. "You just talk to the Cummings woman and no one else, girl," he ordered Sara before backing away.

Leaving Beth and the unsettled situation with Toma and Beng behind, she went down the alley with the stranger. The one he'd called Billy, a tall, heavyset teenager, followed close behind. The pair moved closer to her when they left the alley for the crowded paths of the fairgrounds. They obviously had no intention of letting her slip away from them. Just what did they want with her anyway?

She was alone with them in a narrow street beyond the noise and color of the fair before it occurred to her that this was a really bad idea. She'd been too worried about all the undercurrents and overt threats in the mixed-up situation to think about any danger to herself. Danger? Here she was stuck in 1811 with a malfunctioning magic ring and she hadn't thought about being in danger?

"I am so stupid sometimes," she muttered as she looked around, trying to find a way to slip away from the men.

Much to her relief the first thing she saw when she looked up was Toma, leaning with his arms crossed against the corner of a building they were approaching. She didn't know how the acrobat had gotten to the corner before them, but she found the confident way he pushed himself away from the wall and swaggered up to them infinitely reassuring.

"*Sastipe,*" he said, falling in step beside her.

"'Ere, now," her big escort protested. "Who asked you along?"

"Her father," Toma replied while she racked her brain trying to remember what the word meant.

She didn't suppose this was the time or place to explain the wide gaps in different Romany dialects and that it wasn't exactly her first language anyway. So all she said was, "Hi," when he turned a winning smile on her. She smiled back gratefully, sure that Beng had nothing to do with Toma's showing up to escort her.

"The girl's scared, Cummings," Toma spoke to the guard. "She's never worked for your lot before. Won't hurt to have one of her own to keep her company."

Cummings grunted in answer. "It's a long way to St. Giles," he said. "You know the missus doesn't like to linger in her bawdy house too late in the day."

"Dangerous neighborhood," Toma agreed. "No fit place for a virtuous woman."

Cummings looked as if he didn't know whether to be pleased or insulted at the remark. From behind her Sara heard a repressed snort of laughter from Bill.

She tugged on Toma's sleeve. "If it's not fit for a virtuous woman," she whispered, "what am I?" All the things she didn't know were making her nervous.

Toma took her hand in his. It was comfortingly warm, and she could sense his wiry strength. "My lady," he answered reassuringly. "Your father," he added in Romany, "should never let you deal with Mother Cummings alone. He thinks it's all right because she's only a *gajo* woman. When we're married—"

"Toma!" she cut him off. She didn't want to talk about marriage; she wanted to go home. To deflect him from the subject she said, "I don't want to talk in front of the *gajos*."

He nodded his understanding and they walked on in silence. Sara welcomed his comforting presence by her side, but she was too cautious and confused to try to explain her predicament to him. The streets were narrow, and the upper stories of the buildings they passed leaned inward, blocking the smoke-filled daylight. Garbage and human waste filled the gutters, giving off an almost visible wall of smell. The people they passed were filthy, furtive, unlike human beings at all, really. Sara began to feel as if she were walking through an endless, reeking tunnel populated by suspicious-eyed wraiths, beggars, and the squalling young of an indeterminate species. The ring had brought her to a fantasy world, but the fantasy was dark and threatening—a Regency novel by Stephen King. In this grim setting she forgot about the sweetness of Toma's kiss, the worshiping look in his eyes, the sure strength of his touch.

"Own true love isn't worth the hassle," she muttered as Cummings came to a halt before a narrow, three-story building.

"'Ere we are, darling," Cummings said cheerfully, opening the door. Loud conversation and the concentrated stench of a hundred unwashed bodies spilled out and covered her like a fetid blanket.

By the time she was shown through the low door Sara was shaking with apprehension. Her only consolation was that her sense of smell had finally gone numb with overload. The room was barely lit with smoking lanterns widely spaced along the walls. She noticed a rickety staircase and a great many doors, all of them unpainted and sagging. There were tables and rows of barrels lining one wall. Numb as her nose tried to be, she could still pick out the aromas of sour wine and stale beer.

Mostly she was aware of the thick crowd of people, not as individuals, but as a great wall of obstacles.

Cummings plunged into the wall of bodies and plowed through, shouting and thrashing his great arms as he went. She and Toma followed in his wake, with Billy continuing as a rear guard. They were in a back room with the door closed behind them before Sara realized how many of the crowd outside had been hard-eyed girls, some no older than Beth. Cummings had called this place a bawdy house. Surely those girls weren't whores, were they?

She didn't want to think about it. *1811 is not a fun place to be,* she told the ring silently. *You can take me home any time now.* She tried rubbing her thumb against the stone, hoping to get its attention. Perhaps, like a genie in a bottle, it needed a little tactile stimulation to get its attention. "I hope you're ticklish," she murmured.

"Someday I'll let you find out," Toma answered.

She jumped, having forgotten her surroundings for the moment. When she looked up Toma was cheerfully grinning at her. She looked quickly away from her charming companion and looked at the room instead. The outer room was bare and shabby; this room was luxurious in contrast. The furnishings included a sphinx-footed table, a pair of gracefully curved chairs, a love seat upholstered in gold brocade. The soft glow of candlelight lit the room. A woman in a high-waisted gown was seated at the table. She had sharp eyes above a prominent nose. Her mouth was pursed in a disapproving frown. Sara was willing to bet their hostess wasn't going to invite anyone to sit down.

"About time," the woman said. She aimed an

annoyed look at Cummings. "Did he stop at a flash house along the way?"

"No, Mother Cummings," Billy said quickly. "We come right back."

"Girl didn't want to come," Cummings said. "'Er pa said she's been sick.'"

"She doesn't look sick to me. Did you ask her why the delay?"

"No, pet," Cummings answered. "You just tol' me to fetch 'er and to try not to turn up 'er skirts. So I didn't, and 'ere we are, my lovely."

Who were these people? Sara wondered. Why were they discussing her as if she weren't in the room? She wondered if anyone would notice if she left.

At that moment, Mother Cummings looked at her and rapped out, "Well, girl?"

"Well, what?" Sara questioned back. There were gasps of shock from Cummings and Billy. Apparently Mother Cummings was only in the habit of asking rhetorical questions. "What is going on here?" Sara asked. "Who are you? What do you want with—"

"Don't you take that tone with me, gypsy," Mother Cummings cut her off. "I've sent the runners after better than you for forgetting their place. Haven't I, lads?" There was agreeing laughter from Cummings and Billy.

I really could use a translator, Sara thought at the ring.

Toma stepped in front of her. "No need to frighten the girl, Mother Cummings," he soothed. "She's biddable. You just tell her what you want. I'll make her understand. Gypsy girls are always obedient to their menfolk." He turned his head to give her a reassuring look.

"Biddable?" Sara asked Toma softly.

She disliked the sound of the word. Nor did she like the way Toma just smiled and nodded at her before turning his attention back to the Cummings woman. Sara stared at the back of Toma's head and resisted the urge to tap her foot in annoyance. Or kick him in his cute little butt. *Biddable, eh?* she thought angrily. *Pliable? Obedient? Maybe the other Sara was, but, honey, this Rom girl don't put up with nothing from nobody.* "I think we need to have a little talk," she muttered. She rubbed the ring again. *Just what kind of own true love are we talking about here? One that needs to be housebroken?*

"What I want," Mother Cummings said, "is for your gypsy friend to get back to work. I can't afford for the best cracksman in London to claim she's sick for a month. You owe me, girl."

"Huh?" Sara asked. "What?"

"Well, Sara?" Mother Cummings demanded, "when do I see the gold beetles from Lord Philipston's?"

Sara stared at the cold-faced woman while everyone else in the room stared at her. Except for Toma, their looks were openly hostile. Toma caressed the hilt of his knife with his thumb as he switched his gaze from her to the other men.

"What?" Sara asked again. "Gold beetles?" She looked helplessly at Toma. "What's a gold beetle?"

"Lord Philipston's Egyptian scarab collection," he explained. "I told you about it. Don't you remember?"

Sara shook her head. "Remember what? What am I supposed to do with scarabs? Do they have something to do with the ring?"

"Ring?" Toma asked.

"Steal them," Mother Cummings ordered angrily. "You've kept my buyer waiting long enough."

Steal them? Sara thought. "Oh, no," she said, "I'm not stealing anything."

"She's holding out on you, Mother," Billy said. "Can't trust a gypsy." Both Billy and Cummings took a threatening step forward.

Sara wished she'd kept her mouth shut as the men bore down on her.

From behind the desk Mother Cummings said, "You'll change your mind fast enough when the lads are done with you."

Toma put himself between her and the men. "Now, lads," he said soothingly. Sara noticed that his knife was in his hand, but not exactly pointed at anyone. The men backed off a few steps. "Keep your tempers," he advised, "and leave Sara to me."

"You said she'd do as she's told," Mother Cummings reminded him.

"So she will," Toma said soothingly.

"Are you holding out for a higher price, girl?" the woman asked. "Are you trying to play a deep game with me?" She banged the flat of her hand on the tabletop. The sound cut across the tense air in the room. "Well?"

"No!" Sara spoke quickly. She didn't know if it was the right answer or not. She did know she was willing to say whatever she had to to get away from this woman, her enforcers, and whatever crazy scheme they were trying to push her into. She rubbed her fingers nervously across the ring. "I have to go," she said. "I really have to get out of here."

"Shall I take you home?" Toma asked without turning his head to look at her. Her protector was keeping his attention on Billy and Cummings. Sara had a distinct impression of the two of them being barely leashed guard dogs. "You shouldn't have brought her here," Toma told Mother Cummings. "She's too valuable to damage and you know it. You don't treat the finest dab in the city like one of the bawds in your knocking shop back there."

"Say what?" Sara asked, but Toma didn't answer her.

Mother Cummings ignored Toma and glared fiercely at Sara. "Tomorrow night, girl, do you hear me? I want those beetles tomorrow night."

Sara backed toward the door, while the woman's malevolent gaze bored into her. Mother Cummings didn't need to speak the threat out loud. Sara read in the woman's hard expression all the nasty things that would be in store for her if she didn't steal the scarabs. Discussing the matter wasn't an option. She'd been brought here to have the fear of God put in her by someone who judged herself an expert in getting her own way.

Sara said, "I won't argue."

Mother Cummings nodded emphatically. "Just do it."

Go to hell, Sara thought. "Let's go," she said to Toma. He was by her side instantly, a guiding hand on her arm, his knife back in its sheath. She let him lead her out the door and through the crowd in the main room.

Afternoon had faded into night while they were inside. Sara was glad of Toma's company, though she still dreaded the journey back through the narrow, dark streets. Toma put his arm around her waist as they walked away from Mother Cummings's establishment. Though the night was warm, she still found the heat from his body comforting.

She had no intention of being in 1811 London tomorrow night but she was curious to find out just what was going on. "I thought," she said as they hurried along, "that Sara was a pickpocket."

Toma chuckled. "Say 'I am a pickpocket,'" he instructed.

She needed explanations, not an English lesson, so she repeated, "I am a pickpocket. Does this Philipston person keep his beetles in his pockets?"

He shrugged and she felt the rippling of his wiry muscles all along her side. Before she could ask him to do it again, he said, "Picking pockets at the fair is a lovely hobby, but it is time you got back to cracking houses, the old slut's right about that."

"Cracking houses?" she repeated. She had an image of rolling up to a house driving a large crane with a big steel ball attached to it. He probably had something a bit more subtle in mind. "Breaking and entering?" she guessed.

"And snatching and grabbing," he concluded. "Imagine my surprise to find out you're the best in London." He stroked her hair, then dropped a quick kiss on her forehead. "Did you really learn the trade from your mother?"

Sara didn't answer and they walked on in silence while she absorbed the knowledge that the ring had dropped her into the body of a famous burglar. A burglar involved with some dangerous characters, from the looks of it. "Mother Cummings is a fence, right?" she guessed. "Not just a fence, but the brains behind the whole operation."

"'Course she is," Toma agreed. "Fever addle your memory?" he asked.

He sounded concerned. She was going to miss him. *You can take me home now,* she thought at the ring. To Toma she said, "There's all sorts of things I don't know."

"It's all right," he answered. "I'll take care of you."

His words were meant to reassure a young girl adrift in London's criminal underworld. He meant to be kind and reassuring. Sara recognized his intention, but she didn't like the idea of needing anyone's protection no matter how out of her depth she felt. Then again, considering the respect Cummings and Billy had shown for Toma's knife she had to admit she might have need of a little protection if the ring didn't get her out of this mess soon.

They were close to the river now; their footsteps rang on uneven cobblestones and echoed off the walls of warehouses lining the street opposite dockyards. Sara got a distinct impression of people moving in the shadows near the warehouse walls, contesting rats for the right of way, she thought, if the scurrying sounds coming out of the darkness were any indication.

Every now and then they passed old men carrying lanterns; Sara assumed the old men were the warehouse guards. Not exactly first-rate security teams, she thought. Maybe that was why a teenage girl was a famous burglar, because the guards would all have coronaries trying to catch her.

A nearly full moon was doing its best to shine down through the smoke haze blanketing the city, managing to spark the waters of the Thames into a dull silver ribbon. Sara loved nothing better than water in the moonlight, and the sight drew her. She stopped at a break in one of the dockyard fences to look out across the wide river. The dark shapes of several large, decrepit vessels loomed up on the opposite side of the water, casting ominous shadows across the moonlit water. She could hear the creaking of old timber, and other, darker sounds drifted to them from the ships. Human sounds, like a kind of low, collective moan coming from many voices. There were a few lights on the old ships though they looked as if they ought to be abandoned. There was something very wrong and evil about the boats; just looking at them sent a shudder through her.

Toma drew her closer and his hand strayed upward to just below the undercurve of her breast. To distract herself from the half-formed hope that his hand would do more than just linger, she asked, "Those boats, what are they?"

"Those are the prison hulks," he said. "Where the *bitcherin mush* send little girls like you if you get caught. You've never seen them before, have you?"

"Prison hulks?" She'd seen a documentary on the

history of Australia. She knew about the hulks. "When the prisons got too full the British government locked criminals up on abandoned naval vessels. Sometimes they were there for years before they even had a trial. The conditions were terrible, hundreds died. Then the poor people who lived long enough to be tried were packed into ships that were almost as bad and shipped off to live like slaves in New South Wales." She looked across the river at the horrible reality of the statistics the television narrator had so calmly explained.

Toma turned her to face him. She could see his concerned expression in the moonlight. "That's right, sweetheart," he said. "That's exactly what happens. The sending man comes and puts you on the boat; then they send you to sea. Pretty little girl like you would be whoring for lags and guards alike on your first day." He pointed at the boats. "They scare you?"

Sara tried to disguise her disgust, but she heard her voice shaking with fear when she answered, "Those aren't my idea of first-class accommodations to Australia." When she realized that Toma didn't understand her comment any more than she did some of his, she explained, "They scare me, all right."

"Better not get done cracking the glaze on the Philipston house, then."

She really wished the man would speak English she could understand.

"You'd better not get caught breaking into Lord Philipston's house," he said. "I'd hate to see you imprisoned and transported for stealing from the *gajos.* Let's get back to the fair," he added, as he led her back down the street.

Sara considered the situation while they walked along, hand in hand. Of course, she told herself, it really had nothing to do with her; these people were expecting things from an entirely different person. Dangerous, illegal things. She'd be back in the twentieth century soon, and they would get on with their dangerous, illegal behavior without her. Of course, there was a nagging little fear itching at the back of her mind, a faint worry that maybe she wouldn't get back home.

It was in response to that worry that she said to Toma, "I'm not a burglar. Or a pickpocket. I've never stolen anything from anybody and I'm not going to start now."

Toma laughed. The sound was as silvery bright as the moonlight on the wide river. "That's rich, sweetheart. Lord, what a fine joke."

"I'm not joking."

Toma stopped and put his hands on her shoulders. "But sweetheart—" he began, but a sudden shout from the mouth of a nearby alley interrupted his words. There was another shout, then the fleshy sound of blows, shuffling feet, and angry curses.

"Help! Someone help me!" The pleading voice was that of an old man; the words were in Romany.

Both Toma and Sara ran into the alley. He had his knife, and she grabbed up a loose cobblestone. When she saw the two men she paused, took aim, and let fly, trusting to a lifetime of experience pitching in softball leagues for accuracy. The stone hit the man on the back of the head. He grunted and went down. Sara hoped she hadn't done more than knock the attacker unconscious. She hunted around for another rock as the second attacker turned toward Toma.

She didn't have to worry. The man saw the glitter of steel in the moonlight, glanced quickly down at his felled partner, and ran for the other end of the alley. Sara rushed up to the old man who was leaning against the wall of a building. He was panting and shaking as he clutched a canvas sack for dear life. Another bulky sack rested at his feet.

"They would have taken all I had, Sara. I should never have agreed to come here," he said as his frightened gaze focused on her. "All my stock, my whole livelihood's in this bag. You'd said it would be safe."

He must be some sort of peddler from the fair, Sara decided. Here was someone else she was supposed to know. "You'd better go home," she advised. He looked at her as if he were waiting for her to say more. Toma came up and put his hand on her shoulder. She turned her head to look at him.

He stroked her jawline with his thumb. "We'd better all get home," he said. "Before that one wakes up. What are you doing out so late, Evan?"

The old man pointed at her. "She said to wait for her here." He waved his hand at the bag at his feet. "I brought it," he said. He edged away from them toward the mouth of the alley. "I brought it. Now I'm gone." And he was, disappearing into the night with one last angry grumble.

Sara wondered what was in the bag, but didn't pick it up to look. Whatever it was wasn't really her property, probably not old man Evan's either. It was probably something the girl had stolen and asked Evan to keep for her.

"Well?" Toma asked her, nudging the bag with his foot.

"Let's get back to the fair," she said. She wanted to return to the tent where she'd woken up. She wanted privacy. She wanted to have a long talk with the magic ring.

Toma called after her as she walked back toward the street. She heard him pick up the bag and follow after her. She waited for him. Not only did she enjoy his company, she needed a guide.

They walked in silence until they reached the still-busy fairgrounds. Torchlight illuminated the thick crowds. The hawkers and entertainers were still busily at work. Toma guided her to the quiet, darkened area behind the stalls where the workers made their camp. They stopped next to a fence separating the public walkways from the makeshift dwellings.

"Better separate before your father sees us," he told her. He glanced back toward the fair. "Time for me to give another show before the constables close the place down. It'll keep Sandor from being too angry at my leaving." He put the bag down and took her in his arms. "But before I go . . ."

He brushed his lips against hers. She opened her mouth and kissed him back, her tongue slipping teasingly inside his mouth as he opened it in surprise. She found herself clinging to him while her senses threatened to reel out of control. It happened so incredibly fast, she didn't quite know what she was doing. One moment she was preparing to say good night to the man, the next thing she knew she was all over him, burning with passion at the touch, the taste, the scent of him. He filled her senses, intense hunger for him setting her afire. She pressed closer to Toma, her hands feverishly caressing him, compelled to—

Compelled.

Wait a minute.

Her self-control kicked in as quickly as it had disappeared. Her panting hunger flashed out of existence with an almost audible pop. She blushed hotly as she stepped away from the stunned but dazedly smiling Toma. "I'm sorry," she told him. "I don't normally act like that on the first date." *We have to talk,* she added to the ring.

"You've been wanting to do that all night," the ring answered.

"I don't need any help with my sex life, thank you. You pervert," she added angrily. Just what she needed, a magic ring with an aphrodisiac attachment. It was a good thing she'd noticed the unnatural feel of the ring trying to control her.

"I'm not a pervert, but I am very tempted. We'd better get married quickly," Toma said, thrusting the bag into her hands. He backed away from her. "Before you make me forget you're a good girl." He turned and was gone before she could say a word.

She smiled fondly after him. A gentleman, she thought. Toma the Magnificent was a nice man.

"He carries a knife," the ring pointed out.

Yeah, she thought as she made her way to the tent where she'd woken up, *it's kind of sexy. He's very protective. Sweet, really.* "I'm going to miss him," she added as she lifted the tent flap and went inside.

"Not necessarily," the ring responded.

"Well, I can't very well take him home with me. And just where have you been the last few hours?" she demanded. She put down the bag, then sat down in a shaft of moonlight let in by the overhead smoke hole. She could make out the small form of Beth, sleeping on a pile of quilts next to the dark bulk of the clothes chest. Not wanting to wake the sleeping child, she thought her next comment at the ring. *Well?*

"Recharging," it answered. "You and your true love have been getting to know each other, I trust?"

You've been putting a spell on me, haven't you?

"What? Me? What do you mean?"

You fogged my brain, or gave me temporary amnesia or something, didn't you? she accused.

"What? How? What would I do to—"

I've been trying to get you to take me back home. You haven't paid the slightest attention and now I understand why.

"Oh?" There was a definitely suspicious tone in the ring's sarcastic metallic voice.

You, Sara thought at it, *are a wish ring. I know you're a wish ring. I've been asking to go home—asking, demanding, pleading—but I haven't been wishing. You put a spell on me that made me forget that you have to grant me whatever I wish.*

"I was matchmaking," it answered, not denying her charge. "Giving you time to get to know each other."

Do you know what kind of day I've had? What

this girl is involved in? I could have gotten killed while you were taking a little nap.

"Toma was with you."

"So what? You're driving me crazy," she told the ring. She held it up so that the orange stone caught the light. She wasn't going to argue with it. She wasn't going to hesitate, because if she did the memory of how right it felt to be with Toma might override all the things wrong with the circumstances of their meeting. It was going to have to be enough to have met him. She swallowed the lump of regret in her throat and said firmly, "I wish to return to my own time and my own body. Right now."

"Sorry," the ring responded. "No can do."

"What? Get me out of here. I made a wish, you have to obey it."

"Sara?" Beth questioned sleepily from her pallet.

"Go back to sleep," Sara responded to the note of concern in the little girl's voice. "It's nothing. Why aren't you obeying me?" she whispered to the ring.

"It's after midnight," was its cryptic answer. "I don't do wishes after midnight."

5

What's the time *got to do with anything?*
Sara demanded, her words an angry shout inside her
head. *I wish to go home. Please,* she added in case
politeness would have any effect on the magic ring.

"I would if I could," it answered, "but it's too late."

*I don't get it. What's too late? Why don't you work
after midnight? Union rules or something?*

"It is now August twenty-fifth. St. Bartholomew's
Day is August twenty-fourth."

Yeah, so? Even as she thought the question, Sara
guessed what the answer would be.

"I may only grant wishes on St. Bartholomew's
Day. The day I was made, actually; the saint's day
doesn't have anything to do with it. I'm a one-day-
only wish ring. Sorry."

It wasn't sorry, she could tell by the way the silver
felt against her finger, all cool and smug. She was
tempted to pull the ring off and hurl it across the tent.
Or stomp on it. Rather than give in to impulse she sat

very still and tried to think. From beginning to end nothing had made sense today. All she'd planned on was spending the day at the Renaissance Faire, then going home, maybe ordering a pizza, practicing guitar for a while, and watching television. No adventure, no excitement, no threats of violence. No Toma, either, but so what? She'd never expected to get what she wished for, not even before she met a magic ring.

"I want to go home," she whispered. The words filled the darkness of the hot, still night. "I just want to go home."

"You can," the ring replied. There was something almost sheepish about the way it felt on her hand.

Relief surged through her. *Thank God! How? What do I do? What do I say?*

"All you have to do is wish."

Fine. I wish to go home.

"No, not now. On St. Bartholomew's Day."

But—

"All you have to do is wait a year."

A year!

"Make any wish on St. Bartholomew's Day and I must grant it. You've only got to wait three hundred and sixty-four more days."

Sara stared at the ring in stunned disbelief. What the ring was suggesting wasn't a solution, it was a sentence. She was condemned to spend a year in this hellhole? No. Impossible. There had to be another way.

You can't do this to me.

"It's only a year, Sara. A year with Toma."

She ignored the seductive suggestion in the ring's tone. *Why didn't you tell me?*

"Why should I tell you everything?"

Because . . . because you're magical, that's why!

"You been watching Disney movies, girl? What gave you the idea magic is benign?" The ring's metallic voice grated along her nerve endings. "Magic is power," it went on coldly. "Power just is. It isn't power's job to teach people how to use it. You're stuck in the past for a year. Maybe by then you'll figure out how to use me properly."

She wasn't interested in hearing lectures. She didn't think arguing was going to do any good, either. She thought violence might be an appropriate response, but she didn't know how to go about slapping around a little silver ring. *I hate you,* she told it. *I really, really hate you.* She waited for it to answer, but the ring just circled her finger, barely visible in the fading moonlight. It didn't care what she was feeling; her emotional devastation meant nothing to it. "Power just is," she whispered. "Fine. Be that way."

There had to be something she could do, some way out. Maybe it was all just a weird dream. Had to be, she decided. She stretched and yawned. She was so tired she could barely move, let alone think straight. Hallucination. Nightmare. That's all this whole thing was. She groped her way to the pallet where she'd first woken up and curled up on it without bothering to take off her clothes. This wasn't real, she assured herself as she buried her face in a feather pillow. She was going to wake up in her own bed. It was just a dream.

*   *   *

"I want to go home."

Sara didn't recognize the man's deep voice, but his words drew her out of a comfortable doze. You're not the only one, she thought as she opened her eyes, and discovered she was still in the tent. She groaned and screwed her eyes shut again.

"We all want to go home." It was Beng who spoke this time. The men were just outside the tent opening. "But what can we do? The *gajos* blockade the Channel. We can't leave England."

"Bororavia's a long way," a third man said. She recognized this voice, Evan, the old man they'd rescued from the muggers. "A long way to travel, with war and cossacks every step of the way."

"There are old trails, or so I've heard. Paths only Rom know," the stranger said. "It's getting past the blockade that will be hard. We need a ship."

"We can't get a ship," Beng said.

"Toma says he can," Evan replied.

"Toma." Beng hawked and spat, then went on. "Why you listen to that Calderash boy? He's not even *rom baro.*"

Not a man, Sara interpreted. Oh, great, she'd ended up involved with an old-fashioned tribe where you had to be married before anyone would listen to you.

"I like the boy," Evan said.

I do too, she thought, pleased at the old man's opinion of Toma.

"That's the problem," the stranger said. "He'll never be anything but a boy unless Beng gives in."

"He's not marrying my Sara. He's half *gajo.*"

And what's wrong with that? Sara wondered indignantly. Not that she planned to marry Toma, of course.

"Sara spends most of her time with *gajo*," Evan answered. "Your own sister married one, Beng. If Sara spends more time with the *gajo* maybe she'll want to marry one like your sister did."

"I won't talk about what my sister did. Someone has to deal with the English, and Sara is good at it. That's all there is to it," Beng said. "She earns a good living. She helps the whole *familia*."

"But no one but Toma has offered a bride-price for her," the stranger said. "Men suspect the virtue of one who deals too much with the *gajo*. Not I," he added quickly. "But some do. Toma cares for her."

"Toma is not one of us."

"He's a good lad," Evan defended him. "Let him marry the girl."

"No. And what has Sara's marriage got to do with our returning to Bororavia?"

Yeah, Sara thought, more curious than disturbed by the conversation. She didn't feel as if they were really talking about her. *What's the connection between me and Bororavia?*

"If Toma can get us past the English blockade," the stranger said, "and the French ships beyond the English ships, he deserves the girl for his efforts."

"No," Beng said again.

A voice called them from across the camp before the discussion could go on. The men moved away in response, to see after the horses. Sara wondered where the bathroom was as she got up, then remembered there wasn't one. She was thankful when she spotted a wide-mouthed pot, but not at all happy about having to use it. She was just thankful Beth was already awake and out of the tent so she could answer the call of nature in private.

When she was done she found a jug of water and splashed some over her hands. The water reminded her that she hadn't eaten or drunk anything since she'd woken up the day before. Just thinking about food made her stomach growl. There were copper pots and a small chest next to the fire pit, and a small mound of twigs lying on the ashes of the last fire. Sara thought about where the water came from and decided boiling it before trying to drink it might be safer. Fortunately, it didn't take her long to figure out how to use the flint and steel she found among the cooking things, though it did take a while to get it to work. She found a flat loaf of bread and some fruit in the food chest. There was also a bag of loose tea. She threw some leaves into the pot of water and ate while she waited for the tea to boil. She was waiting for the tea to cool when she noticed the big bag Evan had given to her the night before.

There was something familiar about the curve of the covered shape. She picked the thing up. She untied the cord holding the bag closed, then slid the cloth carefully down, revealing the rounded, honey-colored body of a finely made guitar. She held the instrument up, examining it with critical pleasure. The neck was narrow, dark wood inlaid with mother of pearl. She cradled it, strummed a D chord across the wire strings, then adjusted the tuning pegs and tried again.

"Sweet," she said, as familiar pleasure spread through her at the sound. "Beautiful."

She tried a few more chords, then looked at the fingertips of her left hand. They were already red and throbbing slightly. Sara the pickpocket and burglar had beautiful, sensitive, delicate fingers; their skill obviously made them too valuable to exercise on any rough work.

"Tough," Sara said.

It was going to hurt like hell to get them callused up enough to play properly, but at least she would have music. She hugged the guitar, comforted to have found something to help get her through the next year.

She dropped to sit cross-legged on the floor of the tent and pulled the bag to her. Inside she found smaller bags holding replacement strings and picks carved from thin slices of tortoiseshell, flexible but strong. "All right!" she crowed happily.

She was practicing Segovia scales when Beth came in. She switched to "Stairway to Heaven" after the girl just stood there gaping for a while, round-eyed with surprise.

"What the 'ell is that?" Beth finally blurted out.

"Led Zeppelin. I've always thought Jimmy Page's acoustic stuff is really great but—"

"What are you doing?" The little girl plopped down in front of her. She gingerly touched the body of the guitar. "Where'd you get this thing?"

"It's stolen, I guess. Beautiful, isn't it?"

"I reckon. You know 'ow to play it?"

Sara flexed her aching fingers. "More or less. Maybe

well enough to . . ." she trailed off, then shrugged. "All right, I'll say it out loud. I think, maybe, I've figured out how I can make a living for the next year."

Beth cocked her head. The look she gave Sara was a blend of annoyance and curiosity. "Your fingers are all red," she pointed out. "Can't pick locks if you 'urt your 'ands. Mother Cummings won't like that."

"Do I care? Anyway," she went on hastily, "I think I'm almost pretty sure that I can maybe, like, get a gig, you know, like a street musician or something. Or maybe audition for whatever passes for agents in this time. Maybe play Albert Hall or something. No, it hasn't been built yet. Maybe I could start here at the fair. Today. Maybe." She closed her eyes, then took a steadying breath and looked at the gaping child. "I really hate playing in public, but I'm going to do it."

"Fair's over today," Beth said. She rocked back on her heels and gave Sara a cunning look. "Could work," she said. "You gather in the crowd, I'll pick their pockets. Could make a bit that way." She nodded emphatically. "I like it."

Sara scowled at the girl. "Oh, no. No picking pockets. No stealing. Do you know what will happen to you if you get caught?"

Beth said indifferently, "Transported, maybe 'anged."

Sara's first reaction was disbelief at the girl's casual attitude. She was a child, she reminded herself. She didn't believe in her own mortality. And no one had ever taught her anything about morality. "Where are your parents, anyway?" she demanded. "Don't you have a home to go to?"

Beth looked as if she were about to cry. "You said you'd take care of me. You promised I could stay with you and you'd teach me." She sprang to her feet. "You ain't sending me back to Mother Cummings! I ain't going!"

Sara hastily put aside the guitar and grabbed Beth by the shoulders. "Of course not!" The girl was as lost in this uncaring world as she was. They were both scared. Sara hugged her. "I'll take care of you, I promise." At least for the next year, she added to herself. She didn't dare try to think past the next St. Bartholomew's Day.

Beth stepped back, her panic instantly turned off. "We want to eat, we better earn some money."

Sara couldn't argue with the girl's practical attitude. She did have to swallow hard on her own panic at facing the crowd. The time for stage fright was long past, and she knew it. She could try her hand at being a thief, or she could play in front of an audience.

"Get transported to Australia, or get rotten fruit thrown at you. The choice really isn't all that hard," she said. She picked up the guitar and put it back in the canvas bag to protect it until it was time to play. "Okay, let's go." She wagged a finger at Beth. "No pickpocketing."

Beth grimaced. "You crazy? 'Course I'll—"

"No you won't."

"Dammit, Sara!"

"And no swearing." Oh, God, Sara thought, I sound just like my mother. She almost didn't blame Beth for giving her a disgusted look and running out of the tent.

Sara called after her, but when she got no answer she clutched the bag to her chest and followed the girl to the bustle of the fair. It was a bright and beautiful morning, except for the ever-present smoke in the air. The sky overhead reminded Sara of her one trip to Los Angeles a few years back. "A few years forward. Whatever." *I'm talking to myself. That's crazy. You listening to me?* she asked the ring. It didn't answer. She decided to ignore it as well, and plunged into the crowd.

She was lost instantly, of course. Beth was nowhere in sight. She never had gotten her bearings the day before when she'd had the ring or Beth or Toma as a guide at all times. She wondered where Toma was now, and remembered where she'd first seen him. Maybe she could find him now. Maybe he could help her find Beth and find a place where she could play for the fairgoers. Toma. She got a warm, sweet feeling from just thinking about him. It was disgusting, that was what it was. Pure, mush-brained, romantic tripe. All the ring's fault. She just wished it didn't feel so good.

"Hmmph," she complained, hefted her guitar, and wandered down a jammed pathway that looked vaguely familiar. She smiled triumphantly a few minutes later when she recognized the alley that led behind Toma's stage. The stage must be around the next turning. She hurried forward as fast as she could dodge around the fairgoers, many of them excitedly chattering women. She felt a stab of jealousy at the realization that the women were chattering about Toma the Magnificent. She found herself tossing her dark curls, smug in the knowledge that she was the one Toma the Magnificent wanted to marry. Not that she could marry him, of course, but it was nice to be wanted.

Toma emerged from the alley just as she reached it. He was bare chested, with a blue silk headband holding back his long black hair. Beth was with him. A smile lit his face as he saw her; Sara thought for a second she was going to melt. He took her arm and drew her into the privacy of the alley.

"She's crazy, Toma," Beth said as they looked deep into each other's eyes. "She belongs in Bedlam, I swear!"

Toma gave Beth a stern look. "Hush, mud lark. Let me talk to her." He looked back at Sara. "I don't have much time."

She nodded. "Show time. I know."

"Beth's been raving at me. Is any of it true?"

Sara nodded. "I can't steal."

"You can't do anything else."

He looked so frustrated she wanted to comfort him. She supposed trying to explain magic rings and time travel and reincarnation would only make things worse. "I'm going to play the guitar," she said, since it was the only thing she really could explain. "Instead of stealing. Make an honest living."

"You *see!*" Beth chimed in. "Crazy. Mother Cummings'll kill us all!"

Toma ignored the girl. Sara would have tried to say something reassuring, but Toma had caught her gaze with his, and she couldn't turn away. His look was so intense, so pleading, she didn't know what to do. He wanted something from her. Lost in his gaze she wanted nothing more than to give him anything he wanted.

"I need you," he said. "Do you know how much I need you?" His hands tightened on her shoulders. For a moment she thought he was going to shake her. But he dropped his hands to his sides and balled them into fists instead. "You can't understand." The intensity bordering on anger left his face. "Why do you want to make an honest living?"

She was almost too shocked to answer him for a moment. To her it seemed so obvious, but how could she make someone who had never known anything but poverty and prejudice understand? "I have to."

"Mother Cummings won't like it." He brushed his hand through her curls. "Beng won't like it."

"I don't care."

He touched the tip of her chin. "I can tell. I can read your stubbornness right there."

"Help me," she pleaded.

"Toma!" Beth warned.

He sighed, then nodded. "How?"

She would have thrown her arms around him if it hadn't meant dropping the guitar. "I need somewhere to play," she explained. "Some way to get paid for it. I think you English call it busking. You know, being a street musician. I've seen people do it in Dinkytown back home, over by the university, and in Seattle, but I don't know where your equivalent of Pike Place Market is, so—"

"Sara?" This time he did shake her. "What are you talking about? Where are these places?" He touched the bag, sounding a muffled thrum from the bass string. "Guitar?" She nodded. "Can you really play the thing?"

Sara had to battle a combination of uncertainty and hard-earned, private pride before she could raise her head and say, "Of course."

Toma gave a curt nod. "Very well. Come with me."

She followed him to the steps behind the stage where Sandor waited, shifting nervously from foot to foot.

Sandor frowned at her and said to Toma, "Big crowd for the last day. Ready?"

"Not yet," Toma said. He pulled Sara up the steps. They were standing on the stage before she realized what he was doing. A burst of applause froze her in place. She couldn't bring herself to look out at the audience not twenty feet away.

"What are you doing?" she whispered at Toma.

He made a sweeping gesture toward the crowd. "You said you wanted to play."

"Not here. Not now!"

"If not here, where? If not now, when?" the ring piped up.

"I don't need any comments from you, thank you!"

"I didn't say anything."

"I wasn't talking to you!" Sara heard the panic in her voice and tried to get the better of it. "I mean, aren't you supposed to go on now?"

Toma left her to walk to the front of the stage. While Sara watched in horror, he bowed to the audience, then announced, "A fine gypsy musician to entertain you while I prepare for the death-defying feats to come." He glanced back at her for an instant, smiling encouragement. "Ladies and gentlemen," he went on to the waiting audience, "the incomparable Sara!"

As he stepped back there was a sprinkling of applause. She could feel people staring, waiting, but she couldn't look at them. She took a step forward, then another. She took the guitar from the bag without quite realizing she was doing it. Her blood felt frozen in her veins. It was the same cold fear of facing an audience that she'd always had, but this time she couldn't let it matter. The ring was right, as much as she hated to admit it. She had to do it. Her future in the past depended on it. She looked into Toma's eyes once more as she made it all the way to the front of the stage. He had given her a chance. She had to do it for him. He was there for her no matter what.

Nothing else matters, she thought. Which was also the title of a painfully beautiful love song she just happened to know how to play acoustically. It was as if Toma's caring fueled her courage. She didn't let herself think about the crowd as she began to play.

Toma wasn't anywhere in sight when she finished the song. She'd gone through it by rote, without any great feeling, but at least she'd gotten through it. A few people applauded. Sara looked up in surprise. She was more than surprised. She liked it. She smiled.

"That wasn't so bad, was it?"

She ignored the ring, even if it did mirror her own thought. She managed to look at the audience for a second longer, and give them a shy smile. Then she lowered her head and played a folk song she hoped the people would find familiar. She played two more songs and got more enthusiastic response from the crowd before Toma came out carrying a round velvet cap in his hand. She watched in amazement as he held the cap out significantly and a few coins were tossed onto the stage.

They like me, she thought, *they really like me.* She kept hold of the guitar with one hand while she scrambled to pick up the coins. Toma presented the cap to her with a flourish so she could drop the money into it. Then he graced her with a proud look before he hustled her offstage in order to get on with his own act.

She passed the ever-disapproving Sandor going up the rear steps as she came lightly down. A familiar face was waiting for her in the fenced courtyard.

"Mala?" Sara said in surprise. "What are you doing here?" Sara looked angrily at the ring. "How did she get back here?"

"Please call me Aunt Molly, dear," the woman answered. "You know I don't use my Romany name anymore. The dear late Mr. Macalpine always preferred Molly." She sighed. "May he rest in peace."

"Molly?" Sara questioned the woman who looked just like her friend.

Maybe the woman didn't look exactly like Mala; she was a little shorter and a little rounder, but her dark eyes were certainly the same. She wore a black dress, and a black bonnet covered her graying black hair. Behind them a roar of adoration went up from the crowd. Sandor must have lit the flames beneath

Toma's tightrope. Sara tried not to worry about him performing the dangerous stunt. She concentrated on the woman instead.

"Aunt Molly Macalpine? My aunt?" *Must be more reincarnation stuff,* Sara decided. *My father here looks like my father back home, only with a temper. So in this life Mala is my aunt instead of my math teacher. Right.* Sara smiled weakly at the woman. "Hi, Aunt Molly."

Beth appeared before anything more could be said. She snatched the hat away from Sara and quickly ran the coins through her fingers. "Gawd!" the girl complained loudly. "Call this an honest living. You can't buy a quart o' gin with this."

Sara took back the cap; it felt lighter. She didn't know how much money she'd actually made, but she definitely had less now. Beth must have helped herself to a few shillings.

She held out her hand. "Hand it over." Beth grinned and unashamedly dropped three coins into Sara's palm. "We aren't going to be buying gin," Sara informed the girl. "This is for basic necessities."

"Gin's necessary," Beth answered. "Ask anyone."

"Nonsense," Molly answered. "Nothing and no one is necessary but our Lord and his Commandments. You'd be wise to heed the word of Jesus Christ, my girl."

Beth looked at the woman as if she were about to spit on her. Molly looked at Beth as if she were about to launch into a sermon. Sara got the idea that Aunt Molly was a missionary. She didn't know what to say.

She was saved the need to when another roar went

up, not from the stage this time, but from the entrance to the courtyard. Sara recognized the bellow even before she turned her head to look at the man charging toward them. She smiled wanly at Beng's approach, but Beng's anger wasn't directed at her this time.

"You!" he shouted, halting in front of Molly. "What are you doing here, *mirame*?"

Molly didn't flinch at the insult, but looked Beng squarely in the eyes. "Sara's young man asked me to have a little talk with her. As her only female relative."

"You are no relative of mine. You make me unclean just looking at you."

"Who's asking you to look at me?" Molly shot back. She pointed at Sara. "I'm here to try to save my niece's soul, not listen to your heathen ravings about cleanliness. Mr. Macalpine was the finest man I ever met. How dare you call me dirty for marrying him?"

"He was a filthy *gajo*," Beng stormed back.

"He was my husband and I loved him!"

Sara and Beth looked at each other. Sara could tell that the little girl didn't want to hang around and listen to this argument any more than she did. Maybe they could sneak out before anyone noticed them. Without exchanging a word she and Beth began to sidle toward the alley door.

Beng rounded on her immediately. "What's that thing? What are you doing here? You been talking to this woman?"

Sara halted her retreat and turned back to Beng. "This is a guitar," she answered calmly. "Toma let me use his stage. I haven't actually had a discussion with the lady. I'm going to go back to my tent now, all right?"

"You go to Mother Cummings," he said. "You have work to do."

"For shame!" Molly spoke up. "You keep her away from that horrible woman. No decent woman would—"

"You stay out of this!" He turned his attention back to Sara. "You do what I tell you right now."

Sara looked into his determined face and wondered what she should do. He really wasn't her father, she reminded herself. She didn't owe him explanations. "I'm getting tired of saying this, but I will say it one more time: I am not a thief. I'm not robbing anyone. Leave me alone."

While Beng gaped at her she jammed the guitar back into its bag, took Beth by the hand, and said, "Come on, kid. We're history."

6

"I don't want to talk about it!"

Beng and Molly had followed her back to her tent. Neither of them looked as if they were going to go away. Other people in the camp had abandoned packing the wagons to gather around to stare. Sara had seen several of them make signs against evil at Molly. Molly pretended not to notice.

Sara sighed and said, "All right. Let's go inside and talk about it."

She started to go in, but Beng grabbed her arm. *"She* can't go in there."

"Oh, for crying out loud!" Sara complained. "I hate all this *mirame* stuff. My whole tribe's been accused of it for nearly two hundred years. Will you get with the program?" While Beng gaped at her she gestured at Molly. "The woman is not going to pollute everything she touches just because she married a non-Rom. Sheesh."

"I've been trying to tell them that for years, the poor heathens," Molly told her.

"They aren't heathens, they're Rom," Sara snapped at the woman's smug tone. "Go and get your things," she said to Beth while Beng and Molly looked at her with their mouths hanging open. The pair looked very like brother and sister at this moment. "I'm leaving," she told Beng before he could gather wits enough to yell at her. "I don't know where, but I'm going." She wanted to run straight to Toma, but romance wasn't the solution to her future.

"You're going, all right, to the house in St. Giles," Beng finally managed to answer. He gestured toward the wagons. "We're going to the Salisbury fair. You work for the Cummings woman until we get back." He gestured to include all the wagons again. "You make enough to see us through the winter. You be a good girl."

Oh, no, Sara thought, he wasn't putting the responsibility for caring for the whole *familia* on her. She closed her eyes for a moment. When she opened them again Molly was looking at her sympathetically.

Beng favored Molly with a contemptuous glare. "I won't stay while she's here. You just do what I say." This seemed to settle the discussion as far as he was concerned. He stomped off toward the horse corral without further comment.

"Now what?" Sara said. "What am I going to do?" She wondered if Cummings and Billy were going to come looking for her sometime soon. Mother Cummings had said she wanted the burglary done tonight. Toma couldn't protect her. He was a circus performer scheduled to leave with the others. Toma? She looked at Molly. "You said Toma wanted you to talk to me? About what?"

Molly crossed her arms and looked belligerently at the people who still lingered near Sara's tent. "In private, dear," she said. "You aren't going to that Cummings woman," she added. "You're coming with your aunt. Right now, before Beng can stop us. I'll meet you by the fair entrance." Molly turned and walked away, head held high, before Sara could ask any questions.

Sara decided to ask questions later. It was faster just to bundle up some clothes from the tent, take Beth and the guitar, and get out before Mother Cummings's goons showed up. She missed saying good-bye to Toma the Magnificent, but that was for the best. Her heart got more caught up every time she talked to the man. It kept trying to get her brain to agree to the ludicrous idea of marrying him. Better to go with the well-meaning missionary aunt and forget all about marrying Toma.

"Marry Toma, Aunt Molly?" Sara couldn't help but smile no matter how incredulous she felt at the woman's suggestion.

They were seated in the kitchen of the woman's very respectable inn. It turned out Aunt Molly wasn't a missionary after all, at least not professionally. She and her late husband were committed Methodists who also ran the Blue Rose inn. Now that she was a widow, Molly had decided to devote most of her time to charity work among the Anglo-Romany.

The inn's kitchen was closed for the evening, and most of the guests were in bed or conversing quietly in the common room. Beth was tucked into bed in a small room off the kitchen. Sara had been given a room next door. She'd spent part of the day helping out in the kitchen with Molly and the couple who worked for her, then had played guitar quietly in the common room while the guests ate dinner. Her second public performance hadn't been anywhere near as nerve-racking as her first, but she'd been happy to escape to the kitchen when Aunt Molly suggested a little chat.

She didn't know why she was so surprised when marriage to Toma turned out to be the subject of the conversation. "You said he'd asked you to talk to me. I'd forgotten."

Molly nodded. "He's such a respectful boy. When Beng refused to discuss the marriage with him he remembered that you had one female relative. So he asked me to discuss the marriage with you. I really think you ought to marry him, dear," she repeated. "He's really quite exceptionally good-looking."

"Yes. Yes, he is," Sara agreed. She tried not to sigh romantically. "I . . ." She let her words trail away. How could she explain that she couldn't marry him even if she wanted to? If she had to make explanations she'd save them for Toma. For now she said, "I'll think about it."

"You don't want to disobey your father, do you?"

Sara nodded stiffly.

"I understand," Molly went on. "I know what it's like to go against your family and everything you know." She stood. "Time we got some rest, my dear. Join me in a prayer for wisdom."

Sara stood and bowed her head. When Molly had

finished Sara said, "Thank you for taking me in, Aunt Molly."

The woman waved her thanks away and handed Sara one of the candles on the table. "Off to bed with you."

Gripping the candle by its brass holder, Sara followed its feeble light down the back hall to her bedroom. The room was smaller than the tent and held in the August heat like an oven, but Sara didn't mind calling it home. It had only a narrow bed with a thin mattress, a clothes chest, and a small table for her to rest the candlestick on, but it was better than any other alternative she'd been presented.

"Better than a prison hulk," she whispered as she closed the heavy door behind. "Anything's better than that."

"I couldn't agree more," Toma said, stepping out of the deep shadows by the wardrobe.

Sara jumped in surprise. Her movement snuffed out the candle, which she dropped anyway. A shaft of moonlight fell in a neat square in front of the room's only window. Toma drew her into it. She realized how much she'd missed him as she saw his angular features outlined in the silvery light. She didn't know how it was possible to get attached to someone so quickly, but it had happened.

She touched his cheek, feeling the faintest trace of stubble. "Maybe there is something to this own true love business," she said, not sure if she was admitting it to him, herself, or the ring.

Her confusion disappeared when Toma bent his head and his lips met hers. The kiss was one of gentle greeting at first, but grew more ardent and hungry by the second. She wasn't sure who started it, but before long their hands were all over each other. The hot night, the enclosed room, any questions she had were soon forgotten in the heat that rose from every spot where Toma's nimble fingers touched.

She didn't know when or how they ended up on the bed, but at some point, sometime after he began licking and sucking on her nipples through the thin cloth of her dress, Sara came to her senses enough to ask, "Do you have any protection?"

Toma's eyes glinted up out of the night, over the rounded mounds of her breasts. "I have my knife," he said.

His weight across her was deliciously solid. One of her hands was resting on his shoulder; the other was combing through the silky mane of his black hair. She laughed breathlessly at his answer. "I meant a condom," she told him. "You know, birth control, AIDS, that kind of protection."

Toma rolled off her and propped himself up on one elbow. It was a tight fit for both of them to lie on the bed, and Sara was wedged up against the wall. "Protection? Condom? A skin sheath, you mean? Don't talk like a whore."

His irritated tone immediately annoyed her, but she supposed it was stupid to argue social attitudes with a man from the past. It was even more stupid to want so desperately to make love to him. She couldn't complicate living a year in the past by adding pregnancy to her problems. Besides, making love to Toma once would just make her want to do it again. It was too physically and emotionally risky. She squeezed her hands into fists to keep from pulling him into another deep kiss.

"We'd better stop," she said.

Toma ran his hand down her side, then down across her stomach. "Must we?"

The cajoling promise in his voice sent a pleasant shiver through her. "Yep. Uh-huh. Oh, my, that feels good." She didn't know when her eyes closed as he continued his persuasive caressing, but she managed to pry them open before losing complete control of herself. When she saw Toma smiling at her she didn't know whether to laugh or to smack him, he looked so pleased with himself. "Take your hand off of there," she ordered. "Right now."

He sighed dramatically, but took his hand away.

Before she could ask him to put it back she remembered to ask, "How did you get in here? What are you doing in here? Isn't the circus going to Salisbury?"

He sat up and swung his legs over the side of the bed. Sara moved to sit beside him. His arm went around her shoulder. "Shh," he warned. "We don't want to shock your aunt. I wanted to see you in private. She would have wanted to chaperon us, and she wouldn't like what I have to tell you. I came in the back way, found your room, and waited." He kissed her cheek. "It was worth the wait."

Sara snuggled closer to him. His presence made her feel safe and wanted. He couldn't know how important it was not to be alone in this alien time and place. "You're wonderful," she said. "So sweet. Kind of like Ed on *Northern Exposure.*" But sexy like Chris, she said to herself, only shorter. And if she'd known she was going to miss a year's worth of television she could have at least set a tape.

"Ed who?" Toma asked.

The hint of jealousy in his voice amused her. "Never mind. Why aren't you with the circus?"

"You're more important. I wanted to warn you, help you. You're not safe here, Sara," he went on before she could ask him what he meant. "Mother Cummings knows all about it."

"It? It what?"

"Knows you're here. That you're holding out on her."

"I'm not holding—"

"She doesn't like it, Sara." He brushed his hand across her forehead. "Don't get her angry. She can have you killed." He snapped his fingers. "Just like that." Another snap, right next to her ear. She jumped nervously at the sound. "More likely it's Beth she'll hurt since she still needs you. She knows you care for the mud lark."

"Hurt Beth?" Sara said the words slowly, memories of Cummings's crude comment to the girl and Beth's fear of Mother Cummings playing over in her mind as she spoke. "She's just a little girl." Larcenous and streetwise, but still just a child. "I promised I'd protect her."

"Then you'd better do what Mother Cummings wants."

Sara shook her head. "No. That's not possible."

"But—"

Sara broke away from the safe shelter of his

embrace before he could finish. "That is not an option," she told him firmly. She headed for the door. "I've got to get Beth out of here. Can you take her to Salisbury with you?" she asked as he hurriedly followed her next door to Beth's room.

"I'm not going to Salisbury."

She whirled to face him. "Why not?"

His hands touched her shoulders. "I stayed to look after you."

"Oh." The rush of love nearly overwhelmed her. "Thank you." It was illogical, it was impossible, she'd known the man for only a day, but she knew she loved him. He drew her to him and kissed her, slowly and gently. But worry for Beth drew her out of his arms before long. She stepped away, but took his hand as they went to Beth's door.

Moonlight from a small window fell directly across the bed, but there was nothing there for them to see. The bed was empty. Sara paused in the doorway, her gaze searching frantically, but it was obvious that Beth was not in the room.

"No," she whispered. "Oh, no."

Toma urged her forward. While she stood in hopeless confusion in the middle of the room, he lit a candle, then held it up, slowly turning to search the shadows. Sara followed his movements, and saw the folded piece of paper at the foot of the bed the same instant he said, "Look."

She rushed to snatch it up.

Toma held out his hand. "Let me read that for you."

"I can read it myself, thank you," she said, irritated

despite her worry. He held the candle closer as she unfolded the paper. "I can read, but I'm not sure these jokers can write." She stared at the abysmal scrawling squiggles on the page. Though the message was easy enough to guess, it took her a while before she could decipher the details. "It says I won't see Beth again unless I bring Mother Cummings the scarabs."

"Tonight," Toma added. His arm came around her shoulder. "Sara, it has to be tonight."

"What am I going to do?"

"Do you want to see the mud lark again?"

"Of course!"

"Then do it." He swiveled her to face him. His expression was intense in the gold glow of the candle. "You're the best, sweetheart. Do this one job and they'll never bother you again. I'll see to that, I promise."

"But . . . how?" She searched desperately for some sane alternative to this situation. "Couldn't we call the police? Scotland Yard?"

Toma frowned in puzzlement. "Police? This isn't France. There are no secret police in England, love."

"Who said anything about secret police? I'm talking about getting help to get Beth back. The poor baby's been kidnaped. There must be somebody we can go to."

His laugh was low and harsh. "We're Rom," he reminded her. "No law protects us."

Sara sat down on the bed, too overcome with fear to stay on her feet. She touched the ring, pressing her sore fingertip into the knotwork design. "Can't you do something?" she begged it. It made no response.

Toma faced her. "You're the only one who can help her, Sara." He held out his hand to her. "Come with me. To Philipston House. I can show you the way."

Sara looked up at him in bleak anguish. The man she loved was offering to help her commit a felony. It was wrong. She didn't know how. She was terrified. Beth's life depended on her. "Oh, God," she whispered. "There's nothing I can do." She took Toma's hand and let him pull her to her feet. "All right. If I have to. Just this once." She looked into his deep blue sympathetic eyes. "Show me what to do."

"I can't go through with this."

Toma grabbed her sleeve as she turned to run. "Sara."

"I can't go in there."

They were standing in a park in the center of a square in a fashionable part of town. Mayfair, Toma had said as they made their way to the west side of London. As they passed mansions and parks and gardens, dodged carriages and groups of fashionably dressed people, Sara had felt not only more out of place, but more familiar with the setting. This was the Regency London she knew about, the upscale side of the world she'd discovered the day before.

The house before them was three stories tall, narrow, separated from identical mansions by narrow strips of garden. Unlike other houses in the neighborhood no lights were showing in the windows of Philipston House. There was no traffic on the wide, brick-paved road. It was a quiet night in a quiet neighborhood.

"Too quiet," Sara whispered, pressing her back against a wide tree trunk. Her mouth was dry with fear. This was worse than stage fright. Toma tugged on her hand. "I can't do it," she repeated.

"Beth."

It was all he had to say, and he knew it. He'd been repeating the word to her the whole way, every time she tried to turn back. Beth. He was right. She couldn't do it but she had to. So she would. Somehow.

"Beth. Right," she grumbled. She pushed herself away from the tree. She studied the house again. "You sure there's nobody home?"

"Philipston went to Bath for his gout," Toma told her. "He took his household with him."

"What about alarms?" she asked. "Security systems?"

"What?"

"Large watchdogs with mean, nasty teeth," she clarified. "Things like that."

Toma shook his head. "No. Nothing like that."

"How do you know?" she snapped. Her irritation was fueled by panic. She didn't have time to panic. "Get a grip," she ordered herself. She squared her shoulders and walked swiftly out of the park. She was standing in front of the door to Philipston House before she noticed Toma wasn't with her. When she turned to look she saw him lingering on the curb across the street. The silver threads in his blue head-scarf glittered in the moonlight. It occurred to her that her own colorful long skirts weren't exactly the ideal attire for breaking and entering. "Attack of the ninja gypsy guitarist. How's that for a movie of the week?" The ludicrous image almost made her chuckle. What was her partner in crime waiting for? She gestured with her head. She caught the flash of his white teeth as he grinned before sprinting across the street to join her.

"What do you plan?" he asked when he reached her. "Just to knock on the front door?"

"It's a thought."

"Servants' entrance for the likes of us."

Sara tilted her head thoughtfully. "You're right. There must be a back door. Come on."

They made their way cautiously through a garden to the back of the house. Roses scented the air around them, as romantic as the moonlight. Music filtered across the distance from one of the nearby houses. Sara paused for a moment, struck by the beauty of the setting and the incongruousness of the moment.

"Pianoforte. Mozart." She sighed.

Toma touched her on the shoulder. "How do you know?"

"My mom's a music teacher."

"Your mother worked the *bujo*," Toma answered. "Molly told me."

This was no time to try to explain the difference between herself and the person he thought she was, even if the difference was crucial to what they were about to do. She did take the time to defend her mother. "Mom's a *gajo*. She wouldn't know how to run a con to save her life. Come on, let's get this over with."

Toma gave a confused shake of his head before they hurried on. The flower garden gave way to a vegetable garden. There were stables beyond, and several small outbuildings that Sara guessed were storage sheds. The back door loomed wide and dark up a short flight of stairs in the center of the back wall. There was still no sign of movement inside or out. Not even a stray cat ambled by along the back fence.

"Too quiet," Sara whispered again. She sat down on a stone bench on the edge of the flower garden and stared at the back of the house for a while. What the hell was she supposed to do next? She rubbed the ring. *I'm open to suggestions,* she told it.

Toma paced the pathway in front of the bench, his soft-soled shoes making no sound on the flat, round paving stones. "Hurry," he instructed in a fierce whisper. "Let's get this over with."

He sounded angry as well as anxious. He must be as worried as she was at getting caught, even though the morality of the situation didn't seem to bother him. If he mentioned Beth one more time she thought she might kick him. She stood up and approached the door and turned the knob. It was locked, of course. When she glanced over her shoulder at Toma she saw he was standing with his arms crossed, a sarcastic expression evident even if she could only see him by moonlight.

"It was worth a shot," she told him.

He bounded up the steps to join her. "You could try breaking a window."

"I could," she agreed, "but that would be stupid. If we can get in without being obvious about it, no one is going to know anything is missing until this guy gets home. The less evidence the better, the less chance of getting caught."

He patted her on the head. "Clever girl."

"Yeah," Sara agreed, though she hadn't realized what she was thinking until she'd spoken. Maybe she did have a bit of criminal talent. The notion gave her confidence. She took a step back onto the top stair tread and looked around thoughtfully, looking for possibilities.

"I wonder," she said after carefully looking over the scene. "Maybe there's a spare house key hidden someplace."

"What?"

"Think about it. The place is crawling with servants, right? People must go in and out at all hours. It would be convenient to be able to get in without somebody getting out of bed at three in the morning when the butler comes home drunk on his night off."

Toma looked indignant. "But the butler doesn't—it makes sense, I suppose," he finished thoughtfully. "Can't trust servants."

"Can't hurt to look." Sara began with the stairs. She didn't find anything until she reached the bottom. Then a loose flagstone to the right of the bottom step flipped over as she ran her hands along the ground. "Got it," she said as the moonlight glinted off a shiny metal object. She fished the key out of its hiding place and smiled triumphantly at the watching Toma.

"Well?" he asked. "What are you waiting for?"

His impatience spurred her back up the stairs. He was right; they had to get this over with and get out of here. The key fit smoothly into the lock. It turned without any trouble. Sara let out a tensely held breath as she heard the lock click open. The door opened without a squeak or rattle.

She hurried inside, Toma a few steps behind her, and quickly closed the door. She didn't know what room they were in, but at least they were inside.

"Servants' hall, I think," Toma said before she could ask. It was light enough in the room to show the outline of a door on the opposite wall. "Kitchen through there, maybe?"

"Sounds good to me." She touched his sleeve. "If you were a collection of gold scarabs, where would you hang out? Wait, maybe the ring would know."

"What?"

Well? she asked the ring. *Give me some help here.*

"Try the library," came the bored voice in her head. "Egyptian jewelry is *so* serious."

"Library." She rubbed her chin thoughtfully. "Has to be in the front of the house where there are windows, plenty of light." She tried to imagine the probable layout of the house's interior. Using her imagination she led the way from the servants' hall through the large kitchen and into a dark hallway. Without moonlight coming in through windows to see by she was instantly disoriented.

"How do we find the library?" she asked while waiting for her eyes to adjust to the darkness.

She soon made out a few dark shapes of furniture

lining the walls. There was a thick strip of carpet beneath her feet. She waited for Toma's answer, but none came. She couldn't feel the warmth of his presence, either. Nor the soft sounds of his breathing and almost inaudible sound of his clothes as he moved. A stab of fear shot through her. He wasn't there, was he?

"Toma?"

She turned slowly, not in any hurry to find out she was alone. Putting it off didn't change the fact that he wasn't there. "Toma?" she repeated, voice a husky whisper. A chill of dread settled over her despite the warmth of the night. She took a step back toward the kitchen. All her confidence disappeared in a nauseating rush. Where was he?

She heard a footstep just as her hand touched the kitchen door. "Thank God!" She whirled around, almost ready to collapse with relief. "Don't do that—"

At first she thought the big man looming out of the darkness was Cummings; then another man appeared from down the hall carrying a candle and she saw that the men were strangers. They were dressed identically in gray coats and white knee breeches, and they were both far larger than she was. She lunged for the door handle. It was locked.

She was grabbed from behind before she could run, and spun around and marched ahead of her captors down the hall with her arms held behind her back. No one said a word. She longed to scream out to Toma for help, but she didn't want to risk his being captured as well.

The house was no longer completely dark. The

men took her to a room she decided must be a sitting room. They made her sit in a brocade chair while they took up posts on either side of the room's only door. Then they waited. Waiting for what, Sara didn't know and couldn't find voice to ask. The cops, she supposed. She'd been caught, and there was no way out. She was going to prison. Worse still, Beth was going to suffer for her failure. She could only pray that Toma got away, that he could do something for the child.

The waiting seemed to go on forever. Sara found herself watching a candle flame slowly burning its way through about an inch of wax. The men didn't move, nor would they answer her questions. The air in the room was stuffy and still. A clock ticked on the mantel; the sound was almost on the edge of hearing, but loud enough to eat at her nerves. She wouldn't look at the clock. She was afraid she'd discover the ring had transported her into some sort of limbo where time didn't pass at all.

By the time the door opened and two men stepped inside she almost welcomed their arrival. It meant she was about to be dragged off to jail but at least the wait was over. She stood as they entered and forced herself to confront them. One was tall and graying; the other was young, slim, with long black hair tied at the nape of his neck.

The younger one approached her. She hoped she'd be given a chance to explain about Beth; maybe the police would do something to help the girl. She looked him in the eye as she tried to think of a lucid explanation. His eyes were bright blue. His face was a handsome, sharp triangle above an elaborate starched collar. He tilted his head slightly, a faint flicker of amusement quirking up his lips for just a moment. Lips she'd kissed not that long ago.

"Toma?"

"Hello, Sara," he answered. "You're under arrest."

7

"What?"

"Arrest," he repeated. "You are my prisoner."

He'd taken his time changing, luxuriating in the feel of a hot bath and being dressed in the clothes that were the first stare of fashion. He had also taken his time so the girl would have a chance to contemplate the horrors awaiting her. Imagination was a powerful weapon, and the gypsies were an imaginative, superstitious lot. And, in truth, he hadn't relished the coming confrontation any.

He'd expected the girl to be huddled on a chair in hysterical tears when he entered. Her reaction upon recognizing him was far from satisfactory.

"You could scream and faint," he suggested with a wry smile. "I promise to catch you."

Instead of fainting, Sara dropped back into the chair as if she'd been struck, raised her right hand in front of her face, and said angrily, "My own true love is an undercover cop? What is going on here?"

"Cool little mort, isn't she?" his companion said.

He found the mixture of contempt and amusement in the man's voice irritating but he ignored him. He kept his attention on Sara. He thought he'd come to know the girl in the time he'd been cultivating her and her tribe, but now he wasn't so sure his assumptions about her were correct. The shy, docile, clever-fingered child he'd first met had been acting very peculiar in the last couple of days. He'd been equally intrigued, amused, and worried at her sudden assertive behavior. Perhaps she was mad, but it was too late to abandon the plan now.

"I don't know what 'cop' means," he said to her. "But you are correct about 'undercover.'" He gave her a condescending smile. "Just where did you learn the language of espionage, my lovely?"

She looked up at him, dark eyes snapping with anger. "I watch a lot of television. Who are you really? Where's Beth?"

Her concern for the mud lark was touching. Of course, it was also her downfall. "Safely asleep at your aunt's, I should imagine. I gave her a whole pound to make herself absent for a while."

Sara surged angrily to her feet. "You bastard! I was scared to death for her. You knew it was a trap, didn't you? What's this about, anyway?"

He had the oddest notion that she wasn't addressing him. Not for the first time. "What it's about," he answered, "is that I need a cat's paw, and you're it." He made a short bow. "You have the honor of addressing Lieutenant Lewis Morgan, Royal Navy."

"Lewis Morgan?" She stared at him, her anger tempered by incredulity. "*The* Lewis Morgan? The Hero of the Revolution?"

Before he could ask what she meant his companion spoke. "The girl's beetle-headed, my boy. She obviously won't do. Send for the constables."

"She'll do," Lewis answered. "By the way," he went on to Sara, "meet Lord Philipston. My father."

"The situation hardly requires formal introductions." His father glared down his long nose at Sara with disdain. "I shall have to have the chair burned, I suppose."

He watched Sara's hands ball into fists, but she didn't say anything to Lord Philipston. She kept her attention on him. Anger burned in her, and a growing contempt that made it hard for him to continue to look her in the eye. She was supposed to be frightened, confused, begging. He'd been prepared to deal with tears and entreaties.

Sara bit her tongue rather than answer the older man's rude comment. However, she did spread her skirts and sit with deliberate slowness on the fine brocade upholstery of the chair. "Is there a scarab collection?" she asked. She felt an odd sense of victory in managing to keep her voice quite calm. She wasn't calm; she was about a nanosecond away from total panic. She was tempted to take Toma—Lewis Morgan—up on his screaming and fainting offer. Only the thought of being wrapped in the false safety of his arms kept her from giving in. The ring felt like a lead weight on her finger. It knew what was going on—she could feel it—but it wasn't talking.

Lewis Morgan stood over her. She hoped she didn't look as intimidated by him as she felt. He looked so . . . aristocratic. Not a good sign, she was sure.

"You're not Rom, are you? Not even half?"

His smile was slow, and somehow menacing. "I knew a gypsy girl once, from the Calderash tribe," he said. "She taught me a lot, before her own family denounced her as a whore."

The way they'll denounce you if you aren't careful. He didn't say it, but Sara heard the implication in his tone. She wondered why she'd thought of Toma as a sweet young man. "Everything you've done and said has been a lie." He nodded. "Why?"

"I need you," he said. "I need to control you."

She had the feeling his reasons were going to be treacherous and convoluted. She looked at the intricate knotwork pattern of the ring. She was beginning to realize that the ring liked things convoluted.

"You're a spy, aren't you?" she asked Lewis. None of her father's historical bedtime stories had mentioned anything about Lewis Morgan being a British spy. She did her best to remember everything she knew about him. Anything she could remember would come in handy right now. She hoped. Maybe a knowledge of history didn't help when the history hadn't happened yet.

"I am an officer in His Majesty's Navy," he answered. "And, yes, I am a spy."

The bitterness in his voice did nothing to mollify her newborn hatred for him. "Why did you set me up? What do you want me for?" Lord Philipston snickered lewdly, but she didn't pay him any attention.

Lewis gave his father an annoyed look. He was obviously finding the girl's humiliation amusing. He owed the man a debt of gratitude for allowing him to use Philipston House for this operation. He hadn't minded agreeing to his father's request to "be in at the kill," but now that the vixen was cornered his presence was proving obstructive. "Could you leave us alone, please?" he requested. "State Secrets," he explained as his father turned a dark frown on him. "My apologies, sir."

His father hesitated for a moment, then gave an annoyed nod. "You're cheating me of my fun, lad." He left the room, signaling the footmen to go with him.

Once away from his father's stern scrutiny, Lewis pulled up a chair and sat down facing the girl. "Now, love, let's have a little talk."

"I'm not your love." She twisted the fingers of her left hand around the ring finger of her right hand. She'd been making the nervous gesture quite a bit lately.

He sat back and tried to act relaxed. "Let's just pretend you are."

"Let's not. What's going on here, Morgan?" Her voice was as cold as iron, her expression about as hard.

He'd definitely been mistaken about the girl. He'd approached her thinking his job would be easy. He didn't know when it had gotten complicated, when she had gotten complicated. "You have a choice," he told her. "Cooperate with everything I want of you, or accept the just punishment for your crimes."

"Crimes?" she looked around her. "Breaking in here?" He nodded. She shook her head. "I don't think so. Where I come from this is called entrapment. You can't do this."

"You're a long way from Bororavia, Sara."

"I'm not from Bororavia, I'm from Minnesota."
She ran her hands through her hair in sudden agitation. "Oh, God, this is 1811, isn't it?"

"By the English calendar, it is." He supposed gypsies reckoned the time differently, if the wanderers reckoned it at all. Since he'd started studying them he'd been slowly discovering that they did everything differently.

She knew he wouldn't believe her if she told him she was from 1994. She needed the ring's help, but the ring felt like a dead weight on her finger. Find out what the man wants, she told herself. Work from there.

"You didn't con me into this mess just to send me to Botany Bay."

"Correct," he acknowledged. "But Botany Bay will be your destination if you don't fully cooperate."

"Cooperate with what?"

"My plans."

She got the impression he was embarrassed. Or that the plan was so secret even he didn't know what it was. She started in surprise when he said, "Marry me, Sara."

She stared at him in utter confusion. He was obviously out of his mind. Finally, all she could manage to say was, "In your dreams."

"It wasn't a request."

"But . . . why do you want to marry me?"

"I don't. It's necessary for my mission."

"And your mission is?"

"None of your concern."

She was so frustrated she wanted to hit him. She had never wanted to hit anyone in her life before, but the man had the ability to stir violent emotion in her. "An hour ago I loved you," she said. "I wouldn't marry you now if my life depended on it."

"It does."

The cold finality of his voice chilled her to the bone. She didn't have any choice. She hated not having any choice. It almost choked her to get the words out. It was him or the prison hulks. "I'll marry you."

The look of hatred on Sara's face warned Lewis that he wasn't going to have an easy time of it. "It's late," he said. "We should get some rest." In truth, he wanted the chance to spend the night in a decent bed between clean linen sheets before he had to resume his disguise. "Come along."

He had to take Sara's hand in a tight grasp and tug her forward before he could get the stubborn girl to move. A footman was waiting outside the door with a branch of candles. He preceded them, lighting their way to the storerooms behind the kitchen. He unlocked the vegetable larder door and handed the key to Lewis before stepping out of the way. Lewis waved Sara forward.

"There's no window," he said, "and nothing you can steal. This should suit."

Sara let out an audible gulp as she peered into the narrow, dark room. "You want me to sleep in there?"

From her horrified tone, one would have thought he was throwing her into the mouth of hell. "Can't have the likes of you spoiling my father's bed linen, can we?" he said jokingly.

He pushed her inside and slammed the door before she could scamper back out.

"Toma!" she called to him. He locked the door.

The footman chuckled at her panicked cry, but Lewis walked silently away.

He poured her a basin of water in the kitchen so she could wash the tearstains off her face. She looked pathetic, which was just what he'd intended, broken to his command. It was not a pleasant sight. He did not relish having to spend the next few months in the girl's cowed company. He'd had to summon up every bit of cold resolve he could manage before facing his prisoner. He had to keep reminding himself that she was a thief, and getting off far better than she deserved.

It was just after dawn of what promised to be another hot day. Lewis had not had a pleasant night's rest. He was anxious to be away before his father rose, cup-shot and foul tempered as usual.

"Sleep well?" he asked his prisoner as she dried her face with a dishcloth. Sara flashed him a look of pure hatred. The force of it was enough to send him back a step. "Not too cowed, I see. Perhaps your company won't prove boring, after all."

"Drop dead."

She hadn't slept at all. The room had been stifling hot, airless, the darkness frequently stirred by the sound of rodents. She'd spent a lot of time crying, which made her feel weak and stupid. Lewis and his father's casually bigoted comments kept replaying themselves in her mind, keeping her very unpleasant company. She'd emerged from the storeroom in no mood to put up with anything from Lewis Morgan.

She stretched tiredly. "I want to be home," she said, more to herself or the ring than her smirking companion. "In a hot bath, listening to Richie Sambora. I cannot put up with a year of this."

Lewis grabbed her arms and pulled her to him. He wasn't a large man, but she was much shorter. He loomed over her. He looked coolly angry and dangerous. "Richie who?"

"What do you mean, Richie—" He shook her. "The guitarist with Bon Jovi," she explained hastily. "I really love his solo albu—"

"Is he your lover?"

Sara couldn't keep from laughing. "Don't I wish." She saw instantly that she'd given the wrong answer. Her captor looked so angry that for a moment she was afraid he was going to hit her. Then his expression shifted from anger to contempt. Contempt she could deal with. "My fantasy life is none of your business," she told him. "He's a musician I listen to."

"Spends much time in your tent, does he? While you bathe?"

"I've never met the man. What is your problem? Jealous?"

He dropped his hands so fast he might have been burned. He gave her a smile she would have found charming yesterday. "There's no man in your life but me from now on, darling." He reached out again, taking her by the hand this time. "Let's go, while there's no one on the streets who might recognize me."

He was dressed in his gypsy clothes, back playing Toma again.

"Go where?" she asked, following him out the door.

They were well away from Philipston House before he answered. "Back to your aunt's. She'll be worried about you."

He sounded amused about Aunt Molly being worried, but Sara didn't want to explore the subject of upper class humor. She didn't particularly want to talk to him at all, but there was so much she wanted to know. A chilled, angry silence toward him for the next year might be tempting, but it wasn't very practical. She was still very annoyed about the storeroom.

"So, fiancé, what happens when you want me to get pregnant?" she asked bitterly. "You have some nice, romantic crypt picked out? I can hardly wait to hear your honeymoon plans."

"I'm not interested in children," he replied as he hurried her along the quiet streets. After a significant pause he chuckled and added, "We'll be honeymooning in France."

It took several minutes for the remark to register. "But England was at war with France in 1811."

The fool girl pestered him with questions the rest of the way back to the Blue Rose. He didn't answer any of them. He'd already said too much. He had to remember the gypsy girl was a pawn, not an ally. As they came to the door of the inn he pulled her close and whispered in her ear. "Follow my lead. Do what you're told. Remember what happens if you don't."

Sara heard the chilling menace in his whispered words and any confidence she might have gathered during the long walk back from Mayfair vanished. Lewis Morgan meant business and she had no choice. She was going to get him for this, she promised herself. She said, "I understand." He kissed her cheek. She forced herself not to jerk away from the soft warmth of his lips.

"Come along, love." He opened the door and led her into the inn's common room.

Aunt Molly didn't look worried when she glanced up from talking to a customer. She looked annoyed. "Well," she said sternly as she marched up to them, wiping her hands on an apron. "Well, indeed! I suspected as much. For shame." She pointed toward the back of the house. "Into the kitchen with you two. Scandal. In my house," she added, herding them into the kitchen. "I'll not have it. It's the parson's mousetrap for you two, make no mistake."

"We're sorry to have worried you," Toma said as soon as Molly had sent the servants away. "You know I intend to do the honorable thing by the girl. Don't I, Sara?"

Sara slipped away from his grasp. "Where's Beth?" she asked the outraged woman. "Is she all right? We were looking for her," she added when Molly stared at her questioningly.

"You went out alone? With a young man?" Molly shook a finger under Sara's nose. "Hardly proper, for an English girl or a Rom."

"She's sorry."

Sara ignored Lewis Morgan's sincere-sounding apology. "Beth?"

"Upstairs with one of the maids, learning to make beds." Molly sighed. "The child requires a great deal of supervision, I'm afraid. Thieving ways," she explained in a confidential tone.

"We know," Lewis said. "Sara thought she'd run away last night," he explained. "I helped her look for her."

Molly turned to him. "Why aren't you in Salisbury?"

"Sara found me at the campgrounds before I left. I couldn't leave her alone."

The sincerity in the man's expression and tone made Sara want to gag. "Right," she said sarcastically. "He's just full of the milk of human kindness. Or at least he's just full of it," she added to herself.

Molly beamed. "You're a good lad, Toma. He'll make you a fine husband, my dear," she said to Sara.

"That's what he tells me."

Molly looked between her and Lewis, her dark complexion reddening with embarrassment. "I'm sure nothing—untoward—happened last night, but I must insist that—"

"No need to insist," Toma assured her. "We'll be married as soon as the circus returns."

"Oh, but that's days," Molly said. "I'm sure I can persuade Reverend Wilkins to procure a special license—"

"No!"

Lewis's shout was so unexpected that both women jumped, then stared at him, waiting for an explanation.

"No *gajo* wedding," he said firmly. "We'll be accepted by the Borava tribe or it will be no marriage."

"But—"

"Am I right, Sara?" he asked Sara, cutting off Molly's protest.

The harsh expression in his eyes reminded Sara of the dark shadows of the convict hulks. "Right," she said reluctantly. "Toma wants the marriage acknowledged by the *kris*. You want the tribe council's acceptance, isn't that it?" He nodded slowly. She wondered if he would answer if she asked why.

Molly looked worried. "That will take some doing. You know what happened to me when I married Mr. Macalpine."

Lewis moved to put his arm around the woman. "It will work out," he assured her. It had better, he thought, shooting a commanding look at Sara over the woman's head. The girl's chin lifted stubbornly, but she gave him a slight nod. The gesture reassured him he was in control of the situation. He drew Sara's aunt aside, toward the garden door. "I have to go," he told her quietly. "Take care of Sara for me, please. I'm afraid she might run away from Beng's temper if she's left alone to think too much."

"I can understand that," Molly agreed. "It's going to be hard for the wee thing to face up to him."

"She'll have me by her side."

Molly sighed. "At least you're Rom. You have more chance than I did."

"Keep Sara occupied," he requested. "Don't let her out of your sight if you can help it."

"Don't you worry, dear boy. There are no idle hands in this house. She'll have no chance to have second thoughts."

"Thank you." He bowed and graciously dropped a kiss on the woman's hand before going to the door. He gave Sara another stern look. "Be a good girl and do as you're told."

"He'll be a fine, commanding husband," Molly said admiringly after Lewis Morgan disappeared out the back door.

"That's what I'm afraid of," Sara answered. Molly giggled as though she'd just heard a childish joke.

"Come along, dear," she said, "and help me straighten the private parlor."

Having nothing better to do and nowhere to run, Sara resignedly followed the woman out of the kitchen.

"What are you doing here?" Sara asked as her bedroom door closed behind Lewis.

"It's late. Why aren't you asleep?"

Sara sat on the bed, practicing guitar by the light of a single candle. Aching muscles had been begging her to give it up and get some rest but she hadn't been ready to face being alone in the silent darkness just yet.

He leaned against the closed door, his finger to his lips, his blue eyes lit with amusement. Sara ignored him and went back to playing, even after he came to sit beside her on the bed.

Lewis didn't like this small sign of rebellion in the

girl. He expected to have her attention when he was in the room. "What are you playing?" When she didn't answer, he tried, "It's pretty." She just continued to play, fingers caressing the instrument's six strings in an intricate lullaby. "Something *Richie* taught you?"

Dark eyes flashed as she turned her head to confront him. "I wrote it. Molly won't like you being in here."

He took the guitar from her hands. "Molly is peacefully snoring upstairs." He put the instrument on the floor. He caressed her cheek. "We're all alone, love." She sat stiff and unresponsive beside him. He leaned over to kiss her.

"I thought you said you didn't want babies." Her words stopped him.

"I was only going to—"

"Try touching me and I'll scream rape," she went on coldly.

"I would never rape—"

"An English gentlewoman," she said before he could finish. "I found out last night what you think of Rom."

He had no idea what she was talking about. He hadn't laid a hand on her last night. "But I—"

"So don't ever touch me again, Lieutenant Morgan."

He grabbed her by the shoulders. "My name is Toma, girl. Don't ever call me anything else."

Far from being intimidated she said, "Take your hands off me . . . Toma."

"Sara," he warned. "Remember our bargain."

"I said I'd marry you," she replied.

"That's not enough."

Lewis didn't know what he meant by the words. From the shocked look on her face she obviously thought he meant to force his attentions on her. She was beautiful. He was tempted. He hurriedly moved away from her. He crossed the room so she couldn't see his confusion in the shadows by the clothes chest.

While he stood trying to get his thoughts under control she asked, "Why do you want to marry me?"

This he could deal with. At least here was a truth he could tell her. He turned back to her with a cool smile. "I'm not going to marry you."

She looked as confused as he felt. "Huh? But you set up the whole—"

"No parson's mousetrap for me," he went on. "A gypsy wedding will do for us. It won't be binding by British law. We won't really be married, of course. While you'll make a delightful mistress, marriage is out of the question."

Sara looked at the man in disgust. He was a shadowed, slender outline, full of menace and venom. "You slime."

"You'll like me as a lover, Sara. You wanted me yesterday."

His voice sounded like Toma's. She didn't like being reminded. "That was yesterday."

"I can make you feel like you did yesterday."

His voice was full of sensual suggestion. Sara didn't like the way the heat in the room gathered around her as he spoke. She remembered what it had been like with him, on this bed, about twenty-four hours ago. It had been so full of sweet promise.

She ran her hands through her unruly black curls. "I know what you're doing."

"I should hope so."

The charm the man could exude was palpable. "You figure I'll be easier to control if you seduce me. It's not going to work."

"No?" Lewis winced at her words. She was correct, of course, but he did want her. "Whatever happened to the simple girl I thought I was courting?" he asked.

Sara couldn't keep from smiling at his question. "I haven't been myself lately," she told him. "Is anything about you genuine?"

He stepped into the candlelight. His very tight pants emphasized an obviously genuine part of him. "Would you like to find out?"

"No." She reached for her guitar and took her time putting it in its canvas bag. She was tired, and she wanted to get some sleep. She wished he'd go away. He was still smiling down at her when she finally looked up at him again. "What now?" she asked.

He came closer to the bed.

"That wasn't an invitation," she said quickly.

"Pity."

It wasn't going to do any good to keep sparring with him. "I'm going to sleep now," she said. She stretched out on the narrow bed. "You can leave."

"I'm not leaving."

"Fine. You can sleep on the floor."

Much to her surprise he didn't argue. Apparently the seduction attempt was over for tonight. He padded silently over to the door and settled down in front of it. Sara blew out the candle and turned her back to him.

When she woke up before dawn the next morning he was gone, but her dreams had been aware of his presence all night long.

8

"I won't do it!"

"Listen, kid, if you don't learn some skills you're going to end up back on the streets."

"I like the streets!"

"It's too dangerous. You need—"

Beth stomped her foot. "I ain't going to be no lady's maid!"

"Well, they won't make you CEO of the East India Company!" Sara shouted back.

She'd spent much of the last week trying to domesticate a half-grown street rat. She was just about at the breaking point. Beth's flashes of sweetness and vulnerability didn't quite make up for her stubbornness. Sara admired her strong personality. Most of the time. Toma had sent a message that the gypsy circus was back from Salisbury, camped at the abandoned Bartholomew Fairgrounds. She was going to have to face Beng in a few hours. She didn't need another tantrum to deal with.

The current battle was over Molly suggesting, while they helped Sara dress in one of the outfits Molly had had made for her, that Beth might aspire to being a maid. Apparently Molly considered being a lady's maid a proper career choice. Beth had not reacted well to the kindly woman's words. She'd shouted angrily instead.

Sara took a deep breath while she looked out the window to try to calm down. It was raining, but the view of the kitchen garden was still pleasant. The Blue Rose was a peaceful haven amidst London's vast squalor. Beth's problem was that she had no concept that there was anything beyond the squalor. She was bright and quick-witted and ambitious, but to her ambition meant clawing her way up the sewer to be queen of the rats.

"You want to end up another Mother Cummings?" Sara asked her. "Is that it?"

Beth looked aghast at Sara's question. "Naw. I ain't like 'er." She looked contemptuously around the room, then back at Sara. "I want things like they was. We don't belong 'ere—with the *good* folks."

Sara heard Molly muttering a prayer for the child's soul under her breath. "We aren't going back," she told the girl firmly.

"You promised to teach me all you know." Beth stomped her foot again. "You promised."

"I promised to take care of you," Sara corrected her. "This is better for you."

"I like being a pickpocket. Better'n learnin' 'ow to write."

Sara had no idea how to deal with the girl. She

almost wished Lewis Morgan were here. The girl liked Toma. Everyone liked Toma. He hadn't set foot in the Blue Rose for the last four days. He knew he had her in his power, so he didn't need to hang around to rub it in. She hated knowing he was right. Except when Molly talked about trousseaus and instructed her on how to be a good wife, she pretended he didn't exist.

Sara sat down on her bed and gestured for Beth to join her. She gave Molly a pleading look. The woman nodded and left them alone. When Beth sat down, Sara put her arm around her thin shoulders and asked, "So, what do you want to be when you grow up?"

Beth flashed her a grin. "A princess."

"Pretty dumb job," Sara answered. "You'd have to wear ugly hats and get your phone calls taped." She thought about magic rings and wishes. "But if you want to be a princess I could probably swing it for you."

Beth giggled. "You're crazy, gypsy girl."

The way Sara saw it she was the only person in this crazy time who was sane. "This world won't let you be anything you want, that's the major problem we're facing here," she told the girl. "I know, maybe you could go to America."

Beth looked horrified. "Red Indians'd kill me!"

"Don't be silly."

"I ain't silly."

"No," Sara agreed. "You're not. But—"

"Let's leave," Beth urged her. "I know a flash 'ouse we could roost at. Mrs. Hart'd take us in. There's fences other'n Mother Cummings. We'll do fine, rich in a fortnight! Just you and me." Beth jumped off the bed. She grabbed Sara's hands, trying to tug her up. "Please. I 'ate it 'ere!"

Lewis didn't know what surprised him more when he opened the door on Sara and Beth, the consternation on Sara's face as Beth ran from her, or the way she looked in the jonquil yellow muslin dress. He stared at Sara while Beth slipped past him out the door. Seeing her dressed in the low-necked gown, he was torn between telling her to cover herself and longing to kiss the rich swell of her bosom. The contrast of creamy brown skin next to the pale yellow cloth left him momentarily stunned. Her black hair was arranged on the crown of her head, a yellow ribbon threaded through it, revealing the graceful length of her neck. She was so lovely. Lovely in an alien way, a mockery of an Englishwoman.

"What are you looking at?" she demanded angrily.

"You've no business dressing like that. You're nothing but a—"

She ignored his words as she pointed past his shoulder. "Will you talk to the girl? She'll listen to you."

"Never mind Beth," he said. He closed the door behind him. "You'd better get back into something decent before Beng gets here."

"Decent?" Sara looked down at her dress. "Molly says this is decent."

"Molly thinks like a *gajo*."

"And you don't?"

"We don't have time to argue." He went to the

clothes chest and started looking for her old clothes.

She followed him. "Beng's coming? Here?" She joined him in gathering up skirts and blouses. "He wouldn't come here, would he? I was going to meet him at the campgrounds. You said he'd be at the—"

"My fault," he admitted. "I mentioned where you were to Sandor. Sandor told Beng. Revenge for my not playing the Salisbury Fair, I suppose."

"Or loyalty to a friend," Sara suggested. "How long have you been with the circus, anyway?"

"A month. Don't you know how to count, girl?"

"Of course I know how to count, I'm an accountant."

"I don't care what you are, just change clothes."

The man was right and she hated the fact. Beng was going to be furious to find her associating with Molly. It would be worse if he found out she'd adopted *gajo* habits. She'd end up on a prison hulk if she got herself thrown out of the tribe.

"We wouldn't want to jeopardize your mission." She dropped the clothes she was holding and began fumbling with the back fastening of the dress. Regency clothing looked simple, but needed an instruction manual and a support staff to get it on and off. "Being a lady's maid is really a very high-tech job. Give me a hand with this."

Lewis didn't understand how a girl could be called the cleverest burglar in London and not manage a few hooks and buttons. He was beginning to think tracking her down had been the most unwise move of his life.

He moved behind her and brushed her hands

aside. "It seems I've had more experience at this than you have."

"I bet."

He dropped a quick kiss on the back of her neck. "Do you want to hear about it?"

"No."

"Jealous?"

"Just get the dress unfastened."

He worked as fast as he could, but was just about ready to rip the thing the rest of the way off when the door crashed open. By that time Sara had wriggled out of the sleeves and pushed the dress down around her waist. Her chemise had fallen off one shoulder.

Beng stood in the doorway, large, menacing, red with fury. His eyes widened in shock. Lewis froze, his hands on Sara's waist. Beng bellowed and reached for his knife.

Sara said, "Daddy!"

He's going to kill me, she thought. She tried to push Lewis's hands away, but he clung to her tightly, shielding himself from Beng's wrath.

"It's not what you think!" Lewis shouted at the girl's enraged father as Sara struggled to get away. He hoped she wouldn't get so hysterical he'd have to knock her senseless to protect her. He tightened his grip, prepared to thrust her aside when the man attacked.

"I know what it is," Beng answered him, bitter as well as furious. His hand was curled tightly around the knife hilt. There was pain in his dark eyes. "You get what you want from my girl, Calderash?"

"I—"

Beng looked at Sara. "You get what you want from this half-breed?"

"I—"

"Fine!" He slammed the knife back in its sheath. Then he spat on the floor in front of them in contempt. He caught Lewis's gaze with his own. "Tonight," he said after a long, searching silence. "The wedding is tonight." Without another word, or a glance for Sara, he turned and walked out of the room.

Sara didn't know when she'd stopped breathing, but she was dizzy by the time she caught her breath in a deep gasp. "He—" she panted, "He—said—"

"Wedding," Lewis finished with a sigh of relief. He relaxed against her, his arms went around her, his grasp changed into an embrace. Her back fit neatly against his chest, the bare skin of her shoulders was warm and soft, she smelled of violets. He chuckled in her ear. "Lord, girl, we're getting married."

"I can hardly wait," was her sarcastic reply.

Her cold attitude dashed him back to reality. For a moment he'd gotten lost in the role he played; he'd felt the elation of the loving suitor who was finally getting the woman he'd courted. He let her go. "You'll have to wait," he told her. He went to the door, pausing to blow her a kiss before he went. "At least until tonight."

"Have you seen Beth?" Molly asked as she stepped into the tent.

Sara was surrounded by a trio of women. They

were helping her dress as well as giving her advice.
She'd been listening in silence, hoping to catch their
names from the conversation. They all looked around
furtively when Molly walked in. They stared at the
newcomer in silence, their eyes hard and angry in the
firelight.

Finally, one of them said, "You have no business
here."

Molly waved the woman's cold comment away.
"Nonsense, Darya. I'm not going to miss my niece's
wedding. Beth?" she asked, ignoring the women.

Sara shook her head, jangling the coins edging the
heavy scarf covering her hair. "I didn't see her before
I left the inn." Beng had been in such a hurry to get
her back to the camp and turn her over to respectable
women after Toma left she hadn't had time to see or
speak to anyone.

"Oh, dear." Molly sighed. "I hope she's all right."

So did Sara, but music started up outside the tent
before she could ask any questions.

"It's time to go," Darya said. The women closed
ranks around her, pushing Molly aside. They escorted
Sara outside the tent, Molly following after. Sara
glanced back at her once as she was led toward a
torchlit circle where Lewis waited with the other men
of the caravan. Molly gave her a smile and cheerful
wave, before melting into the shadows beyond the
firelight where the other women and children
watched.

The women parted ranks at the edge of the circle.
Hands pushed her forward. Someone giggled at her
reluctance to move. Sara's gazed darted around the

gathering, looking for some last-minute rescue, and came to rest on the grinning Lt. Lewis Morgan. He wore a clinging scarlet silk shirt tucked into tight black breeches, his hair held out of his face by a wide red headband. He looked like a rock star ready to take the stage. She felt like a human sacrifice. Beng stood next to him, scowling ferociously. He beckoned her forward.

Sara walked stiffly toward the men. This wasn't real, she reminded herself with each step. But she could feel the anticipation and good wishes of the crowd, all of it centered on Toma and her. It was real to them. To them she was a *bori,* a happy new bride. The smile on Toma's face looked real. His hand felt real when he stepped forward to meet her and helped her to kneel in the center of the circle. His name wasn't Toma, and this wasn't real.

She remembered other weddings she'd been to, weddings that had been real. Her memory of those genuinely happy occasions helped her know what she was supposed to do. Lewis knelt on his left knee, she knelt on her right as they faced each other.

"You're beautiful," he whispered to her as Sandor approached them.

Sandor carried two freshly sliced pieces of fine white bread. At least the ceremony would be over soon, Sara knew. Marriage was a private matter between two people; weddings were a chance for everyone to celebrate.

"Let's party," she whispered to Lewis as Sandor scooped salt out of a dish Beng held for him.

Sandor sprinkled the salt on the two slices of bread

they balanced on their legs. Lewis picked up the salted bread from her leg. Fingers trembling, she took his. They held the bread up for a moment. Sara was afraid she was going to drop hers. If it fell into the dirt it would certainly bring the marriage bad luck. Which would serve Lewis right, she supposed, but she didn't drop it. She held it to her lips and took a bite instead. Lewis did the same. People cheered and applauded.

While they finished eating the salted bread Sandor recited, "Great fortune and happiness be with you. Even if salt and bread become enemies, may you live in love and contentment."

The cheering was louder as Lewis sprang up and helped Sara to stand. He put his arms around her in a quick embrace. He felt as though he should kiss the bride, but such a public display would be improper. "Smile," he whispered in her ear as they were surrounded by well-wishers. "You look like you've just been condemned to hang."

"I should be so lucky," she whispered back.

They were pulled apart before he could think of an answer. He was drawn into a group of men; Sara was surrounded by women. He was soon inundated by a flood of husbandly advice. He could only assume Sara was receiving wifely instructions from the women. He hoped those instructions included how to be pleasing and obedient to her new master. Not that what Sara was doing right now was important to his plans. He'd just achieved one of his objectives: he was now accepted by the men of the tribe. It was a few hours yet before he was supposed to disappear into his *bardo* with his bride. It was plenty of time to start work on the next phase of the operation.

He made his way to the campfire where several of the older men sat talking. Sandor and Evan came with him, and Beng followed, still looking as if he'd rather stab him than welcome him as a son. Lewis ignored Beng as he squatted on his heels next to Hadari, the bear leader. The man slept in the same tent with his bear and smelled like it, but as the leader of one of the tribe's faction he was worth cultivating.

"There's a smuggling ship I know of," Lewis said. "Large enough to hold us all—*bardos,* horses, everything. It leaves Dover in three days."

"They'll ask me in the morning if you were chaste. Of course I'll say you were."

Sara ignored Lewis's words while she finished looking around the lamplit interior of his living quarters. The *bardo* was a sort of horse-drawn RV, equipped with a quilt-covered bed and several painted wooden chests. Blue-and-yellow striped curtains covered the curved opening at the front of the wagon. They'd entered through a narrow door in the back.

"How quaint," she said, looking at him at last. "I've read about these things and seen the ones at the Renaissance Faire, but I've never been inside a real one. My tribe abandoned *bardos* the minute the internal combustion engine was invented."

He was looking at her curiously, but she didn't care. Let him think she was crazy. It was his job to pretend he was somebody he wasn't, not hers. She yawned and stretched. "By the way," she told him. "The state of my chastity is none of your business."

Lewis sat down on the bed and pulled his shirt over his head. Once he was bare to the waist he held his hand out to her. "Come here."

Sara pulled off the heavy scarf and shook out her hair. The jangling from the coins edging the cloth had been irritating her all night. She also took off the heavy silver earrings that had been part of her wedding costume. "Is that a feather mattress?"

Lewis patted the spot beside him. "It's soft. You'll like it."

"I'm sure I will," she agreed. "And a strip of Turkish carpet on the floor. How luxurious."

"I'm glad you approve." He made an expansive gesture. "This is your home now."

"The floor's yours," she responded.

Lewis glared at her. "What?"

"The floor," she repeated. "You'll be sleeping on it from now on."

"No," he said firmly. He slammed a fist down on the mattress. "This is my *bardo*. You'll sleep with me in my bed."

She shook her head. "We're not really married, right?"

He knew where this was leading. "Sara," he warned.

Sara twisted the ring around her finger. It felt dead, like nothing more than a small silver ring. She was definitely on her own. Just her against James Bond, Jr., here. "As long as I'm stuck with you and without cable in a tiny little wagon you're sleeping on the floor."

"You're my—"

"No, I'm not."

"Prisoner," he finished. He jabbed a finger at her. "Remember your position, girl."

"Ah," she said, pointing back at him. "Slave. I see. That translates as sex toy, right?"

"I—"

"Wrong." She noticed the man at least had the decency to blush at her accusation. "I'm not some stupid kid you can manipulate," she went on. "I'll only put up with so much blackmail, and screwing you on command is not part of the deal."

"I see." Lewis ducked his head for a few moments, contemplating just how thin and uncomfortable his pretty rug was going to be to sleep on, she hoped. When he looked back at her a slow smile spread across his undeniably handsome face. "Very well, I concede your point."

For tonight. He didn't say it, but he didn't have to. The look of challenge in his eyes said it all. Sara sighed.

Lewis hid his annoyance behind a smile. It wasn't important, he told himself. Bedding the girl was only a diversion, a reward he'd promised himself for all the unpleasantness of this mission. It would wait. He got up off the bed. He gestured her toward it. "Sleep well," he said, moving aside for her. He blew out the lamps as she climbed onto the mattress without taking off her clothes. He wondered if he should offer her his knife for reassurance, but decided that after her show of temper he might need it for himself.

He waited until she was settled before he stretched

out on the wagon floor. "There will be a meeting of the *kris* tomorrow," he told her before turning on his side to sleep.

"Why?" came the curious question out of the dark.

"You'll find out," he replied. "And you'll play the good, quiet wife while the men talk, won't you?" He waited, but when no answer came he eventually drifted off to sleep.

"It's crazy. No, it's suicidal," Sara said as soon as the *bardo* door closed behind them. "You can't drag these people all the way across Europe to Bororavia."

Toma had watched her carefully throughout the hours the gypsies had argued through his plan. She'd been tight-lipped the entire time the *kris* debated. She'd sat with the women, a red silk scarf covering her heavy black curls to indicate her status as a married woman. Because of his new status as a married man the tribe had listened to him. Even though it took a lot of talking, the men had voted in favor of his plan. Very few of the women spoke during the meeting. He'd been surprised when his bride hadn't been one of them. Now he saw that she'd saved her words for a private argument.

"They want to go home," he said. "They've been exiles for ten years. I'm only showing them the way."

She sat down on the bed. She rubbed her temples wearily. "I know they have to go home, I've heard the story all my life about how the *familia* returned. But the story doesn't mention that there was a war on, it just sort of glosses over that part. This is stupid. People are going to get killed."

He saw that she was afraid and her fear bothered him more than her rambling words. He sat down beside her. He would have taken her hand in his, but she pulled it away. "I'll look after you," he promised. He wouldn't let her come to harm; he owed her that much.

"I'm touched," she grumbled. She looked him in the eye. "I'm not worried for myself. You're using a lot of innocent people to cover whatever you're up to. I feel responsible for them."

"Nonsense," Lewis replied. "There's nothing innocent about that lot of thieves and scoundrels. Gypsies are born survivors."

"They're expendable game pieces to you, you mean." She sighed. "You're a spy. You can't afford to have a conscience or care for anybody. You might lose your edge if you did."

Her bitter words stung, but he acknowledged their truth. "When did you get to be so smart, little girl?"

Despite the worry compressing her heart like a fist, Sara couldn't keep from smiling. "Little girl? How old do you think I am?"

"Sixteen. Or so you told me on the day we met."

"And how old are you?"

He gave her a superior smile. "I was born in 1785."

"I can do math," she told him. "That would make you twenty-six. Guess what? So am I." It was her turn to flash a superior smile. Should she tell him? Oh, what the hell. "I'll be born in 1968. I'm an Aries."

He laughed. "What nonsense."

"I'll concede that astrology might be nonsense. But I'm still going to be born in 1968." The annoying part was that he wasn't even looking at her as if he thought she was crazy. He was looking at her as if she was the most amusing creature he'd ever encountered. Maybe she was. This wasn't a particularly amusing time. "Okay, spy," she went on. "I know a little history, maybe enough to make this mission unnecessary."

He put his arm around her and pushed her back on the bed. He couldn't help it. Her words confused him, and piqued his curiosity. Every word was a lie, but she told her lies in such a charming manner he truly enjoyed listening to them. Her attitude was forthright, her speech clever. Damn, but the minx had a delightful way about her.

He hovered over her, his arms planted on either side of her, his face close to hers. "You've a pretty tongue, but I can think of better uses for it than storytelling."

He was grinning, and he was going to kiss her, she could see it in his eyes. "Now wait a min—" she began, but his mouth descended on hers before she could finish.

The man's lips touching hers sent a shock of sweet lightning through her. Which made no sense, all things considered. Her toes curled inside the thin leather of her shoes, her nipples hardened almost instantly as his body pressed against hers. She found herself clutching his back when she'd meant to pummel it. His tongue explored the inside of her mouth with heated thoroughness. She sighed against the softness of his lips, acknowledging that her overwhelming attraction to Toma still existed despite knowing exactly what Lewis Morgan was.

Overwhelming or not, she wasn't going to let him use it against her. "Sex," she said pushing him away, "isn't all it's cracked up to be." Her words came out in a breathless pant.

He was still grinning at her when he rolled onto his side and propped himself up on his elbow. He began playing with a loose strand of her hair. "What could be better than sex?" he asked.

His teasing tone galled her. "Self-respect," she answered. She scooted off the bed to stand and straighten her clothes.

Lewis stayed where he was, his shirt open, tight pants straining against muscular thighs, a lock of hair falling rakishly across his forehead, a devilish gleam lighting his bright blue eyes. He looked good and he knew it. She was considering throwing something at him when someone knocked on the wagon door.

Molly was inside before Sara could answer it. "Is it true?" she asked breathlessly. "Is the *familia* returning home?"

"It is," Lewis said, getting to his feet. He wasn't happy with the interruption. Besides, this woman's presence might jeopardize his new standing with the gypsies. "What do you want?" he snapped.

"Apparently," Sara answered her aunt's question. Molly held out a familiar canvas bag to her. "My guitar. Thank you. Beth?" she asked, taking the instrument. She sat back on the bed, pulled the guitar out, and began tuning it.

Molly shook her head. "I still haven't seen her." She looked appealingly at Lewis. "Do you know where the child might be?"

The mud lark's whereabouts was hardly any of his concern now that she'd played her part in his scheme. He shrugged as both women looked at him anxiously. "I wouldn't know," he answered.

Sara looked at him steadily over the sensuous curves of the guitar. Her slender fingers moved across the strings without her seeming to notice their movement. Her dark eyes looked searchingly into his. He got the distinct impression she was looking for his soul, but decided he was as hollow as the instrument she held. "Don't know, or don't care," she said at last, and looked away.

Sara put down the guitar. "I have no idea where to look for her." She rubbed the ring. *Do you?* she asked it. *Should I try at Mother Cummings's house?* The ring tingled faintly in response, but gave her no answer. The thing had gotten her into this mess, but it wasn't being any help. "Come on, Aunt Molly. Let's go find her."

Lewis blocked the door when she tried to leave. "You're not going anywhere."

"There's a child out there who needs me."

He shook his head. "The brat doesn't want your help."

"I know. That isn't the point."

She tried to get past him but he wouldn't let her. "You're not leaving the camp."

"Oh, really?"

He wasn't impressed by her dangerous tone. "You're staying with Beng to help with the packing," he informed her. He took her arm. "I'm taking you to him right now."

"But—"

"Go home, Molly," he added to Sara's aunt. "There's nothing either of you can do about the girl." He opened the door and dragged Sara outside.

She had to squint against the sunlight of the hot August afternoon. People bustled around the scattered tents and wagons, hurriedly packing. She saw faces full of joyful anticipation as Lewis dragged her through the crowd to Beng's campsite. The laughter of children playing filled the air. These people truly looked forward to going back to Bororavia. They didn't know what Lewis Morgan was getting them into.

"You heartless scumbag," she said to him as they reached Beng's *bardo*.

"You're too kind," was his mocking reply. He swept her a courtly bow. "You've no idea what your flattery means to me, my dear."

"Give me a hint," she returned, but he turned and walked away without another word.

"Arguing already?" Beng asked, coming up beside her. "Good."

9

Saffron Hill was the rookery's name. With a name like that it should have been a pretty, quiet little neighborhood. But Lewis knew as he walked through the filthy, narrow streets that he was in one of the worst slums in London. He didn't know why he was here, not really, but he didn't have time to brood. He was too busy concentrating on watching his back while he made his way to his destination. The flash house didn't have a name but the owner was called Mrs. Hart. His father had once kept her as his mistress when she was young and pretty. Now that she was neither she rented the rooms of her house to young bawds and thieves.

Beth had grown up here until she'd been sent to Mother Cummings to learn the craft of pickpocketing. When he'd heard of the child's connection to the Hart woman he'd purchased her services in his game to ensnare the top burglar in London. He suspected Beth might be his half-sister. Which was why he was here, really. He didn't owe the mud lark anything, but it galled him that a gypsy thief showed more concern for the child than any of her own kindred ever had.

He ignored the girls who approached him as soon as he stepped through the door. "I've a pretty wife waiting at home," he told the most persistent of the pack. "Where's Beth?" he asked when the gray and drawn owner of the house approached him.

"I told 'er she 'ad no right comin' 'ere," the woman assured him. "Wait 'ere, sir, while I fetch 'er for you."

Lewis nodded and found a seat near the room's one window. The chair was rickety, the paint was faded to an unrecognizable color, the floor hadn't seen a scrubbing in ages. A reek of boiled cabbage from the kitchen blended with sour sweat in the close air. At least two of the girls lounging in mended and dirty shifts were heavy with child. Lewis shook his head while he waited, and ignored the girls' looks of open invitation. There was a pretty girl waiting for him at home. And by God she could kiss! His body ached to find out what more she could do. Besides, his muscles also ached from time spent resting on floors. Such uncomfortable sleeping arrangements were going to have to be altered.

He was smiling with anticipation when Beth came hurtling down the stairs. "Toma!" she crowed happily. He was barely out of the chair when she threw herself in his arms. "Oh, Toma, Toma, Toma!"

He ruffled her hair. "You missed me, mud lark."

Bright eyes shone up at him. "Oh, yes! Where's Sara?"

"You ran away from Sara," he reminded her.

"Did not! I ran away from Molly."

"I should send the mite back to Mother Cummings," Mrs. Hart said, coming up to them. She put her hand on Beth's thin shoulder. "Lord knows I can't afford to feed her much longer."

Lewis sighed. "Better being a thief than a whore?" he asked.

"The girl needs to earn her keep somehow."

"True, true," he agreed. He pulled coins from his vest pocket. They disappeared into the woman's apron almost before he handed them over. "Don't worry, Mrs. Hart. Beth's my responsibility now."

Beth crowed with delight. She grabbed his hand, pulling him toward the door without a glance or farewell for the woman. Mrs. Hart didn't bother bidding the child Godspeed, either. They were well away from Mrs. Hart's before Beth asked, "Where we going?"

"France," he answered with a grin.

Her eyes went round. "Ooh! You and me and Sara?"

He nodded. "Sara misses you, mud lark."

"Why are we going to France?" she demanded. "What are we going to steal?"

The little girl certainly had the right of it. He chuckled. The street around was empty but for a flock of bold pigeons that barely moved from feeding to let them past. "Pigeon's blood," he said. "That's what the color's called."

"What?" She tugged impatiently on his hand. "What's pigeon's blood?"

"The ruby," he said. He ruffled her hair again. "We're going to France, mud lark, to steal a ruby brooch."

The girl cooed like one of the birds at their feet. "Oooh! That sounds like fun!"

Fun? He shrugged uncomfortably. Sara wasn't going to think so.

"Of course I'm coming."

Sara tried not to flinch as Beng's dark glare was turned on her. The crowd muttered at her back and hot sunlight poured down on her head, but Sara stood her ground next to Molly's garish wagon. "Tell her she is not going with us," Beng ordered.

"Tell her yourself," Sara answered. "She's your sister."

Molly planted her hands on her hips and tilted her chin stubbornly up at her brother. "I'll follow in your dust if I have to, but I'm going home."

Beng swept his arm out. "You made your choice, woman." The muttering from the Rom witnessing the confrontation grew louder, more threatening.

"I'm going with you," Molly insisted.

Sara didn't know why a nice lady with a comfortable inn wanted to face the hazards of the trek across Europe, but the tribe's hostility was even harder to fathom. Oh, she understood *mirame*—uncleanliness—intellectually, but she didn't have to like it. Or put up with it. She rounded on the crowd.

"Do you know where we got this pollution crap? We brought it with a major inferiority complex out of

India when we started traveling a thousand years ago. It was a caste thing; the Rom were somewhere very low on the social scale and it's kept us humble ever since. We don't live in India anymore, people! Okay," she ranted on to their uncomprehending stares, "we need our customs to keep our identity. I'm proud of who I am, but I won't honor any custom that perpetuates that inferiority complex!"

Beng touched her on the shoulder. She swiveled her head to look at him. "What?" he asked, confusion warring with his usual angry expression.

"Just let the woman come along, okay?"

"Sara's possessed," one of the women in the crowd said. "Her words make no sense."

It was Evan who spoke up for her. "I don't know," he said, rubbing his gray-stubbled chin. "My mother was taken back into the tribe after that Welsh sailor raped her and she had me. Molly was exiled for marrying a *gajo*."

"She abandoned the *familia*," Beng stated.

"She's back now," Evan pointed out. "With a fine *bardo,* and gold to help with the journey."

"We don't need her *gajo* gold," Beng said.

"Could come in handy," Sandor said. "It's a long way to Bororavia."

One of the older women scratched thoughtfully at a wart on her jaw. "She's a widow, a woman should have a husband."

"Your son's been a widower for a month!" Beng stormed. "Hadari would rather share his tent with the bear than have trash like her."

"I remember what a fine cook she used to be,"

Hadari said for himself. "Do you still fry cucumbers with cream?" he asked Molly.

Sara covered her mouth to keep from laughing at the look of consternation on Beng's face. She backed away as the conversation continued. Molly was as strong-willed as her brother and perfectly willing to fight her own battles.

"You've developed quite a way with words," Lewis said as Sara turned around and saw him leaning against their *bardo,* watching her. He'd arrived just in time to overhear her speech to the shocked gypsies. Most of it had made no sense, but he found himself admiring her force of character. And, he had to admit he was curious about the things she'd said. He'd learned very little of gypsy history in the studying he'd done to assume this role.

"Just expressing my own opinion," she said as she came up to him. "And most Rom in my own time don't agree with it. Except . . ." She looked back at the debating crowd. "The Borava," she said on a sigh. "What you might call a dysfunctional *familia.*" She groaned. "If you weren't a slime I'd apologize for that bad pun."

Lewis put out an arm and snagged her to his side as he noticed several people looking their way. Playing the devoted bridegroom was easy when it meant having her soft curves nestled close to him. But her beauty could only distract him momentarily from her odd behavior. "Be careful what you say," he warned. "I've worked too hard to get into this tribe to have you get us both tossed out."

She flashed him an annoyed look. "Just helping a friend. Get your hands off me," she added as his fingers rubbed slow circles on her hip. It made her tingle; the tingling implied that far more serious sensations could result from his touch.

"Come inside," he urged with a slow, seductive smile.

"Oh, no." She shook her head. "I promised Janitza I'd help her finish packing." He ignored her and pulled her up the step into the wagon. "Now, wait a minute—Beth!"

The girl jumped off the bed as Sara pushed past Lewis to reach the girl. "'Allo, Sara," Beth said as Sara grabbed her shoulders.

"Where have you been? Molly and I have been—"

"She's coming with us," Lewis said. "I've promised her a trip to Paris."

Sara looked over her shoulder at the spy, narrow-eyed with suspicion. "*You* found her? Why?"

Lewis read her thoughts on her face and felt himself blush for the first time in years. He couldn't blame her for thinking he would use Beth against her. Since he'd done it already. "I thought you wanted to take care of the girl," he said. "If you'd rather not—"

"Of course I want her." She hugged Beth, then swung around. "Paris?" she questioned sharply. "What do you mean, Paris? The place Napoleon lives?" He nodded. "Why—"

"'Cause of the pigeon—"

"Not now," Lewis cut off Beth's rush of words. He smiled coaxingly at the child. He beckoned her toward the door. "Why don't we get you settled in with Molly."

"Molly!" she complained. "Why Molly?"

"You'll only have to sleep in her wagon. You can spend most of your time with us," he explained. He led her outside while Sara looked on in angry confusion. The caravan was nearly ready to leave the encampment. He'd deal with Sara when they were safely on the road. He winked at Beth. "Me and Sara need to be alone nights," he explained.

"So you can tumble her?"

He nodded. "She's my wife now."

"Really?" Beth looked delighted at the notion.

No. It was all an impossible game. "Yes," he said. "Really."

"Bet you didn't think I could handle this back-to-nature camping-out stuff, did you?"

Lewis frowned at Sara's odd question. "Why wouldn't I?"

"'Cause I'm a city girl. My dad used to make us go camping every summer when I would have been happier at home playing softball. Sometimes we got together with friends and roughed it for two weeks. Dad said it was good to remember the 'old ways.' I think he just wanted a cheap vacation." She gave a self-satisfied smile. "I think I'll start some sourdough tomorrow. I even know how to bake it in warm ashes."

"It's a common way of baking bread," Lewis told her.

"Not where I come from."

Sara stirred the pot hanging over the small cook

fire. She liked the smell of the woodsmoke. She liked the smell of the air now that they were well away from London. The heat of the day had been cooled by a soft evening breeze. The caravan was camped by a stream on the edge of a field of what she'd been told was hops. She'd been assured the farmer who owned the field used Rom field hands at harvesttime so they didn't have to fear being run off.

"I don't suppose there's such a thing as state parks and camping permits in this era," she said.

"What?" Lewis peered at her in the growing dusk. "Why do you say such odd things?"

Sara looked up. "This is the best time of day, isn't it? When the sky still has some blue in it, with pink on the edges and the trees are just black silhouettes hanging on the edge of night."

Lewis couldn't fight the twinge of affection he felt toward the girl. It wasn't just that she was beautiful. Her face, illuminated by firelight, was turned up in wonder at the early stars overhead. She glowed, not just because of the fire, but with life and wit and intelligence. Intelligence? He shook his head. "You're mad," he said.

She leveled a sharp gaze on him. He was halfway ready to swear the girl looking at him wasn't the girl he'd been courting for the last month. A shiver ran up his spine. "What are you up to?" he asked her.

"About five foot in this body. I'm not used to being short," she added. "And I don't like it."

"You're a pocket Venus," he told her. The compliment came easily, despite his growing misgivings. "A week ago you could barely manage a few broken sentences of English, now you're spouting poetry to the sunset. Where did you learn to read? To play music? What sort of spell have you fallen under?"

Sara settled down cross-legged across the fire from Lewis. Onion-scented steam rose from the boiling pot but it didn't obscure her clear view of the puzzled man opposite her. They were hidden from the rest of the camp by the dark bulk of the wagon at Lewis's back. She could hear people nearby caring for the tethered horses, but the two of them were quite alone for the moment.

She held up her right hand and looked Lewis Morgan in the eye. "This," she said. "It's a magic ring."

Lewis peered at her hand. "You're not wearing a ring."

Sara cast a look of deep annoyance at her hand. "It's invisible. It says it can only be seen when it wants to be seen. Convenient for it, but—"

"What nonsense." Lewis gestured angrily. "Do you really believe in magic rings?"

"Not until recently." Sara touched the citrine stone. "You could say something," she suggested to it.

"Talk to him? Not on your life."

"Why not?"

"He's not ready to believe in me yet."

"That didn't stop you with me."

"That was different."

"Right." She glanced at Lewis, who looked disgusted. "It's up to something," she told him. "First it transported me from the future. Then it tried to make me think you're my own true love—"

"He is."

"I'm not talking to you."

"Then who are you talking to?" Lewis asked.

"I was talking to you."

"You just said you weren't."

"No, I didn't. I was talking to the ring."

"You're not wearing a ring."

"Yes, I am. You just don't think I am. I could take it off and show it to you, but I'm not handing over a potential secret weapon to a spy."

"I—see." He didn't, but it seemed useless to argue about it anymore. She was mad. Or dangerously clever. Or he was mad. He certainly didn't feel clever. He was intrigued despite himself. "From the future?" He knew he shouldn't get involved in her flight of fancy, but he found himself anxious to find out where it led. "The ring brought you here from the future?"

She nodded enthusiastically. "Exactly."

"For its own mysterious purposes."

"That's what I think, but it won't tell me. It's a wish ring," she added. "I'm going to wish myself back to 1994 when it'll let me."

"Let you?"

"It only grants wishes one day a year," she explained. She chuckled. "I just realized it granted me a wish I didn't know I wished for. I must have made it before midnight." He narrowed his eyes questioningly, but when he didn't ask, she said, "You were spouting all this Cockney and Regency slang and I remember wishing you'd use language I understood. And you have ever since."

She looked as if she'd just presented him with

some sort of proof she was indeed possessed of magic. Come to think of it, he hadn't been using much slang. . . . He forced the thought to a halt before he could finish it. He was not going to let himself get involved in this. "You're practicing the *bujo* on me," he decided.

Beth and Molly arrived to share their supper before she could refute his accusation. Sara turned her attention from their conversation, and him, with a speed he found disconcerting. In fact, with the other women for company, she had no trouble ignoring him for the rest of the evening. Eventually the women went off to the stream to bathe and wash the dishes. He went off to sit and smoke with the men, but he soon got bored. He left the men joking about the impatience of bridegrooms, though he would have sworn he wasn't anxious to be alone with Sara before hearing the teasing jests as he walked away. But he found that he did want to be alone with her. As he mounted the step to the *bardo* he was wondering what it would be like to kiss her so much she'd have no chance to get a word in before he laid her down on the featherbed.

It felt good to be clean even if the shallow water in the stream had been colder than she'd expected. She found a clean shift to sleep in and left it on the bed while she braided her damp hair. She planned to have the lantern out and be in bed before Lewis got back to the wagon, but her luck didn't hold. He walked in just as she was pulling the shift over her head.

She wasn't wearing anything underneath and knew he got a good view of everything even though it took her only moments to cover her body. It wasn't that she was particularly body conscious, except that she was very aware of Lewis Morgan's body. She wished the linen shift wasn't so thin because he could no doubt see that her nipples were puckered into hard peaks. When she saw the hot gleam in his bright blue eyes she knew that he'd liked what he'd seen. She supposed it would be downright stupid to ask him what he was looking at.

"I'm, uh, going to bed now," she told him. "Good night."

He stepped forward. The *bardo* was small and narrow, and it took him only two steps to reach her. The wagon was crowded; there was nowhere to go when he put his hands on her hips and shoved her down on the bed. The bed was just barely large enough for the two of them. His body pinned hers and his fingers flew, untying the drawstring she'd barely had time to fasten. The gown was halfway off and his mouth had closed around her left breast before she knew what had happened.

"Now, wait a minute . . . you can't . . ." She pulled on his hair. The tip of his tongue flicked across her nipple. Sparks flew to the very core of her and very nearly disconnected her brain. Her back arched up as he continued to tease and suckle the sensitive tip.

"Oh, yes," she breathed. "Very nice."

He weighted the other breast in his hand, kneaded it, made slow circles with his palm. Then he raised his head to look at her, while his hand moved down to the juncture of her legs.

The look of triumph in his eyes restored her to her senses. She kept her legs clamped firmly shut. She shook her head. "Get off me," she said. "Get off me or I scream."

"I want you," he said, voice rough with desire.

She could feel him against her thigh, hot and hard. "I know." She pushed at his shoulders. "You can't have me." His hand probed. He kissed her throat. Her blood simmered beneath the skin where he touched her. "No," she said, with more conviction than she felt. "I'm going to scream now." She filled her lungs with air.

Lewis sat up, too quickly; he ended up falling off the bed. The floor shook at his hard landing. He looked up at the girl, seething with need and anger. "What is the matter with you?" he demanded. "Do you want me or not?" He was tempted to force her, to give her what he knew she wanted. "No one will come if you scream," he pointed out. "You're my wife."

"We've been through that."

She pulled her shift up over her lovely, soft breasts. She was shaking. She stared at him with eyes as round as saucers and full of turbulent emotions. He didn't know whether she was reacting from anger or wanting him. It occurred to him that it might be fear. He didn't want her to be afraid. He supposed he'd frightened her enough already.

The thought was enough to kill desire, or at least shame him out of the notion of forcing her. "I'm not going to hurt you," he said, as much to reassure himself as her.

Sara considered reminding him that everything he'd done to bring them to this place, this situation, had hurt her. But she saw no use in beating the subject to death at the moment. Talking about it wouldn't change his callous disregard for her. She did say, "You don't want me, just a body."

He didn't deny it. He flashed the charming Toma grin. "It's a very enticing body."

"I'll try not to expose it anymore," she promised. Damn it, she was talking to him!

"I don't mind."

She scooted down on the bed. It was too hot for a blanket but she pulled one over her anyway. She wanted all the barriers she could get. "I'm going to sleep now," she said, and rolled over. She hated having her back to him—it made her feel vulnerable— but it was also a denial of his presence. She registered darkness on her eyelids when he blew out the lamp. She heard his steady breathing for hours. Eventually she drifted off to sleep.

She found a sheathed knife on the pillow beside her when she woke up. Lewis Morgan was gone from the wagon. She held the knife in her hands for some time, not sure what he meant by leaving it for her. She wondered if it was a joke, some sort of mock protection against his unwanted advances. They both knew he wouldn't have any trouble disarming her if he wanted to. Still, she had to admit she felt better when she tucked the knife between the mattress and the wall where it would be close if she ever needed it.

10

Fog would be a blessing, Lewis thought, looking up at the clear night sky. It was too late for the smuggling ship to turn back now; they were well out in the Channel, prey for the taking by French or British navy. Lewis tried to reassure himself with the knowledge that smugglers had plied the trade between the coasts of the two countries for hundreds of years. The brandy merchants weren't going to let such a paltry thing as a blockade interfere with their business. He hoped. He had to get into France. He didn't want this to take any more time than necessary. He was responsible for all these people's safety— Lord, where had that thought come from?

He wound his fingers tightly around the ship's railing. Sailors moved like wraiths across the deck, only moonlight shone to light their path; rigging and timber creaked. The gypsies and their possessions were crowded into the hold, well out of everyone's way. The water was far from calm, but the choppiness was not unusual for the English Channel. There was nothing he could do; the crossing was out of his hands. He hated not being in control of every situation but tried to resign himself. He might as well get some sleep.

He went down into the hold. His father had sent him to sea young, so he'd had years to get used to the inconveniences of life on board ship. He paid no attention to the rats whose eyes glittered evilly out of the dark, but took a lantern from a peg near the stairs and used it to find his way to his own wagon.

The interior of the *bardo* was stifling hot. Sara lay curled on the bed, retching feebly. Lewis shook his head and put the lantern down beside the clothes chest. He took a silver flask out of the chest.

He sat down beside the seasick girl and brushed hair out of her sweat-streaked face. "A drink might help," he told her. He held the flask to her lips. She pushed it away.

Dramamine would help, she thought. "I want to go home." She groaned. She wanted him to go away and leave her alone. "I don't like boats."

He propped her up and presented the flask again. "Drink this."

She screwed her eyes shut. "Go away."

"No."

The sea kept rolling beneath them. She'd never experienced anything more turbulent than a waterbed. This was the water bed from hell. The last thing she wanted was anything in her stomach. "I'll just throw up."

He made gentle circles on her temple with his

fingertips. "Trust me." He pressed the rim of the flask to her lips. She took a drink.

The stuff burned down her raw throat and exploded in her empty stomach. It went straight to her head. She took another quick gulp. Numbness was replacing pain. "Can I die now?" she requested. He urged another drink on her. She didn't argue.

It didn't take more than five swallows before she passed out in his arms. She wouldn't feel any better when she woke, but at least the brandy would help her get some rest. Lewis settled down beside her. He held her in his arms, and hoped the rhythm of the sea would relax him.

She fitted neatly against him. Despite the heat he found the warmth of her body comforting. The last two days had been miserable. She'd shared the wagon seat with him as they traveled the road to Dover. She'd fixed him his meals, she slept in the wagon, but she spent every possible moment in the company of Molly and Beth. Or she'd practiced her guitar.

She'd even played for a group of sailors at a dockside tavern while the ship was being loaded. Other women had moved among the crowd telling fortunes, but as Lewis stood in the doorway watching, he'd been all too aware of the lustful attention directed at the girl with the guitar. He hadn't liked it one bit, even if his own attitude was just as lustful. He'd wanted to drag her out of the tavern and remind her that she wasn't just any man's whore, she was his. Except he wasn't quite sure what he meant, and she hadn't even noticed the men watching her. She never noticed anything when she was playing. He was beginning to wish she'd turn the same look of concentrated devotion on him as she did on the wood and wire instrument.

"Silly creature," he whispered, and kissed the side of her throat. Her skin was salty with sweat, and delicious. He buried his face in her hair and twined his fingers around her right hand. Odd, how he enjoyed being beside her. She was a criminal of the lowest class, and insane to boot, but sometimes he thought she might just be—

"Your own true love."

Lewis didn't know where the voice came from, but he denied it instantly. "Don't be absurd."

"Trust me on this one."

Sara shivered violently before he could form another thought. She pulled away from him with a miserable groan. She heaved upward, leaning over the side of the bed. "Oh, God, I'm gonna hurl!"

Lewis searched for a basin while Sara began to retch. As he hunted around in the dark, barking his shins on the clothes chest, he decided that no matter how long the actual crossing took, this was going to be the longest voyage of his life.

Sara looked at the words Lewis had written on the paper he'd brought her. She couldn't make out a single one. She frowned up at him. "Am I going to have to teach you and Beth how to write? Didn't you go to Oxford, or something?"

He gestured her to silence. Even though they were alone in their wagon, the door was open and he worried about being overheard. "No," he admitted, leaning close to whisper the word. He looked at the paper. She'd asked for things to write with. He'd purchased the paper, ink, and quills in a village outside Le Havre while the gypsy caravan moved inland. Then he'd written a few lines from a poem across the top of the first sheet of paper.

"Is this English?" she asked, squinting at the scrawled words.

"It's Byron," he answered. "I'll wager you really can't read."

Sara gave him a superior look, then put the paper back on top of the chest, inked the quill, and began writing beneath his lines. It took her some time, some swearing, much ink spattered, and she tore through the paper completely with the quill point once, but she did produce legible words.

"'She walks in beauty like the night,'" he read when she was done. "'Of cloudless climes and starry skies.' What's this?" he asked.

"Byron," she said with a proud toss of her head. "I don't know the rest of it."

If there was one thing he knew, it was Byron. In fact, he knew Byron. He was a rakeshame scoundrel with a way with words. Lewis would not want to introduce Byron to Sara. "That's not Byron."

"Is too. I remember some English actor reading it on a PBS show about British literature. I only watched it because *Quantum Leap* got preempted for a hockey game."

"Not Byron," he insisted.

"He probably hasn't written it yet," she countered

with her usual mad certainty. "I probably had to read it in high school, too."

He put his hand on her shoulder. "That brings up an interesting point. Who taught you to read? And write? Was it Richie?"

Sara was not surprised by his thunderous frown. The man had been acting distinctly weird for days. He kept *looking* at her. The only description she could think of for that look was darkly proprietary. It couldn't be easy for anyone with eyes as bright blue as Lewis Morgan's to manage dark looks, but he was getting better at it all the time. "Jealous?" she asked, only partly serious.

"Yes," Lewis answered before he could stop himself. His grip tightened on her shoulder. "Who taught you to read?"

Sara couldn't remember a time when she couldn't read. "My parents, I guess. And *Sesame Street.*" Wait a minute, she thought, why was he jealous?

"Guess."

The ring hadn't said anything in days. She wasn't interested in talking to it now.

"Your father can no more read than—"

"Sara, dear, I brought my Bible for Beth's reading lesson," Molly announced as she stepped up to the wagon. "Where's Beth?" she asked as Lewis automatically put a hand out to help her inside. "Thank you, Toma, dear. He's such a gentleman," Molly added to Sara. "So like the late Mr. Macalpine." She gave them a benign smile as she settled on the edge of the bed. She passed the heavy, leather-bound Bible to Sara. "I must say I'm amazed at how quickly you learned to read, child. I remember that time last year when you sneaked into the Blue Rose when that Bow Street Runner was looking for you. I tried to teach you a few verses from the good book but you just cried and cried and said it made your head hurt."

Sara twisted her fingers together. "Yes, well, that was last year."

She refused to look at Lewis. She would just encounter a triumphant smirk from the aristocratic spy. It was odd, she thought, how they were honest with each other in private, but they both played the public roles of a young married couple. She just knew that it was easier to pretend with others than it was with Lewis, even if he didn't believe her. Of course, it was safer to pretend to be the girl they thought she was, and so satisfying to irritate her pretend husband with the truth.

"And I'm so glad you've mended your wicked ways, my girl," Molly went on. "And found this fine, loving man."

Lewis's hand landed on her shoulder again, so she exchanged a falsely adoring look with him, playing to their small audience. "Yes," she said with a strained smile. "Isn't it? Don't you have to go practice juggling sharp, possibly lethal, objects, darling?" she added to her erstwhile husband.

"Why, so I do." He bent to brush her lips swiftly with his before exiting the *bardo*. Wait until he got her alone that night, he thought before he left. He'd kiss her all over, even if he had to quote Byron all night to do it.

Sara traced her fingers across where his lips had just

touched. She resented the tingling sensation he left. It was just a game, she reminded herself. Thankfully Beth appeared in the doorway before she had time to think about just how pleasant the sensation was.

Beth bounced in and onto the bed, a round loaf of bread clutched in her hands. She sniffed. "At least you cleaned up."

"Don't remind me," Sara said.

Cleaning up the wagon had taken most of the day and had not been a pleasant task. All she remembered of the Channel crossing was Lewis holding her through the worst of the seasickness. She had no recollection of how the caravan got unloaded and on the road, though she'd recovered after she'd been on land for a few hours. They'd come to a stop in a willow grove late at night and she'd spent the day cleaning and doing laundry in a stream with the rest of the women. She knew they were camped near a village, but had no idea where they were, other than somewhere in France.

"Beng wants to give a show tonight," Beth said. She held out the bread. "Look what I got."

"Where'd you get it? Reading or writing first?" she asked Molly.

"Perhaps Beth should recite the alphabet," Molly said. "I've been trying to teach it to her as we rode along, just the way Mr. Macalpine taught it to me."

"I got the bread in the village," Beth said. "I sneaked in and snatched it," she added proudly. "Right off the baker's shelf. They talk funny over 'ere, don't they? Don't know what she called me, but she couldn't run."

"Snatched it?" Sara and Molly said together. They exchanged appalled looks. "Beth!"

"What?" the little girl answered.

"Did you steal that bread?" Sara asked.

"Said I did, didn't I?" Beth flashed an inordinately proud smile. Sara groaned.

"Oh, dear," Molly said. She clapped her hands to her cheeks. "Oh, dear, oh, dear."

"Did anyone see you?" Sara asked worriedly. "Were you chased? Are you all right?" In England the child could have been hanged or transported for the offense. Sara didn't suppose the law was any less strict in Napoleonic France. Come to think of it, just being English in Napoleonic France might get the little girl hanged. Pretty, green-eyed Beth didn't look like a Rom, which might get them accused of child stealing. "Another fine mess." She groaned.

Sara was out the door and marching up to Lewis before she knew what she was doing. He dropped the knives he was juggling as she approached. The children who were standing around watching him dispersed at a gesture.

"My love." He smiled warmly at her.

Sara planted her fists on her hips. "This is all your fault," she announced.

His brows shot up under his crimson scarf. "What? I—"

She held out one hand. "Do you have any money? French money? And how much is a loaf of bread?"

He dug a coin out of his vest pocket. "What are you talking about?" he asked as he passed her the money.

"Which way's the village?"

He pointed. "Where are you going?" When she didn't answer he sprinted to catch up with her. He grabbed her arm. "Sara?"

"I've got to find the bakery," she said. "Fix this thing before the cops come looking for the kid."

Beth, he guessed, had been stealing again. "I don't understand the problem."

She walked on. "Of course not," she said over her shoulder. "You," she grumbled as he kept pace with her, "have the ethics of a corporate raider."

"Is that some sort of pirate?"

"In an expensive suit." He took her hand. "What are you doing?"

"He's worried about you," said the ring.

You keep out of this.

"Did you hear someone say something?"

Sara almost smiled at the puzzled look on Lewis's face. She almost explained, but decided she was in too much of a hurry to straighten out Beth's misdemeanor to get into a discussion about magic rings right now. "Will you let go of me?"

"No. Where are we going? To the village bakery?" She nodded. Lewis could tell by the stubborn set of her jaw that there would be no stopping her short of force. "Why?"

"To pay for the bread. I won't have a child arrested for robbery."

"Is this the same girl who was chased by the Runners not so long ago?"

"No." She wasn't going to get into it right now. "Do you speak French?" she asked as they approached a rutted road. She could see buildings in the distance.

"Of course." He tilted his head curiously. "Do you?"

"Sort of." She'd battled through four years of French classes in high school. She'd conceded defeat long ago. She would have to remember enough to make do. "I think bread is called *pain,* though I'm not quite sure about the pronunciation."

Lewis sighed. "I'll do all the talking."

"Fine."

It was sweet, he thought, if completely foolhardy, for Sara to concern herself with Beth's welfare. She was so appealingly anxious to keep the girl away from a life of crime. Sara obviously had no inclination toward thieving herself now, even if it was a skill and way of life as natural as breathing for a gypsy. At least, it was supposed to be. But Molly was a respectable, God-fearing woman, and he'd had to force Sara into a crime she had no stomach for. Guilt twisted in his gut at the memory of that night at his father's house. He'd done what was necessary for his country, but—

"But you acted like a complete bastard, didn't you, Lieutenant?" he heard a voice say.

Yes, he agreed reluctantly with his conscience. He'd just have to take good care of the girl to make up for it.

"Hush," Sara said as she wrenched her hand out of his.

"But—" He let it go, never mind that he hadn't spoken. He had to keep in mind that she was subject to fits of madness. They were on the outskirts of the village, no longer alone on the road. This was no time to get into one of their strange discussions.

He led her the short distance to the tiny town square. Women gossiped around a well in the center of the square. They stopped talking to stare when they approached. A heavyset woman in a flour-covered apron stepped out of the doorway of the bakery, blocking them from entering. *"Interdites aux tsiganes."* She waved them away. The baker's face was red with anger, her eyes full of contempt.

No gypsies, Sara translated. She had to bite her tongue from making an acid comment to match the burning of the words on her pride, but she didn't suppose her French was up to what she wanted to say. She saw Lewis's eyes narrow with annoyance, but he smiled at the woman, sidled closer, and began speaking in rapid French. The baker was smiling in girlish delight within thirty seconds. The man was lying pond scum, but he sure had charm.

Sara listened with half an ear to his explanation of their daughter forgetting to pay for the bread she took while he passed coins and compliments to the flattered woman. While the two of them laughed at Beth's childish mistake several of the younger women by the well separated from the group and approached Sara. Three women surrounded her, openly hostile, but equally curious. One of them held out her palm and demanded loudly to have her fortune told.

Sara didn't have the faintest notion how to read palms, but she didn't want trouble, either. She forced herself to bend humbly over the woman's callused palm and traced her fingers along the ridges and whorls. She could feel the women's hostile fascination as they waited; it washed over her in a nauseating wave. She didn't want to talk to them.

"Tell her she's pregnant with child number five," the ring suggested.

Is she?

"Would I lie to you?"

Sara gave a silent, skeptical snort. She informed the woman that she was with child.

"Ah," the woman said. The other women laughed knowingly. They waited for Sara to go on.

"Soldiers are coming to draft her husband and son."

Sara dutifully repeated this prophecy. The women shuffled and muttered nervously. "When?" one asked.

"In about ten seconds."

Sara heard the tramp of feet as the ring spoke. A group of soldiers in blue uniform coats marched briskly around a corner and fanned out in the square. The women by the well dispersed, the three surrounding Sara going with them. Sara was left staring at the soldiers, several of whom looked her over with blatant interest.

Lewis took her arm and drew her slowly away from the bakery. He didn't look at the soldiers.

"They looking for spies?" she whispered to him as they reached the road that would take them back to the Rom camp. She thought they were out of sight of the soldiers, but she could still feel their gazes on her back.

"Worse," he answered. "The Grand Army's drafting every able-bodied man it can lay hands on." He shook his head. "We'd better get the caravan away from here."

"Why?"

"Because they might not balk at pressing gypsies into service."

"Why do they need . . . oh, because Napoleon's invading Russia next year."

"Probably as early as next year, yes."

"Wait a minute." She stopped in the middle of the road. With Lewis standing in one of the deep ruts they were just about eye to eye. "Why are you in France? Are you gathering information on troop buildups, and stuff like that?"

"No," he answered. "The Russian invasion is a certainty. I have another assignment." He looked back toward the village. "Let's go."

"Then why—?"

"Not now." He took her arm and hurried her along. He wasn't just worried about getting drafted. Several of the troopers had looked at Sara as if she were a fine, rich dessert. He wanted to get her safely away from them.

"He's going to lose, you know," she told him as he set a swift pace. "Big time. Napoleon," she clarified when he gave her a questioning look.

"You can tell fortunes later," he told her. "We need to get off the main roads," he added. "Gypsies are supposed to have their own trails." He paused under the shade of an oak tree and looked at her accusingly, as if she were hiding secret knowledge from him. "How do you find gypsy trails?"

His frustration was more amusing than annoying.

The man had been passing as Rom on pure luck; he really didn't know as much about the culture as he thought. "You have to know what signs to look for," she said. "Even I know that. Marks left on the ground or on fences, odd bits of rags on the roadside, that sort of thing. I took a class in it once."

His eyebrows went up. "Gypsy school?"

"A seminar on ethnic heritage." She smiled wryly at the memory. "The teacher was a *gajo*."

They were standing near a crossroads. The roads bordered ripened fields and sheep pastures; the fields ended at a deep stretch of woods. The roads were lined with short hedges and tumbling-down dry-stone walls. From the ruts the intersecting roads looked to be heavily traveled.

"Crossroads are traditionally good places to find signs left by Roms who've come the same way. Also a good place for musicians to make deals with the devil," she added.

As usual, he looked at her as if he thought she were crazy, but he said, "Show me what to look for."

Sara walked to the middle of the crossroads. Lewis came to stand behind her, his hands on her shoulders. She didn't let the warmth of his nearness distract her. "Well?" he questioned. "What do you see?"

She didn't actually expect to see anything, but a spot of red in a forked branch of a tree caught her attention. She pointed. "Maybe that's something."

The tree was on the edge of the woods. After a few moments of searching the nearby undergrowth, Lewis said, "There's a faint trail here." He gave her a triumphant smile. "It goes southwest."

"Is that good?"

His eyes glinted with merriment. "Trust me."

"Deal with the devil, you mean?"

"Why not? You've been doing it for weeks now, gypsy girl. He hasn't eaten you yet."

He took her hand and kissed the palm. The light touch of his lips sent a shiver through her. "Not yet," she agreed.

Lewis grasped her hand and hurried her back down the road. "We've got to get the caravan moving while there's still light to travel."

11

The evening was cool. Lewis welcomed the comfort of the communal fire as he squatted on his heels with the caravan's other married men. Sandor was on one side, and Beng, stalwart as granite and smelling of the horses he'd just finished tending, was on the other. The day had been warm, but he had noticed some trees along their path were beginning to turn. Sara had quite a skill for finding isolated paths, but the way they had taken toward Paris certainly wasn't the fastest route. It had taken them twelve days to reach the outskirts of Nanterre, just a few miles from the sprawling city. They'd have to be even more careful, and probably slower, through the rest of Europe.

"It's a long way to Bororavia, Toma," Sandor said, echoing the thought crossing Lewis's mind.

He nodded. "I don't fancy traveling in winter."

Evan chuckled around the stem of his pipe. The aroma of his tobacco blended with woodsmoke and roast rabbit. "You've got a pretty bride to keep you warm."

Beng grunted in annoyance, while Lewis's gaze strayed across the fire to where Sara sat with a group of women. Her guitar was by her side, but for now her arms were full of Maritza's infant daughter. Maritza looked on proudly while Sara fussed over the naked baby. Sara's dark skin and hair were gilded by the firelight. The rounded fullness of her breasts strained against the fabric of her blouse as she lifted the gurgling baby, passing the child to its grandmother. What would she look like, he wondered, with a baby at her breast?

He found himself smiling fondly at his beautiful wife as she picked up her guitar and carefully checked the tuning pins. As if she felt his eyes on her, he saw a faint blush coloring her skin. It made his smile widen, even though several of the men chuckled, ready to tease him about his attention being too much on his wife.

Beng nudged him. "You giving me a grandson soon, Calderash?" he asked gruffly. "You good for at least that?"

"I'm good for it," he answered. There was quiet laughter from everyone but Sara's father. He still had no liking for his son-in-law, though he couldn't deny Toma his place among the *rom baro*.

Sara began to play, the music sad and sweet. It had become an evening ritual; Sara would play, and sometimes the women would dance. Evan often joined her with a battered old mandolin and Vastarnyi on violin, and several of the women would add to the rhythm with tambourines. He sighed contentedly as he gazed around the small camp, his senses lulled by music and firelight.

"How you going to give me grandsons sleeping under your wagon?" Beng asked, interrupting his pleasant mood.

He felt the other men's gazes settling on him, waiting for an explanation. He met Beng's eyes. "A woman is *mirame* when she bleeds," he reminded him. "We all sleep under the wagon once a month." He threw a disgruntled look at Sara while Beng counted ostentatiously on his fingers.

"I think my daughter maybe threw you out of the wagon," he said, wiggling his fingers. "Tell her she can come back to her tent if she wants."

He wasn't going to argue with the man. How he lived with his wife was no one's business but his own. If she spent most of her time scouting ahead for the caravan, it was his concern. And if he crawled under the wagon to sleep because the tension that sang between when they were alone was too much for him when she kept telling him no, it was also only his concern. Just because his body ached for her and the increasingly cold water in the streams where he bathed wasn't helping any didn't give anyone cause to bring the subject up.

After a considerable silence while the music played on and the men waited to see if he'd reply to Beng's comment, Andrei finally brought up the subject of whether or not they should set up the circus. Beng was against it, of course. Debate got underway quickly. Even as Lewis took the lead in the discussion he could feel Sara all around him. Her soul was in her music and her music covered him, guitar notes falling like a rainstorm around him.

Things had to go his way and he was silver-tongued enough to make sure they did, but every moment he spent with the gypsy men he was thinking of the gypsy girl not so far away.

"Where are you going?" Lewis asked, coming up to her as she turned from putting her guitar in the *bardo*.

"I thought I'd spend some time with Molly and Beth," she answered. She would have moved away, but he took her arm and pushed her ahead of him into the wagon. She nearly tripped over the guitar. "Hey!" she complained as he pushed it out of the way with his foot. He pushed her onto the bed and stretched out beside her without bothering to light the lantern. "Are we due for another wrestling match?" she questioned sarcastically as he pinned an arm across her breasts.

His eyes glinted at her out of the dark. "No." His mouth came down on hers.

She resisted the probing of his tongue for a moment; then her will deserted her and her lips opened for him. His kiss left her hot and eager, but she groped for words as he moved to nuzzle her throat. Her fingers tangled in the silk of his hair. She didn't know if it was a caress or if she wanted to pull him away. This was happening too quickly, and he was too much in control. "Oh, no," she said, pulling on his hair. "Not now." He lifted his head to look at her face. "Not ever," she added. "Get out of here."

"Your father wants a grandson," he answered. He

kissed the base of her throat. "I think you should give him a grandson."

"You said you weren't interested in having children."

His hand reached down to stroke slow circles on her abdomen. "I changed my mind." He began inching up her skirts.

"Stop that!" She tried to slap him away. "I'm not your wife," she reminded him.

He hadn't forgotten, not in whatever compartment of his mind logic lived, but the emotions that ruled his day-to-day life were in charge at the moment. He felt like Toma, and Toma wanted his wife. "Never mind the baby," he said. "I want to make love to you."

She rolled away from him, and fell onto the floor with a loud thud. "Ouch!" He busied himself with his clothes while she got up and fumbled with lighting the lantern. Sara turned around and gasped. Her dark eyes went round as buttons. Color flooded her cheeks.

Perhaps she'd never seen a naked man before. He gestured down the length of his body. "Now you see why I'm called the Magnificent," he said with a guileless smile.

Sara dropped her face into her hands and began to shake. With laughter. Toma laughed with her. "Stop being cute," she ordered when her laughter subsided. She raised her head to look at him. "Okay, I'm impressed," she admitted.

He beckoned her. She shook her head. "Please?"

She put her hands on her hips. She tried to keep her gaze on his face, but it kept flicking up and down his compactly muscled—magnificent—body. "Lewis Morgan," she demanded, "what has gotten into you?"

He rested his chin on his hand and looked up at her from under thick black lashes. "The problem is what hasn't gotten into you." He sat up, and snatched her around the waist so quickly she barely realized he'd moved until she was sprawled on top of him.

"Lew—" His kiss stopped her words. It went on for a long time and she was just as hungry for it as he was. She'd kissed her way down his chest and was beginning to flick her tongue across one of his tight little nipples when she noticed what she was doing. She raised her head to look at him. The look of uncontrolled pleasure on his face made her want to go right back to what she'd been doing. This had to stop, right now, or there wouldn't be any stopping at all. She saw a bite mark she'd made on his throat and touched it in surprise. With his eyes closed he put his hand over hers then brought her hand up to kiss her fingertips. The soft touch of his lips on the pads of her fingers sent a jolt of fire through her.

She was aching with need when she rose from the bed a second time. He groaned and reached for her, but she backed quickly to the door. She was outside and running to Molly's wagon before he could get off the bed. He shouted after her, but she heard no sounds of pursuit. How could her body be such a traitor? she asked herself as she hurried through the quiet camp. *And don't give me any of this own true love nonsense,* she warned the ring as she reached Molly's *bardo, because I won't believe it.*

*   *   *

What are you so cheerful about? Sara asked the
ring sourly as a tingling of expectation woke her from
a miserable dream.

"Oh, nothing," was the falsely innocent reply.

*If you start whistling I'm going to smash you
between a couple of rocks.*

"Aren't we just full of sweetness this morning?"

Shut up.

"You should have stayed with him."

She wasn't going to talk about it. She sat up and
scrubbed her hands across her face. She had not slept
well. When she had finally slept it had been accompa-
nied by shockingly erotic dreams. Shocking even by
her late-twentieth-century standards. They'd all featured Lewis, of course. The slime.

The slime came sauntering out of their *bardo* and
toward her as she made her way across the camp. It
was just barely dawn but many a cook fire was
already lit and people were moving about purposefully. A baby was crying in one of the wagons, drowning
out early morning birdsong. She noticed that Lewis
was wearing a wide-sleeved, sky blue shirt opened to
the waist, with a matching headband holding a heavy
wing of black hair out of his eyes. She was reminded
of how he looked the first time she'd seen him.
Except that when they met in the center of the camp
he looked tired, and his eyes were full of wariness. He
took her arm and silently led her back to the wagon.

Inside, he stood in front of the door and pointed to
the bed. "Sit," he ordered.

Sara did, gingerly, on the very edge of the bed. She looked nervously up at him.

"Don't worry," he told her. "I'm not going to touch you."

Actually, she hadn't been worried about that at all. She could tell he had something other than sex on his mind. "You look like Lewis Morgan, not Toma."

"I'm glad you can tell the difference."

"What's up?" she asked.

"It's time you went back to work," he answered.

So they'd decided to set up the circus after all. They could stand to earn some money and they'd heard the mood around Paris was festive at the moment. "The natives should be generous," she said.

She was reaching for the guitar when Lewis said, "I'm not talking about music."

The coldness of his tone froze her blood; the only warm spot on her whole body was where the thrumming ring circled her finger. She looked up slowly. Lewis looked as if he were made out of stone, hard and unmovable. For a moment Sara was paralyzed by fear; there wasn't enough air in the tight confines of the wagon. Then she shook the fear off, refusing to give in to it. "The ring is being weird, you're being weird. What's going on here?"

Lewis had been up all night, thinking, or at least trying to think. He'd reached the most important part of his mission only to be lulled by the mindless life of the road and distracted by roaring lust for the girl who was his pawn. The night had been spent in hell and he was in no mood to argue with the mad wench this morning. "You're here to perform a robbery, not play the bloody guitar. That's why I brought you here and that's what you're going to do." He folded his arms and glared angrily at her outraged expression. "Don't say a word. Just do as you're told." He ran his thumb warningly across the hilt of the knife on his belt.

Sara snorted with laughter. "Yeah, right. I'm terrified."

Lewis's shoulders slumped. "Sara!" He shook a finger at her. "I should beat you."

She crossed her arms and mocked him with a glare of her own. "You wouldn't know how to start."

"I've treated you more kindly than you deserve, little thief. It's time you repaid—"

"I'm not a thief."

He felt like beating his head against the sturdy wooden wall. They were going to have one of their mad discussions after all, weren't they? He did spin around and pound a fist against the door; then he turned back to her. "It worked out beautifully until you went insane. I wish you'd stop being insane and let me get on with my assignment."

She gazed at him, looking almost amused, almost serenely calm, almost as if she sympathized with him. "What's worked out beautifully?" she asked. "Take it step by step, Lewis Morgan."

"What?"

"I want to know how we got to this place, you and I. And why?"

He sat down beside her. "Why? Why do you want to know?"

"I'm forming a theory."

A theory. He blinked. Why was it she often sounded better educated and more sophisticated than he was? "Why can't you just be a simple gypsy burglar?"

"Why can't you be a simple Rom acrobat?" she countered.

"Point taken," he agreed with a sigh. "How did we get here?" He didn't know why he was talking to her, other than that it seemed better than arguing with her. He put his arm around her shoulder and drew her close. She didn't resist. When she was snugly fitted beside him he went on. "It's all been fortunate coincidence," he told her. "I learned my acrobatic skills and the language from some gypsies who were impressed onto a ship I served on. I was fifteen and agile as a monkey and—"

"What about the Calderash girl?"

"It was a lie to frighten you."

"Thanks."

"I disguised myself as a gypsy once or twice when I began to work as a spy. When my current assignment required traveling first to France and then to Bororavia I was lucky to discover a circus of Bororavian gypsies anxious to return to their homeland. Traveling with them seemed the perfect way to cover my movements. But they didn't want to accept me even if Sandor was willing to work with me. But coincidence was still in my favor." He squeezed her shoulder, feeling far more affection than he knew he should. She made a noise somewhere between a pleased murmur and a request for him to continue. "I knew I would need an expert thief to help with part of the assignment so I set out to find the best cracksman in London. My investigations led back to the gypsy circus and the prettiest girl in the tribe, the girl I'd already been considering marrying so I could be accepted by her people. My plans all fell neatly into place. The rest you know. Pure coincidence, all of it."

Sara pulled away from him and sat rubbing her fingers as she often did. She was smiling. "It wasn't coincidence."

"It couldn't be anything else, sweetheart."

She held up her hand. "Oh, yes it could. We're not dealing with coincidence; we're dealing with magic."

He slapped his hand forcefully against the mattress. "I'd hoped you were having a lucid spell."

"I think spell might be the operative word here," she said agreeably. She wiggled her fingers.

For a moment Lewis thought he caught the sparkle of an orange stone on her finger. He reached out, but they both jumped in surprise as a loud banging sounded on the back of the wagon.

Lewis had just gotten to the door when Beng flung it open. "Sara!" her father called nervously. "Soldiers are here looking for you. Hide!"

"Soldiers?" Lewis questioned. Fear twisted in his gut. He turned back to Sara. "Why?" She shrugged. "What did you do?"

She didn't know why anyone would be looking for her. "I didn't do anything!"

"This is no time to argue with the Calderash," Beng said. He glanced over his shoulder. "They're coming this way."

Lewis grabbed her shoulders and shook her. "Were you seen robbing a house after you ran away last night?"

"What? No! Let go of me!"

He should never have been lulled into believing her protests of innocence. If she'd ruined his mission . . . "We've got to hide you."

"I hate it when you act like a jerk," Sara told him as she kicked him in the shin to get him to let her go.

She didn't know what soldiers could want with her. She hadn't done anything wrong. In fact, her only contact with the French had been to play and pass the hat at a few inns along their route. There had been soldiers at the last inn. Their officer had clapped loudly, given her quite a bit of money, and suggested that she accompany him upstairs. But he'd been a perfect gentleman and withdrawn the offer gracefully when she'd pointed out she was married. He'd even let her keep the money. She remembered that his name was Captain Custine and that the two blues songs she'd played reminded him of slave music he'd heard when he'd served in the Louisiana colony. She'd liked him.

Which had nothing to do with soldiers in camp looking for her right now, she reminded herself. She thought about running, but where could she go? Running away might put the others in danger. She wouldn't put anyone in danger if she could help it. She gave Lewis a bitter look, placing the blame for any trouble they got into squarely on his shoulders, and stepped out of the *bardo*. With Beng beside her and Lewis standing on the wagon step she spotted four uniformed men who were walking around the remains of last night's bonfire. She raised her arm and waved to get their attention. Behind her, Lewis hissed an oath.

"I'm Sara," she called to the blue-coated soldiers.

The man in the lead hurried forward, grinning beneath a bright red mustache. "Of course you are, my dear," he said, coming up and taking her hands in his. "I was hoping the right band of gypsies was trespassing on my cousin's estate."

"Captain Custine?" Sara had to look a long way up to meet the tall man's gaze. Laugh lines crinkled up around his green eyes. She couldn't help but smile back; he looked so honest and open and reassuring. "How nice to see you again," she said, and meant it. She heard Lewis whisper something under his breath but didn't turn to look at him.

Captain Custine squeezed her hands gently. "The hands of an artist. Odd, how I told my cousin so just last night and today I find you just a mile away from his house. What good fortune this is!"

"Is it?" she asked, and felt a sharp tingle from the ring in response. Apparently it was. "Good fortune, indeed. Your cousin," she guessed. "You want me to play for him?"

His smile widened. "Lovely, clever girl."

She tried to draw her hands from his. "I'll just get my guitar." She had to go with him. Not only was he being amiable, the men he'd brought with him were armed with rifles. He had a sword at his belt, and the authority of the French army, besides. She noticed that Custine was looking past her. She turned her head to find Lewis glaring angrily at the captain.

"Your husband?" Custine asked her.

"Toma," she said. "And my father." She tilted her head toward Beng, hoping to draw the French officer's attention away from the British spy. "I'll get my guitar," she repeated.

He let her go and stepped back. "It'll wait for tonight, my dear." Custine gave her a look full of smoldering promise. It made her blush from her hair to her toes. He leaned forward and spoke softly in her ear. "I'll be seeing you at the chateau tonight."

She gulped nervously. "Tonight?"

Lewis appeared at her side. His arm came around her waist, pulling her hard against his side. She spared him a quick look. Murder blazed out of his bright blue eyes at the French officer. This was no time for the spy to forget that circumspection was the key to survival. She poked him in the ribs with her elbow. Custine noticed and chuckled.

She gave the Frenchman an annoyed look. "You want me to play guitar for your cousin," she reminded him.

"Marshal Moret," he supplied his cousin's name. "Tonight?"

Custine nodded. "The marshal is hosting a small celebration to honor the birth of the emperor's son. You will be part of the entertainment."

"And when shall I bring my wife to the chateau?" Lewis spoke up. "In time to play during dinner, perhaps?"

Custine acknowledged Lewis's presence with a reluctant nod. "That would be acceptable, gypsy," he agreed stiffly. "If she isn't there by nine I'll have you whipped," he added cheerfully before he turned and walked away. His soldiers laughed at his words. One of them made a threatening gesture at Lewis; then they hurried to follow their commander out of camp.

Sara relaxed against him as the Frenchmen disappeared from sight. "Charming," she said. "I don't think he likes you," she added.

Lewis nodded to Beng, then took Sara back into the wagon. "He'd like me to stand aside while he seduces my wife," he said once they were inside.

"I'm not your wife," she reminded him.

"So I'm supposed to let you be seduced by him?"

"I'm not going to get seduced by him."

"Why not?" Lewis demanded. He knew he sounded foolish but he couldn't keep from adding, "He's handsome. He's tall. Gallant."

A teasing smile lifted her lips. "You're handsome. You can be gallant—well, Toma can be."

"I'm not tall."

"No, but you're kind of cute."

"Do you like me?" Lewis shook his head, then pressed the heels of his hands to his temples. "What am I saying? I'm blathering like a fool when I should be crowing with delight."

Sara eyed him suspiciously. "Oh, yeah? What's to crow about?"

"Because it's Marshal Moret's house I've brought you here to rob."

"I'm not robbing anybody's house."

"Yes, you are." He did not want to go through it again.

"It's using us, you know. It has been all along. What is it you want?" She was looking at her right hand when she spoke.

Lewis was getting sick of this magic ring fantasy. He grabbed her hand and began pulling on her ring finger. "There's no magic rin—" A silver circlet appeared as he spoke. "You are wearing a ring!" Where had it come from? She hadn't been wearing a ring, then she had. "But . . ."

"I told you it was invisible. Unless it wants you to see it."

"But . . ." The ring had a small orange stone. It had its own inner glow. It seemed . . . alive. Lewis gave Sara a confused look. "Magic?" She nodded. "Nonsense." He touched the stone.

"Surprise," said the ring.

He'd heard that voice before, inside his head. "But? . . ."

"Articulate, aren't you, Lieutenant?" the ring said scoffingly.

"It's always like that," Sara said. "You get used to the sarcasm."

"But . . . magic?"

"I told you."

"I . . . see," he said slowly. "I've joined you in your delusion. We're insane together."

"That's a possibility," Sara agreed.

"Nonsense," the ring told them. "You're both as sane as I am. I want you both to calm down so we can discuss how you're going to get the brooch."

Lewis tightened his grip on Sara's hand convulsively. "The brooch," he gasped. "How do you know about the brooch?"

"What brooch?" Sara asked.

"My brooch," the ring answered.

"The duke of Bororavia's brooch," Lewis told her. "That's what I need you to steal."

"My own true love," the ring added. "We'll be together again at last."

Sara looked from the ring to Lewis, then back again. "You're nuts," she told them. "Both of you. I refuse to be involved in this—"

"Please, Sara," man and ring pleaded together. "I need you."

Introducing them had been a bad idea. One was looking at her like a begging puppy. The other was projecting hopeful longing with the intensity of nuclear radiation. She tried to block Lewis's look and the ring's longing with angry resentment. She hadn't asked to get into this mess! But trying to pout didn't work for more than a few seconds. There was no way she could hold out against both of them.

Sara swore under her breath, then said, "All right, I give up. I'm not going to get any peace until I help you steal this brooch, so we might as well do it."

12

It was a bujo, this ring business, Lewis decided as he paced outside Molly's wagon. Some sort of elaborate hoax. A deception, that's all it was. There were no such things as magic rings. She'd been playing him for a fool all along, drawing him into her tales of magic so thoroughly that when she finally revealed the actual piece of cheap jewelry he accepted her elaborate lies as real. "That's all it is," he mumbled as he paced. "Lies. She's trying to make a fool of me. But why?" He pondered the question as he tramped restlessly back and forth.

He'd spent his day juggling and running the tightrope. The crowds had gathered to cheer and he'd taken his bows as if it were a normal, sunny autumn day. But all the while his mind had raced with plans for the night, with images of Custine's covetous attention to Sara, and growing anger at himself for believing, even for an instant, in a magic ring. "Nonsense," he grumbled again. "What trick is she playing on me? Sly little gypsy. And what's taking so long in there?" He banged impatiently on the side of the cart.

Beth stuck her head out of the curtained side window and called, "Give it a rest, Toma. She's almost ready."

"It didn't take her this long to get dressed for our wedding," he called back. Beth laughed and ducked her head back inside.

It was twilight, and Sara was in the wagon preparing for her appearance at the Moret dinner party. He didn't know why she was making such a fuss. Why couldn't she just wear a clean skirt, a fresh headscarf, and the blouse she'd mended the day before? Was she trying to make herself look beautiful for Custine? That *gajo* didn't need any encouragement to think she was beautiful.

He looked down and discovered that his hand was resting on the hilt of his knife. "Hurry up!" he shouted.

The door banged open a second later. Sara stood in the entrance. He glanced up and felt his mouth drop open. She wore a fashionable white dress that showed off her amber skin and raven hair to perfection. The neckline was square and low-cut, and her curls were swept up in an elegant style threaded with a scarlet ribbon. She looked as if she were ready to walk into a London ballroom, and Lewis didn't like it one bit.

She stepped down from the wagon and twirled around in front of him. Molly and Beth took her place in the doorway, both of them smiling happily at their handiwork.

Sara stopped turning and said, "Well, what do you think? Stylish, but modest, or so Molly says. She says

French women wear thin muslin and then soak it in water. Sort of the wet T-shirt look, I guess." He continued to stare until she waved her hand in front of his face. "You in there? What are you thinking, Toma?"

"I think," he said, voice low and caustic, "that you should not try to ape your betters."

Sara looked at him in dumbfounded confusion that grew quickly into smoldering anger. "Better than what, you—?"

"Put on some decent clothes," he interrupted before she could work up to an angry tirade.

"You sound just like Beng," she shot back.

That moment Beng came up, looked her over, and said, "Are you going to let her dress like that?"

"No, I'm not," Lewis said. He reached for Sara.

She jumped back before he could grab her arm. "I've seen prom dresses that show more skin than this."

"It's indecent," Beng and Lewis said together.

"Why?"

A crowd was gathering. Sara heard murmurings of *mirame* in the background. Here we go again, she thought with an inward groan. "Excuse me," she called above the growing noise. "It's just a dress." She brushed her hands down the fabric of the skirt. "Look at it objectively, okay? Rom dress code says that women don't show their legs. There is no leg showing here. There are no rules being broken." She glared fiercely at Lewis. "Can we go now?"

She let him take her arm. He grasped it hard enough to bruise but she didn't mention that he was hurting her. They stopped by their wagon for her guitar, then headed out of camp. They walked along in silence for a while as the sky turned to dark velvet and the stars came out.

"So," she said as they approached a tall wrought-iron gate, "you ticked off because I look *gajo* or because I don't look Rom?"

Lewis blinked in confusion. "It's one and the same."

"No, it isn't." She smiled to herself. "Think about it."

He didn't want to think about anything. "You have a job to get on with."

Sara's secret smile widened. They stopped at the gatehouse and Lewis explained their business. The guard nodded, let them through, and pointed the path toward the servants' entrance to the chateau.

Once they were out of the gatekeeper's hearing she said, "I've got a gig. All I'm doing is playing guitar, then I'm out of there." His grip tightened. "Ouch! Dammit, let go!" To make matters worse the ring sent a shocked jolt of emotion all the way up her arm. "Ow! Stop that!" The guitar dropped out of her numb grasp with a loud clatter.

Lewis covered her mouth with his hand. He drew her tightly to him in the shadow of a tall, flowering bush. The scent of night-blooming flowers mingled with the scent of her skin and the metal taste of fear in his mouth. When she would have struggled he forced her to be still.

"Be quiet!" he whispered fiercely in her ear. "I didn't come this far to fail. Toy with me now and so help me, I'll slit your pretty throat."

She heard his desperation and she believed the threat. How could she make the man understand that she just couldn't do it?

"Please," the ring said. "I can't get to the brooch without your help."

The ring sounded desperate, vulnerable, not at all like the arrogant magical being she was used to. What was it like, she wondered suddenly, being a magical being?

"Lonely," the ring answered.

Its plaintive sadness got to her. Lewis's hand came away from her mouth. He stroked her throat and collarbone gently, sending warm tremors through her.

"Sara," he whispered. "Please. I'll never ask another thing of you."

You've never asked anything of me, she wanted to snap. *You just make demands.*

"He doesn't know any other way. He's a lord, you're a peasant. He doesn't know how to ask for help," the ring said.

He should learn, she thought bleakly. *You both should.*

His breath brushed against her ear. "Help me," he pleaded.

This is probably just an act, she told herself, but it worked better than threats. Suddenly she wanted to help him. But she wasn't a thief. The ring needed her. Lewis needed her. She was in the wrong place in time and nobody understood what it was doing to her.

She slumped against Lewis. He kissed the nape of her neck. She was so torn with warring emotions she didn't know what she was going to do.

She turned in the circle of his arms. Lewis dropped his hands to his sides and looked silently at her, his stance tight-muscled and tense. His sharply drawn features were etched in darkness and bright moonlight. She couldn't read his expression, but she felt herself drawn to stroke her fingertips across his wide cheek and down the sharp angle of his jaw.

Lewis waited. He'd finally realized the decision was Sara's to make. He couldn't force her and he couldn't beg her; he'd just have to wait until she made up her mind. If she couldn't do it, she couldn't. He'd just have to find another way. When her hand touched his face it brought a comfort he hadn't realized he needed. She didn't have the hands of a soft English lady. Hers was an artist's hand, callused and clever. He loved the feel of it caressing his face. He sighed, frustration mixed with pleasure.

Sara took a step back. Lewis reached a hand toward her, hesitantly. She took off the ring and handed it to him. He made a soft, surprised sound as the ring touched his palm. "You'll have to do it. The two of you working together."

"But, Sara—" Lewis began.

"Chill out, Lewis," the ring told him, "I'm real. Just put me on and do what the woman says."

He could feel the powerful reality that radiated from the small jewel. Never mind that its reality sent the logical world spinning out of control, out of his life forever. It was real. Sara wasn't mad. Or a liar. Or a thief, though that was what he'd been trying to make her.

Lewis's hand shook so hard he didn't know how

he managed to place the ring on his finger. The fit was perfect even though it had been circling Sara's much smaller finger only a moment before.

"A function of magic," the ring pointed out. "I fit whoever wears me."

Of course, Lewis agreed with the voice ringing in his head. "Ringing," he said out loud, wry amusement sedating all his other roiling emotions. "What else would a ring do?"

Sara picked up her guitar. "We'd better hurry. Captain Custine said I go on at nine." She walked on, with Lewis following close on her heels. "How long do you think you'll need to find the brooch?"

Lewis had a feeling she was talking to the ring. "Can you find it?" he asked it.

"I can feel it from here. On the second floor, in the south wing, near the back of the house."

Lewis repeated the ring's words to Sara. "I'll find a back staircase from the kitchen," he added. "Most of the servants will be occupied with serving the banquet."

"So, what, ten minutes? An hour?"

He put a reassuring hand on her shoulder as they reached a back courtyard between the stables and the servants' entrance. People moved around them purposefully in the light of torches set in tall stands in corners of the courtyard.

They were no longer alone, so he pulled her into a tight embrace and whispered confidently, "Play for the party. Enthrall them so that they don't notice the time passing."

"A diversion," she said. "I think I can do that much."

He had meant the words as a compliment to her

playing, but he wasn't going to pass up the offer of any help if she was offering to keep the party occupied while he stole the brooch. He kissed her. "Thank you," he said. "Do what you can if there's anything you can do."

"Don't get caught," she ordered.

"I won't," he assured her. *I hope,* he added to himself.

"Don't worry about it." The ring intruded on his thoughts. "Come on, let's go."

A footman was waiting at the door. He looked Sara over boldly, and said, "The captain's entertainer's arrived at last. Hope you're expecting a lively night, slut." Sara considered slapping the lewd grin off the man's face, but decided discretion was safer for getting Lewis and her through this crazy situation.

"My wife's come to play for the company," Lewis said in a low, cold voice.

The man gave Lewis a brief, disdainful look as he grabbed her by the arm. "Your pimp can wait here if he wants, but it's going to be a long night." He pushed Sara inside. "Don't worry about your fee, *tsigane,*" he added to Lewis before closing the door in his face, "your wife's pretty enough to earn you a fortune."

It took Lewis a precious instant to recover from the shock of the servant's insolent words. Then rage flooded him, turning the world red and driving all thought of the brooch out of his head. But when he would have pounded angrily on the door he found himself frozen in place. His limbs felt weighted down by bands of silver.

"Live with it, gypsy," the ring said coldly. "Or remember that you're not a gypsy and get on with your mission."

I won't have them treating her like a whore!

"She can take care of herself. That's why I picked her for this job."

You picked—I thought I picked—what is this job? Sara had said the ring was manipulating them. He no longer dismissed anything she'd said as insane ravings.

"We both want to get the brooch to Bororavia, Lieutenant," the ring said. "Let's just concentrate on that for now, shall we?"

Lewis sighed, and felt control of his muscles returned to him. The ring was right; there was much to do. *But I'll kill anyone who harms her,* he added as he looked around for a way into the chateau.

"Fine," the ring said. "I'll be happy to help you. There's a kitchen maid coming this way from the dairy. Try exerting a little of that Morgan charm on her to get us into the kitchen."

A pretty girl came hurrying toward him a moment later. Lewis didn't bother asking the ring how it had known the girl was coming; he just fell back into his role between one breath and the next. He moved to intercept her without hesitation, summoning up a boyish smile to turn on what looked like an overworked child. Within minutes he had in his helpful hands the heavy bucket she was carrying. It took only a few more coaxing words before she'd invited him into the buttery to keep her company while she went about her work. Keeping her company proved taking more time offering kisses and compliments than he liked, but she wasn't one to be rushed. She had to hide him from the butler when he came in and fussed at her about the quality of the cream. Eventually she went off to the kitchen to fetch her hungry new friend a bowl of potage. He followed the ring's directions to the back stairs as soon as the girl was out of sight.

"You were magnificent," Captain Custine told Sara as he took the guitar from her hands. He handed the instrument to a footman and drew her up off the chair where she was sitting.

They were standing near a gigantic fireplace in the rear of the huge dining room. She'd been sitting on a spindly little chair with her back to the roaring fire. The diners sat at a long table covered in scarlet cloth beneath a row of ornate crystal chandeliers. Everything in the room was red and gold, and bright and glittering and larger than life. Sara felt dwarfed and intimidated by everything around her. Even Captain Custine was red and gold, including his red hair and the gold buttons on his scarlet coat.

Sara looked around his broad form to the rest of her audience. She'd played through three long courses while the guests chattered to each other and the servants moved silently around her. Her hands and arms were aching from the effort and sweat was gathered on her back and between her breasts. She'd played everything from Hungarian folk ballads to L.A. Guns, but no one paid any heed to her at all, then or now, as Custine led her through the room and out a tall glass-paned door into a garden.

All she wanted was to get her guitar back and get away from the chateau. It didn't look as if there were anything she could do to help Lewis and the ring. She hoped they'd already gotten the brooch and gone. How long would it take for Custine to notice a jewel robbery? Her mind was full of questions as the captain urged her down on a marble bench. Would the Rom performers be suspected immediately? Would they be chased? Arrested? What would happen if they found out Lewis was a British spy? Stupid question. He'd be executed, of course. The rest of the caravan would probably be executed for harboring him. She scarcely noticed Custine's arm going around her shoulders.

His kiss came as a genuine surprise. His mustache was soft as silk, but the mouth that covered hers was harshly demanding. His tongue sought entrance and she opened her lips rather than try to fight him off. She felt nothing as he probed and explored; she just closed her eyes and wondered if she'd get a chance to tell him diplomatically that she wasn't interested, or punch him in the groin if it became necessary.

Eventually he lifted his head and told her, "You're delicious. I knew you would be."

She put her hand on his chest when he bent to kiss her again. "But I'm married," she reminded him.

"As am I. Shall I take you to Paris?" he asked. "Set you up in a little house? Introduce you to the theater owners?" He stroked her shoulders, baring them as he eased down the material of her sleeves. "Your skin's like dark honey, you exotic little creature."

She didn't mind the exotic, but the creature part

made her want to hit him. "You want me to be your mistress," she guessed.

His hands drifted down to cover her breasts. He weighed them in his palms while he spoke. "I wanted you when I first saw you in that filthy little inn. A pity I didn't have time to woo you properly then. Isn't it lucky we met again?"

"I don't think luck had anything to do with it." She grasped his wrists and tried to push his hands away. "I don't think this is a good idea, Captain Custine."

"Not private enough for you? You're shy," he said with a smile. "I liked that from the first. Except when you play. I watched you put your soul into your playing and knew I wanted to see you look at me like that when I made love to you. I love watching you play. I want to watch from an audience and know I'm the one taking you to bed after the crowd has gone wild. How they'll envy me."

She was really beginning to want to tell him just what he could do with his plans for her future. This turkey made Lewis look good by comparison. Where was Lewis, anyway? She hoped he'd gotten away. "Uh, thank you," she said, since Custine seemed to be waiting for a response.

"Do you want to be famous?" he asked. "I can help you conquer the Paris stage."

"First Paris and then the world?" she asked.

"Of course." He smirked and preeningly stroked his mustache.

Sara thought a little simpering might be in order while she tried to think of a safe way to get away from him. "You French do seem to be good at conquering things."

"The world is ours for the taking, little one."

You're going to deserve Euro-Disney, she thought maliciously. He drew her to him and kissed her again. While she ignored the forceful exploration of her mouth it occurred to her that in a future life Custine was probably going to be incarnated as Joe Malkos, the guy she'd dated through high school and most of college, who had dumped her to marry an aerobics instructor he'd gotten pregnant. She'd been more relieved than upset, even if the experience had soured her enough to turn her into a guitar-playing couch potato who watched more television than was good for her.

While her mind replayed scenes from her life in the future, he urged her to her feet, still kissing her. He lifted his head and said, "Shall I carry you to my room?"

"I can walk," Sara answered, then realized her words implied a consent she certainly didn't mean. "But, I—"

The big man swung her up in his arms. "Such a tiny thing you are," he murmured. Sara would have struggled, but he turned toward the house and dropped her back to her feet before taking a step. "What's that?" he asked, looking up toward a second-story window.

Sara saw it too, brief flashes of light behind the curtains, one red, one orange. They touched, then flared to impossibly white brightness, strobed, then vanished. Something wonderful and right had just happened. Sara felt the pleasure of the lights' reunion down to her bones. It set her shuddering with delight.

She wanted to throw her head back and laugh with joy.

"What the devil was that?" Custine demanded worriedly. "Don't be afraid," he added, stroking her face.

He must have felt her shaking; he obviously hadn't experienced the emotional rush accompanying the light show. It was the ring, she knew. Even if she wasn't wearing it she was still linked to it. Lewis must be up in that room. She wondered if the emotional backwash was stronger closer to the source. Was Lewis passed out on the floor with a deliriously happy smile on his face?

"I'd better go see what that was," Custine said. "Wait here." He began to stride manfully away.

Sara jumped after him in panic. "Wait! Don't go!" She grabbed his arm. She had to keep the man from finding Lewis. She'd promised Lewis a diversion and she had to come through for him somehow.

Custine swiveled around and grabbed her arms. When he started to thrust her away she grabbed the decorated front of his coat and pulled his head down to hers. She kissed him, with enough simulated passion to drive the idea of investigating anything but her out of his head. She pressed herself against him, grinding her hips suggestively against him. It was only moments before he'd taken her in a tight, possessive embrace.

"Don't leave me alone," she whispered seductively. "You promised to take me to your room."

"Very well," he agreed. "It must have been no

more than a dropped lantern. Come, we'll make our own fire."

He grinned and she felt his hardness pressing against her thigh. Oh, dear, she thought as he hurried her back into the house. He swung her into his arms again and carried her up a dark staircase, Rhett Butler style.

"Oh, dear," she whispered as he kicked open a door. He took her briskly to a big bed centered in a square of moonlight cast through a high, square window. "Oh, dear," she said again, and clutched at him as he laid her down. Her fingers dug deep into his shoulders but he mistook her panic for a sign of passion.

"Wild little animal," he said and kissed her.

When he'd kissed her before, she'd suffered it with indifferent patience; it hadn't seemed like a threat at the time. Now his tongue delving into her mouth served to block a scream of fear. She'd gotten herself into this; she was going to have to get herself out, but as he began caressing her roughly through her clothes she felt building hysteria threatening to rob her of all control.

She didn't want him touching her! She didn't want him on top of her! She pummeled his back with her fists, but that just made him laugh.

"Such a passionate creature," he said. He started to pull off his clothing.

He was down to his trousers and she'd rolled off the opposite side of the bed and was considering jumping out the window when the shouting started.

"Fire! Fire! Help!"

A new fear shoved Sara's hysteria out of the way. The house was on fire! She had to find Lewis! She ran for the door.

Custine caught her before she got there. He set her firmly back on the bed. "Wait here," he ordered as he pulled on his shirt. "It's nothing. You're perfectly safe. I'll be right back."

Sara bunched up fistfuls of bedcovers in furious frustration, but she didn't say anything. She just nodded and then made a face at him when he turned his back. She waited a full ten seconds after he was gone before she sprinted out of the room.

13

"Sara!" She had to be close by! *"Sara!"*

Lewis kept low as he moved along the smoke-filled hallway. Logic told him she was safely out of the burning mansion, but he didn't believe in logic anymore. A sixth sense told him she was up here on the second floor, perhaps trapped, probably frightened. "Sara!" he called again as he hurried from door to door. Where was she? What had Custine done to her? For if she was here, it was the French captain's doing. "If anything happens to her he's a dead man," Lewis threatened angrily.

He touched the brooch pinned on the inside of his vest. It was cool now; when he'd found it in Madame Moret's jewel case it had glowed like a burning coal as he snatched it up. Things had happened then, magical things. He couldn't remember any of it clearly. There had been light, and then a long, giddy ride down to darkness. When he'd woken, he'd wandered downstairs, almost mindless with joy, mindless of any danger. He'd felt protected, loved, things he'd never felt before.

Then the shout of "Fire!" went up and he came to his senses. Or as much as he thought he was likely to from now on. What he should have done was get the brooch away from the chateau as quickly as his legs would carry him. Instead he'd dashed upstairs to search for the gypsy girl.

He heard shouts and heavy, running footsteps and someone coughing on the smoke in the distance. He eased warily around a corner and headed for the first door on the left side of the corridor.

"Sara!" he shouted again, just as she jerked open the door and ran into him. They fell together onto the floor. His arms went around her in a tight embrace. "Are you all right? Did he hurt you?"

"Are you okay? Did you get the brooch? Did you start the fire?" she questioned rapidly.

He hauled her to her feet. "No, of course I didn't." Her hair tumbled loosely around her shoulders, her clothes were disheveled, and her lips swollen. "It's obvious what you've been doing."

"I was trying to cover your butt," she answered angrily. She stalked off toward the stairs. Smoke curled around her head as she moved away from the annoying Englishman. She was so angry she wasn't sure if the smoke was from the fire, or if it was coming out of her ears.

Lewis raced up and grabbed her arm. "You were trying to protect me?" He hurried her along. "Stay low," he directed.

"Yes," she answered as they reached the back

staircase. They ran down them. Sara could hear the distant roaring of flames when they reached the ground floor.

"Thank you," Lewis said as they paused for a moment in the rear hallway. He looked around and tried to recall the way to the servants' entrance. "I think the kitchen's on fire. Perhaps we should try for the front of the house. Which way?"

"What?" Sara had been standing in the smoky dark next to Lewis immersed in odd emotions having to do with his actually having thanked her for something. His question surprised her into thinking about their situation. She led him toward an intersecting corridor. "This way. I think I remember how to get to the garden door."

"Garden door?" he asked. "What were you doing in the garden?"

"Fooling around," she admitted.

He heard the amusement in her voice and said, "I see."

"Custine was fooling around. I was trying to keep him from investigating the lights upstairs. That was you and the ring, wasn't it?"

"Yes," he agreed. People were shouting in the distance but they were alone as they entered the dining room. He stopped her in a bar of light from one of the tall windows. He pulled off the ring. "Here. This is yours."

She looked at the silver and citrine ring cradled in his palm, then slowly up at his face. A warm wave of pleasure spread through her. The ring bestowed power, maybe a weird sort of power, but any kind of power was valuable. Lewis, loyal British military man though he was, wasn't trying to take that power for himself or his cause. He was freely giving it back to her. "Maybe there's hope for you yet," she said and plucked the ring out of his hand before he had a chance to change his mind.

"It's yours," he answered.

"What about the brooch?"

"That I am keeping."

"No, I meant, did you get it?"

He smiled. "Indeed." He flipped open his vest to show her a ruby in an ornate gold setting. "The ring says I'm to wear it next to my heart. Come on, let's get out of here."

She nodded, and ran for the garden door with him right behind her. They found the garden path and ran for the woods at the edge of the estate grounds. They were nearing the woods when Sara halted abruptly. Lewis ran into her. He grabbed her around the waist, steadying them both before they fell.

"What?" he demanded.

"My guitar!" she shouted as she lunged back toward the house.

He held on tight. "No! Are you mad?"

She struggled to free herself. "I have to get my guitar!"

The desperation in her voice was frightening. "No you do not," he said firmly. "It's too late, Sara, love. Come on, before someone sees us." They'd been incredibly lucky so far; he didn't want to gamble on getting caught now that they were so close to getting clean away.

She pushed against his restraining hands. There

were tears in her voice when she spoke. "You don't understand . . . that guitar, it's perfect. Like it was made for me. I have to get it back. You have to help me. Please?"

He wished she didn't sound so desperate. He wished she hadn't asked for his help. "I would if I could, sweet, but—"

"Let go of me!" she shouted, and began to struggle harder.

Lewis looked back. They were beyond sight of the house, but the sky behind them glowed red-orange. "It's too late," he told her, as gently as he could, considering she was fighting him like a hellcat.

He winced with guilt, but he didn't really feel as if he had any choice when he spun her around and planted his fist in a square, hard blow against her jaw. She collapsed, unconscious. He caught her limp body and hoisted her over his shoulder. She was a little thing, but carrying her did slow him down as he hurried up the path through the woods. It wasn't far to the gypsy camp; the night was still, clear, and crisp. He heard none but his own near-silent footsteps on the mossy path. He breathed a sigh of relief as he came around a turn in the path and saw the caravan's campfires in the distance. Home. Safe. Mission accomplished. Not another single magical or unexplainable occurrence could possibly occur to confuse his mind tonight.

He found the guitar, snugly wrapped in its oiled canvas bag, leaning against a tree only a few feet farther on. He refused to be confused, bemused, or even a little bit curious about how it had gotten there.

He just adjusted Sara's limp weight on his shoulder, picked the guitar up with his free hand, and continued on to the camp.

Sara woke up knowing only that her jaw hurt and that something very essential was missing from her life. She was lying down on a soft, familiar surface, a faint light bathing her eyelids. When she opened her eyes she saw the flicker of flame from the lantern set on top of the nearby storage chest. She was in her own *bardo,* curled up on her side with a pillow under her head. She let her breath out in a slow sigh, curious but lethargic. Why did her jaw hurt? Why did her soul hurt? She closed her eyes again and rolled onto her back. With a groan she put her arm over her eyes.

"Awake at last."

Lewis's voice was rough, as if he'd been smoking. Her throat felt raw, too, come to think of it. As if she'd been smoking. Smoke. Smoke inhalation. They'd been in a fire. At the chateau. The ring. The brooch. She sat up abruptly.

"My guitar!"

Lewis stood over her, wearing only his trousers and his headscarf. He grinned at her like a half-wild Cheshire cat. Then he nudged her legs over and sat down on the bed. He handed her the guitar. She hugged it to her like a beloved child.

"Oh, Lewis, you did go back for my guitar!"

"I found—" She turned such a loving look of gratitude on him he couldn't bring himself to explain further. He just smiled and said, "Everything's all right now, love."

A ripple of deep pleasure spread through her at his words. Edgy pleasure, as if maybe everything wasn't quite all right, but maybe it was going to be. A tension that had been coiling tighter and tighter inside her for weeks began to unwind as she met his bright blue gaze. Heat spread through her from the contact.

Without knowing what she was doing she set the guitar on the floor and reached out to touch Lewis Morgan's face. A sooty-lidded, blue-eyed fox, she thought, running her fingers along the dark arch of his brows.

Lewis sat and waited, almost holding his breath as Sara moved closer to him. He wanted to take her in his arms but he let her come to him. She pushed her fingers under the headband he wore, pulled it off, and ran her hands through the loosened strands of his hair. He closed his eyes, loving the feel of her fingers combing across his scalp. He'd always loved it when a woman played with his hair. Sara seemed to know instinctively how to arouse him. He caught his breath in a hot gasp as she traced her fingers down to his throat. It set his pulse pounding when her fingernails danced in light circles around the edges of his nipples. He grasped the sides of the feather-stuffed mattress in a death grip as her artist's fingers moved on sensually to massage the tight muscles of his chest. Then the tip of her tongue touched his lips. He opened his mouth at her gentle urging, nearly drowning in passive heat as she hungrily searched his mouth. His head spun and his blood pulsed with need. He grew hard with hunger as her hands moved over him, cleverly exploring. Her breasts pressed against his chest, the hard peaks of her nipples separated from him by only the sheer width of her muslin bodice. He wanted to feel her naked skin against his and within moments he conceived a deep hatred for the inoffensive cloth. He felt the heat from her skin; the scent of her filled his senses. He kept his eyes closed and his hands off her, though he could feel his fingers gouging holes in the mattress cover.

He'd let her take whatever she wanted. He wasn't touching her, he vowed, not until she wanted him to. She could have him, but he wasn't going to take. He'd taken enough from her. The passion she was building in him was intense, and she was making it a gift.

Sara didn't know quite what she was doing, but she couldn't stop touching him. Desire twisted deeper inside her with every small noise Lewis made. She played him, calling forth sounds of need and pleasure with her fingers and her lips, making music with small, passionate bites, and quick, sharp licks of her tongue.

She didn't remember pushing him onto his back, or freeing his hard shaft from his straining trousers, but when she brushed her lips across the sheathed tip Lewis called out her name. His hips bucked convulsively; he sat up and tangled his hands in her hair. He pulled her up the length of his body. The next thing she knew she was on her back and he was holding a knife.

Lewis had plucked the knife from under the top of

the mattress. With a deep sound in his throat, he used it to slice into the material of her *gajo* dress. He tossed the knife away and ripped the fabric with his hands to get at the lush, soft curves of her body. He couldn't fight for control anymore; wanting her was a burning agony he had to end. She was hot velvet under his hands. Her back arched passionately as he drew her breast to his mouth. He slid his hand up her thigh to the juncture of her legs. There he found and stroked her, glorying in the shivers of desire from her taut body. He wanted only to bury himself in her, to sheathe himself in consuming heat.

Lightning shot through her at his intimate caress and all Sara could do was flow on the ravaging current. He moved over her then, quick and sinuous as a cat, stroking her until she purred and the purr turned into a plea for more. She brought up her knees and he slid between them and into her in one swift, possessive motion.

Sara bucked uncontrollably at the sudden burst of pain. All her senses, already centered at where their bodies joined, jolted in response. "Lewis!" she called out, and he froze, poised over her, inside her but unmoving. She felt tearing pain.

"I'm hurting you." His words came on a grindingly ragged breath. Sweat beaded on his face and dripped onto her breasts. "God, Sara, I can't . . ." His hips stabbed forward. She groaned, but lifted herself to meet the thrust, trying to make it easier for both of them.

She didn't understand it; she'd been so hot and ready for him, but this felt like the first . . .

"Oh, dear," she choked out, grasping at his shoulders. "Lewis, I think I'm a virgin!"

"I—you *were* a virgin," he answered on a wild laugh. Despite the distraction of the moment she couldn't help but notice how inordinately pleased he sounded about this development.

"Men," she complained, then closed her eyes and gave herself up to the slow rhythm Lewis was setting up inside her. Her body rocked with him, the pain receding more with each smooth thrust. She felt inner muscles pulse tightly around his questing shaft as heat began to center once more on where they joined. It wasn't long before nothing but the building heat mattered.

She flowed into it, with it, like riding a lava flow back to its source until she fell into dark, delicious fire. It was a phoenix fire, bringing her to life even as it consumed her. She soared for a long time on the flames. As the fire faded she was caught up briefly in a passionate dance as Lewis reached his own peak and his spirit seemed to swirl and fuse for a moment with her own.

The images faded as she fell back into herself, but the memory of the moment of fusion stayed with her as she found herself lying on her back, cradling Lewis's head on her breast.

She sighed sweetly and murmured very softly, "Again!"

When he came to, sated, all Lewis wanted to do was lay his ear over her heart. He wanted to hold her close and be lulled to sleep as his own pounding pulse settled to join her calming heartbeat. He just wanted to be with her forever and ever. She whispered something, but he was too tired to catch the word.

"Sleep," he said, moving to hold her close in the darkness. He groped for a blanket to cover them. The lantern was long since out of oil. He kissed her hair. "Just go to sleep, sweetheart."

Sara got up to use the chamber pot just before dawn. The sound of others in the camp stirring as she hurriedly washed and dressed in the cramped quarters had a comforting regularity about it. She'd gotten used to the routine of the traveling life in the last few weeks. Having Lewis in her bed was not part of the routine. She turned and watched him sleeping. He looked young, and rather sweet, as he lay on his side, his hands cradling his cheek, a wing of black hair covering his eyes.

She sat on the end of the bed and picked up the guitar. Oh, yes, very sweet, she thought, not quite sure of her own mood. But how had he gotten in her bed? Wasn't she supposed to have been invulnerable to his charm? She had been wronged. She'd held the moral high ground, which had not only been a lonely position, but had gotten damned shaky under her feet of late. She sighed. It was done. It had felt great. She'd been as responsible as he was. No use slinging recriminations when he woke up.

"Question is," she murmured, "is it going to happen again?"

Lewis opened his eyes when he heard Sara's voice. He had to swipe hair out of the way before he could actually see. "Very unfashionable," he grumbled, "long hair." He rolled out of bed and made quick work of cleaning himself up and getting dressed. Sara sat on the bed and played something sad on her guitar. When he was done he came back and half sprawled on a pile of pillows. He would have been happy to start the day off with bedding Sara again, then polishing off an enormous breakfast, but they had a lot to talk about first.

"What's that you're playing?" he asked, trying to get her attention.

Sara looked at him sideways, with one of her cryptic, superior smiles. "I call it 'The Good Woman Having a Bad Hair Day Blues.'" While he digested this latest bit of nonsense she put the instrument down and turned toward him. "So," she said. "How'd you know where I hid the knife? And you can apologize for ruining the dress, too."

"I thought using the knife was a rather fetching dramatic gesture."

"You weren't thinking at all."

"Perhaps not too clearly," he admitted. "You were driving me mad, vixen. As for the knife, I am a spy, Sara. It always pays to know where all the weapons are hidden."

She nodded. "I can see where it might come in handy." She looked away from him. "Last night was—"

"Magnificent," he supplied for her. He reached his hand out to her. "Let's repeat it, shall we?"

Sara shook her head, and groaned. "I hate ethical predicaments."

"I wish you'd stop saying things like that," he said. Lewis wished he hadn't decided they needed to talk. What was there to discuss? Very little, really, if they kept magic rings and the thousand questions he wanted to ask out of the conversation.

"How am I supposed to talk?" she asked. "Like an adoring Rom wife?"

Before he could answer, the door of the *bardo* was thrown open. Beng stuck his head in. "The Frenchman's come looking for you, Sara."

"Custine?" Sara jumped to her feet. "What's he doing here?" She looked frantically at Lewis. "He must know about the brooch!"

"The devil with the brooch," Lewis said. "He wants you!"

Beng spoke up. "I haven't enough of his *gajo* language to make much sense of his words. I think he says you were in the fire. Has he come to arrest you for burning down the castle?"

"No," Sara told Beng. "That's not why he wants me. He wants me to be his mistress."

"He what?" Lewis shouted angrily.

Beng glared at Lewis. "You going to protect your woman, Calderash?"

"I'll protect her, all right," Lewis declared. "Stay here," he ordered Sara, and charged out of the wagon. Beng had to jump hastily aside to keep from being bowled over.

"Custine!" Lewis shouted, intent on murder as he spotted the red-haired Frenchman approaching the wagon. He was tackled from behind at the same time he noticed he hadn't put on his belt when he'd gotten dressed. His knife was back in the *bardo*. Never mind, he'd strangle the bastard with his bare hands!

As he struggled to rise he heard Beng explaining in his broken French, "My son-in-law jealous man."

It was Beng who was holding him down! What was the matter with the man? Did he want him to defend Sara or not?

"I'm sorry," Custine said brokenly. "I'm truly sorry."

What was the matter with the Frenchman? Sandor appeared, then Andrei and Hadari. The men hauled him to his feet and held him back when he struggled to get at Custine.

"What's the matter with you?" Sandor whispered fiercely in his ear. "You attack the French captain, you'll get us all killed."

Sandor's words splashed over him like a bucket of icy water. He slumped in the men's tight grasp. Lord, what had he been thinking? A moment ago he'd been willing to risk his entire mission for the honor of a bit of skirt. Honor? He blinked and shook his head as if to clear it. Beng had said he was jealous, but it hadn't been just jealousy. He'd rushed off to defend a gypsy girl's problematic honor. Ridiculous.

When Custine stepped up to him he was almost able to speak rationally to the man. "What do you want?" he demanded.

Custine's eyes and face were red and swollen. He looked as if he had been crying. The expression in his eyes was a little wild. "I'm sorry," he said again. "I don't know if your kind is capable of love, but she was your wife. I can see you felt something for her."

"Felt?" Lewis repeated. Felt? The light suddenly dawned. The Frenchman thought Sara was dead. "Killed in the fire?"

The question had been more to himself than to the Frenchman, but Custine answered. "She was the only one trapped inside. I was hoping that perhaps she got out and made her way back here. I can see from your face that she didn't." He wiped his sleeve across his eyes. His wide chest heaved in a sigh. "I'm so sorry."

Lewis found himself looking up at the clear blue autumn sky. A faint haze drifted above the trees in the direction of the chateau. He looked away from Custine to keep from laughing in the man's face. He also looked away to keep from seeing the genuine caring the man felt for Sara. He wanted to sneer at the romantic fool. At the same time he felt a deep stab of shame and envy at the man's simple, uncomplicated attachment to the girl.

Lewis didn't have the luxury of being uncomplicated. "My wife!" He let out a dramatic howl toward heaven. "He thinks Sara's dead," he explained in Romany to the others in between ragged sobs while Custine looked on in anguished embarrassment.

"So that's his problem," Beng said. "I thought maybe he wanted to buy her."

Sandor spat. "Filthy *gajo*." He patted Lewis's shoulder as if comforting him. "Too bad we can't let you kill him."

"Better to skin him," Beng said. "That's the way to take care of your wife, Calderash. This one's ripe for the *bujo*, I think."

Beng turned to Custine and switched back to pidgin French. "What you give us for the loss of my daughter?" He pointed at Lewis. "Toma lost a good wife. Now we have to go all the way back to Bororavia to get him another one. Gypsy law," he added at Custine's confused expression. "Now he must marry her sister. Sister is in Bororavia. We must go to Bororavia to mourn our dead properly too." Beng's gesture took in the whole camp. "You cause us much trouble."

Custine's gaze followed Beng's hand. Lewis began crying louder for emphasis. Sandor and Andrei joined in, but not so loudly as to disrupt negotiations. "You have all my sympathy," Custine told them. He shuffled his feet nervously.

Beng pounded his chest with his fist. "I don't have my daughter. You can't give me my daughter."

"I would if I could, believe me."

"We go to Bororavia now." Beng pointed at Custine. "You help us get to Bororavia, maybe the old women not curse you and all your generations for this."

"Help you get . . ." Custine stared at them blankly for long seconds. Lewis might have held his breath in anticipation if he hadn't been busy setting up a mournful racket. He prayed that Sara didn't take it into her head to come see what the noise was all about. He could practically see the watchworks of Custine's brain turning as the Frenchman churned through the possibilities of what Beng wanted from him.

Finally Custine spoke. "I could, perhaps, be of some help. I could arrange travel papers for you.

That might make it easier for you to cross the empire."

"Many borders between here and Bororavia," Beng pointed out. "Papers. Yes." He nodded emphatically. "Papers help us return home swiftly. Mourn Sara at home. Get new wife for wronged son. Women not curse you." He put his hand on Custine's slumped shoulder. "You good man, Captain. Come." Beng turned him and headed him out of the camp. "I come with you to get papers." He threw a look at Lewis over his shoulder. He spoke in Romany. "Have the caravan ready to leave when I get back."

Lewis nodded. The other men released him and ran to hurry their women's packing as Beng and the French officer disappeared from sight. Lewis stood alone for a few moments after they'd gone. He looked up at the sky again and laughed. The sound was full of triumph as much as amusement as both Toma and Lewis reveled in having gotten the best of the foolish French *gajo*.

14

The fingertips brushing across the tip of Sara's breast were cold; that alone was enough to bring an instant response, never mind what they were doing. Which was so stimulating that she had to grit her teeth to keep from waking up the whole camp with her reaction.

"You're awake, I see," she said from behind her gritted teeth. Lewis grunted in response, while his cold hand stroked down across her waist and stomach. "You slept with your hand outside the cover, didn't you?"

"Umm," he responded as his lips found and began nuzzling her ear.

"Ah," she whispered as his fingers reached the top of her thighs. She opened her legs without any urging. At the same time she reached for his head and brought his mouth to hers. She kissed him, with her hands tightly fisted in his silky hair while his fingers made magic with delicate little swirling strokes. One thing led quickly to another then, and the next thing she knew she was lying cradled beside him, warm and sated and slightly embarrassed by the ease of the entire process.

It kept happening. For days now, one thing had kept leading to another. Every time she told him to go away he ended up sharing the bed. They didn't talk about it; they hadn't talked much about anything since the night they stole the brooch. In fact, she spent most of her time with Molly and Beth and he was either with the other men, or entertaining the caravan's adoring children. The kids followed him as if he were the Pied Piper. She played the guitar and sometimes caught herself sulking if he wasn't looking at her over the width of the campfire. Then he would look at her and the outcome would be inevitable. Deliciously inevitable, despite her mild protests that they shouldn't. They always seemed to end up sleeping together, though.

She had to admit it felt nice, not just the sex, but the sleeping in the comfort of shared warmth as the days grew cooler. She'd lost track of the time. She wasn't sure what month it was. In fact everything that had happened before stealing the brooch was wrapped in a sort of haze, and every day since had been gone through in a daze.

The brooch, she thought, then lifted her head to look at Lewis. "The brooch," she said. "What are you going to do with the brooch?" Of course the question should more properly be asked of the ring, but Lewis hadn't known about the ring when he set out to steal the brooch. "And why'd you want it in the first place?"

Lewis had drifted into a light doze after making love. He didn't particularly want to wake up just yet. He didn't want to talk; talking brought the world too close. He liked the world distant and all fuzzy around the edges, the way it had been the last several weeks. He didn't want to talk, but Sara's tone told him she wasn't going to be put off.

He sighed. "I don't want it for anything," he answered.

"Yeah, right," she replied skeptically. She shifted in the narrow confines of the bed, propping herself up on one arm. Lewis opened one eye to look at her. "So," she said, glad she had his attention, even if it was her bare breasts he was looking at. "What's it got to do with the defeat of one Napoleon Bonaparte? You know," she went on, "to me Napoleon's the name of a pastry, but my dad knows all about him."

"What does Beng know about Napoleon?" he scoffed. He brushed hair out of his eyes and adjusted the pillows so he could comfortably look at Sara without actually having to sit up.

"Not Beng," she said, "my father. Who is probably Beng in this life, but the man I think of as my father is named Paul. This reincarnation thing is complicated."

"I knew a Hindu man from India once," he said. "He explained reincarnation to me. It doesn't make any sense. I didn't know gypsies believed in it," he added.

"The Rom are from India originally," she told him. "Though I don't think the linguistic connection to India has been made yet. In the early eighteen hundreds, I mean. Maybe. I might not know too much about

Napoleon, but I'm pretty good with Rom history, if not much good at remembering dates. So, why'd you steal the brooch?"

He had hoped she'd gone off on enough of a tangent to forget about her original question. "Because I was ordered to," he answered.

She tapped him on the chest. "Not good enough."

He gave her a sour look. "Why should I tell you?"

She wiggled her fingers threateningly. "Because I know where you're ticklish."

He grasped her wrist, then brought her hand to his lips. "A formidable weapon, this," he said after he'd kissed and nibbled on her fingers and palm for a while. He released her hand, and she began combing her fingers through his hair. Little ripples of pleasure radiated out from his scalp, but he ignored them to answer her question finally. "Britain is negotiating a port treaty with the duke of Bororavia. Negotiations with his overlord, the czar. It's a very delicate matter."

"Why?"

He sighed. "Why would a foolish little gypsy girl want to know?"

Nails dug suddenly into his chest. "How about," she said coolly, "because the foolish little Rom girl has a degree in economics, and doesn't like being condescended to?"

Her voice held a sharper edge than his knife. It cut into the fiction he'd been trying to maintain about his lover. She said she was from the future. He didn't want to think about it. He certainly didn't want to face it straight on. He decided it was better for his sanity just to answer her question rather than ask any of his own.

"Napoleon has been trying to ruin Britain's trade for years," he answered. "It's part of what he calls the continental system. He's been fairly successful in keeping British ships out of European ports."

"The blockade we had to run to get to France?"

"Yes. But the blockade's not completely effective. What we've lacked are countries willing to risk Napoleon's wrath to let British trading vessels in."

"Hmm." He paused at her thoughtful sound. After a few moments she said. "It's 1811. Wellington has started kicking butt in Spain by now, right?"

"Nosey's won a few battles, yes."

"But Napoleon's mostly concentrating on building the army he's going to lose in Russia."

"I'm glad you're so confident he's going to lose."

"I'm not, I've just seen at least two versions of *War and Peace.*"

Lewis didn't ask for her to clarify any further. "The brooch was the original topic of conversation, as I recall."

"The brooch has something to do with trade negotiations with Bororavia," Sara summed up. "What?"

"The brooch belongs to the grand duke of Bororavia. I believe he lost it to Madame Moret gaming a few years back. Or perhaps she was his mistress for a time and he gave it to her. I'm told he changes his story from day to day."

"Oh," she said. "The mad duke. I know about him."

"I don't know that much about him," Lewis admitted. "I was just given the assignment to bring the brooch to the British ambassador conducting the negotiations."

"Why?"

"The duke wants the brooch back, as a token of good faith from the British."

"So the British can trade with Russia?"

"Bororavia," he corrected.

She snorted. "Please, Lewis, I know my Bororavian history. The treaty that Sara negotiated was on behalf of—of—"

As her voice faltered he felt the hand resting on his forehead go cold. "Sara?" She was staring off into space, color drained from her dark honey skin. He sat up and took her by the shoulders. "Sara?"

She nodded. "Sara." He saw her throat move as she swallowed hard. "I'm very good with finances, you know. So was . . . she . . . Sara . . . the regent." She swallowed again. "Nah."

"What are you talking about? What regent?"

Sara was looking at her hand. At the invisible magic ring, Lewis supposed. "I'm out of here next August," she said. "Bororavia is not my problem. I'm not . . . her!"

The wildness in her voice worried Lewis. "What's the matter? What's the ring saying?"

She slowly met his gaze. "Nothing. The ring's not saying anything." Her expression was guarded. She shook his hands off. "It's time we got dressed. You promised to help the kids go foraging today."

He nodded at her reminder. He could sense fear in

her and was reluctant to let her go, but he did. It was better not to ask, he told himself. Whatever it was that was bothering her was between her and the ring. But what was happening in August? She'd mentioned the date before. Maybe he knew and just didn't want to think about it.

He wouldn't think about it. He got up and got dressed instead. He did say, "Come with us," to her when he was ready. He held out his hand. "Keep me company today." He wanted to spend all of today with her. All of tomorrow.

Sara was warmed by the intensity of Lewis's look, by the eagerness of his voice. "All right," she answered. "I'll go nuts-and-berries hunting with you."

Being with him would keep her mind off what she suspected the ring had in mind.

"What happens in August?" Lewis asked.

He hadn't meant to. He hadn't wanted to. But the question had raced around in his head for hours, and eventually, as they approached a small, steaming pool, it just came out. There was a faint smell of sulfur in the air from the water. It reminded him of his one trip to Bath.

Sara wrinkled her nose and said, "Yuck. Smells like a catalytic converter."

He didn't want to know about that either. "August," he said. "What happens in August?"

Sara fanned her hand in front of her nose. "Could we leave? This place stinks."

"You won't notice after a few minutes." He began to strip off his shirt. "Let's have a soak."

Sara pointed distastefully at the faintly yellow, steaming water. While she watched he pulled off his boots and dipped his foot into the pool. She half expected the Swamp Thing to reach out and pull Lewis to his doom, but Lewis just sighed contentedly as he wet his toes.

"Perfect," he said. He quickly finished undressing. "Come along," he said when he was naked. "We can have a hot bath while we talk."

They'd spent much of the day walking through forested hills, helping four of the younger children forage for food. While they'd been with the children they hadn't talked much, but the children were now on their way back to camp with a couple of hedge-hogs and a basket of greens to boil in the communal pot. They were alone in an autumn red glade, and Lewis looked inviting even if the water didn't.

"Mineral springs are healthy," he coaxed as she continued to look dubiously at the pool. "The trail that led here looked well used. The locals must have been coming here for generations." Sara's expression changed as he spoke. She looked nervously around. Lewis followed her gaze and asked, "What?"

"Maybe we shouldn't be here."

"We're alone," he assured her. "There's nothing to worry about."

She pulled her blue wool shawl tight around her bosom. "What if we get caught?"

"Caught?"

Sara shook her head. He didn't understand. He'd

been living among the Borava tribe for all this time and he still didn't understand. "They won't like Rom polluting their water," she told him. "Rom are filthy animals, remember?"

"Nonsense." He saw instantly that she wasn't going to be reassured by his airy dismissal of danger. "Are you afraid of a few ignorant peasants?" he asked her.

"Yes," she answered. "Ignorant peasants are a leading cause of mortality among Rom."

He sighed and slid into the heated water. It covered him to waist level, bubbling gently and tingling against his skin. "It feels wonderful," he told her. He held his arms out. "Don't be afraid. I won't let anything happen to you. You're not going to let anything scare you," he added, smiling encouragement. "Not my brave Sara."

She shook her head. "I'm not brave. I just come from a place—a time—that's a little bit better." The thought of a hot bath was inviting, she had to admit. And Lewis thought she was brave.

It took her longer to shed her layers of clothes than it had Lewis. By the time she'd jumped in beside him he was looking serious. The water did feel good. She edged gingerly around the slippery bottom of the pool until she found a spot where she could kneel with only her head out of the water.

"Ah," she said as the bubbling sulfur water began to work wonders on her muscles. The air surrounding the pool was crisp and cool, a delicious contrast to the water's steaming warmth. A bird began singing in a nearby tree. She closed her eyes for a moment to listen. "This is nice."

Lewis waded over to join her. "Only a little better? Your world is only a little better?" he asked. "What happens in August?"

She saw the worry deep in his eyes, and it tore at something inside her. Her throat grew so tight with pain that she could barely speak. "You know what happens in August."

She didn't know how many times she'd told him she was going back to the twentieth century on the next St. Bartholomew's Day. Of course, she'd told him a great many things he hadn't believed before he knew the ring's magic was real.

"Why go back?" he asked. "If it's only a little bit better than now."

"What have I got to stay for?" she answered, which wasn't at all what she intended to say. She hoped her desperation for him to give her some reason to stay didn't show in her eyes. A moment ago she hadn't known the desperation was there herself.

He wanted to tell her to stay. She had a magic ring. She had a place in the future. It sounded like a very different place from the one she occupied in the present. "How did you get to this time?" he heard himself ask. He ran his fingers along the delicate high arch of her nose. "How did you become the Sara I thought I knew?" She blushed as he spoke and looked away. "Oh, dear," he murmured, amused despite himself. "The tale must be very wicked."

Her temperature was rising, and she wasn't sure it had anything to do with the natural warmth of the mineral spring. Was it embarrassment, or just because Lewis was so close?

"Well?" he coaxed. "How did you get to the past?"

"The ring."

He snorted at her answer. "Not how, then, but why?"

"I, uh, made a wish."

His fingertips brushed her temples. She closed her eyes. "What wish?"

She grimaced, but she couldn't keep from answering. "To meet my own true love." She felt her pulse quicken as he continued to gently massage her temples. She made a small, pleased sound.

He tilted her head back so he could kiss her throat. "Have you found him?" he asked when he was done tasting the moist smoothness of her skin. The water washing over them added a bittersweet deliciousness to his kiss. "Have you found this true love of yours?" He reached down to circle her small waist with his hands. He drew her slowly upward, sliding moist skin over moist skin. She made another soft, needful sound as she moved against him. "Well?" he whispered in her ear.

Sara balled her hands into fists. She knew she was only seconds away from losing all self-control. She'd be all over him then, and it would be wonderful, but it wouldn't settle anything. Sex was a panacea; it wasn't a cure. It wasn't a bridge for the gulf between them.

"I'll let you know when I find him," she answered, then gave in to the need.

"I think Beng is beginning to like me," Lewis said as he joined Sara beside the small fire next to their wagon.

She wrapped a heavy quilt tighter around her legs while Lewis spoke. She didn't look up from the fire. "I've noticed," she answered. "Scary, isn't it?"

Lewis chuckled. "He actually agreed with me about pushing on through Poland rather than finding a place to winter." It felt good actually to have his stubborn father-in-law's support for once. The men had talked and debated for hours, but in the end, with Beng's help, Toma's opinions had prevailed. "He said I was right."

"Good for him."

"We should reach Bororavia soon, if the weather holds."

"Yeah."

"It's a good thing we have those travel papers from Custine," he went on, well aware that Sara wasn't really listening. "It's been faster to travel the main roads."

"Uh-huh."

The night was dark and cold, moonless. It was early in November. "We're lucky there hasn't been snow yet," he said, hoping to catch her interest in some conversational topic.

She looked up at last. Her eyes caught gold from the fire. "I don't think it's luck," she told him. She held up her right hand. "It won't talk to me," she said worriedly. "But I think it wants to get to Bororavia as quickly as you do. I know what it wants from me," she added in a barely audible whisper. "But I won't do it."

Lewis scarcely heard her last words. Something else she'd said struck him like a blow. "As quickly as

I—" Lewis sat down abruptly as a stab of anguish shot through him. He found himself staring into dancing flames while a part of his mind cried out. He didn't want to reach Bororavia!

He wouldn't be Toma anymore when they reached Bororavia!

He wasn't Toma. But if he wasn't Toma, who was he? It was just a part he played. He'd played parts before, but this time the part was playing him. "This is all a dream," he whispered. "A mad, twisted dream."

He looked slowly up at Sara. Her gaze was averted once more, and she didn't seem aware of him at all. "What are you thinking?" he asked, rather than give in to confusion.

Sara got up and pulled the quilt around her shoulders. She walked to the *bardo* entrance before she looked back at Lewis and spoke. "I was trying to remember what year Sara Morgan's first child was born. I think it was 1812," she added before he could ask any questions, and disappeared inside the dark wagon.

"Sara Morgan?" Lewis asked the empty space where she'd been. "Who's Sara Morgan?" It was a foolish question and he knew it. So he sat and stared into the fire until it died and tried not to think at all.

15

If she's pregnant, *she'll stay.*

The thought rolled and rolled around Lewis's head as the long sleepless night wore on toward dawn. They shared the bed, body warmth, and the pile of quilts, but Sara slept peacefully while he knew he couldn't have bought sleep with a dozen bottles of port.

Did he want her to stay? Did he want her to have his child? Yes. A half-breed bastard? No. For the child's sake, no. Still, he'd love a child she gave him, give it all the love he'd never known. He kept smiling at the thought of presenting Beng with a sturdy, dark-eyed grandson. Or a laughing little girl. They'd look like Sara, of course; their children should all look like Sara. She was so beautiful. They? Lord help him, but he wanted to raise her children.

Sara Morgan. Sara. Morgan. Marry her? She'd been joking, of course. A ruse, perhaps, to trick him into marriage. Impossible. It wasn't done. Wasn't ton. The scandal of marrying a gypsy would instantly ruin him. His father would disown him. His father would be delighted to disown him; he was the throw-away third son anyway. He'd be forced to resign his commission. He'd be ostracized from his none-too-stable place in society. What would he be then? Could he live his life as nothing more than Toma, the gypsy acrobat? Toma, husband of Sara, father of many. Impossible.

It was so tempting.

If she was pregnant, she'd stay.

If I'm pregnant, I'll have to stay.

The thought alternately terrified and elated her. She couldn't sleep for all the scenarios racing through her mind. All she could do was lie still and occasion-ally take her mind off her problems by silently cursing the man who slept like a baby beside her. He held her close in the circle of his arms, but she was aware of how false the protectiveness really was. The man didn't know who the hell he was, let alone who she was, or what was going on between them.

She kept counting up how long it had been since she'd had a period, then recounting because she didn't like the numbers. She wished she wasn't so good with numbers. Then she swore at herself a lot for letting it happen. How could she have been so stupid, so thoughtless, so *horny* that she hadn't let one thought of getting pregnant cross her mind since she'd gone to bed with the man? Had she thought a magic ring was a birth control device!

I'm not going to stay, she thought. *I'm not.* She

wanted electricity, equal rights, her mommy and daddy. She wanted—someone who didn't have to wear a mask to love her. Why hadn't she just wished for guitar lessons from Joe Satriani instead of an own true love?

When she wasn't cursing Lewis or herself, she was cursing the ring. It wanted her to stay. To go to Bororavia. To be the Heroine of the Revolution.

It might be kind of fun, actually.

No! If Lewis were anything like the Lewis Morgan of legend, maybe, but he wasn't. He was a jerk. Well, maybe not that much of a jerk. He was . . . improving. Maybe if he said he was sorry . . .

Talk to me! she shouted silently to the ring. *Tell me what you're up to! Tell me why!* It didn't answer. She could feel it pulsing with power and life, as if there was a really great party going on inside the little orange stone. Sometimes it felt as if she were wearing a concentrated magnum of champagne on her finger. She ignored it most of the time, but tonight she wanted some answers. None were forthcoming.

If you want me to run a revolution, she complained, *you could at least tell me why. Generations of Bororavian legend is not enough to prepare me for this. Sara was this great leader; she changed the Borava tribe's culture, opened their minds, and educated them. She ran a country for a few years. Okay, Bororavia's a little country, very little, more like a postage stamp than a country, really, but it's still a big responsibility. I do not want that kind of responsibility.*

But if she was pregnant, and it always came back to if she was pregnant, she was going to have to stay.

If she stayed she knew she couldn't live without Lewis. Which meant something was going to have to be done about his bad attitude. If she stayed they couldn't start the revolution without her.

So, how did one start a revolution? Was it any wonder she couldn't sleep?

"I'm thinking about marrying Hadari," Molly said as she took a seat beside Sara and Beth at the tiny fold-down table in her wagon.

Sara held her hands out to the faint warmth of the candle in the center of the table. Beth didn't look up from the open Bible in front of her. Sara did notice that the little girl's lips stopped moving as she read the words to herself and curved into a brief, knowing smile.

Sara looked at Molly and accepted the cup of tea she'd just brought in from the outside cook fire. "Oh," she said. "Hadari?"

Molly nodded. "Yes. His mother approached me yesterday. She's been eyeing me for months, you know."

"Yes, I know. But I didn't know if anything would come of it." Sometimes Sara couldn't tell if the *familia* had accepted Molly back or not. She was allowed to travel with them, but no one but Sara associated with her very much. It was nice to know somebody was making a friendly gesture finally. Sara wondered what they would do if they knew Toma wasn't even the half Rom he claimed. Lord knew it was bad enough Toma was from a different tribe. Or it had been. He was certainly treated like a beloved son of the Borava these days.

She wondered what Molly would say if she told her she was pregnant. No she didn't. Molly would be delighted. Everyone would be delighted. Toma would be delighted. He'd go strutting around the camp smirking and acting as though he'd invented sex. Which, considering how he made her feel, maybe he had. Except his name wasn't Toma. She wanted to cry.

"You don't look well, dear. Are you all right?"

Sara had to yawn before she could answer Molly's concerned question. "I just didn't sleep very well last night. Actually, I didn't sleep at all."

"Oh." Molly took a few sips of tea. "I thought you might be breeding."

Sara blinked. "I beg your pardon?" Beth giggled.

"It's an English term, dear. It means with child."

"Oh. Let's talk about you and Hadari. Are you going to marry him? Do you want to? What about the bear?"

Molly looked thoughtfully into her tea for a bit. "I think perhaps I do," she said at last. "I loved the late Mr. Macalpine, but Hadari's a good man. Attractive in his own way. His bear's a gentle creature, really, takes honey right out of my hand. Hadari's mother is a good woman, and she could certainly use help raising his children. Mr. Macalpine and I couldn't have children. Hadari had five with his late wife."

"I know," Sara said.

The oldest of Hadari's children, Rose, was a precocious fourteen-year-old with a hopeless crush on

Toma. All the girls had hopeless crushes on Toma. Sara couldn't help but take a certain smug pleasure in knowing he was hers. Until they got to the British embassy in Bororavia, at least. She didn't want to think about it.

Molly was a handsome woman, probably no more than in her early thirties. Not too old to have children, even in this day and age. Children. Have children. She didn't want to think about that, either.

"I hope you have lots of babies," she said anyway. "Beng will make a doting uncle."

Molly laughed. "He'll make an even more doting grandfather."

"I don't want to think about that."

"Why not?" Molly asked. She put her hand over Sara's. "I've never seen a happier couple than you and Toma. You'll make wonderful parents."

Sara met the other woman's reassuring gaze. "Are we a happy couple? Is that what it looks like to everyone else?"

It was Beth who answered her uncertain questions. "Lor', Sara, 'e's crazy mad for you. Got 'im eatin' out of your 'and, you 'ave, like 'adari's old bear."

"Say 'him eating out of your hand.'" Molly corrected the girl's pronunciation, not her statement.

Guess we've got everyone in camp fooled, Sara thought. She stood up. "I'd better go," she said. "We have to break camp soon. Beng wants the wagons at the border ford by nightfall."

Tonight they would be entering Bororavia. She and Toma only had a few days left. She had no idea what to do with them.

* * *

"So," Sara said as the wagon rolled slowly along the rutted track leading to the Drovan River crossing, "if I was knocked up, would you feel any responsibility for it?"

She hated how tentative her voice sounded. She didn't like the way her fingers twisted nervously together in the fabric of the quilt covering her lap. At least Lewis's hands were occupied with driving the team of horses. All she had to do was sit on the box beside him and think.

It was growing dark, but not so dark she couldn't make out Lewis's stone-still profile. She could hear rushing water in the distance. She'd been startled earlier to hear the howling of wolves hunting in the forest. The sound had been eerie and beautiful and reminded her of home, of camping on the north shore of Lake Superior. The howling had brought a pang of home-sickness that only added to her confusion.

"Knocked up?" Lewis asked after a considerable pause.

"It's an American term," she explained. "It means breeding."

"Are you?"

She couldn't read any emotion at all in his voice. "It's a hypothetical question," she replied. "If I were, what would you do?"

He knew what his heart wanted to say, but his heart was a fool. His heart had always ached for some impossible thing he couldn't name. Hadn't been able to name until this mission both complicated and simplified his life. He had no words for Sara; he had none for himself. He just drove on in mute misery. Their *bardo* was the first to reach the bank above the ford. The other wagons, and people on foot and horseback, followed behind them. Lewis stopped the wagon, set the brake, and stood on the box to scan the tree-lined riverbank.

"Oh," Sara said finally. "I see." He didn't want to talk about it. Fine. They wouldn't talk about it. What was there to talk about? He'd go back to the Royal Navy. She'd raise the kid on her own. It all sounded like that awful song about "Gypsies, Tramps and Thieves" Cher had done back in the seventies. "At least Cher got a shot at dating Richie Sambora," she grumbled under her breath. "All I get is to be stuck in the nineteenth century."

Lewis shot Sara a fierce look. She was talking about Richie again. He didn't know what the man meant to Sara, but he wished him cheerfully to hell. "The river looks high," he said rather than make the jealous comment that sprang to his lips.

There'd been many rivers and streams to cross between the border of France and this last crossing. There'd been bridges and fords and ferries all along the route. This was just another ford. Except this one was on the border between Bororavia and Poland. They'd eluded a border patrol on this side once today already; there would be patrols on the other side as well. The duchy wasn't very large, just a small, mountainous corner of the Russian-dominated land of Lithuania. It was, however, crucial to Britain for its deepwater Baltic port of Duwal. It was reported to have a large population of settled Rom. The Borava *familia*'s circus had left their home village to perform in England years ago, and now the wanderers were almost home. His assignment was almost over. He did not want to cross this river.

"Well," Sara questioned. "What are you waiting for?"

She was right. Polish cavalry could appear to stop them at any moment. The wind was picking up and it was beginning to snow. He glanced back at the line of people and wagons waiting for him to begin, then started his reluctant team of horses forward.

The crossing wasn't easy; the current was swift even though the water was shallow in this narrow part of the channel. The caravan's seven wagons had to move slowly, but they crossed in an orderly fashion, massing in an open glade on the far side of the river as they waited for the last of the riders and people on foot to make it across.

Sara got down from the wagon box to stretch tired muscles. Lewis got down to check the horses, to pat and quietly praise them for their work. He had lumps of sugar for them in his pockets, she knew. They knew it too, and nuzzled him insistently for their treats. She watched him with the animals for a while, amused and touched by his easy affection for them. *Sometimes, Lewis Morgan,* she thought, *it's easy to love you.* She walked away, hugging herself tightly with her shawl.

Sara went to stand on the bank of the river above the crossing. A pool of dark water swirled and gurgled a few feet below where she stood. The snow was getting heavier by the moment and the dead gray winter light was almost gone. But it wasn't so dark that she didn't see the two horsemen in red uniform coats appear on the far side of the river. The snow muffled the sound of their horses. One of them raised a rifle. Nothing could have muffled the crack of gun-fire.

Lewis came running up to her as the report of the shot filled the twilight. "Sandor!" he shouted as the last man across fell slowly from his horse.

Women screamed. Men ran forward to haul Sandor's body out of the water, to catch the bolting horse. Across the river the soldiers could be heard laughing. Sara wished she had a gun. They wheeled their horses and rode away. She supposed they'd ful-filled their duty to protect the border.

"Or maybe it's just open season on Rom," she said. "Again." The taste of the words was bitter in her mind as Lewis ran down the gentle slope to where people were gathered around the man they'd fished out of the water.

"Please, God," she whispered, as she turned and walked back to stand beside the wagon, "don't let him be dead."

"Dead," Lewis said when he came back a while later.

His voice was bleak and tired. She couldn't see his expression in the darkness. She didn't ask for details, or what they were going to do about it. She just balled her fists into tight knots. She felt as if she should do something but she didn't know what. Cry-ing for Sandor wouldn't change anything. When

Lewis picked her up and carried her into the *bardo* she didn't make any protest. She could feel him shaking in reaction and found herself hugging him tightly as he put her down on the bed.

"Stay here," he said as he stepped away. "I'll be back as soon as we bury him."

Stay here, she thought, rubbing the ring as Lewis went away. Of course. Where else was there for her to go?

She slept for a long time. She knew it was a long time because there was daylight coming in the *bardo*'s tiny window when she woke up. She felt better. Her dreams had been full of nightmares, but the nightmares had driven away the demons that had been torturing her waking thoughts lately. She didn't approve of wallowing in self-pity. It was time to get her life straightened out.

The wagon rumbled onward over a rough track as she washed and quickly re-dressed in her rumpled clothes. When she looked out the window she saw that last night's snow had been no more than a dusting. It wasn't preventing the caravan from traveling away from Sandor's unmarked grave.

At least she assumed it was an unmarked grave. She supposed she should jump out the back of the slow-moving wagon and go say a word to his widow. Then she decided it could wait until they made camp. There were a few things she wanted to say to Lt. Lewis Morgan right now.

She went to the front of the wagon, pushed aside

the heavy canvas curtain separating the driver's seat from the living quarters, and sat down beside him on the driver's box. He automatically passed a folded quilt to her.

He waited until she'd tucked the covering around her legs before he asked, "How are you feeling?"

"Tired," she admitted. "I don't know how long I slept, but I feel tired."

"Like the weight of the world's descended on you?" He nodded. "I know." Lewis sighed. "I'll miss the old thief."

There was genuine regret and affection in his words. Sara wished she could deny the "old thief" part, but Sandor had not been the most honest of men. Or sober. Or clean. Still, "It's your fault he's dead," she said, with less anger than she'd thought she would.

"I've been thinking about that," Lewis replied. He looked straight ahead, paying careful attention to the rising road. They'd passed through only one village so far today. The inhabitants had stared at them in sullen, angry-eyed silence. He was alert for trouble. Besides, he didn't want to look at the Rom girl beside him and see hatred looking back at him.

Sara had been prepared to sermonize. Instead she asked, "So, what have you been thinking?"

"I've been thinking that you were going to accuse me of being responsible for his death. And you did."

"You are," she said. "He'd be in London now."

"Drunk on cheap gin while he sent his wife out begging."

"But he wouldn't be dead if it weren't for you and the ambitions of the British Empire."

"I'm fighting a war, Sara," he answered wearily. "I'm not interested in my country's ambitions, just stopping Napoleon's."

"Right," she granted. "You're a good soldier."

"Sailor," he corrected. "And I'm not responsible for Sandor's death." He risked a quick glance. Her face was hard with anger, but maybe she didn't hate him. He sighed.

"You got him—us—into this."

"But a Polish border guard killed him. It was a *gajo* who killed him."

"Yeah, but—"

"Do you hate the *gajo,* Sara?" he asked on a quick, desperate breath.

"No!" she answered. The word was a knee-jerk reaction of her twentieth-century self. After a short, painfully thoughtful pause, she said, "Sometimes."

"Me, too. Sometimes."

"You are a *gajo.*"

"I know." He wished she'd reach out and touch his hand. He wanted some contact from her. When she didn't, he said, "That guard just thought he was doing his duty. I have to remember that."

"You're just doing yours," she was quick to reply. Before he could.

"Yes."

"It's all your fault." She banged her fist on the seat between them. "None of this would have happened if you hadn't dragged these people across Europe as your cover. We're all just camouflage to you. We don't mean anything to you."

"You do," he answered sharply.

"Yeah," she said bitterly. "I'm the bimbo in your private James Bond movie."

"What?"

"My role in your life is sex toy," she explained slowly and carefully. "Concubine for the duration of the adventure. Bed warmer. I'm not blaming you for that. I let it happen." She banged the seat again. "Why don't you take the responsibility for this, Morgan?"

The sky overhead was iron gray and ugly, dotted with ravens. Ice on the road crunched beneath the horses' slow footsteps. The countryside, empty fields and barren woods, was anything but inviting. "I helped your people get here," he said. "This is Bororavia, the place they wanted to be. If you want me to take responsibility for helping your people do exactly what they wanted, I will. Gladly."

"But your reasons—"

"Hardly altruistic," he agreed. "But I meant them no harm."

"No," she said. "You didn't mean them harm. You didn't give a damn about them one way or another."

"True," he admitted. "I didn't."

"You'd do anything you had to."

The accusation in her tone burned like fire. "Yes."

"You'd have sent me to the hulks without a second thought."

He nodded. "You didn't mean anything to me."

"We're all just a means to an end for you."

"Yes. Yes. Yes." He wanted her to stop telling him the truth. "Enough," he said. "We both know what I am."

"Yes," she said, her throat constricted with pain. "Bastard."

He looked at her straight on for the first time. "We both know what I am," he said again. "But what are you, woman from the future? Who are you? Are these people yours any more than they are mine? And," he added before she could respond to the fear in his bright eyes, "just how much of all this is that ring you're wearing responsible for?"

16

As Lewis's words sank in, Sara shuddered. A chill crept over her, deeper than the one brought by the November wind. "Good questions," she had to acknowledge. "Who am I?" She thought about it for a minute, putting thoughts about the ring on hold. "I'm a Rom of the Borava tribe," she said at last. "Only I was born in St. Paul, Minnesota."

"Which is somewhere in North America," he surmised.

"Yes. I don't think there's been any European settlement there this early in the nineteenth century. I'm not sure. My family came to America after the Communist takeover after World War Two."

"Communist? World War? The second one?"

"How complicated do you want this conversation to get?" she asked.

"I don't want to know the future," he said. "At least no more than I need to know about you."

"Fine with me," she agreed. "So, my father's family moved to America. My grandfather's family, well, we used to own a small circus. Maybe it's this one because we had it for generations, I don't know. A lot of my relatives who were in the circus were killed during the war."

"World War Two?"

"Yes. Some were resistance fighters. Some—" She struggled with things she wanted to tell him, things that had relevance to her life in ways he could never understand. How could she explain concentration camps when she couldn't really comprehend them herself? "The world hasn't gotten better," she said, "just more organized. No, things are better in the future, I refuse to be cynical and depressed about some of the bad things. There is more justice, better quality of life. But I'm trying to tell you about me."

He gave her a subdued version of his glowing smile. "Go on."

"The Borava tribe isn't as into the *mirame* taboos as some other Rom."

"Really?" he asked skeptically. "I hadn't noticed."

"What about Molly?" she defended.

"That's your doing," he told her. "They wouldn't have taken her back if you hadn't talked them into it."

"I think it's because we interpret our Rom heritage in a more liberal manner than some other tribes. We won equal rights in Bororavia during the rev—early on," she concluded hastily, remembering that the revolution hadn't happened yet. Might not happen the way things were going. "Anyway, there are plenty of *gajos* in my background. My father married an Irish girl from St. Paul, and I'm their spoiled-rotten only child. I went to the University of Minnesota, worked for an accounting firm—I think you'd call me a countinghouse clerk. I own my own place. Playing guitar is my hobby."

He looked surprised. "You're not a professional musician?"

"No."

"You should be. I mean that as a compliment," he added hastily.

"Thank you."

"You attended university, you say? In this Minnesota?"

"Yes."

He didn't challenge her words further. "You have a husband? Suitors?"

"Neither."

He was silent for a few moments. "You're wealthy and independent, then. Are you happy in Minnesota?"

She didn't challenge him on his assumption of her wealth; by his standards she supposed she was. Happy? "Yes," she said. "I have a good life."

"Then you'll be going home come St. Bartholomew's Day."

His words were more statement than question. She didn't know how to respond, but the words came out before she could think about them. "No. I'll be staying in Bororavia."

Staying. He breathed a silent prayer of thanks. She'd be staying. He hadn't known until this moment how badly the thought of her disappearing tore at his soul. She was staying. He wanted to ask her why she'd be staying. He wanted to hear her say it was because she loved him, but he felt too fragile to risk her giving a different answer. So he just nodded. "What about the ring?" he asked instead.

The ring. It was time she got some answers from the ring. Sara looked down at the silver band tightly circling her finger. The stone winked alertly up at her. "Well?"

"People don't make magic. Magic makes people," was its cryptic reply.

"Oh, that's very clever. Excuse me," she said to Lewis. "We have to talk."

"We are talking."

"Not us. Me and the ring."

"Ah," he said with a nod. "Yes. That might be wise."

So, she thought angrily at the ring, *don't I deserve more than fortune-cookie philosophy?*

"Certain events need to come to pass. My duty is to see that they do. You and Lewis are the means to achieve those ends. I cannot work without help. I had to find humans who can cope with magic. Most people can't, you know."

No, I didn't know. You could have asked for volunteers.

"You have to be chosen, you can't volunteer. You do get to live happily ever after as a by-product."

Right.

"Besides," it added, "the other Sara wished to save her people as well as her own soul. I need you to do that."

Sara rubbed her temples. "I definitely don't want to hear this."

"What?" Lewis asked.

"It wants me to lead an uprising against the mad duke," she told him. Lewis gaped at her.

"Tell him the rest."

She folded her hands in her lap. "And you're going to help," she concluded in the most rational tone she could manage. "We're going to be the Heroes of the Revolution. I know," she said as he continued his openmouthed stare, "I don't like it either. But I think we're stuck with it. It's part of this magic we're caught in." Oddly enough, having said it out loud finally, she began to feel more comfortable with the notion. "Not that I have any idea how to run a revolution. The most politically radical thing I've ever done was join the Nature Conservancy."

"What revolution?"

"The Bororavian one. It hasn't happened yet. My father's always said it didn't make the headlines when it happened because Napoleon was bigger news. The revolution will make Bororavia the most progressive area in the Baltic. I hope that means we get indoor plumbing soon," she added wistfully.

Lewis made a skeptical noise. "Revolutions don't bring progress."

"Of course *you* prefer the status quo, you're an aristocrat."

"Life isn't as easy for the aristocrats as rabble-rousers seem to think."

"Oh, yeah? How many meals have you missed?"

Before he could answer, Hadari, who had been riding a little way ahead of the caravan, turned his horse and came up to them. Lewis brought the wagon to a halt at Hadari's gesture. "What?"

"The village we're headed for," Hadari said, "Jurmla. It's in the river valley just over this hill. I remember the place." Hadari looked back nervously.

"But?" Lewis prompted.

Hadari shook his head. "It's been burned to the ground," he said. "Not a building standing. No one in sight. We all had family in Jurmla," he went on worriedly. "What has happened to them?"

Lewis swore fiercely at this ugly news. While he spoke Beng and some of the other men came up to see why they were stopped. Hadari quickly explained. Everyone began to talk worriedly and all at once.

Sara listened anxiously. Finally she said, "If Rom villages are being burned, it's time we got off the road. Why don't we camp in the woods above the river for tonight? Then Toma and I can scout for hidden ways."

"Hidden ways to where?" Hadari asked.

"I don't know. Away from the burned village, at least."

"We need to head toward Duwal," Lewis said. "The capital will be a good place for a circus."

"Countryside might be a better place to hide," Beng said.

"Hide from what?" Lewis pointed up the road. "We don't know why that village was destroyed."

Hadari spat on the ground. "Cossacks don't need reasons."

Sara plucked the slack reins from Lewis's hands. "You men can argue all you want," she said, turning the animals off the road to head for the woods. "We women have children to tend."

"Some women have children to tend," Lewis said as she drove the *bardo*. He glanced behind them and looked back, smiling when he saw the others were following. He crossed his arms over his chest. "Do you have a child to tend, Sara?"

Her features twisted in a stubborn, unhappy frown. "I don't want to talk about it right now. I just want to get these people settled somewhere safely out of the way."

They were going to talk about it, he decided. It was time they both stopped being cowards and got some things settled.

"Come back to England with me," Lewis said, coming to kneel by Sara who was adding sticks to the small fire she'd built.

Sara looked into his eyes as he took her hands. Hers were warm from the fire; the fingers that gripped hers were cold as ice. "Come back to England," she repeated. "Why?"

"It's too dangerous for you here," he said. He'd meant to tell her he loved her and that was why he wanted her to return with him, but the news he'd just heard intruded on his emotional intentions. "You saw the Borava who came out of the forest just as we were making camp?"

She nodded. "Three families' worth. Maritza and Molly are helping to settle the women and children."

She would have helped too, but there had been an unpleasant incident involving her throwing up at about the same time the newcomers arrived. The women had assured her it was perfectly normal even though she hadn't said anything to anyone about maybe, possibly, being pregnant. She'd still been told to stay by her *bardo* and rest.

"There's been a poor harvest," Lewis said. "The men told us that Grand Duke Alexander has decided that the Rom have cursed the Bororavian fields."

"That's crazy!" Sara declared angrily. Then she added, "Well, there must be a reason he's called the mad duke."

"Ambassador Tate has sent back reports saying the man's a bit unstable." He chuckled quietly. "Britain's so used to having a mad king we don't think anything of dealing with mad dukes. At least King George is safely locked away, and sane men run the country. As for Duke Alexander," Lewis continued, "he sent troops to burn some of the Rom villages in reprisal for the bad harvest. The Rom weren't expecting it." He shook his head sadly. "They tell us they've always had good relations with the *gajo* peasants. Unfortunately, most of the duke's troops are German mercenaries. The peasants are being taxed out of their livelihoods to support the soldiers. There's a great deal of unrest here, Sara. It isn't safe for you to be here."

Sara took her hand from his and touched his cheek. He looked so sincere and worried she hated to remind him of why she'd ended up in Bororavia in the first place. Still, she thought, maybe he needed the reminder. "You brought me here," she said. "It's my country," she added. "I'm staying."

"Yes," he said with a slow nod. "I brought you

here, and I'm sorry I did, but this isn't your country. You're from Minnesota. I can't take you back there, but I can see you safely to England."

He was sorry. He'd actually said he was sorry! She was instantly ready to forgive him, even if she wasn't so sure it was a good idea. If she forgave him, she might end up letting him talk her into anything he wanted. Deep down she had this urge to please him, because, well, because she loved him.

"I don't want to go to England," she said firmly. "This is my country, ethnically and spiritually, even if I wasn't born here." She wasn't sure she believed her words; she was quite proud of being American. "The ring thinks I have the skill to run a revolution. So, apparently, these people need me."

"The devil with the ring!" He was just barely able to keep himself from shouting. There were too many people around for shouting. He didn't want a public quarrel. He stood up, yanked Sara to her feet, and pushed her in front of him into the wagon. "Now," he said once they were inside, "women do not run revolutions. I do not believe in revolutions. You are coming home with me." This was out of hand. He wasn't saying what he'd intended at all.

"It's cold in here," Sara complained. She sat down on the bed. She could barely make out his expression in the shadowy interior of the wagon, but she read the frustrated annoyance in his stance and voice. She wasn't going to argue with him about the revolution. She wasn't so sure she believed in it, anyway. "I have no idea how to organize a revolution," she admitted.

He sat down beside her. "Then come home with me."

Silence descended in the dark little wagon. Both of them waited in the cold, both of them felt alone and vulnerable, and both knew it. It was Sara who finally had to take a deep, hesitant breath, and ask, "Why?"

Lewis knew he couldn't let this moment pass. If it did it would never come again. He'd never opened his life and his heart to anyone, never been taught how to trust. He had won medals, he could dance on a thin rope over an engulfing fire, but he'd never felt brave. He was almost too frightened to let the dangerous words out.

His mouth went very dry. He swallowed hard, and said, "Because I love you."

The silence stretched out again after he spoke. If he'd been hoping for her to throw herself passionately into his arms, it didn't happen. Instead, after an achingly uncomfortable while, she said, "Is this Toma who loves me, or Lewis?"

It was the most valid question he'd ever heard. "I love you," was all he could answer.

She knew he was waiting for her to tell him how she felt. She didn't know how she felt. All right, she loved him. So? She gulped. "All right," she said. "I love you. I don't know if there's anything we can do about it," she added, "but no way am I going to let you be braver than me."

He took her hand. "Words are the most dangerous weapons of all, aren't they?"

"Oh, yeah," she agreed, leaning against his hard-muscled side. She put her hand over his heart. "I shouldn't love you. You blackmailed me."

"I know. I'm sorry."

"You locked me in the storeroom. There were *things* in there."

"Vegetables?"

"Mice. It was dark."

He stroked her hair. "I'm sorry. It won't happen again."

"You didn't even think about it, did you?" She didn't know why she was pouting about the incident at Philipston House now, but it suddenly stung more than anything else he'd done to her. "I was scared."

"I'm sorry." God, sorry wasn't going to be good enough, was it? It had been a thoughtless, callous gesture. The vegetable larder had been a convenient place to store a bit of gypsy trash until he had need of it. Gypsies, after all, had no place in civilized society. "I'll make up for everything," he promised. "I'll buy you a house. A beautiful quiet place where no one will ever bother you. I'll take such good care of you. I'll give you everything you need."

He kissed her, hoping to seal a bargain with passion, to heal the wound his indifference had inflicted on her. "I love you," he whispered as his body grew tight with desire.

He laid her back on the soft mattress. His hands roved over her, undressing her, warming her flesh with skilled caresses.

Sara closed her eyes as his touch claimed her. Every time they made love she felt as though she belonged to him a little bit more. She suspected he felt the same. Together, like this, they became whole. The rest of the time she felt half of herself missing. She was naked before she knew it, as was Lewis.

Then he was poised over her, then deep inside her and she felt complete again.

It was cold in the *bardo* but she stopped feeling it after the first few moments of lovemaking. The cold came back with a sharp bite as soon as he moved from her to sit up.

"Lewis?" she questioned, touching his arm, hoping to draw him back.

He looked down at her. She could make out the white line of his teeth as he smiled. His eyes glittered in moonlight let in by the window. "You never call me Toma." He stroked a finger across her cheek and outlined her lips. "You never think of me as Toma, do you?"

"No."

He felt her answer in his fingertips. "Why?"

"Because I know who you are."

"Do you?"

She put her hand over his and squeezed gently. "I'm lucky, my name is Sara in both times. And I don't have to pretend as much as you do."

"You must be hungry," he said, rather than continue the conversation. "I know I am." He rose and began to dress.

Sara wrapped herself in a quilt and sat up. "I am most definitely not hungry."

"You're always hungry after making love," he teased.

"Not tonight." She felt a faint wave of nausea as she spoke. "Nope. Definitely not hungry." She lay back down, closed her eyes, and tried not to think about throwing up. "I'm not sure sex was such a good idea."

Lewis stretched out beside her. He pulled her close. "Are you feeling well?"

"I'm fine," she lied. "Perfectly fine. Just tired." She didn't want to think or talk about how she felt, or why. "So," she said, returning to their earlier discussion. "What sort of house do you have in mind?"

Lewis grinned with relief. "Somewhere quiet, out of the way. You'll have a rose garden."

"Why would I want a rose garden?"

"Because I like roses," he said. "I want a house full of roses when I visit."

"Visit." There was a significant pause before she said, "Visit? Would you mind explaining what you mean when you say *visit?*"

"I have my work," he hedged, then admitted, "I'm offering to keep you as my mistress, Sara."

When she moved to sit up he let her go reluctantly. "I'm your wife," she said.

She sat with her back to him. He sat up and put his arms around her from behind. "Sara."

"I'm your wife. Don't try to bargain about it."

"I can't marry you," he said bleakly. "I'm not saying I don't want to, but I can't. It's not because there's already a Mrs. Morgan," he added quickly when she tried to jerk away.

"Yes, there is," she said. "Me."

"We aren't wed," he answered. "Not by English law."

"We are by Rom law."

"But—"

"If Rom law isn't good enough for you, equal to your own, then we have nothing to talk about."

"It isn't that easy!"

"Yes, it is."

"You're asking me to give up everything I am for you!"

"No, I'm not!" she answered, voice fierce with angry pride. "Just accept me as your equal and we'll be fine."

"I do! But I can't—"

"I won't be your mistress."

"You already are," he reminded her, and let her go, knowing she was going to whirl around and slap him. After she did, and his head was ringing from the strength of the blow, he said, "I'm sorry, but it's true."

A long moment passed.

"Yeah, you're right," she agreed reluctantly. "I can see how you can think that. I don't see it that way."

"How do you see it?"

"We're lovers, equally responsible for our actions. But if you want to have a permanent relationship—"

"I do," he hastened to tell her.

"Then we're married."

"We can't." He grabbed her hands, as much for comfort as to keep her from hitting him again. "It isn't possible, it isn't done, it doesn't have to matter."

"The hell it doesn't."

"Marriage has nothing to do with love," he pointed out. "Among your people or mine. That is one thing we have in common."

"I'm not sure this has anything to do with love, either," she said. "It has to do with respect."

"I don't understand."

She explained. "If you don't admit that you're married to me, then you don't respect me, or my people. I won't live with a man who believes Rom are less than *gajos*."

He laughed. "Since when do the Rom respect *gajos*? Your people are just as bad as mine."

"No, they aren't," she defended. "Not the Borava. Not in my time."

"We aren't in your time. Damn it, Sara, I don't want to argue with you. Be my mistress and I will love and cherish you forever."

"Hmmm," she said thoughtfully. "How come it's all right for me to be your mistress, but you freaked when Custine offered me the same job?"

"Custine," he said angrily, "is a filthy swine."

"No, he's not. He was sweet, and my first groupie."

He heard the affection in her voice and wanted to shake her. "Do you want to be his mistress, then?"

"No. Lewis, let go of me." He dropped his hands before he did anything foolish. "You don't get it, do you?"

"Get what?" The words came out cold and hard. "If you mean I don't understand what you want, you're correct. I don't."

"I'm just trying to say that you're no different than Custine."

"Rubbish! I love you."

"Yes, you do," she acknowledged, "but not the right way."

"There is no right way to love someone."

"Wrong." Oh, hell, she thought, too frustrated to go on with the discussion. It was all going in circles, anyway. She got up and hurriedly got dressed. Lewis sat on the bed and watched her. She could feel confusion and anger coming off him in invisible sparks.

"Where are you going?" he asked when she went to the door.

"I want to be alone," she answered. "Maybe you do too."

"Stay with me."

"Now or forever?" she asked quietly.

"Both."

She wanted to go to him, to hold him and tell him, yes, of course, we're own true loves, aren't we? "We both need to do some thinking," she said instead. "Don't worry." She tried for an Arnold Schwarzenegger imitation. "I'll be back."

17

She didn't know what time it was, but there was no activity in the camp when she went outside. It was dark and cold and everyone was huddled in their wagons or tents. Somebody was probably watching the horses and a guard would be patrolling the perimeter of the camp, but Sara felt as if she were completely alone.

The fire had burned down to glowing embers. Sara built it up again, then put a pot of water on to boil. She'd left a small supply box next to the wagon. She got tea out of it and tossed dry leaves into the pot. She let the aroma drifting up with the steam fill her senses. There was something very soothing about the scent of tea. She was sipping on a strong cup of it while gazing into the fire when she finally let herself think.

What was she going to do?

"The answer to that is obvious, isn't it?"

The flames danced and crackled. *I wasn't talking to you,* she complained.

"Oh, then what were you doing?"

Crying out in anguish to the universe, I guess.

"I see. Feeling sorry for yourself, were you?"

Yes, she admitted unashamedly. *You got a problem with that?*

"No, no indeed. Everyone deserves a bit of self-pity sometimes. Just don't be too long about it, all right?"

She obviously wasn't going to get any sympathy from the Bartholomew Ring. "You're a real pain, you know that, don't you?"

"Magic is not easy. I've mentioned that before."

Yes, it had. Nothing was easy. Life wasn't. Love was impossible. "He doesn't understand," she heard herself whine at last. "And, honestly, neither do I. We do not communicate on the most fundamental level."

"Oh, yeah? What about junior in there?"

She felt as if she were being poked in the abdomen with a sharp finger. "That isn't communication, that's sex."

"It's a fundamental way of communicating."

Maybe, she conceded. *Sometimes. I don't know. Okay, Lewis and I communicate on a primal level. How do I communicate with him on a more objective level?*

"Who says you need to be objective?"

"I—" She took a sharp breath. "I don't know. We need some kind of compromise," she admitted. "Some middle ground where we can just be ourselves."

"His world won't permit it."

"I figured that out."

"Neither will the Rom world."

"Yeah, I know," she grumbled. She drank more

tea. "Something ought to be done about that, you know?"

"Yes, I do. That's why you're here. To do something about it."

"Me?" she asked skeptically. "What?"

"You're being deliberately obtuse again. I brought you here to be the Heroine of the Revolution and I think it's about time you got to work."

"But—"

"What you have to do is simple, and it isn't even for the good of the people. You, Sara, if you love the man the way I know you do, have to create a middle ground where the two of you can exist as equals. That's it. Turn Bororavia into the place you need to be happy."

"That's *it!*" The ring was out of its little rock-headed mind. "You're crazy!"

"You're sitting in a field on a cold winter night yelling at a ring, and I'm crazy?"

"You're the ring. Besides, I'm not yelling." She knew her voice hadn't been raised above a whisper during the whole conversation.

"Inside your head, you're yelling."

Sara made herself calm down, to think logically. "You brought me here so I could live happily ever after?"

"Correct."

"But I'm the one who has to make it work?"

"Of course. Why should happily ever after come easy? Everything's got a price, kid."

"Thank you, I'm so happy to hear that." She rubbed her jaw, then tapped her finger against the tip of her chin thoughtfully. "What about the brooch?"

"What about the brooch?" came the wary reply a few seconds later.

"What's in it for you and the brooch? What happens when Lewis returns it to the mad duke? What's going on with you and the brooch? Is it magical too?"

"Never mind the brooch," the ring responded stubbornly. "We're discussing you and Lewis."

"But it's all connected, isn't it?"

"All right." It sighed. The sensation was like a warm breath across the fingers of her right hand. "While Lewis wears the brooch and you wear me, we're all united. We need you and Lewis to live happily ever after so we can."

"Aha. I suspected it was something like that. But what happens when the brooch is given back to the duke?"

"We'll get it back. I have faith in you and Lewis."

She wished she did. She also decided to concentrate on her own problems and let the ring worry about its ruby companion. It obviously didn't want to answer questions about the brooch. She wasn't sure she wanted it to. "This magic stuff is so complicated."

"That's why so few humans have ever been any good at it. Let's concentrate on changing our little part of the world, shall we?"

The ring was right. The only way she and Lewis could be together was in a world they made for themselves. She didn't know if he was willing to help make that world; he hadn't been favorably disposed toward the notion of changing anybody's status quo so far. It was time she got started, though.

"Okay, so what do I do?"

She felt the ring tingle with pleased anticipation. "You need an organization. There's a man named Alze who came in with the refugees. Talk to him. He's got some ideas, and contacts with the village councils. He was in Jurmla before the soldiers arrived. He got most of them out of town and on the road to Duwal before the place was destroyed. He brought the rest of the people here."

Alze sounded like a man of action. The village councils, she recalled as she stood, were the traditional ruling body of the Bororavian peasants. The village and town councils, the *kris,* which was the Rom tribal council, and the noble class had formed the congress during the revolution. They'd turned the country into a constitutional monarchy, well, duchy. Or rather, they would, once she was through with them.

She tossed the rest of the tea into the fire, which hissed and smoked as she turned away. "Let's wake up this Alze," she said confidently, "and get this show on the road."

She didn't return to the *bardo* until after dawn. Lewis wasn't there. He'd left a note for her on the bed, but when she sat down to read it she couldn't make out a word. She shook the paper in frustration. "The man should have been a doctor! Do you know what this says?" she asked the ring. "Where is he?"

"He needs to think," the ring answered. "That's a good sign," it offered helpfully.

Maybe it was, she agreed reluctantly. At least he

hadn't just walked out on her. Still, the narrow living quarters of the wagon seemed larger without his presence. She was instantly lonely. Even when she'd been making him sleep under the wagon she'd at least known he was there. The bed was going to be cold without him. And empty and lonely, and she didn't want to think about it.

She got up and rummaged through the clothes chest. "At least he took warm clothes. I wonder how long he'll be gone?"

"Don't worry about it," the ring advised as she sat down and picked up her guitar. "There are plenty of other things for you to think about."

Yeah, she thought, like why did Alze act as if he knew her? She'd woken the man out of a sound sleep and he'd greeted her like a long-lost friend. He'd given her a report on the underground movement without waiting for her to ask. It hadn't made a lot of sense.

"Correction," she said as she carefully tuned the metal strings of the guitar, "it didn't make any sense."

"They're hungry for a leader," the ring offered.

"An outsider? A woman?" She played a few chords. "Well, it won't hurt to have their trust from the beginning."

She and Alze had talked for a long time. He'd told her about the violence against all the villages, not just the Rom. About the nobles' worries over the duke's bringing in German mercenaries. The duke had fired all the aristocratic officers except for the captain of his palace guard, replacing them with hired outsiders. He was negotiating with every power in Europe.

There was fear that his bungling diplomacy could bring down the wrath of everybody on tiny Bororavia. He was consulting mystics and fortune-tellers while persecuting the Rom for being mystics and fortune-tellers. Maybe worst of all, he was holding a continuous rowdy party while the people faced a harsh, hungry winter. It was said that entertainers summoned to the palace didn't come out again. She'd come to the conclusion that Alexander was known to history as the mad duke for good reasons.

Alze had advised that she return to lead the resistance in Duwal while he continued to rouse the countryside. To talk to Mikal the silversmith. "Return?" she questioned now as she played. "What did he mean return? I've never been to Duwal."

"It's probably a language problem," the ring responded. "You two were speaking different dialects, you know."

"Yeah, it was pretty hard to understand him sometimes. But why'd he act like he knew me?"

"Perhaps it's just his way. He seems like a friendly sort."

"I guess." She started playing her favorite blues song. "You think Lewis will be back soon?"

A shadow crossed in front of her. "Oh, there you are," Sara said. She went back to stirring the pot hung over the fire. She was wearing a pair of worn gloves and two shawls to fight off the cold. Her head was covered with the scarf worn by all married women.

Married. Lewis sighed.

"I hate taking care of horses," she said as he stood silently by her side. "You know I hate taking care of the horses. It's been two days," she added, looking up at him. "You want me to rush into your arms and show how happy I am to have you back?"

"I'd like that," he answered. "Are you?" It wasn't an easy question to ask.

She sat back on her heels and smiled. It warmed him more than his nearness to the fire. "Yes."

He held a canvas bag out to her. "I brought you a chicken for the pot."

"Did you pay for it?" she asked suspiciously.

"What?" He was so surprised at the question he almost dropped the bag. "Of course."

"You can never tell with Rom," she told him. "They're a thieving bunch."

"Point taken," he agreed. He knelt beside her and leaned forward to sniff the steam rising from the pot. Potatoes, and probably not very many of them. The meat would be a welcome addition to the meal.

"There's a joke in my family," she said while he tried not to grab her into a fierce embrace.

"Oh?"

"Do you know the recipe for gypsy stew?"

"What?"

"First, steal a chicken." He looked at her, a smile tilting up his lips. She pointed at him. "It's only funny if we Rom tell it," she told him. "Remind me to explain political correctness to you sometime."

"I missed you," he said. "I missed you very much."

"So," she asked, her words sounding too carefully casual, "where have you been?"

He'd been traveling alongside the caravan, actually, as it moved toward the outskirts of Duwal. He'd been worried about the large number of green-coated soldiers patrolling the countryside. He'd passed more burned villages and bands of refugees as his course paralleled his own gypsy band's. He'd wanted to be close enough to be of any help if there was trouble, far enough from Sara to clear his mind. When his thoughts refused to cooperate with his plan to get them sorted out, he gave in and came back.

"I suppose you thought I'd struck out for the city on my own."

"No." She reached forward to stir the pot.

He took her hand, rubbing his thumb restlessly across the rough material of her glove. "It would be faster, I know. You probably thought I'd left you."

"No," she said again.

This time the word actually registered with him. "Oh." He narrowed his eyes as he peered at her. "Why not?"

"You said you'd be back."

She trusted him! He almost laughed with delight. "The fool girl trusts me when I don't trust myself!" He drew her into his arms and a deep, sorely needed kiss. Just the touch of her tongue gliding against his lit fires in him. "I can't leave you," he said when they stopped kissing. "I can't."

Sara rubbed her fingers across her lips. They still burned with pleasure. "I'm going to get chapped lips if we keep this up," she told him. She grinned. "I'm willing to risk it." She stood and held her arms out to him. "Let's go somewhere quiet where we can fool around."

"In private," he added, bouncing lightly to his feet. "What about the chicken?"

"This is no time to be practical." Still, she picked up the bag and took it to the communal fire in the center of the camp. After she'd handed it to one of the women working there she came back and took Lewis's hand. As she led him into the *bardo* she explained. "There's a party later tonight. Molly and Hadari are getting married."

Married, he thought, and sighed. He tried not to think about it as he followed her to the welcome homecoming inside.

Their reunion was bittersweet and delicious. Lewis just wanted to lie on Sara's breast and sleep when they were done. Sara, however, had other plans for the evening. She kicked the quilt aside when he tried to wrap them in a warm cocoon. He complained with a weak moan.

"We have to get dressed," she said, pushing him to sit up. "I'm not missing Molly's wedding." She chuckled. "She risked a lot not to miss mine."

There was no getting out of it, he supposed. He rolled over and his stomach rumbled. The gnaw of hunger reminded him of the chicken stewing on the central fire.

"Never mind the wedding," he said, getting up as she lit the lantern. "I'm hungry."

Her eyes went round. She swore. "My soup!" She

hadn't taken off many clothes for their lovemaking. She straightened them hurriedly before she ran out to check her forgotten cooking.

Lewis took his time about getting dressed, taking Toma's finest shirt, vest, and silk headband out of the clothes chest. He washed, shaved, and carefully combed the snarls out of his long black hair. When he was presentable, he put his heavy greatcoat on over the gypsy finery and went outside.

Starlight glinted coldly overhead, along with a sliver of moon. There was a glow of light on the horizon from the port city a few miles away. Britain wanted that port. The grand duke's palace was in the center of the lighted city, with embassy buildings clustered closely around it. He belonged at the British embassy.

He turned his glance to the small fires by the tents and wagons. Someone was scratching out a mournful tune on a violin. He could make out Vastarnyi practicing the knife juggling he'd spent the whole trip teaching him. He saw Hadari lead his smelly old bear to a stake driven in the hard ground near the main fire. Apparently the trained bear wasn't to miss his master's wedding. He belonged at the British embassy, but he wanted to be here.

He walked up to Sara and took the long wooden spoon from her hands. He'd made the spoon; Beng had taught him how to carve it. He stared at it for a long moment, holding it as if it were made of gold. "Get ready," he told her when he glanced up to find her looking at him curiously. "I'll see that your soup doesn't burn. I won't have you looking like a just-tumbled wanton at my friends' wedding."

"Even if I am?"

"Even so. Go on."

She smiled, kissed his cheek, and hurried back inside. Married, she thought, and sighed.

There must be three hundred people here, Sara decided as Lewis led her through the crowd. They'd arrived in the large Rom enclave only a few hours before, but news of the wedding at the newcomers' campsite had spread fast. Elders had shown up to greet them as well, and they'd had a lot of news to pass on to the elders from the world outside Bororavia. People gathered quickly for the tales and the wedding and the hastily arranged communal feast. It was a boisterous crowd, too. She noticed the bottles and jugs being passed from hand to hand to add to the merriment and warm up a cold night.

Lewis looked at the happy crowd of gypsies around him and worried. He didn't like it that so many were gathered in one place when the duke had all but outlawed their presence in Bororavia.

"This doesn't make sense," he said to Sara, drawing her into the shadows just inside the large tent set up for the ceremony. People were congregating around lanterns hung up in the center, but no one took notice of them on the edge of the crowd. "Why have the gypsy refugees flocked to Duwal instead of scattering into the countryside?"

Sara shook her head. "Beng told me he'd heard a rumor that all the *kris* were told to gather for a meeting in Duwal. Besides," she added, "it might be easier to survive the winter in the town than in the countryside." She tugged on his hand. Outside, the noise was getting louder, and some of the shouting was almost hysterical. "It's starting. Let's get closer." He nodded, and they moved forward.

Hadari's aged mother stood in the center of the tent. She held up her hands for silence. After the crowd quieted down she spoke, voice high-pitched and carrying to be heard over the party outside. "We have seen death already coming here. Sandor died without the chance to forgive us any wrongs we may have done him. We can only pray his ghost walks to feed among the Polish *gajo* who took him too quickly to see our mourning. He spoke at our last wedding, making the bride and groom married, but we pray he is not with us tonight."

Sara and Lewis exchanged a shocked look. He felt her shudder, and when he realized he'd made the sign against evil he felt himself blush. He found himself saying a quick prayer for the dead under his breath, a simple Anglican prayer. He could only give in to superstition so far.

"I wish she hadn't brought that up," Sara whispered in his ear. "It's so morbid."

"It's just her way of cursing Molly's marriage without pointing out that she's unclean," Lewis whispered back.

"Or protection," Sara countered. "If anything goes wrong we can point the finger at Sandor's ghost and not the ex-*mirame.*"

"Not a bad strategy," he agreed. "I just wish she hadn't brought us into it."

Sara gave him a sidelong look, then turned a cool smile on him. "Don't you want to be reminded of your wedding day? I seem to remember you being so anxious for us to get married."

"Sara," he warned quietly, and squirmed inwardly.

"Beng will speak for Hadari and Molly," Hadari's mother continued. She gestured and Beng and the bride and groom stepped forward. They knelt facing each other, on one knee. They smiled at each other. Hadari's mother placed bread and salt on their knees. Beng stepped forward and began to speak.

Molly looked lovely, Sara thought. She hadn't helped the bride get ready; the women had politely sent her away when she'd volunteered. "It's because you're pregnant, dear," Molly had explained.

"I never said I was—" she'd protested.

"Well, we all suspect that you are. That makes you—you know—unclean."

"Molly!" She'd been shocked at her aunt.

Molly had only shrugged. She had to follow some of the rules. Sara frowned now at the memory. Beth wasn't in the tent, either, not that the little girl cared about not getting invited to a wedding because she was a *gajo*. She was outside partying with Rom friends her own age. Sara thought that Beth having friends was a good sign, more important than whether she got invited to a wedding right now. And it sounded like quite a party out there. She wondered what all the shouting was about. It was definitely getting louder. It sounded like people were riding through the camp. Horse races in the middle of the night?

Lewis's arm tightened around her waist as he pulled her closer. She relaxed against the warm strength of his body.

Lewis was thinking that he'd do it over if he could. Not just the wedding. Everything. Especially the wedding. He looked at Sara; their gazes met. It hurt so much he almost laughed. "Reality—how would you put it—sucks?"

"Tell me about it," she agreed.

As the bride and groom got to their feet, horsemen crashed into the tent. People screamed, shouted, ran from the heavy, hurtling bodies. Swords flashed. Sara stood frozen, aware suddenly that all the noise was a riot going on outside the tent. But the cavalry was charging around inside it. Lewis hauled her outside, out from under the hooves of a rearing horse, before she could make any sense of what she was seeing inside the tent.

Outside was worse. People were running frantically. Men in green coats, with swords and guns and lances were chasing them down. There were screams of pain and fear. People were swearing and fighting back. Knives flashed against swords in the surreal flickering of the fires. The air was frosted with the breath from screams and the smoke from gunfire.

Only one thought flashed in Sara's head as she and Lewis plunged into this frightening scene. "Beth!" she screamed. "Where's Beth?"

Lewis wanted to get Sara to safety, but she was right; they had to find the child. He wished they could find all the children and get them safely away. They crouched on the cold ground behind the tent. He pulled his knife. He wasn't entirely surprised to see Sara do the same. He wondered how long she'd been carrying the knife he'd given her?

"Since we got to Bororavia," she said when she saw him look at the knife and his eyebrows go up.

There was a horrific crash as the soldiers turned over one of the *bardos*. "Where is she?" he muttered frantically.

"I don't know!"

"In Maritza's tent!" said a familiar metallic voice.

"In Maritza's—"

"I heard! Stay here!"

"Get real!" she shouted and ran after Lewis as he sprinted away from the tent toward the perimeter of the camp.

He was going to try to circle away from the center, where the Bororavian troops were attacking in force. Sara glanced quickly back. She couldn't tell what was really going on, if the people were being killed, or if the soldiers were out to beat and frighten them and destroy what little they had. There were bodies on the ground; she saw soldiers kicking them. She did see a lance protruding from one still form; it was Hadari's tame bear. The bastards had killed it. She turned and hurried after Lewis. They had to get to Beth!

She saw the glint of light off the saber before she saw the tall man holding it. He came silently out of the night, a gigantic form, sword raised, right in front of Lewis. Lewis's left arm came up to block the man's arm, his knife hand flashing out stiffly. The swordsman jumped back before Lewis connected. The saber slashed again, across Lewis's arm and chest. Lewis fell slowly, face forward onto the frozen earth.

Sara did not scream as the man moved to stand over Lewis, about to finish off the fallen man. She wanted to scream. Instead she stepped forward and almost calmly stabbed the soldier in the back. She shoved his body aside as he fell, so she could get to Lewis.

18

It was Beth who found her. The girl came running out of the dark as Sara rolled Lewis gently onto his back. She could hear screams and sounds of fighting in the distance but it had a faded, far-off quality as she glanced quickly up at Beth.

Beth's hand touched her shoulder. "Is 'e dead?"

"I don't know." She felt blood, hot and sticky, on her hands as she ran them down Lewis's chest. "What are you doing here?" she heard herself ask. A part of her was worried about the girl's safety even while most of her attention was taken up in trying to find out if the man she loved was still alive.

The girl crouched down beside her as Lewis's eyes opened. His hand came up to capture Sara's wrist in a tight grip. He moaned.

Sara let out her breath in a sob. "You're alive." She didn't know how badly hurt he was, but at least he wasn't dead. "We need a doctor." The girl beside her gave a cynical laugh. It was enough to remind Sara of who and when they were. "Beng, then." Sara spoke quickly. "I've seen him treat people as well as horses." Okay, so she'd only seen him set a broken arm and pull a couple of teeth, but Beng was all they had. Lewis moaned again. "We have to find Beng."

Beth jumped up and looked around. "Fighting's dying down. A man came looking for you, Sara," she added. "'E's at Maritza's. I'll get 'im to 'elp."

The girl was gone, racing back toward the camp before Sara could say anything. She pulled off a shawl and draped it over Lewis. The cold could not be doing him any good. It was too dark for her to tell how badly he was bleeding. He was wearing a heavy coat; maybe that had shielded him somewhat from the saber slash. Had she actually killed someone? Were there dead among the Rom? What were they going to do? Where was Beth? What were they going to do?

She bent over Lewis, peering into his shadowed face. His eyes were open, but unfocused. "Don't you die on me," she ordered. "Don't you dare die."

He made a sound like a pained chuckle. "Wouldn't—dare."

"And don't talk." She looked around wildly. "Where's Beth?"

"Love you," he said. Then she felt his body go slack under her hands.

She wanted to scream. She searched for a pulse instead, and started crying when she found it, fast and light, but it let her know he was still alive. She tried to think, but she couldn't remember a thing about first aid. By the time people surrounded her and pried her away from Lewis so they could take him back to camp she was incoherent with shock and terror. She wasn't sure how they got Lewis back to their wagon. She wasn't sure how she got back there herself. Lewis woke on the slow journey back. She heard him fight not to groan with every step the men carrying him took. His efforts left her sobbing.

Beng turned to her after they got the lantern lit and Lewis settled on the bed. He put his arm around her and led her to the door. "You go now. I'll get him drunk and sew him up, then you can tend him. You see to the camp. Help look after things. Keep busy."

Sara was ashamed of herself, but she didn't protest. She had no idea what she could do to help Lewis right now. So she nodded and stepped outside. An icy blast of wind caught her in the face as she jumped down from the wagon; it slapped her around enough so that much of her shock wore off. She looked around her, and for some reason saw a great many people looking back. A crowd was gathered around her *bardo,* most of them people she'd never seen before. In the flickering light of torches held by several of them she read the crowd's stunned expressions. She got the impression they were looking to her for leadership. Maybe they were waiting for Beng to come out and lead them, she didn't know. She did know that something had to be done to put the camp to rights.

She was feeling more like a coward than a leader, but if she didn't do something to keep her mind off the possibility of Lewis dying she was going to go crazy. So she nodded decisively at the waiting people and many of them nodded back.

Beth tugged a tall, slender man forward as Sara came into the crowd. "Mikal," Beth told her.

Sara vaguely recalled the name from somewhere. He was a stranger, but he did seem familiar. Maybe it was because he looked a lot like Jeff Goldblum. He gave her a decisive nod; it almost seemed like a secret greeting. "I came from Duwal," he said. "Tell me what to do to help."

"Mikal," she said slowly. "Mikal the silversmith." He nodded again. She stepped into the crowd, with Beth and the tall silversmith at her side. "First, let's find out who's injured and get them all to one tent and keep them warm. Cala the midwife can organize that."

She continued to give orders and people carried them out. Shelters were found for people whose wagons and tents had been destroyed, debris was picked up. The bodies of two dead soldiers and one dead bear were disposed of. Weapons were distributed and guards were set to defend against the troop's return. Plans were made to disperse the Rom refugees out of one central location so they wouldn't be so vulnerable to attack.

Sara worked through the night, but the work didn't help keep her mind off Lewis. Sometime after dawn she made her way back to the *bardo* at last. Mikal walked with her. It was the first time she was alone with the revolutionary.

"We started the school," he said as they walked along.

"Good," she said.

"I think you should come back to Duwal with me. Stay with my family, they'd like you to."

"I have to look after my husband," she said as they reached the wagon. Beth had been bringing her reports on his condition all night. She knew that Beng said the cuts across his arm and chest were deep but probably not fatal. Probably. She did not like the sound of the word; it was so fatalistic. It was time she made herself take a look at the damage herself. Maybe there was something she could do about it, nurse Lewis back to fine, glowing health, hopefully.

Mikal put his hand on her arm as she mounted the step into the wagon. "Come home with me. We'll care for your husband at my house. It will be warmer than the *bardo,* at least."

Gratitude swept through her as she smiled at the man. "Oh, yes," she said. "Thank you. He needs all the help he can get."

He nodded pleasantly. "I'll hitch your horses for you, and drive carefully into town. He won't even have to leave his bed to get to my house."

"Door-to-door service. Thank you."

"I'll talk to your father about the horses." He helped her up the step. "You care for your man."

My man, she thought, pleasure at the words distracting her from worry for a moment, and stepped inside. Lewis was on the bed, pale and unconscious. Beth was crouched on the floor next to him, wrapped in a quilt.

Sara knelt briefly beside the half-asleep girl to say, "Get your things from Molly's wagon. We're leaving," before turning her attention to making Lewis comfortable for the ride into Duwal.

"I saw something funny when Mikal was showing me around." Sara talked even though she wasn't sure Lewis was actually conscious enough to listen. She held his hand and occasionally stroked hair off his brow and talked. She'd been talking for at least an hour now. He hadn't been aware of the slow trip, or of being moved onto a hastily set-up cot in the back room of Mikal's shop. But his eyes opened and followed the glow of the candle she carried when she'd come in after settling Beth in the room the local Rom used for a school. She'd put the candle on an upturned box next to the cot, taken his hand, and begun talking to him. His eyes kept fluttering open and closed; occasionally he mumbled. She was cheered by his every small movement and kept on speaking.

"Maybe if I irritate you enough you'll wake up long enough to tell me to shut up," she said as she tenderly stroked the bare chest showing just above the bandages. "Mikal's wife said she'd bring you some broth after she got her children to bed. She has four so it'll be a while. About the sign," she went on, "it's funny. I mean, I thought it was a political slogan from my century, but there it was, written out in Bororavian in 1811. It just goes to show that there's nothing new, you know?"

"Sign?" he mumbled. His eyes opened a little, hardly more than slits, but he looked at her curiously. "What sign say?"

"It said, It's the Economy, Stupid," she answered, knowing that hugging a conscious Lewis probably wouldn't be wise no matter how much she wanted to. She squeezed his hand and asked, "How do you feel?" He gave a faint smile. "Okay," she agreed. "Dumb question. Stay here." She hurried out and came back with a bowl of broth a few minutes later.

"Stay here?" he asked incredulously when she sat down beside him. "Stay here?"

Sara almost spilled the broth. She hastily put down the steaming bowl. "Feel like eating something?"

"No."

"Fine. Let's get you propped up and get started." She worked carefully to arrange pillows beneath his head and shoulders. Then she sat down on the edge of the bed with the bowl and dipped up a spoonful of the broth. "I'm not good at this angel-of-mercy stuff," she warned. "So don't push your luck. Open wide," she added with a cheerful smile.

"I hate you," he complained, but opened his mouth for her.

"That's not what you said a few hours ago."

"I must have been feverish. This is good."

She fed him a few more spoonfuls before she said, "Beng says you bled a lot but he doesn't think it's serious. He said he cleaned the wound with vodka. I hope that was antiseptic enough."

"What's antiseptic?"

"Stuff that kills germs."

"What're germs?"

"Drink your soup," she said. She was probably worried for nothing, she told herself. Lewis was going to be fine. He had a good appetite, and he wasn't exactly deathly pale. He was going to be fine. "You're going to be fine," she said, trying to convince herself with the words.

"Had worse," he answered. He hurt like hell, but he was alive, which he hadn't expected to be the outcome when he saw the big German with the saber coming at him. Damn long-armed bastard. "What happened?" he asked. "Where are we?"

"At a friend's. In the city."

He looked around. He'd already noticed that he was truly warm for the first time in weeks. "There's a fireplace," he said. "Lovely things, fireplaces." He looked back at Sara. She looked tired, and drawn with worry. "Beautiful Sara. Never looked lovelier. What happened to the guardsman?"

She looked away. The color drained from her cheeks. "I don't want to talk about it."

Lewis considered her reticence. He recalled that Sara had had a knife. It could only mean one thing. "You saved my life, didn't you?"

She put down the bowl. The spoon clattered against the earthenware. "A little." She looked back at him. "I don't like to think about killing somebody." But if she was going to run a revolution she supposed she was going to have to think about it. About minimizing violence on both sides, certainly.

"Don't think about it," he told her. "He deserved it."

She wasn't going to debate with Lewis on that subject, especially because deep down she agreed. "I couldn't let him kill you."

"Thank you," he said. He wished he could hold her

but he didn't think moving at all right now was likely. His chest and upper arm burned like fire. And he was light-headed with the knowledge that she cared enough for him to risk her life for his. "It's the most wonderful gift anyone's ever given me."

Sara blushed and got awkwardly to her feet. "I think you need to rest now," she said. "Look." She pointed at the floor, out of his line of vision. "I've got a pallet set up next to the fireplace. If you need to use the pot I can get Mikal to help."

Lewis found that eating and a bit of conversation had totally exhausted him. He wanted to talk to Sara, to look at her, to ask just who the devil Mikal was, but more than anything else he needed the rest. "I think you should call Mikal," he conceded, giving in to mundane necessity. "I'd be grateful for the help."

In two days Lewis had not gotten any better. Sara tried to tell herself that he wasn't any worse, but even she could tell that he was running a fever. Nothing wrong with running a fever, she'd been told. The man had a sword wound; of course he was going to run a fever. She washed him with cold water for the fever, and helped Mikal's wife, Ana, change the bandages, and kept up cheerful conversation, but she was scared to death.

She'd spent the morning with Mikal and some Rom elders. Alze had arrived with news from the outlying villages. She begrudged every minute away from Lewis. She hurried to his side as soon as she could get away. He'd asked her for music when she'd left Beth watching him that morning, so she brought her guitar with her when she returned.

"Where's Beth?" she asked when she found him alone in the room.

He waved his hand. "I sent her out to play. She told me she made a new friend when she went to the market with Ana. A boy who speaks English. She likes speaking her own language." He gave her a weak smile. "You brought your guitar. Good. I heard you retching this morning," he added, and his smile turned downright smug. "When do you think you're due?"

"I don't want to talk about it," she answered.

"Why not?"

She sat down and started tuning the guitar. "I want to wait until you're healthy enough to put up a proper argument."

"Why would I want to argue?"

"You will," she assured him. "Right now you're sick enough and grateful enough to do anything I ask."

"I'll do anything you want," he assured her. "I love you. Let's get married."

"I love you too, Lewis, and we already are. Let's fight about it when you're better." He was looking at her longingly, devotion shining out of his fever-bright eyes. It was definitely time to change the subject. "Beth's picked up a lot of Romany, don't you think? Mine's gotten a lot better too, come to think of it."

"Sometimes I don't notice what language I'm speaking," he said. A look of confusion crossed his face.

She put down the guitar to take his hand. "We're speaking English right now," she told him. She laughed softly. "I've noticed that we switch back and forth a lot depending on who's around. Then sometimes when we're alone we use both languages and never miss a beat. We've got our own pidgen language."

"I like that," he said with a wistful smile. "A language all our own. We'll pass it on to the children."

"We're not discussing children right now, Lewis."

His eyes narrowed with an effort at looking stern. "When I'm better we will, madam. We always make love in Romany," he added. "Have you noticed that?"

"I'm going to play guitar now," she said.

Instead she gazed at him thoughtfully, for so long that he eventually asked, "What are you thinking?"

"I was remembering a conversation we had a while back. When I told you about me."

"An unbelievable tale. Or at least an unintelligible one. I believed every word I understood," he added hastily before she could make any protests. "Magic, and souls brought back from the future to lead past lives. It's the most nonsensical truth I'll ever be confronted with."

"Never mind all that. I wasn't thinking about me."

"Then, pray, what were you thinking about?"

"You." She gazed at him with an affection he had never really noticed from her before.

"What about me?"

"I told you about me, but I don't know about you. How'd you end up being a spy? And being that creep Philipston's kid?"

"Creep?"

Sara hunted for a contemporary word. "How about blackguard? I'm not sure what it means, but it doesn't sound very nice."

"You only saw my father for a few moments, how can you tell he's not very nice?"

"Well, he didn't act as though he liked you for one thing. He certainly didn't like me."

"He would have liked you well enough," Lewis answered seriously. "In his bed. He has a taste for pretty girls."

"As mistresses?" she wondered.

He took exception to the arch innocence of her tone. "I thought we weren't going to discuss our future right now?"

"We're not." She leaned forward, chin cupped in her palm. "Tell me about you."

He put his head back on the pillow and looked at the low, beamed ceiling. He started by saying, "My father isn't very nice. You're right, he doesn't like me. When he thinks about me at all, that is. He married my mother for her dowry. He was a widower with two sons when he married her, and he took no interest in another child. I was eight when mother died, and he sent me to the navy when I was nine."

"Nine!"

"My mother's brother was a ship's captain, so he took me as a cabin boy. My father did eventually buy my commission."

"Nine?" she repeated. "But you were just a little boy. What kind of childhood is that?"

"Not," he said blandly, "idyllic."

He heard her take in a sharp breath, but she didn't

offer any pitying remarks. "So how'd you end up a spy?" she asked.

"I volunteered. After I was wounded at Trafalgar—"

"Big naval battle," she said. "With the Armada or something."

"The battle did involve a Spanish fleet, but under French command," was as much correction as he felt able to make without laughing so hard he'd burst his bandages. His lady from the future was no historian. "Well, I did my duty there and got wounded. I ended up spending nearly two years in England attending balls and frequenting gaming hells and dancing at Almack's with virginal misses when I wasn't whoring and drinking. Had the time of my life, though I was living on half pay and winnings from gambling," he added. "I did get to know my father over the gaming tables at Watiers."

"Hope you won a lot of money off him," Sara commented.

"I did." He smiled fondly at the memory of those bitter victories. "I got to know my older brothers as well, but I felt more like an outsider than a pink of the ton. I grew restless, running with the bucks, and waiting for a simpering, rich heiress to fall in love with me wasn't enough. Then my uncle reminded me that I was still a naval officer. He'd gone on to work in the diplomatic service. He asked me to do a small job for him. I started out as a courier and went on to other things. Spying's not the most honorable profession for a gentleman," he concluded, "but I've a talent for it. And cloak-and-dagger work suited my flair for the dramatic."

"And it's something to do with your life," she added. "Sounds like you'd rather work for a living anyway."

"A sad failing," he agreed. His wounds hurt and the fever made him tired. He wanted to sleep, but sleep would rob him of the chance to be with Sara. He so enjoyed talking to her, and felt they had such little time left to be together. The fever, he supposed, was making him morbid.

She stroked his hair. "I like your sad failing. I think I like you, Lewis Morgan."

"I thought you loved me."

"I do, but like lasts longer."

Before he could puzzle through this statement the door opened. Beth came breezing in, a small whirlwind in layers of clothing. A boy in a caped coat came in with her.

"This is Max," she said, introducing the boy. He swept off a fur hat, revealing brown curls, and bowed to Sara. "'E's a toff," Beth added, almost in apology. "But 'e speaks English, so I don't mind." She faced Sara with her hands defiantly on her hips. "Max's run away from home. I told 'im we 'ave a circus and we'll keep 'im."

Sara ignored Beth's belligerent posture and saw the pleading in the girl's green eyes. "Max," she said, turning her attention from Beth to the boy, "why do you want to run away from home?"

"Cause 'is pa's crazy," Beth answered for him. "Isn't 'e, Max?"

The boy's fair cheeks blushed bright red. He gave Beth a beseeching look. She took his hand. He looked back at Sara. "I have chosen not to live under my father's roof," he said, his English slow and formal. He shuffled his feet. "I met Beth the last time I ran away." He gave the slightly taller girl a look of adoration. "She said you would help me, Madam Sara."

Sara noted the way Max was dressed, his manners and his obvious education. His crazy father was obviously rich. She had a horrifying image of some wealthy noble accusing the Rom of child stealing. "Beth," she said, "I think we've got a problem here."

Beth shifted anxiously from foot to foot. "Please, Sara! Let me keep 'im! I promised I'd teach Max to be a *buzman*."

Sara looked at Lewis. "A pickpocket," he translated.

"No," she said firmly to Beth.

"And that you'd teach 'im guitar." Beth stepped closer, dragging Max with her. "'E loves music. You can teach 'im."

Max slipped away from Beth's grasp and picked up the guitar leaning next to Sara's chair. "This is beautiful!" He held it out to her before she could say anything else to Beth. "Play for me." It wasn't so much a request as a command, but without any arrogance to it. He smiled, showing deep dimples. "Please?"

The kid had a lot of charisma. She couldn't resist his imploring look. She took the guitar. "All right."

From his bed, Lewis said, "Good. You promised me you'd play half an hour ago."

Beth went and sat next to Lewis on the edge of the bed. "I still love you best," she said as Sara readjusted the tuning. "But I think I'll marry Max," she added, "since Sara's got you."

"Wise of you," Lewis told her. Max sat down cross-legged at Sara's feet. Lewis closed his eyes and drifted into the music as she began to play.

She'd just started a fourth song when the sound of raised voices beyond the door stopped her. Mikal said something; the tone was urgent but the words unclear. A man with a deep, authoritative voice answered. Then a woman spoke, polite but anxious.

Max jumped to his feet as Sara stood and started toward the door. He grabbed her skirt. "Hide me!"

He obviously recognized the voices. His reaction told Sara what was going on. "Your parents?"

He shook his head. "My governess. And Captain Rudeseko."

"Captain?"

"The captain of the—"

The door swung open before the boy could finish. A large man filled the entry and glared down at everyone present. He was wearing the dark green uniform of the Bororavian guard. With lots and lots of braid and gold buttons. He had a saber and a pistol hanging from his belt.

"Do you mind?" Sara said, stepping protectively in front of Lewis's bed. "There's an injured man in here."

The guard captain ignored her as he stepped into the room. "There you are," he said to Max. The relief in his voice was obvious. "Do you know how badly you frightened Miss Meinstad?"

"Don't scold the boy, Stefan," a slender woman said, pushing her way past the big man. She stepped up to Max and folded her hands in front of her. "You can leave the scolding to me. You must stop this, Maxim," she said to the little boy. She gestured around the room. "Do you want to get these poor people in trouble?"

Max hung his head. "No, Miss Meinstad."

"Then you'd best not do it again."

"Yes, Miss Meinstad."

"I'm just glad I recalled your telling me about your new friend before Stefan ordered the town turned upside down. Think what a bother that might have been."

"Yes, Miss Meinstad."

"Think of your father's reaction."

"Yes, Miss Meinstad."

"That's enough thinking for now," she concluded. "I'm just happy we found you where we thought you'd be."

Sara studied the woman. She was small, fine boned, and attractive, with blond hair, a pink porcelain complexion, a high-arched nose, and large blue eyes. Blue-violet, Sara decided, when the woman turned her gaze on her, and smart.

The woman smiled at her. She'd been speaking in English to Max; now she switched to slow, thickly accented Bororavian. "I'm sorry to intrude so abruptly, but we feared for Maxim's safety."

"Sara speaks English, Miss Meinstad," Max said. "So does Beth. May I bring them home with me to practice? Father wants me to practice English," he wheedled.

"I know that better than you do, Maxim," the governess answered. "That is why he engaged me. My mother is English," she added to Sara. "And you are?"

"Sara," Sara answered. She gestured toward the bed. "My husband, Toma."

"This is Beth," Max said, taking the girl's hand. "May I keep her?"

"No," Miss Meinstad said. "Though I'm pleased to meet you at last, Beth," she added. "Maxim has told me a great deal about you." She smiled at Sara and gave a concerned glance toward Lewis. "That's a lovely instrument," she added, looking at the guitar.

Miss Meinstad, Sara noticed, seemed unconcerned that she was standing in the back room of a shop talking to a Rom woman in ragged clothing. Now that she'd seen that Max was safe, Miss Meinstad seemed ready to settle down and ask for a spot of tea and conversation.

"That tea smells lovely," the woman said, eyeing the pot sitting on the warm hearth.

Captain Rudeseko stepped up to the bed and peered down at Lewis for a few tense moments. Lewis looked back with open hostility. "I heard about the raid on the gypsy camp," Rudeseko said finally. He looked from Lewis to Sara. "My men had nothing to do with it. Come, Denise," he said, taking Miss Meinstad's arm. "Maxim." He nodded politely to Sara. "We're going now."

Both Miss Meinstad and Max looked as if they were going to protest, but the guard captain had them both out the door before they could say a word.

Once they were gone, Sara sat down hard on her chair and held out her arms for Beth. Beth came to her and Sara pulled her onto her lap.

"I like 'im," Beth announced. "Max'll run away again. We'll be together forever and ever."

Sara nodded. She couldn't help but chuckle.

"What?" Lewis asked. She looked at him. He was looking puzzled. "Do you know who those people were?"

Sara nodded. "Do you remember when you told me you wanted to be a princess, Beth?" The girl nodded. "I think you're going to get your wish." She looked back at Lewis. "There's a Bororavian legend," she told him. "About Grand Duke Maxim's beloved English wife. It's about how she dazzled the courts of Europe by stealing their silver. I do believe our little girl has found her future husband."

"Course I 'ave," Beth declared firmly. "Max."

"And Max is—"

"The heir to the duchy of Bororavia," Sara finished for Lewis.

Lewis let his head fall heavily onto the pillow. "Oh, good Lord," he said.

19

"He's not getting any better," she whispered. "Why isn't he getting any better?"

As the slow winter days passed Lewis's fever just kept getting higher. The wound was infected. She suspected he'd developed pneumonia. He wasn't getting any better. All anybody could or would do was stand around and shake their heads sympathetically. Sara was at the point where she wanted to wring a few sympathetic necks.

Sara knelt on the hearth to add more wood to the fire. From there, she looked over her shoulder at Lewis who lay sleeping on the cot across the room. The distance wasn't far, but Sara felt it, not just in inches but in time. Each of the one hundred and eighty-two years that separated them was between her and the sick man on the bed. He was desperately ill and there was nothing she could do about it. "All he probably needs are some antibiotics," she said. "A few days in intensive care, and he'd be fine."

Sara looked at the ring; the little orange stone took

on light from the fire. The glow was pretty, but it didn't look in the least magical. It was just reflected light. "Well?" she demanded of it. "Can't you do something?"

"No."

"Then what good are you?" It took almost more restraint than she had not to fling the ring into the fire. "I need some help here. You healed this body," she reminded it. "You said she died from a heart condition, but you fixed it."

"That was on August twenty-fourth," the ring reminded her. "I don't have the strength for that kind of magic right now."

"Well, you ought to!"

"He needs a doctor."

"I know that!" she snapped, full of nervous anger. "But I can't get him one. The duke's forbidden doctors to treat Rom."

"I know," the ring answered with stony patience. "But you're forgetting something very important."

Sara sat back on her heels at the force of the realization; then she shot to her feet. "He isn't Rom!"

"You're slow, but you do get things eventually." The ring's sarcastic voice rang in her head.

Sara hurried to Lewis's side. "Does the British embassy have a doctor?"

"Yes," the ring answered.

"Then I have to get him to the embassy." She struck the heel of her hand against her forehead. "Why didn't I think of this before?"

"Because you've been letting yourself think like someone who belongs nearly two centuries in your past," the ring replied. "Very dangerous. Disgustingly romantic."

"Or maybe I just want him to be a Rom. Which is equally dangerous and romantic," she added before the ring could make any snide comments. "I just hope I haven't killed him."

"Get him to a doctor."

Sara took her usual seat next to Lewis's bed and enfolded his hand in hers once more. She spent a lot of time just sitting and holding his hand. He hadn't been lucid, or even really conscious, for days, but he seemed to be comforted by the contact. She knew she was. "Let's be logical about this," she said. "They're going to want some proof that this guy is Lieutenant Lewis Morgan."

"There are papers in the *bardo*," the ring told her. "The clothes chest has a false bottom."

She sighed with relief. "That takes care of proving who he is. What about the brooch? They might not help him if I don't turn it over with him."

"You don't trust the *gajos* to protect their own?"

"No," she admitted, "I don't. I've developed a few prejudices of my own in the last few months."

"Not without cause," it agreed. "Don't worry about the brooch. It belongs next to Lewis's heart."

"But it's supposed to be given to the duke."

"Don't worry about it," the ring repeated. "You worry about your flesh-and-blood lover, I'll worry about the ruby."

Fair enough. Since the ring wouldn't tell her what was going on between it and the brooch anyway, she might as well let the magical being worry about the magical stuff.

"Fine," she said, and stood up. She looked down worriedly at Lewis, and brushed sweat-damp hair off his hot forehead before saying, "I'll get those papers, then Mikal can help me get him into the *bardo*. I just hope the ride won't kill him."

"It won't," the ring assured her. "He'll be fine."

Easy for the ring to say, she thought as she left the sickroom. It was immortal.

The butler looked from her to the wagon parked in front of the elegant residence, then beyond, to the tall facade of the palace across the street. "You don't belong here, girl," he said. He looked as if he wished he'd never opened the door. "Be off with you."

"No way."

"Gypsies are not wel—"

"Shut up and listen!" She thrust the leather case holding Lewis's papers at him. "You will note that I speak English," she said. She drew herself up to her full miniscule height and tried to match the butler's arrogant look. He was very tall and she had to crane her neck to look him in the eye. "Take these papers to Ambassador Tate immediately." She waved him away. "Be off with you."

Thank God Lewis had mentioned the ambassador's name and she'd remembered it. Surprise broke through the butler's coldly impassive demeanor as she spoke. The case was the size of a file folder, of brown leather, with the gilded initials *LM* worked on the front. The papers she'd found in the case at the bottom of the chest were sealed with impressive, official-looking blobs of red wax. She'd decided it might look better if she didn't open them and find out what was inside. It might look more authentic if the seals were intact; after all, Lewis was arriving under very odd circumstances.

The butler sniffed indignantly, but he took the case. "Wait here," he said. He stepped back and slammed the door in her face.

"I wouldn't think of going anywhere," Sara said, between clenched teeth, to the ornate brass door knocker. It took her a few seconds to get her indignation under control. After she reminded herself a few times that the important thing was to get Lewis to a doctor she managed a philosophical shrug. Then she turned warily to study her surroundings.

The street was narrow, paved in red brick. The wrought-iron fence of the palace and a group of patrolling guards weren't very far away. Sara had not been comfortable parking the *bardo* so close to the palace but there hadn't been any choice. She just hoped she could get Lewis safely inside before the Bororavian guards decided to amble across the street to see what was going on.

Fortunately she didn't have to wait long before the door opened again. The butler was back, but he'd brought with him a couple of flunkies in red-and-white uniforms, and a serious-looking man with graying hair and expensively tailored black clothes.

The man in black said, "Where's Lieutenant Morgan?"

Sara sighed with relief. "In the wagon. He's very ill," she added as the man gestured the footmen forward. "Do you have a staff physician?"

The man nodded curtly. "How was he injured?"

"A sword cut. When the soldiers attacked the Rom camp."

"They thought he was a gypsy?"

"Yes. Are you Ambassador Tate?"

"I am. Thank you for bringing him to us," he added as the footmen carefully carried Lewis up the embassy stairs.

Sara stood aside to get out of their way as he was carried inside. "He's going to be all right, isn't he?" she asked the ambassador worriedly. She was starving for reassurance though she was aware that the authoritative man didn't know any more about Lewis's chances than she did.

"I'm sure he'll be fine," Ambassador Tate said. He blocked her way when she tried to follow the footmen inside. "Thank you for your assistance, young woman. We'll care for him from now on."

Sara looked up into chillingly blue eyes. "He needs me," she said. "You don't understand," she went on, "I'm his wife."

The man's expression went from distantly polite to cynically amused. "Really?"

Bad move, Sara realized, never mind that it was the truth. If Lewis wasn't able to accept their marriage as the truth, it was going to be worse with his countrymen. "I want to help nurse him." She tried another tack. "I just want to help."

"Admirable," Ambassador Tate replied. "But not necessary." He gestured toward the palace. "I don't care one way or another for your kind, but Duke Alexander would frown on my harboring one of you.

Good day," he said firmly. He stepped back inside. The butler slammed the door in her face again before Sara could say another word. The last thing she saw was his nasty, superior smile.

"No!" she screamed. She leapt forward, her shoulder jarring into the solid wood. She pounded on the door. "Lewis!" She grabbed the brass knocker and banged it as forcefully as she could against the door. She shouted until she was hoarse. Eventually the footmen reappeared. One of them was carrying a short leather whip.

"What were you doing at the English house?" Captain Rudeseko asked as he picked her up off the street.

Sara was thankful for all the layers of clothing she was wearing. She was even more thankful neither of the men had had any enthusiasm for their job. She thought they'd been more interested in getting her to go away than in actually hurting her. She was bruised and aching and humiliated, but not really hurt. She'd only pretended to be unconscious after she'd rolled down the steps to get the footmen to go away. They'd gone.

She didn't know where the guard captain had come from. Then she remembered the embassy was only a few feet from the palace. She wondered how much Rudeseko had seen.

"Well?" he asked, tilting up her chin with his fingers. "What were you doing there?"

A jolt of fear went through her at his question. It

wouldn't help the Rom for the grand duke to find out they'd been harboring a British spy. "Begging," she answered him. Her gaze slid away from him. "Just begging, sir."

He grunted. "Odd," he said. "I thought you might have come looking for help for your husband."

"No!" she said, too quickly. "I was hungry. I was just begging for food."

He made another suspicious sound, but he didn't challenge her story again. He gently wiped the mixture of dirt and tears off her face. "Looks as though you picked the wrong place. Are you hurt?"

She shook her head, and ignored the fact that it made her a little dizzy. "No."

He smiled. "Good. I'd hate to have to take you to my lady for nursing."

"Lady?"

"Maxim's governess, Miss Meinstad. We're betrothed." His fond smile was not for Sara. "Denise doesn't much care for propriety. If you were hurt she'd insist on caring for you."

"That could be awkward," Sara said dryly.

He nodded. "You'd better get your cart out of here," he added. "Before I have to arrest you since you aren't hurt."

Why hadn't he arrested her already? she wondered. Never mind Denise, Rudeseko worked for the duke. She carefully didn't ask questions as he guided her by the elbow and took her over to the *bardo*.

He helped her up on the seat and handed her the reins. "Go," he said. He slapped the horse nearest him on the rump.

Sara called "Thank you," as the wagon rolled forward, but her mind was far more on losing Lewis than on her encounter with the guard captain as she drove back to Mikal's.

"It's for the best," the ring kept saying. "He'll be fine."

After a while she didn't know if it was the ring who kept repeating the words in her head, or if she was just talking to herself. She did know she didn't believe it, no matter who was doing the talking.

Beng was waiting at Mikal's when she returned. He helped her with the horses in silence. Once they'd left the stables for cups of strong tea from the samovar in the kitchen he said, "Why did you take Toma to the British?"

Sara sat down heavily at the table. She looked up at the man who thought he was her father. She felt a wave of affection for him as she looked into his worried gaze. She decided to tell him the truth. "He is British," she said. "Not Anglo-Romany, not Calderash, but British."

He didn't look as if he believed her. She almost smiled as she remembered how much Beng had disliked Toma originally. "Toma is a *gajo?*"

She nodded. "A British military officer. A spy."

He rubbed a hand across his stubbled jaw. "And a good one, I'll wager."

"What?" There'd been pride in Beng's voice when she'd expected him to be scoffing and furious.

"My son-in-law would be good at whatever he does," Beng declared. "What does he call himself when he isn't Toma?"

"Bond," she said without thinking, "James Bond. Why am I joking about this?" she asked, incredulous at her own flippant words.

"Because if you don't laugh at this it will crush you," the ring answered quickly.

"It's really Lewis Morgan," she corrected. "I don't know what I'm saying sometimes."

"James Bond Lewis Morgan." Beng rubbed his jaw again. "I've known Anglo-Romany named Morgan. So my grandchildren will be called Morgan."

"Yeah. I guess." She put her hand protectively over her abdomen, and sighed worriedly.

"Why did you take him to the *gajo*?" Beng asked again.

"There was nothing we could do for him. He needs a doctor."

"What for?" Beng demanded. "So they can bleed the life out of him?" He shook a finger under her nose. "You should have sent for a wise woman, girl, not put your trust in *gajo* medicine."

Maybe she should have. She didn't know. She just wanted Lewis to get well. She looked at Beng in miserable silence.

He said, "Drink your tea."

Before she could Mikal came in with two other men and a stout older woman. The woman was the widow of a printer named Madelinki. Her husband had been killed when the duke's soldiers had destroyed his press. There was a rumor that the press had been repaired. The two men she'd met before. One was a merchant with a booth in the busy square near the palace. The other ran an employment service that supplied domestic help to wealthy households. She had plans for ways to use all these people.

While she couldn't put the worried thoughts of Lewis out of her mind, she made herself focus on the reason she'd asked for this meeting. Maybe if she was able to concentrate on hope for Bororavia's future she wouldn't think too much about how bleak her own would be without Lewis in it.

Mikal got them seated around the kitchen table, then stepped back to stand guard by the door. With everyone's attention centered on her, Sara took a fortifying sip of strong tea and got started.

"Communications and reliable intelligence reporting are invaluable for what we have to do. We have to know what the duke and his supporters are planning at all times so we can counter their every move. We need to organize a network of spies."

"We need weapons," Beng said. "We can't fight the *gajo* without weapons."

"I know," she agreed. "But we also need to know exactly how many we have to fight and where they're the most vulnerable and who will help us. A disorganized revolt is known as a riot. Riots might start revolutions, but they don't win them." Now, where had she gotten that slogan from? she asked herself as Beng gave a grunt of agreement. She looked at Madam Madelinki. "And we need to spread the word of what we're doing, what the enemy is doing, and what needs to be done in every corner of the country." She put her hands earnestly over the older woman's and looked deep into her worried eyes. "I need your help."

For some reason they listened to her. People had been listening to her ever since she'd arrived in Bororavia. She didn't know why. Maybe she was just the only person who'd offered any solutions to the duke's tyranny. She knew she was just stumbling around blindly, doing insane things and trying to sound as if they made perfect sense. People were following her. She hoped it wasn't blindly. Maybe she was the Heroine of the Revolution.

She just hoped Lewis lived long enough to be the Hero.

"What about Captain Rudeseko?" Sara said.

She'd asked the question in response to Mikal's wondering who was going to lead the force they were recruiting and training in the winter woods. He stared at her response, big brown eyes full incredulity. They were alone in the kitchen for once. While Ana put the babies to bed they sat by the stove, drank tea, and talked about the future.

"Well, why not?" she went on. One thing Sara didn't want to talk about was the present. The present was a horrible limbo of days that passed with no word on whether or not Lewis was still alive. She had set a constant watch on the British embassy but no word had yet come back. She knew she was going to have to get someone inside as a servant. Maybe she could get hired as a scullery maid. But infiltrating the British embassy wasn't the subject of the discussion; the coming confrontation with the duke's German mercenaries was.

"Rudeseko?" Mikal scoffed. "He's captain of the guard!"

Sara folded her hands around her glass teacup. "Yeah," she agreed. "But I got the impression he doesn't like his job very much."

"He still won't side with peasants against the nobles."

"That's why we're working to get the nobles on our side," she reminded him. "We know we can depend on some of them already. Rudeseko could help win over more."

Mikal snorted his disagreement as he picked up his tea. Before the rim of the cup reached his lips the man's big eyes got even wider with shock, and the cup dropped from his hands.

As glass shattered on the tiled floor Sara rose and whirled to face what had caused Mikal's reaction. She'd been sitting with her back to the curtained doorway that led into the shop. When she saw the big man standing in the entrance, one hand holding back the black curtain, she blurted out, "Captain Rudeseko, we were just talking about you!"

Dumb, she told herself as he turned a puzzled look on her. Dumb, dumb, dumb. "I mean," she went on hastily, "I was wondering about Max—his highness—and Miss Meinstad, and you." Her voice trailed off as he continued to stare. "Hi," she finished lamely. Behind her, Mikal busied himself with cleaning up spilled tea and broken glass.

"Good evening," Rudeseko said at last. He moved from the doorway, filling up the room with his large presence. His gaze didn't leave hers. "Your husband, how is he?"

Sara was at a loss at how to answer the grave question for a few moments. Finally, she swallowed hard and decided to say, "He's dead, Captain."

Rudeseko nodded. "My apologies, Sara. I'm sorry for your loss," he went on, "but your loss makes my duty easier."

"Duty?" The word came out as a frightened squeak. She backed up a step; then the solid table stopped any further retreat. He took a step closer to her. She considered vaulting over the table and running for the back door.

Rudeseko's hand closed around her forearm. She knew there was no breaking that grip. "I've come to take you to the palace," he said.

The palace? The mad duke's palace? The palace of the mad duke she was organizing a revolt against? She was being arrested? Taken to prison? To be tortured? Executed? What if they questioned her? Would she spill her guts? Betray her people?

"Oh, dear God," she whispered. She felt as if she was going to faint.

"Gather your things," Rudeseko said.

"Things?" she whispered. She shot a frightened glance at Mikal, but Mikal was no longer in the room. Off to gather up Ana and the children and escape, she hoped. "Things? Why would I need things in prison?"

"I'm not taking you to prison," the guard captain said. "I'm taking you to the palace. You, and your guitar, and the child Beth have been sent for." He gave her a reassuring smile. "Hurry up, it's a cold night and the snow is growing thick outside."

20

Fingers brushed across his temple, cool and light. "Do you think he'll be returning to life any time in 1812?"

Lewis heard the words, but he didn't recognize the voice, and they certainly didn't make sense. What year was it? Where was he?

"Sara? Where's Sara?" His hand groped out, encountered a fabric-clad arm. He clutched at the arm and croaked, "Sara?"

"There he goes again," a weary, worried voice said. "I thought you said the fever had broken, Dr. Ames. He's been delirious for a fortnight."

"The infection is most insidious. The fever comes and goes. I bleed him, but the humors are not cooling."

"Sometimes I think Western medicine is useless. I think I'll let Dr. Liang have a look at him."

"Liang!" The indignant protest grated on Lewis's nerves. He was very nearly awake. He tried desperately to push himself further toward lucidity, but he simply couldn't make the final effort. He was forced to remain a mute victim while the man's anger ground over him. "You'd turn my patient over to that heathen Chinaman you found in the sewers of India? That's madness, Tate!"

"You're clearly not doing the man any good. Dr. Liang's a scholar, and a friend, so mind your tongue when you speak of him. I should have thought of calling him in earlier. But he's been holed up in his room translating some Sanskrit manuscripts for weeks and I very nearly forgot his existence." The speaker made a thoughtful noise. "Yes, Ames, I definitely think Dr. Liang will be in charge of the lieutenant's case from now on."

"Well!"

Things banged, there was the heavy sound of feet stomping across a hardwood floor, a door slammed. The noises hurt so much Lewis wanted to scream. Fingers brushed across his temple again. "Sara?"

"You've seen the last of your gypsy temptress, lad. You rest now."

The next time Lewis came awake his head was full of memories of a smiling old man. The old man had told him that he had lingered on even when the foreign-devil excuse for a physician had nearly killed him because his soul was intimately linked to the strength of another. They were two souls with much to work out. Lewis vaguely remembered Sara's saying, "Tell me about it," but the voice had been his own.

The old man had also stuck needles in him and

massaged him and forced horrible concoctions down his throat. He had been faintly aware that the old man had been a doctor and that the whole regimen had been by way of a cure for his festering wound and aching lungs. The whole experience had been far more pleasant than the bleedings, purgings, and horrible concoctions he'd had forced on him during other illnesses.

When he opened his eyes the old man was bending over him, his wrinkled face very close. "Chinese," Lewis said. What voice he had was a rasping whisper. "I thought you were Rom. You spoke to me in Romany."

The old man straightened, and proved to be barely five feet tall. He wore long black robes trimmed in bands of scarlet and had a long but not at all impressive white beard. His smile was warm, and revealed very few teeth. "I found your mixture of languages most interesting. When you spoke I answered in an Indian dialect that you seemed to understand." He stroked his long beard. "I have taken quite a few notes of our very interesting exchanges."

"India," Lewis said. "Sara said her people came from India."

"We'll speak of this later, Lieutenant. Before you ask," he added, "I have no idea who or where Sara is." He smiled, bowed, and left the room before Lewis could say anything else.

Lewis rested his head on a pile of feather pillows and looked up at a ceiling full of naked-bottomed cherubs painted in pink and gold. It would appear he was back in the civilized world. He had to admit he didn't much care for the civilized world's taste in decorating. He felt almost too weak to run his hands through his hair, but he did anyway, and found that someone had chopped most of it off.

"Damn!" he grumbled. "Don't they know a man's strength is in his hair? Foolish *gajo*, no wonder I've been sick." He laughed weakly at his own superstitious reaction, but he didn't like having had his hair cut. "Sara won't like it either."

Where was Sara? He couldn't remember feeling her presence for the longest time. "Probably off playing guitar somewhere," he grumbled. If he had one rival it was the girl's blasted guitar. He smiled at the memory of watching her play. Her music had been in his dreams, but he didn't think she'd been there, playing for him in the flesh.

The Chinese doctor had said he didn't know who or where she was. "That doesn't sound promising," Lewis said, and threw back the bedcovers. When he tried to rise he fell back on the pillows, weak as a kitten. "Damn!" he said, looking resentfully up at the cherubs' rumps. "Damn, damn, damn."

"Yes, well, you are still something of an invalid," a rich, familiar voice said. "Pity. Though you've been missing a perfectly splendid winter, you lucky man."

Lewis slowly turned his head to look at the man who'd spoken. He hadn't heard anyone come in. Or perhaps the speaker had been there all along, because when Lewis finally spotted him, Sir Horace Tate was standing next to a tall window. The ambassador held back the velvet curtain with one hand while he gazed out at swirling snow. Lewis became aware of the high howling of wind as Sir Horace turned and approached the bed.

"I miss India," the ambassador said. He put his hands behind his back. He gave Lewis an encouraging smile. "You've been swearing like the sailor you are for days now, that's how I knew you were going to recover."

Sir Horace was an old friend. Lewis was happy to see him; he was happy to be alive; he had no time for pleasantries. "Where's Sara?"

Sir Horace's ice blue eyes narrowed significantly. "I thought it was the fever that had you obsessed with the gypsy."

"Where—"

"How the deuce would I know? Frankly I think you should be ashamed of yourself," Sir Horace went on sternly.

"Ashamed? But—"

"I don't know what nonsense you told the girl but she came here believing she was your wife. She was in a desperate state. I had to have the butler threaten to have her beaten to get her off the doorstep."

"What?" Oh, Lord, no! Lewis struggled to sit up. Panic gave him the strength he needed. "You did what?" Sara was hurt? When? How long had he been ill?

"It was only a threat," Sir Horace went on. "The poor mort deserved better for trying to save your miserable hide but it was the only way to get her off the premises."

"Well, why the devil didn't you let her in?" Lewis shouted at the ambassador. "She's my—"

"Hold your tongue," Sir Horace shouted back. "Lie down before you faint." He put a hand on Lewis's shoulder and gently pushed him back onto the pillows. "We've more important things to discuss than your pretty ladybird."

Lewis grudgingly settled back on the bed. He closed his eyes. "I have to find her." He looked at Sir Horace again. "This is all my fault."

"It certainly is. Don't be alarmed, all this happened weeks ago. She's back with her people, and has forgotten about you, I should hope. Where's the brooch?"

"She's going to kill me, you know. She's going to be delighted I'm not dead, so she can kill me herself."

"The gypsies are a fierce people," Sir Horace agreed. "Did you get the brooch?"

"It's worse than that. You see, she has this magic ring."

"Magic ring? Lad, you're more ill than I thought."

"I'm fine. She's not an ordinary Rom."

"No?"

"No. She's from the future, you know."

"Of course she is," Sir Horace said soothingly. "Dr. Liang must have been feeding you opium. Don't worry, the delusions will go away soon."

"Things are different in the future," Lewis went on. "Not better, just different. She said that. Sara. She's proud, and intelligent and loving—and pregnant." He sat bolt upright again. "Oh, God, the baby!"

"You got the girl with child?" Sir Horace demanded angrily.

"I think so. I know so. She doesn't want to talk—"

"You swine." Sir Horace punched a fist into his palm. "I wish I'd given her some sort of reward for bringing you in. She'll need it if she's got a half-caste bastard to raise."

Lewis seethed with anger at the man's words. He also winced with shame. "I have to find her."

"Yes," the ambassador agreed dryly. "I rather think you do. You should have taken better care in your dealings with the girl. When I received your letter saying you would be traveling with a gypsy band I was concerned you'd become friends with them. Now it seems you've done more than that."

"Friends?" Lewis repeated. He closed his eyes and let his head drop wearily back onto the pillows. "Oh, yes," he said, groaning. "I most certainly have become friends."

"Give yourself time and you'll get over it."

"No," Lewis said. "I won't."

"Hmm. I see. What you need right now is rest. But first," the British ambassador insisted, "do tell me where you've hidden that blasted ruby brooch so I can give it to that fool of a duke."

Maybe Sara had the brooch. The ring would have wanted Sara to keep the brooch. Then he remembered how the ring was invisible most of the time. Maybe the brooch was the same. He looked at Sir Horace and said, "Bring me my vest. Or did you burn my Rom clothes?"

"The housekeeper wanted to." Sir Horace went to the door and gave orders to a footman waiting outside. A few minutes later the footman came back with a bundle of clothing. Sir Horace sorted it out. He dropped all but the vest onto the floor, then handed the vest to Lewis.

He radiated impatience while he waited for Lewis to search the material. "I've no use for the grand duke," he admitted. "He's a creature of whims and no honor. Personally, I think his rule is as doomed at the late French king's. There's revolution brewing in the winter landscape of Duwal, but while Duke Alexander rules I have to deal with him. Having that brooch will make my job quite a bit easier. He asks about it daily. As if it were some sort of magic talisman."

"Perhaps it is," Lewis said as he found the ruby pin. He unfastened it from the vest and held it out to Sir Horace.

"It's merely a goodwill token," Sir Horace said as he peered at the jewel on Lewis's palm. "Though a fine-looking one." He took it from him. "Where the devil did you hide the thing, lad?"

Lewis supposed it was safer to ignore any reference to magic. He'd already said too much about the ring. So he shrugged and offered a sly smile. "I have my ways."

Sir Horace returned his smile. "So you do. You'd best rest now." The ambassador went to the door. "I suppose you'll be looking for your gypsy girl as soon as you're fit enough to get about."

"Yes," Lewis said, "I certainly will."

The man nodded. "Good. I've decided I want you to keep up your contacts with the gypsies."

"Why?" Lewis asked suspiciously.

"Rumor has it that the gypsies are at the heart of the growing unrest."

Lewis concealed a rush of excitement. "Oh?" he said blandly. As if he didn't already know who was at the heart of the rebellion.

Sir Horace nodded again, then glanced toward the window. "I don't imagine you'll have any difficulty finding your Sara," he said. "The gypsies set a watch on the embassy weeks ago."

"What?"

"They haven't been subtle about it, and I'm not blind. Or deaf. Every now and then the palace guard drives him away, but he always comes back. So, when you're up to it, you can have a little chat with the gentleman who begs and plays violin on the corner."

"You'll be accompanying me to the palace tonight," Sir Horace said as he entered Lewis's room. Lewis looked at him in the mirror as he finished dressing. "Duke Alexander wishes to meet you," the ambassador went on.

He was going to find Sara, and the devil with the duke. There was no use mentioning this to his amiable superior, however. He finished tying an elaborate knot in the stiffly starched whitestock before answering. "Why would the duke want to meet me?"

Sir Horace sighed. "The duke and I were discussing circus acts. The duke loves those sorts of performers even though he's outlawed public entertainments. I made the mistake of mentioning that I have a young man on my staff who was a dab hand at juggling."

Lewis's eyebrows went up. "Juggle?"

"With knives. You can still manage the feat, I trust?"

"I believe so," Lewis admitted modestly. He shook his head. "There are food riots on the docks and the duke is having another banquet?"

The ambassador nodded. "This one is to celebrate Bororavian and British goodwill. They're stringing banners as decoration from the embassy to the palace even as we speak."

"I've heard the hammering since dawn."

"As for the disturbance near the harbor," Sir Horace told him, "I suspect the rebels were merely staging a diversion so they could raid the East India Company warehouse where we're storing the arms shipment we haven't yet turned over to the duke."

Lewis whirled from the mirror. "We're supplying the Bororavian army? Did the rebels get the weapons?"

"We're dangling the weapons for some treaty concessions. And, no, the rebels failed to get their hands on them. This time," he added with an enigmatic smile. "I really dislike Duke Alexander."

Lewis was chafing to get out of the house. Sir Horace's tailor had provided him with a fine wardrobe. He'd been offered the services of a valet but preferred taking care of himself. He knew he might not look the first stare of fashion at present, but he was presentable.

He felt fit at last, and Dr. Liang had finally given

him permission to venture out. The ambassador was too wary of the duke's spies to let him send any messages while he recovered. Sir Horace had no objection to his taking a stroll to enjoy the brutally crisp air. He was going to Sara today, which was all that mattered.

He picked up the heavy caped coat he'd laid out on the bed. He put it on, then a beaver hat, not that he thought the bloody thing was going to keep his fashionably shorn head warm. A gentleman didn't worry about such inconveniences as the weather. Or so Beau Brummel, the dictator of fashion, would insist. Beau Brummel had obviously never spent a winter in Bororavia.

"I'll be off now," Lewis said.

Sir Horace nodded and opened the bedroom door for him. "Good hunting, lad."

Lewis was momentarily stunned by the cold as he stepped out-of-doors for the first time in several months. Overhead the flags of Britain and Bororavia, suspended from a strong rope, flapped sharply in the high wind. Lewis gave them a passing glance as he hurried down to the street.

He had some memory of December, but then time had disappeared in a fever haze and he was just now stepping into February. He worried about what had happened to Sara in the intervening weeks. Time might have stopped for him, but he was sure she was caught up in the dangerous center of the rebellion.

"We'll just see about that," he said as he strode up the cobbled street to the ragged street musician who stood on the corner, sawing inexpertly on a fiddle.

Lewis threw a coin into the hat at the man's feet as their gazes warily met. "Hello, Beng," he said. "I didn't know you played the violin."

"Vastarnyi was sick today," Beng said. As he lowered the violin he looked Lewis over critically. "I always thought you looked too much like a *gajo,* boy." Lewis flinched as Beng lunged toward him, but he was caught up in a tight hug before he could duck away. "It's good to know you're alive."

Lewis threw off his surprise at this show of affection. He stepped back from Beng's arms and asked anxiously, "Sara? Where's Sara?"

Beng shook his head. "The cossacks took her away."

Fear colder than the Bororavian winter clutched a tight fist around Lewis's heart. "Away? Where?"

Beng pointed toward the white marble edifice of the palace. "She was taken by the guard captain."

Oh, God, Lewis thought. Not just arrested, but probably arrested for high treason. Was she even alive? She must be; surely he would have felt her death wrench his soul. Besides, the duke preferred gaudy public executions. The whole country would know if she were dead.

He remembered the guard captain calmly studying him when he'd been lying sick at Mikal's. "Captain Rudeseko."

"That's the big cossack's name," Beng agreed. He touched Lewis's shoulder. "I been thinking maybe you talk to the captain. Maybe he listen to a rich Englishman."

Lewis nodded slowly, grasping for any plan to help Sara. "I'll talk to him." He'd do more than talk to the man if Sara had been harmed in any way.

Beng pushed him back toward the embassy. "You go, then, Toma James Bond Lewis Morgan. You free your wife from the mad duke."

"I will," Lewis promised. "I'll do just that."

Lewis prowled the perimeter of Sir Horace's study one more time. "You don't understand! An innocent woman has been imprisoned!"

Sir Horace folded his hands on the table before him. "Innocent? Didn't you tell me the girl was organizing the rebellion?"

"Innocent—except for that," Lewis conceded.

"Then her arrest was perfectly justified."

"What has justice got to do with anything?" Lewis raged. "We're dealing with a dictator here! This is a righteous revolution!" Lewis stopped pacing as his own words rang in his head. When had he come to believe in revolution? "Legality doesn't matter," he proclaimed. "We have to save Sara."

"We? Why?"

Lewis hunted for a reason that might appear practical to the ambassador. "What if the duke rejects the treaty? You told me he's making more demands than you can accept. What if you can use the rebels against him? Don't tell me you aren't already considering the possibility."

Sir Horace nodded reluctantly. "But I don't know what I can do for your young woman."

Lewis came forward. He leaned across the table, his hands flat on the smooth surface of the wood. Voice lowered he said, "Let me talk to Rudeseko. Perhaps he can be bribed into releasing one female prisoner."

Sir Horace looked as if he'd just tasted something sour. "Get dressed for dinner," was all he said. "If you should by chance meet Captain Rudeseko at the palace this evening I certainly have no control over any *private* conversation you might have with him."

Lewis nodded. "I realize, of course, that the British government has no knowledge of my private affairs. How much am I authorized to offer for Sara's release?" he asked.

"As much as it takes," Sir Horace answered. "Since I'm sure you intend to anyway."

Lewis smiled. "I'm so glad we understand each other, Sir Horace."

"The ruby is lovely, Sir Horace," the grand duke said with a beaming smile. He touched the brooch pinned to the lapel of his gold satin coat. The ambassador, seated next to him at the banquet table, nodded agreeably. "But I've been thinking that I should like some new diamonds to go with it," the duke went on.

"Indeed, Your Highness?" Sir Horace said cautiously.

"Yes. I'm told India is the place for diamonds. I

think I should like to go to India. You've been to India, haven't you, Sir Horace?"

"Yes. I served the Crown and the East India Company for many pleasant years there."

"Do you know about Hindus?"

"I do."

"I'm told their sexual practices are amazing."

Sir Horace gave a small, polite cough. "Perhaps my physician, Dr. Liang, could be of assistance with such knowledge."

"Splendid!" the grand duke exclaimed. He slapped the table, rattling the china and silverware. "Send for the heathen. And arrange to give me a palace in India."

"A palace?" Sir Horace asked.

"The English have plenty of Indian palaces to spare. I've decided I want one. And diamonds," he added. "Lots of diamonds."

"I shall convey your requests to London immediately, Your Highness."

"Splendid."

Lewis, watching from the seat opposite the ambassador, was amazed at the man's ability to retain his bland affability through each outrageous demand. The duke, he had decided the moment he'd been ushered into the same room with him, *was* mad. The mad duke, as Sara had so often referred to him, was tall and handsome, except for his staring blue eyes and darting movements. To Lewis he looked like an opium-eating heron in need of a fresh pipe. His demeanor was arrogant, but no more than any ruler's. His behavior, however, was dangerously erratic.

So far, during the long evening meal, he'd ordered his mistress banished to a convent for wearing a dress the same color as his coat. This was after being reminded that he had chosen the poor woman's dress himself. Then he'd regaled his dinner guests with readings of various broadsheets that had been published about him by an underground press.

No one had known whether they were supposed to laugh, jeer, or applaud as he read the news to them. The grand duke had merely looked up briefly as he tossed each sheet of paper to the floor, then gone back to reading. He frequently guffawed, but his court sat in miserable silence through the meal. Lewis had been relieved when Duke Alexander turned his attention to the British ambassador.

Through it all, while he pecked at the splendid meal and tried to be ignored by the mad duke, Lewis worried about Sara. He tried to frame the words he would say to Captain Rudeseko if he ever got the chance to approach the man standing watchfully by the banquet hall doorway.

Lewis was so caught up in his own thoughts that he didn't react at first when Duke Alexander said, "Now we will have the English juggler. Then music."

Silence followed the duke's statement. A silence so penetrating that Lewis eventually noticed it and looked up. To find everyone in the room staring at him.

"What?" he asked, looking to Sir Horace for direction.

Sir Horace looked pained. "His Highness wishes to see you juggle, Lieutenant."

He'd been so intent on saving Sara that he'd forgotten why he'd been invited to the palace in the first place. Lewis stood instantly. He bowed to the grand duke and started gathering up cutlery. The woman he loved was in terrible danger. His mind was full of images of the horror she must be enduring, but the performance must go on.

21

"What was that?"

"A bi-dextral hammer-on," Sara said when she finished playing. Maxim continued to stare up at her in
extreme confusion from his seat on the nursery floor.
Then he and Beth exchanged long-suffering looks.

After a moment Sara grasped what he'd been asking. "Oh, you mean the song. Sort of kind of vaguely
Van Halen."

"It was pretty," Max told her. "I like what you play
better than what my music master teaches me."

"That's my little head-banger." She reached out to
ruffle his curly hair, then put the guitar down. "I love
this thing but I miss electricity. I've got an Ibanez Voy-
ager at home," she told the attentive children. "Mostly
I just run it through a practice amp and use head-
phones, but sometimes I crank up the Crate to ten and
drive the neighbors to drink." She sighed wistfully. "I
bet they don't miss me at all. Mrs. Dahl swore I was
making her cat go bald. Personally, I think it was her
son who's got this garage band that's really into

grunge. Seattle's a nice town but I wish they'd keep their music to themselves, except for Queensryche, of course. Do you think Lewis is all right?"

Beth shook her head. She got up and went over to Denise as the governess came into the bedroom from the schoolroom. "Sara's talking crazy again."

Sara knew she was. She babbled constantly when she wasn't occupied with practical matters. She would start talking and say anything that came into her head to keep from thinking about the only thing that really mattered. Oh, the revolution mattered, but there was only so much time she could spend being the selfless political organizer, especially since she was forced to work from inside the guarded walls of the palace.

Denise put her arm around Beth's shoulder and they crossed to where Sara sat with Max. Beth was dressed in a white dress with a wide blue sash, and blue ribbons were fastened in her shining hair. Max adored Beth and insisted that his constant companion have the best of everything. Not only did Max adore her, so did his governess. Sara had to admit that she was a little jealous of the close relationship Beth had developed with Denise. She was also delighted that Denise and Max were capable of channeling the girl's wild nature in more civilized directions. She certainly hadn't had any talent for it.

"I'm going to make a terrible mother," she said as Denise came up and took a seat beside her on the closed lid of the toy chest.

"Nonsense," Denise assured her briskly. "You look lovely," she added.

Like Beth, Sara no longer wore rags. She was a privileged and pampered court musician, until such time as the duke remembered she was Rom and decided to have her executed. Because she might be called to perform at tonight's banquet she was dressed in a gown of deep red velvet with matching hothouse roses twined in her hair.

"Thank you," Sara answered belatedly after she realized she'd been staring off into space for a while. Had leaving him at the embassy been the right thing? Why hadn't word gotten back to her about him yet? What was the use of setting up an intelligence network if nobody had the intelligence to report to the person in charge? Which wasn't fair since she got plenty of news from the outside, just none of it the news she was praying for.

"I'm not sure it's such a good idea to use the children as couriers," Denise said, as if she'd read Sara's thoughts. "Don't you think Maxim's father might get a bit upset with him if he knew the boy was working to overthrow his rule?"

"He'd have my head cut off," Max said confidently. "Beth and I are careful," he added.

"Perhaps," Denise agreed. "But it isn't wise for you to keep sneaking out of the palace. I realize you're only trying to help your people, and that's very commendable, but it's interfering with your lessons."

Sara didn't understand Denise Meinstad at all, but she liked her a lot. "You're right about using the kids," Sara agreed. "Clever as they are, I'm worried about their getting caught."

"We won't!" Beth spoke up.

Before Sara or Denise could answer they were disturbed by a knock on the door. A maid stuck her head in a moment later, and said, "You've been sent for, Sara."

Sara sighed tiredly and picked up her guitar. She was tired and her back ached and being near the duke made her skin crawl, but she had no choice but to go. She was one of a number of entertainers imprisoned in the palace, well treated but permanently at the duke's beck and call. At least tonight was a simple party gig. She'd spent several nights since she'd been brought here in the duke's bedchamber, playing blindfolded, providing music for orgies going on only a few feet from where she sat. It had all been terribly embarrassing.

"You'd better hurry," Denise encouraged her as Sara walked reluctantly toward the door. "I'll get the children to bed, and by the time you're done I'll have some hot cocoa waiting for you. With schnapps," she added with a warm smile.

"Not in my condition," Sara said.

"Which you don't want to talk about," Denise added for her.

"But thanks for the hot chocolate. I'm going to need it."

Max came up to her and took her hand before she could leave. She turned to him. "I'm sorry, Sara," he said earnestly.

Sara ruffled his curls. "For what, sweetheart?"

"For mentioning you and Beth to my father. He never would have had you brought here if I hadn't told him how much I enjoyed your playing. I'm not sorry I said I wanted Beth for a playmate, but I didn't mean to make either of you prisoners."

"I know that, honey," she answered. "It's all right."

"Now you can't ever leave. It's all my fault. So I don't want to stop being your courier," he added in a whisper. "I want to help you save the country."

Beth came up and touched Max on the shoulders. "She's got to go now," she told him firmly. "Come on, we're going to 'ave—have—a story."

"It'll be all right," Sara assured Max. She smiled at Beth. "Good night, kid."

"'Night, Sara," Beth said as she tugged the heir to the duchy of Bororavia back toward his waiting governess.

"Everything's going to be all right," Sara said to herself as she left the nursery to hurry to the banquet hall. "Please, God, let Lewis be all right too."

"A pity you weren't here earlier," Stefan Rudeseko said to her as he met her in the corridor outside the banquet hall. He paused to add a small, formal bow to the smile he was already giving her. "You look beautiful tonight, Sara."

Sara returned his smile. Captain Rudeseko was invariably polite, invariably kind, and he invariably turned a blind eye to her subversive activities. It was because of him that she felt safer inside the palace than outside, where the duke's mercenaries were ruthlessly searching for the leader of the rebellion. She knew that besides her own efforts to overthrow Duke Alexander with a popular uprising there were factions inside the court looking to depose him. Everybody approached Rudeseko for help eventually, but the guard captain remained loyal to the ruling family.

To Sara that meant that Stefan Rudeseko was going to protect Max from all comers. She liked him for his loyalty to the kid. It was also why she knew he was eventually going to give his complete support to her instead of anyone else trying to take over the rule of Bororavia. He knew she'd never let anything happen to Max, either. After all, besides really liking the kid, she knew Bororavian history.

This was neither the time or place to discuss politics. "Why should I have been here earlier?" she asked him as he offered his arm to escort her into the hall.

"There was a juggler invited to dinner," he answered. "As fine as any gypsy entertainer, but brought by the English ambassador. A fearless fellow who juggled knives."

"Oh?" Sara said, more out of politeness than curiosity. Then she halted in her tracks as they reached the wide double doors. She looked up slowly to meet Rudeseko's mild gaze. Her heart was beginning to hammer so heavily she could barely hear herself speak. "Did you say knives?"

He nodded. "A familiar-looking fellow," he added. "But I couldn't quite place him."

"Blue eyes?" she questioned eagerly. "Black hair? A sharp, triangular face? Medium height? Kind of skinny but with a really great butt?"

"Guys don't notice that kind of stuff," the ring pointed out. "Of course it's him."

"How do you know?" she demanded before she realized she was speaking out loud to the ring. The ring hadn't said anything in weeks. She figured it was sulking even though it had voluntarily given up the brooch to help Lewis.

"How do I know what?" Rudeseko asked. "That the fellow looks familiar? He does. And you've described him well enough, though I didn't actually look at his butt."

"I know it's him," the ring told her, "because I can sense his presence near the brooch. They belong together the way you and I do."

Lewis was alive! Lewis was alive! Lewis was alive! And well and in the next room. What was she waiting for? Sara very nearly jumped up and down with happiness. Grinning like a fool, she punched the air with a fist and crowed, "Yes!"

Guards and servants in the hallway looked at her strangely, but Captain Rudeseko just gave an accepting nod. "So," he said. "I suspected as much." He rubbed his strongly cleft chin. "Best not to cause a scene." Sara was ready to rush into the banquet room and start shouting for Lewis. Rudeseko firmly took her arm again. "Come with me."

He drew her into a nearby alcove where a tall gold fountain bubbled like overflowing champagne into a circular base filled with white and yellow water lilies. There was a mural of a blooming rain forest painted on the little room's walls. Gold planters of scarlet and pink and purple orchids bloomed beneath a glittering crystal chandelier. He gently pushed her onto one of the curving marble benches that circled the fountain.

"Wait here."

She complied in frustration. She'd give him five minutes to bring Lewis to her, no more; then she was going to find him herself. Meanwhile, to keep from pacing or screaming with impatience she remembered she was carrying her guitar. She fiddled with the tuning for a bit, then started to play.

Lewis was happy enough to escape from the banquet. The doors connecting the dining room with the ballroom had been opened and Duke Alexander was busy conducting the orchestra at present. The result was not pretty. People were trying to dance to the noise, anyway, which meant dodging around the edges of the crowd to avoid couples lurching to what was supposed to be a waltz. He felt momentarily safer once he and Rudeseko were in the hallway.

What he wasn't happy about was that it was the captain of the palace guards who had asked for a word in private with him. Of course he was anxious for a private word with the man, but being singled out by the captain held alarming possibilities to Lewis.

"Yes?" he demanded before Rudeseko could say anything.

"I think you'll want to be alone for a while," the captain said, motioning him toward an open door. Lewis could see flowers and dancing water beyond. Then he heard the music. A string instrument being strummed so softly it was barely audible above the muffled sound coming from the ballroom.

His heart twisted with joy. "Sara?"

"I'll return shortly," Rudeseko added as Lewis hurried forward. Lewis paid no attention to him.

She looked up as he entered, her eyes filled with delight as she saw him. He grinned like a madman and hurried to her. The guitar dropped to the floor with a thrumming thud when she jumped up to meet him.

"You're alive!" they said together.

Then they laughed and their lips met in a hungry, desperate kiss. At some point Lewis tasted the salt of tears; whether they were his or hers he didn't know. "Oh, Lord, Sara," he whispered after a while. "I've been scared to death."

"Me too." She rubbed her head against his shoulder. "You're alive." She lifted her head and looked at him. "You've lost weight."

He held her away from him, his hands on her waist. "You've gained some weight."

Sara put her hands on his shoulders. "I don't want to talk about it," she said automatically. She touched his hair. "Oh, Lewis, I liked it long."

"It'll grow." He pulled her close again. She smelled of roses and he felt the softness of velvet under his hands. "You are so beautiful," he told her; then he chuckled just before their lips met again.

Sara's head pulled back. "What's so funny?" she demanded with narrowed eyes.

"I am," he acknowledged. "I am." He shook his head. "I am such a fool."

"Yeah, okay, I'll go along with that," she agreed.

He gave her an amused glower. "I'm your long-lost—"

"Own True Love."

"You're supposed to say I'm wonderful and would never, ever act like a fool."

"Yeah, but I know better," she reminded him. "We're both fools, okay? Now let's fool around."

"I thought you wanted to know why I laughed."

"It could wait."

He recalled that they were in the middle of the enemy camp. They might not have much time, and there were some things he needed to say. "I love you," was the first one.

"I love you too." She ruffled his short hair. "I love you so much."

"Even though I'm a fool."

She stepped back and crossed her arms. "I'm horny and you want to talk. You could drive me to drink, Lewis Morgan, if I weren't, well, you know."

"With child," he said, and gave her a look that dared her to deny it.

She winced, but said, "Yeah. That."

"With my child."

Her hands went to her hips, and fire blazed in her dark eyes. "And just who else would be the father?"

He held his hands up in front of him. "No one. My baby. I'm delighted."

"You'd better be, you lying *gajo* scum."

His heart warmed at her words. "She loves me," he announced to the orchids. "She really loves me."

"I thought you were dead," she said, turning serious once more. "I was so afraid for you."

"I thought you were imprisoned," he told her. "I was going mad with fear of what they'd done to you."

"Oh, really." She grew sarcastic. "Worry from the man who was going to send me to the prison hulks."

He felt the color draining out of his face. He couldn't look at her when he spoke. "That was—" He made a helpless gesture. "A lifetime ago."

The dark red velvet dress suited her like nothing else he'd ever seen her in. He found himself wondering how she dressed in the time she really came from. More importantly, he remembered in detail everything she'd worn since she'd appeared in his time. And everything she hadn't worn, as well. He shook his head. "It's taken me so long to realize that you're you. You're the same, no matter what you're wearing or where you are, you are you." He paused. "You've become more real to me every moment I've known you. And I've become a stranger to myself in the process. I love *you*. What you are doesn't matter, but what I am does."

Sara put the guitar on the bench, then folded her hands across her stomach. "Are you going to grovel over treating me like an object? A pawn? A less than human thing?"

"I was planning on it," he said. "You deserve a thousand apologies."

She shook her head. "One's enough. Accepted. Let's just cut to the chase, okay?"

He sat down beside her. The guitar was between them. "I don't understand," he told her.

"I know. It's this class thing. You were raised to think your class is better than anyone else's. You're a preppy, hon. Worse, you're an English noble who's scared to death he won't be accepted anymore if he

makes one little false move—like marrying a Rom."
She reached across the guitar to put her hand over
his. "You just have to get over it, babe."

"I am over it." He spoke with painful slowness,
because turning his back on the only life he'd ever
known was hard even though she was worth it. She
was the only thing that made the future they were
going to have bearable. "I'm taking you home with
me," he said. "I'll make you my wife no matter what
my father or anyone says."

Sara's hand tightened painfully on his. "Damn it,
Lewis, I am your wife!" she told him. "And it doesn't
have to be that bad. I've got other plans in mind."

Before he could ask what precisely she had in mind
Rudeseko came in. Sir Horace was with him. Lewis
stood protectively over Sara as the men entered.

Sara stood, and glared at the ambassador. "Oh, it's
you," she said. "Bring your horsewhip along?"

Sir Horace looked startled. "I beg your pardon,
young woman?"

"That's Mrs. Morgan to you," she said haughtily.
"Isn't it, Lewis?"

"I—uh—"

"Lewis!"

"You're wanted now, Sara," Rudeseko said before
he could find any words.

The guard captain gave him a searching look, and
Lewis shook his head. Sara obviously didn't see the
danger she placed herself in by claiming a relationship with a British spy. She didn't seem to fear Rudeseko, and it was Rudeseko who had arranged their
reunion. But why? Lewis had to be cautious for both

of them until he found out on whose side the captain was playing.

"Now, Sara," Rudeseko ordered. "His Highness is asking for you." The man's gaze swept over Lewis and the ambassador. "My master is not one to be kept waiting," he reminded them. "Go, Sara," he said when she hesitated. "I'll deal with these two."

She grumbled a curse, but grabbed her guitar and hurried out the door.

Lewis squared his shoulders and faced the big Bororavian. "After the performance," he announced, "Sara is leaving with me."

"Sara," he was informed, "is the permanent guest of the Grand Duke Alexander. She stays in the palace, Englishman."

"She goes with me."

"My boy," Sir Horace said warningly.

"She leaves with me, and you're not going to stop me."

"I am," Rudeseko replied calmly.

"You and what army?" Lewis asked.

"No army," the captain answered with a slow smile. "I do have the palace guard under my command, if you recall."

Which, of course, Lewis hadn't.

22

"*We might have been* able to reason with the man if you hadn't insisted on causing such a row," Sir Horace complained as the embassy door closed behind them. He handed his coat to the butler. "That is the first time in my long career that I have ever been forcibly ejected from a celebration held in my honor."

Lewis did not want to talk about it. "I've got to get Sara out of there," he said, pacing up and down the embassy's front hall. He started for the door but Sir Horace stepped in front of him.

"Young man," he announced angrily, "we have more important matters to discuss than your love life."

"No, we don't," Lewis answered shortly. "Get out of my way," he ordered his superior. "I'm going back to the palace."

"You're doing no such thing." Sir Horace put his hand on his arm. "Not just yet, anyway. Tomorrow is soon enough. Your ladybird is quite safe for now."

The man's words were so calmly reassuring they almost penetrated the red fog of anger that had come over Lewis when Rudeseko had refused to let Sara leave. He calmed down enough to realize that arguing with the ambassador was futile. He sighed. "Very well," he said. "I'll stay put. For now."

"Good." Sir Horace urged him toward his study. "Come along, have a brandy with me. We need to talk." The butler hurried ahead of them to serve the drinks. Lewis would rather have gone straight to his room instead of wasting time, but he went reluctantly along with the older man.

"I have a task for you," the ambassador said when they were alone.

Lewis stood by the window, looking across the street to the palace. Outside, the flags hung like drying laundry in the still night air. He could see Sir Horace's reflection in the glass. The older man stood by the fireplace, swirling a snifter of brandy in one hand. Lewis had decided to decline the offer of a drink; he wanted to keep his head clear.

If he didn't get on with the conversation he'd be here all night. "What task?" he asked roughly.

He'd wanted a direct answer, but instead Sir Horace said, "I've had quite enough of the duke. I'm beginning to see why all the broadsides he read to us tonight refer to him as the mad duke. A palace in India, indeed! My boy, something has to be done about that madman!"

"So you can get the treaty signed and go home?" Lewis found himself asking. It annoyed him that he was going to allow himself to be drawn into a political

discussion when he had a more important task to perform. He turned from the window. "You've decided
to aid one of the factions in overthrowing the madman," he guessed. "It must be the Rom faction, or
you wouldn't need my help."

"Just so," Sir Horace agreed with an emphatic nod.
He put his glass on the mantel and crossed the room
to his writing table. Lewis came to stand beside the
table while Sir Horace opened a drawer and brought
out a key. "That opens the East India Company warehouse on the docks," he told Lewis.

"The one where the weapons are stored?"

Sir Horace nodded. He tossed the key to Lewis. "I
want you to deliver it to the gypsy leader. This
evening. Why are you grinning at me like that, you
insolent pup?"

Lewis didn't just grin; he threw back his head and
laughed. When he stopped laughing Sir Horace was
looking more disgruntled than before. "Because," he
told his old friend, "the Rom leader is the girl you
wouldn't let me rescue earlier tonight."

Dark brows drew down over Sir Horace's sharp
blue eyes. "Sara is truly the one leading the rebellion?
You're sure?" Lewis nodded. "I thought you were
joking. That pretty little gypsy girl?" he asked, obviously not willing to believe that Sara was more than
just one of the rebels. Lewis nodded again. "Your
ladybird?"

"My wife," Lewis corrected firmly. He was surprised that he didn't feel odd finally saying it. Just a
great deal of pride. The memory of kneeling with her
in the firelight and sharing bread and salt and vows

flashed through his mind. Of course she was his wife.

"So she's your wife now, is she?" Sir Horace questioned. "Since when?"

"She's always been my wife," Lewis admitted. "I just didn't know it until a moment ago."

"Well. I see." Sir Horace shook his head; then he smiled conspiratorially. "I suppose you'll just have to go rescue her then, won't you?"

"Yes," Lewis said, affectionately smiling at the ambassador. He looked toward the window. "Don't worry, Sir Horace, I have a plan."

Lewis was glad there was no wind and that the night was dark and that the flag rope was a strong one. He wasn't at all happy about the frigid temperature. He was in stocking feet, with his shoes tucked in the pockets of his black coat, standing on the roof of the embassy. He looked at the rope stretched across the narrow distance between it and the palace roof, then reached a foot out to test it delicately one more time. It seemed taut enough. He nodded and edged forward.

In a moment both feet were on the rope, his arms held out at his sides for balance. The rope was stiff with the cold. So were his toes. He took another cautious step. He wanted to run, just to get it over with, but he was out of practice, so it was very important to make himself move with deliberate care. He took each step slowly; it seemed as if it took years to cross the street on the rope slung two stories above it.

The fall was not a long one, he reminded himself

as he inched along, but he couldn't afford the noise of
crashing down to the icy cobbles, never mind the
prospect of a rather messy death. The point was not
to alert any guards. Falling *might* not kill him, but
this was a one-way trip. The important thing was to
be unseen, to get in, get to Sara, and find a way out.
She was no tightrope walker. No time to worry about
how they were getting out just now, he knew. One
thing at a time. One step at a time.

He was sweating despite the cold when he reached
the other roof. He let out a sigh once he was standing
on the flat, gravelly surface, and hurriedly put his
shoes on. Once shod he looked around for a way into
the building. He moved forward, trying to be silent,
hoping his tread would not be heard in the servants'
quarters that must be tucked in the attics below the
roof. Sir Horace had told him that he'd never noticed
any guards patrolling the palace roof. As Lewis circled above rearing rows of chimney pots, searching
for an entrance, he prayed he was alone while cursing
the darkness at the same time.

The opposite side of the roof was in dark shadow,
caused by the curving wall of a marble facade that
reared above the actual roofline. Lewis headed for the
wall, hoping to find the access door hidden by the
facade. The door he was searching for opened and a
small cloaked figure stepped out just as he reached
the wall.

His prayers were answered. "Sara?" he whispered,
hurrying the short distance forward.

"Stefan?" a woman's voice questioned as she
turned his way.

Lewis froze in his tracks, a fist of disappointment tightening around his heart. "You're not Sara."

The woman threw back her hood. Even in the faint light he could tell her hair was pale blond. "You're not Stefan," she said.

Where had he heard that voice before? He associated it with music. And pain. He recalled the back room at Mikal's, and the visit from the child, and his governess. "Miss Meinstad," he said. He found himself giving her a polite little bow despite the ludicrous circumstances of their second meeting. "How nice to see you again," he added. He wondered if he should force her to take him to Sara, or politely wait here for the firing squad?

"You're Lieutenant Morgan, aren't you?" Miss Meinstad asked. She didn't seem at all disconcerted by his presence on the palace roof. "I knew that if you survived and really loved her you'd come. Sara's told me all about you," she went on. "Have you seen Captain Rudeseko?" she added. "Sara told me he wanted to see me on the roof, but I think near midnight on February twenty-third is hardly the best time for a rooftop tryst. Don't you agree? I don't think I'll wait for him. I don't suppose you're waiting for him too?"

"Uh. No." What else could he say. "Sara?"

The governess took his arm. "I suppose I'd best take you to Sara now," she said.

"Thank you," he said as she opened the door and led him to a dark stairway.

"Can't have the guards, even dear Stefan, interfering in dramatic rescues, now, can we? This *is* a dramatic rescue, isn't it, young man?" she questioned sharply.

"Uh. Yes."

"Good." They descended the last of the stairs to a hallway lit by candles in wall sconces. "This way," she directed. "Sara's going to be so happy about this."

"I've got to get out of here," Sara said. She stopped before the hearth to look at the ring in the firelight. "Lewis needs me," she told it. "The revolution needs me. It's time I got out of here. Why don't we grab the brooch and make a run for it?"

"Never mind the brooch," the ring answered. "Let's just go."

"Never mind the brooch? I felt you drooling over it the whole time I was trying to play. It's your fault I was so bad tonight," she added as she recalled her pitiful performance. The duke had shouted at her a lot before ordering her out of his sight. "It's a wonder the duke didn't have me executed."

"You were thinking about Lewis."

"Of course I was thinking about Lewis. You were thinking about your ruby friend. It was a fiasco."

"Indeed. Let's not quibble over who's to blame, let's just get out of here."

"Fine with me. How?"

"Good question," the ring answered just as the door opened.

Sara's room was right next to the governess's, so she was used to Denise coming in at all hours. In fact, she recalled that Denise had promised her cocoa just before Lewis Morgan came back into her life. Sara looked up to greet Denise, but barely noticed her as her gaze found the man accompanying her.

"Lewis," she said as he stepped in behind Denise, and quickly closed the door behind them. She ran forward. "Oh, Lewis!" Which, she realized, was an incredibly dumb thing to say when she should be asking him why he was risking his neck to come to her. And what he'd meant by not admitting she was his—

He took her hands and said tenderly, "Hello, Mrs. Morgan."

Oh. Well. Everything was all right, then. The love shining out of his eyes nearly melted her. "Hello," she replied. The simple word was completely inadequate to what she was feeling. What she was feeling was going to take years to articulate. She began by saying, "About time."

He nodded. He drew her to him in a tight embrace. "I'm a very slow learner," he whispered in her ear. "I love you and you're mine."

"I love you and you're mine," she repeated. It felt as if they had just taken their marriage vows all over again and this time it was really real.

"I'm glad that's settled," Denise chimed in. "Now," she went on as Sara and Lewis looked at her, "don't you think you should be leaving? Don't worry about Beth," she added as she took off her cape and handed it to Sara. "She's safer here with me. And happier too, I think."

Sara couldn't deny it, so she nodded her agreement at Denise's words. "Can I leave my guitar here too?" she asked, putting on the cape. She hated leaving it more than she did Beth, but it was probably not good to be loaded down with bulky objects during daring escapes. She touched her abdomen, glad that she wasn't all that bulky yet herself. Denise smiled and nodded to her request.

Lewis took her arm. "Come on," he urged. "Before Rudeseko shows up to find out why Miss Meinstad didn't meet him on the roof."

"He wanted you to meet him on the roof?" Sara asked Denise. "Why?"

"I wouldn't know. You're the one who told me."

Sara looked at her friend in utter confusion. "No, I didn't."

"But—" The door opened before Denise could finish. It was Captain Rudeseko. "Oh, dear," she said. Then she folded her hands in front of her, lifted her chin, and looked her betrothed in the eye. "Stefan, dear," she said. "The Morgans are leaving now. Would you mind showing them out?"

Rudeseko opened his mouth to speak, but no sound came out; he just stared at Denise for a while. He looked as though he were frozen in place. Sara wondered if she and Lewis could sneak out behind him.

"I—" he finally said. "Uh—" He took a deep breath and turned to Sara. He pointed at Lewis. "Do you want to leave with this Englishman?"

Lewis put his arm around Sara's shoulder. "Why wouldn't she?"

"Will you be safe at the embassy?" Rudeseko persisted.

"Why wouldn't she be?"

Sara cast a wary look at Lewis. "We aren't going back

to the embassy," she told him. "We have to find Mikal."

"Yes." Since Rudeseko continued to glare at him, Lewis asked her, "Why does he think I'm going to hurt you?"

"Not you," she answered. "I've told him all about you. He doesn't want me to go back to the embassy. I don't want to go back there, either."

Lewis didn't understand Sara's hostility any more than he did the guard captain's. "Why? Ambassador Tate is a wonderful man. He sent me to—"

"He had her beaten when she brought you to the embassy, Englishman," Rudeseko cut him off. "When she was only trying to save your life."

What Lewis felt was as much shame as it was a slow, cleansing anger. He turned Sara to face him. "Sir Horace told me he had the butler threaten to beat you to get you to leave."

She shook her head. "It wasn't a threat." She watched Lewis go white with anger. His fingers tightened on her shoulders. She was inordinately pleased by his reaction. "They didn't really hurt me," she admitted.

"But they humiliated you." She blushed, and nodded. "The butler and I will be having serious words," he promised her. Sara was right; they weren't going back to the embassy, or to England. They weren't going anywhere where she could be hurt or humiliated by her inferiors. Which meant, he supposed, that they were staying right here in Bororavia and getting on with her blasted revolution.

"Come," Rudeseko said. "I will show you to the gate."

Sara turned a grateful look on him. "Thank you." She smiled at Denise. "Thank you both."

Denise waved her toward the door. "You'd better get going. We'll talk later."

With the guard captain as their escort no one challenged them as they made their way through the palace and grounds. Sara paused at the gate and put a hand on Rudeseko's sleeve. She whispered to keep any of the soldiers on patrol in front of the palace from overhearing. "You aren't going to get into trouble for this, are you?"

He shook his head. "It's time I started handling trouble. Be careful," he added. "His Highness has his German mercenaries hunting the houses for the rebels' printing press tonight."

She nodded. "We'll be careful," she promised. "You know," she added, "when you walked in just now, I was scared you were coming with the order to execute me."

Rudeseko blushed, and rubbed the back of his neck. "I was. Godspeed, Sara," he added, before turning and walking back through the palace gate.

Lewis took her hand and quickly led her in the opposite direction.

"It's a cold February night," Sara said, "and I'm from Minnesota. I know better than to go out for long walks in less than thermal underwear and goose down this time of year. But am I wearing them? No. Do I have frostbite? Yes."

"Are you trying to tell me you're cold?" Lewis

asked as they approached the house Sara had identified as Mikal's. He had no memory of the house, merely of pain mixed with comfort in the back room. "A lady," he added, "never admits to being affected by the weather."

"In Minnesota," she went on as if she hadn't heard him, "I have at least six different weights of coat in my closet. Do I have any of them with me? No. Why? Because of a dumb wish ring that didn't bother explaining the rules before we got started on this little escapade of ours."

"Most ungentlemanly of it," Lewis agreed. It had been a long walk, and yes, it was very cold, but he was having a wonderful time. Why? Because Sara was with him. "Love," he commented, "causes the most ridiculous state of mind."

"Don't it, though," she agreed. She looked around. "The street is quiet. Too quiet."

"Perhaps," he said, pausing to take a look up and down the shabby, shop-lined street. "It is past midnight."

Groups of mounted soldiers had passed them at irregular intervals throughout the trip from the palace, but they hadn't been stopped. They had seen other people stopped, questioned, some taken away. He'd kept a firm hand on Sara and they kept moving. Lewis attributed their luck to their being a well-dressed couple who walked along hand in hand, with deliberate casualness.

The front of the silversmith's shop was dark. Sara led him to an alley and around to the back of the building. Light spilled out from a small window, and warmth greeted them after Sara knocked and a tall man came to open the door. A broad smile spread over the man's drooping features and he hurried them into a small, crowded kitchen. Beng was seated at the kitchen table. He pushed to his feet as Sara ran to him and threw herself into his arms.

"So, James Bond Lewis Morgan," Beng said sternly over Sara's head, "you've brought my daughter back from among the *gajos*. And yourself." His voice was stern, but the Rom patriarch was smiling.

Lewis nodded. "That I have."

"None too soon," Mikal said. He touched Sara's arm. "Come. I have something to show you." He picked up a lamp and they followed him into the back room.

When she saw what was in the storeroom Sara groaned. "The printing press. You brought the press *here?*"

"We've set up shop here, but we'll have to break the press up and move it soon," Mikal told her. "It's too dangerous to keep it in one place for long."

"That's for sure," she answered. "The city's crawling with troops looking for that thing."

"We barely got it out of Madelinka's before the cossacks came," Beng said from the doorway. "They burned the old woman's house. Mikal sent her and his family to a camp we set up in the Ozersk Forest. Molly organized that," he added. Sara couldn't help but notice that Beng sounded proud of his sister. "The men are in the city," he went on. "Waiting only for more weapons before we take the palace."

Lewis smiled and stepped up to Beng. He took the

key out of his pocket. "This will get you into the East India Company warehouse," he told his father-in-law. He smiled. "I'm sure the guards will be looking the other way when you show up to use it."

Beng reached for the key, but it was Mikal who came up and took it from him. The tall man clapped a hand on his shoulder. "Thank you," he said earnestly. "This will save many lives. You truly are a Hero of the Revolution."

Behind him Lewis heard Sara mutter, "I do all the work and he's the Hero of the Revolution. Typical."

"I think you'd better hurry," Lewis said to the men.

Beng nodded. "We go now. Come, Mikal."

After the men left Lewis came up to Sara, who was staring intently at the printing press. "What are you thinking?" he asked. He put his arm around her shoulder.

She took her gaze from the press to look at him. "I was wondering," she said, "if there's any way we could make that thing look inconspicuous."

He lifted his eyebrows questioningly. "Inconspicuous? Like a piece of very uncomfortable furniture, perhaps?"

"Yeah." She gave him a teasing smile. "Think we can find enough flowered chintz to make a really big slipcover?"

He didn't want to answer her; he wanted to kiss her, but the soldiers smashed down the storeroom door before he had the chance to do either.

23

"This is another fine mess you've gotten me into."

Lewis brought her hand to his lips and kissed the tips of her fingers. One of the men guarding them snorted derisively at the gesture. "I'm sorry," he told Sara. "I am so sorry."

On the other side of the throne room the British ambassador was talking very fast. Grand Duke Alexander was sprawled on his throne, looking more bored than anything else. The walls were lined with the duke's well-armed German mercenaries. The mercenaries' attention was on Lewis and her. Neither Captain Rudeseko nor any of his men were anywhere in sight. Things did not look good for them, Sara had to admit.

She turned a gentle smile on her husband. "It's only an old joke," she told him. "I didn't mean to make you feel guilty." Despite their dangerous situation, she found herself yawning tiredly. "Long night."

"I am guilty," Lewis said. "Sir Horace isn't going to talk him out of executing us."

"Probably not," she agreed. "You know, it wasn't supposed to end like this," she mused. "The legends say Sara and Lewis lived to a ripe old age and had many children."

"Legends lie," he answered. "A pity the officer who arrested us recognized both of us. Now we've both been accused of spying and sedition."

"Well, at least we're guilty of it," Sara said with a cheerful grin. She didn't feel cheerful, but Lewis was taking this thing far too seriously. Okay, so they were going to get executed, but she didn't want him to die thinking it was his fault. She jerked a thumb at the mad duke. "He was going to have me executed for giving one bad show. Now that is a bad review. If I'm going to get killed I want it to be for something I can be proud of. Not that I want to get killed at all."

"Of course you don't."

She'd almost forgotten about the ring. She wondered if there was anything it could do to get them out of it.

"Think about it," the ring answered in its usual annoying, cryptic way.

"If I'd known it would come to this six months ago . . ." Lewis's voice trailed off with a sigh. He kissed her hand again. "If I'd believed in you, us, sooner . . . I love you. Now I'm going to lose you."

"Six months," she said as she touched his cheek. "Has it only been six months? Then again, it hardly seems like any time at all since I wished to meet my own true love." Six months? Something teased at the back of her mind.

"It was a bad wish," he said. "I wish you'd wished something else. You'd be safe now."

"But I wouldn't have met you." She made a face. "This is the most disgustingly mushy romantic conversation I have ever heard."

It was Lewis's turn to give a cheerful grin. "People who wish to meet their own true love shouldn't complain when they end up having romantic conversations with them."

"Under trying circumstances," she added, looking around the throne room again.

The danger was thick enough to cut with a knife. Duke Alexander was on his feet. Sir Horace, called out of his bed to defend the British government against charges of spying, had stepped away from the throne. Several officers had taken his place. Without looking at them, the duke pointed at where she and Lewis were standing. The officers bowed and came toward them.

"It don't look good, hon," she said.

He followed her gaze. "You do have a gift for understatement, my dear."

Orders were given; men surrounded them. Lewis's fingers were tightly woven with hers as they were hustled from the throne room. Dawn lit the sky as they were led outdoors. Sara was exhausted, frightened, distracted, but the cold blast of the winter air brought her fully alert. They were taken to the square in front of the palace and made to stand before a wall. The surface of the wall was pitted with bullet marks.

Sara saw the evidence of other executions and gulped hard. "Oh, dear."

"Stand here," the officer in charge ordered. A half dozen soldiers with rifles were lining up not more than ten feet from where they stood.

"Think they'll miss from that distance?" she asked when Lewis waved away the offer of blindfolds. She heard the effort to remain calm in the high pitch of her voice.

"Highly unlikely," he answered, voice equally strained. How did one say good-bye in such circumstances? Lewis wondered. "I feel that I've hardly had time to say hello," he told the woman he loved. At least they weren't tied, not that he supposed her dying with her hand in his was much comfort for her.

"Time," Sara said, voice distant and thoughtful. "Time. Six months." She looked at him. For some reason her eyes were lit with hope.

Her expression was almost enough to make him believe she'd found a way out of this totally desperate situation. He ignored the noises of the firing squad loading their guns as he gazed at her. "What?" he whispered.

"I think I got it."

"What?" he repeated.

Sara didn't know whether to groan with frustration or giggle with relief, not that she had time to do either. Time. Six months. "What's the date?" she asked Lewis.

He looked confused, then thoughtful, then answered, "February twenty-fourth, I believe."

She punched the air with her fist, just as the firing squad raised their guns to their shoulders. "Yes!"

"Sara?"

"You know," she had said to Mala, *"I wish I had six months free to do the research about what really happened. I'd start in London and go all the way to Bororavia. Follow their trail and find out what really happened."*

That had been her first wish, *not* meeting her own true love. She just hadn't known it was a wish when she made it. But the ring had. The ring had granted it.

Well, she'd found out exactly what had happened all right. "It's been exactly six months," she said.

"Not exactly six," the ring responded.

"Close enough," she argued. "Are you going to help me? Or are you going to split hairs while we get shot?"

"Sara?" Lewis asked anxiously.

Nearby, the officer in charge said, "Ready."

"I suppose we could take different time zones into consideration."

"I think we'd better." She looked at Lewis. "Don't worry," she told him. "How about the kid?" she asked the ring.

"He'll be fine."

"Aim."

Him, huh? She gave a satisfied smile. "We're going to have a boy," she told Lewis.

"Oh, God!" His words were a strangled whisper of pain. He grabbed her in a tight embrace.

Looking up into his anguished face Sara said, "Don't panic." She touched his beard-stubbled cheek. "Don't worry. It'll be fine. Hit it," she said to the ring.

A nanosecond later the whole world was yanked away from her. Correction, she was yanked out of it.

Sara went limp in Lewis's arms at the same instant the commander shouted, "Fire!"

The first difference she noticed was the temperature. It felt as if she'd been tossed out of a freezer into an oven. "More like out of the frying pan into the fire," Sara said as she opened her eyes in Mala's tent. "Was that all a dream?" she wondered as she looked around.

"No, it wasn't." The acid voice of the ring rang in her head.

Sara sighed, and wiped a hand across her sweat-beaded forehead. "Good," she said with a fond smile for all the memories she'd brought back from six months in the past. She stood, then swayed and almost fell back onto the pile of colorful pillows. Her body did not feel at all as she remembered. She felt big and clumsy and not at all like herself. "Okay," she said to the ring. "Where do we start?"

"I'm not allowed to tell," it answered sheepishly.

"Oh, for crying out loud!"

She could hear the noise and laughter from the Renaissance Faire outside the tent. She had returned to the same twentieth-century afternoon she had left, probably only a few moments before. She dismissed the sounds and world beyond the tent walls without a second thought. She wasn't in the least bit tempted to walk out of the tent and return to the life she had known. She had to get back to Lewis. Before he was executed.

"I'm not in the mood to put up with any 'magic is complicated' technobabble from you."

"I can't help it!" the ring answered in a metallic shout. "That's the way I was made. You've got to figure the next part out for yourself. It is fairly simple," it added in haughty challenge.

Sara looked at the ring, and noticed her square, short-fingered hands instead. She had never liked her hands. "I wish I still looked like the other me," she said wistfully. A moment later, after a shriveling blast of pain that drove her to her knees, she did.

While she was still trying to catch her breath, the ring said, "Next?"

Sara's aching head cleared at the question. She threw back her head and laughed. "Of course! I made a wish. It's still August twenty-fourth here. I can wish for anything I want!" She held her hand up so that the orange stone caught light coming in from the roof of the tent. "I wish for you to bring Lewis into the future. Right here, right now."

"Sorry. I can't do that."

"What!"

"It has to do with transmigration of souls," the ring explained. "Try again."

"Why are you giving me trouble?"

"I'm doing the best I can. Try using your brain. Hint—does the word 'anomaly' have any meaning for you?"

"Anomaly? Anomaly." What was the ring talking about? Wasn't time traveling to a former incarnation anomaly enough? No, she corrected herself, that wasn't anomalous; it was just plain crazy. "Okay, so what anomaly are we talking about here?"

"I can't tell you."

"Twenty questions with a magic ring." She folded her hands together and tried to remain calm. "I can do that," she said. "What happened in the past that was an anomaly? What the heck's an anomaly, anyway? An irregularity. Something weird you can't explain." She shrugged. "Plenty of things like that happened back in the past."

"Such as—?"

"Well, take the guitar," she began thoughtfully. "How come she stole a guitar when a guitar was just what I needed? And where do you suppose Sara found a guitar perfect for these little hands?"

"Good questions. Where do you think?"

The exasperation in the metallic voice in her head triggered the obvious realization. Sara slapped her palm against her forehead. "I'm the one who gave me the guitar? No way!"

"Way," the ring insisted.

Sara hugged herself and laughed. "But? . . . Why? . . ."

"Rules of magic won't allow you to interfere in history directly. You have to be subtle about it. You have to direct things from behind the scenes."

"The rules of magic are a pain in the butt," Sara said.

"Tell me about it. Shall we get started?"

"But . . . how?" Sara asked.

The ring sighed dramatically. "It requires your being in two places at once, more or less, that's all."

"That's all?"

"Piece of cake. While the you that lives in 1811 is traveling through Europe, the you from right now moves around in time, providing yourself with the things you'll need."

"Oh." She didn't understand it. She wasn't going to try.

Sara got to her feet. What should she do first? Get back to the past, she supposed. "How about," she said to the ring, "I make a blanket wish for you to give me stuff and take me where I need to go without having to waste any more time with this twenty-question game?"

"Very good," the ring replied in its usual sarcastic way. "Consider it done."

Maybe it sounded sarcastic, but she could tell by the way her finger tickled that the ring was pleased with her suggestion. "Okay. London. August twenty-four, 1811. I need to see a man about a guitar."

"If that's what you want, Sara," Evan said, taking from her the guitar that the ring had provided. Before he turned to go he looked at her strangely. "I'll meet you with this at midnight, girl. But tell me, what is that thing on your blouse?"

Startled, Sara looked down, to discover that while her body had changed, she was still wearing her twentieth-century clothes, leggings under a very long, loose red T-shirt. "It's a moose," she said.

"Oh." Evan shook his head and walked away.

Sara was glad the old man hadn't asked for any further enlightenment. She wondered if she should have the ring give her more appropriate clothes, but then decided defiantly against it. Somehow, a Rocky-

and-Bullwinkle T-shirt seemed like the perfect attire for this escapade.

"Where to next?" she asked the ring.

The next moment she was standing in the kitchen garden behind a tall, imposing house. She looked around quickly. "Nobody around. Where are we?" She was holding something, a key. "Oh. This must be Lewis's dad's place." Sara chuckled. "You mean the key wasn't really hidden under a rock at the bottom of the stairs?" The burglary had seemed awfully easy, come to think of it.

"It will be in a moment. Hurry up."

Sara gave another cautious look around, then knelt at the bottom of the stairs and worked loose the stone she'd found the key under when she and Toma had come here—uh, would find when they came here tomorrow night.

"What next?" she asked when the key was safely hidden.

"Guess."

Sara sat back on her heels while the sun beat down on her head and the rank London air filled her nostrils. "What do you mean, guess? I thought you were going to cooperate."

"I am. But why should I do all the work?"

The ring was out to drive her crazy. It always had been. She knew it. She closed her eyes and thought. What next? What other anomaly had she encounter— "Got it!" she said as she popped up off the ground. "France. The crossroads—with a little Eric Clapton as background music, if you please."

"Don't push it," the ring complained as it complied.

"Gypsy signs, indeed," Sara said, standing in the center of the crossroads outside the village where Beth had stolen the bread. "Secret ways known to but a few. Ha!"

"They are secret ways known to but a few," the ring replied. "You and me. We have to mark them all the way to the outskirts of Paris. Shall we get started?"

"Mark them with what?" Sara asked. Then she laughed, remembering that the trail signs she'd found had all been scraps of red cloth. She hadn't noticed at the time that the cloth was cotton knit T-shirt material. She shook her head. "I took so much for granted." She fingered the hem of the shirt she wore. "Good thing this is really big, or I'd be naked by the time we get to Paris. I'll take a pair of scissors," she told the ring. "No way am I going to try to tear this stuff with my teeth."

She fastened bits of her clothing at a dozen stops between the crossroads and the village of Nanterre, preparing the way for the caravan to follow. Once in the clearing where the Borava would eventually make their camp she sat down on a tree stump, cradled her chin on her fist, and considered her next move.

"Custine," she said, remembering the handsome, red-haired French officer. She stood, and before she could blink she was standing inside the chateau where she'd nearly found herself in bed with Custine.

She ducked behind a heavy velvet curtain as she heard people approaching. She pressed herself against the window glass, and noticed that it was a beautiful, moonlit night on the other side of the pane. She peeked cautiously from behind her cover to watch a half dozen liveried servants carrying silver dishes toward the dining room. The sound of guitar music played in the distance. Tempting aromas lingered in the hallway after the servants had gone. She guessed that the kitchen wasn't too far away.

"Come to think of it, I did end up in bed with Custine," she recalled. She edged out from behind the curtain, and listened to the distant music. "That's my playing."

"Correct."

"This is the party I entertained at?"

"I thought that would be obvious."

Maybe it should have been, but it wasn't. She wasn't going to argue about it. She had to hurry; the music had stopped. Even now Custine was taking Sara outside to fool around in the garden. Lewis and the ring were stealing the brooch. Custine was going to notice the light in the window and want to investigate. Sara was going to be desperate to create a diversion and only one thing was going to come to mind. Soon she and Custine would go upstairs.

"No way am I—she?—me, going to sleep with him!"

"Then you'd better do something fast."

An oil lamp burned in a gilded bracket near where she stood, and the kitchen was nearby. Sara remembered the house fire and went to take the lamp from its holder. The oil was going to come in useful for helping to spread a fire from the kitchen to the rest of the mansion.

Sara rubbed her hands in satisfaction once she was certain that the blaze would spread throughout the lower floor of the building. She stood outside in the shadow of the stables and looked back at the house while servants shouted in alarm. "I don't remember hearing about anybody getting hurt. Nobody does, right?"

"No. Everyone will be fine."

"Good, let's go." The ring made no move to transport her away. Sara shook her hand. "Time's wasting. Come on. We need to get to Bororavia and get the rebels organized."

"You're sure you want to leave so soon?"

"I want to get this over with," she said in exasperation. "I have to get back to Lewis."

"Well, all right. If you wish to let the guitar be destroyed I have to obey you."

"What are you talking about? Of course I don't want to get the guitar destroyed."

"You left it in the chateau."

"Yeah, but Lewis found it for me." She gave a fond smile as she remembered waking after they'd escaped the blaze to find Lewis smiling as he gave her her guitar.

"True, Lewis did find it," the ring told her. "But where?"

A frown replaced her smile as she thought about what the ring had said. "You mean he didn't go back to brave the flames for me?"

"For the guitar, you mean. He did go back to save you, but asking him to go back for the instrument was a bit much on your part."

"He didn't?"

"No."

"Oh." So much for that romantic gesture. At least

Lewis would be making enough romantic gestures in the time between the fire and the firing squad to make up for bending the truth a bit tonight. Sara started back toward the burning building. "Let's go get the guitar."

Once she'd left the instrument leaning against a tree by the path back to the camp she gave a cackle of laughter and said to the ring, "The Emerald City—Bororavia—as fast as lightning!"

"I in no way resemble a broomstick," the ring said as she materialized outside the door to Mikal's silver shop. "Even if you do bear a striking resemblance to the Wicked Witch of the—"

"Can it." She interrupted the ring's complaint and walked into the shop, then strode purposefully upstairs. Mikal, Alze, and several others were gathered in what was going to become a schoolroom.

"I'm Sara," she announced when they looked up in surprise. She came forward. She picked up a quill from the table, dipped it in ink, and wrote a slogan in large letters on a piece of paper. The men stared while she stuck the paper onto a nail in the wall. "What we have to do," she said, turning back to the wide-eyed gathering, "is educate our kids, train them for jobs, get rid of the outdated tax structure, reorganize the military and health-care systems, and overthrow the mad duke. Let's get started. Any questions?"

It took her a while to get them to listen to her, then act on her ideas. Eventually she said to Mikal, "I'll be back."

Then she said, "Hit it," to the ring, and found herself in a familiar hallway in the nursery section of the palace. She blinked dizzily, and put her hand against the wall for support. "Rough landing," she said. She heard a door open across the hall from her.

"Sara!" Denise called out as she looked up. The governess hurried to her. "Are you feeling well?"

Sara straightened and gave her friend a reassuring smile. "I'm fine."

"What an odd costume," Denise said as she stepped back to look at her. "Do you have to play at one of the duke's silly midnight masquerades?"

"Yes," Sara agreed quickly. "Yes, I do."

"What a shame. You must be tired. And I was looking forward to a chat with you over warm cocoa."

Sara smiled. "But we couldn't have the chat, anyway," she told Denise. At the other woman's curious look she went on. "Stefan stopped me as I came up to change," she extemporized. "He asked me to ask you to meet him on the roof."

"The roof? Are you sure you heard him correctly?"

Sara gave her skeptical friend a conspiratorial smile. "Oh, yes. I think he wants to have you alone for once. You two hardly ever have a chance for a little private romance."

Denise nodded slowly. "That is true. The roof." A smile lit her violet-blue eyes. "How wickedly improper. I'll fetch my cloak."

"Good," Sara said once she was alone in the hall. "Lewis now has someone to help him find me. I don't have to worry about him getting caught. What was he doing on the roof, anyway?"

"Walking a very fine line," the ring answered. "A

cold, dangerous one. Let's get out of here, shall we?"

She knew the ring wasn't going to explain any further. She'd ask Lewis when she saw him again. "Anything else? Are all the loose ends tied up now?"

"All anomalies now accounted for," the ring answered.

"Great. Get me back to Lewis," she ordered.

"Not quite yet."

Before she could ask she was back in Mala's tent at the Renaissance Faire. She looked like her twentieth-century self again.

"What the—!"

"Just one more little thing." The ring cut off her protest. "You have to go back to the body you left at the execution."

"Of course I do," she agreed. "I've got a kid to look after."

"So this Sara has to be left behind again."

Sara sat down on the piled pillows. "What happens to this body when I go back? What happens to me?" she asked, remembering that she was the person she was leaving behind. "You've been through this all before," she realized. "You know."

"I know that you and Lewis live happily ever after. At least you'll grow happily old together and be smothered in many grandchildren. Then—"

"Yes?" she prompted.

"Sara and Lewis Morgan will fade into legend. You will wake up at the Renaissance Faire."

"In this body?"

"Yes."

"Then what? Will she—I—think it was all a dream?"

"No. You'll remember."

"But . . . What about Lewis? I want to be with Lewis."

"Your own true love, you mean?" -

"Yeah. The guy back at the firing squad."

"You will find your own true love again." For once the ring sounded serious instead of sarcastic. "Don't worry. It's meant to be. Speaking of the firing squad," it added, "we'd better go."

Lewis hardly noticed the sound of gunfire as Sara's limp weight pulled him to the ground, saving him from the salvo fired by the firing squad. While bullets passed over his head to ricochet off the wall behind them he flattened himself against his wife's lifeless body.

It was a futile protective gesture. She was already dead.

He could sense no spirit animating her small, delicate form. One moment she had been smiling into his eyes; then everything that made her Sara flicked away, like a candle being carelessly blown out. He cursed the inefficiency of the executioners who had left him to suffer even a few moments without her.

He heard the commander shout the order to reload.

In the distance other voices shouted. Many voices. The cobblestones beneath him rumbled with the echo of many running feet. Lewis, vision strained with tears, looked up as a mob roared into the square before the palace. Some members of the mob halted, raising British-made rifles to aim at the firing squad.

Shots rang out; gun smoke filled the morning air. The soldiers, still reloading, were instantly overwhelmed. Lewis saw Beng and Mikal and Captain Rudeseko in the forefront of the triumphant crowd. The palace guard appeared, not to put down the riot, but to join it. The mercenaries left in the square ran for their lives.

The revolution, it seemed, had begun. Rescue was at hand. Lewis didn't care. Sara was dead. He sat on the ground and cradled her in his arms as Beng came running up to them.

"We did it, my fine young *rom baro!*" Beng called out triumphantly. "What's wrong with that lazy wife of yours?" he asked on a deep laugh. "Sleeping through her own rescue?"

"No," Lewis choked out as Beng squatted on his heel beside him. He brushed his hand across her hair. Curls twined around his fingers with a life of their own. "She's—"

"Heavy," Sara complained as she stiffened in his grasp. Small hands pushed against his chest. "Come on, move, hon, you're heavy." Sara opened her eyes as he stared at her in aching wonder. Her smile brought him back to life. "Hi."

Somehow, someway, she was back. She had been gone. He had felt her wrenched away from him, felt it in the part of his soul firmly and permanently attached to his lovely Rom wife. She was back, and he was whole again.

"But—"

She grabbed his hair and pulled him into a kiss before he could say anything else. "Shameless," he heard his father-in-law complain before he was lost to the sensual heat only Sara could arouse in him. The kiss might have gone on forever. It might have gone on for only a few moments. He was left grinning with delight, and aching for more when Sara pushed him away.

"We'll continue this later," she promised him.

"At great length," he promised her.

"For the rest of our lives. Now let's wipe these silly smiles off our faces and get to work."

He nodded, and helped Sara to her feet. They couldn't help but embrace and start kissing again.

"Do you mind?" the ring shouted, so loud they both heard it. "You're not the only ones with an own true love, you know."

"Right," Sara said to it. She took Lewis by the hand. "We'd better go rescue the ruby from the mad duke." He nodded his agreement. He was happy to go with her anywhere. "What is with you and that brooch?" she asked the ring.

"That," the ring told them, "is another story."

She didn't say anything more to the ring. She turned her attention to Lewis, who put his arm around her waist. She touched the slight swelling at her abdomen. He put his hand tenderly over hers. He smiled at the thought of his soon-to-be son, and at the teasing light in her eyes.

"So," she asked as they began to follow the mob into the palace, "what do you think of naming the kid Richie?"

"No."

COMING NEXT MONTH

CHEYENNE AMBER by Catherine Anderson

From the bestselling author of the Comanche Trilogy and *Coming Up Roses* comes a dramatic western set in the Colorado Territory. Under normal circumstances, Laura Cheney would never have fallen in love with a rough-edged tracker. But when her infant son was kidnapped by Comancheros, she had no choice but to hire Deke Sheridan. *"Cheyenne Amber* is vivid, unforgettable, and thoroughly marvelous."—Elizabeth Lowell

MOMENTS by Georgia Bockoven

A heartwarming new novel from the author of *A Marriage of Convenience* and *The Way It Should Have Been*. Elizabeth and Amado Montoyas' happy marriage is short-lived when he inexplicably begins to pull away from her. Hurt and bewildered, she turns to Michael Logan, a man Amado thinks of as a son. Now Elizabeth is torn between two men she loves—and hiding a secret that could destroy her world forever.

TRAITOROUS HEARTS by Susan Kay Law

As the American Revolution erupted around them, Elizabeth "Bennie" Jones, the patriotic daughter of a colonial tavern owner, and Jon Leighton, a British soldier, fell desperately in love, in spite of their differences. But when Jon began to question the loyalties of her family, Bennie was torn between duty and family, honor and passion.

THE VOW by Mary Spencer

A medieval love story of a damsel in distress and her questionable knight in shining armor. Beautiful Lady Margot le Brun, the daughter of a well-landed lord, had loved Sir Eric Stavelot, a famed knight of the realm, ever since she was a child and was determined to marry him. But Eric would have none of her, fearing that secrets regarding his birth would ultimately destroy them.

MANTRAP by Louise Titchener

When Sally Dunphy's ex-boyfriend kills himself, she is convinced that there was foul play involved. She teams up with a gorgeous police detective, Duke Spikowski, and discovers suspicious goings-on surprisingly close to home. An exciting, new romantic suspense from the bestselling author of *Homebody*.

GHOSTLY ENCHANTMENT by Angie Ray

With a touch of magic, a dash of humor, and a lot of romance, an enchanting ghost story about a proper miss, her nerdy fiancé, and a debonair ghost. When Margaret Westbourne met Phillip Eglinton, she never realized a man could be so exciting, so dashing, and so . . . dead. For the first time, Margaret began to question whether she should listen to her heart and look for love instead of marrying dull, insect-loving Bernard.

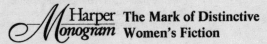 **Harper Monogram** The Mark of Distinctive Women's Fiction

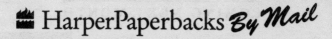

YESTERDAY'S SHADOWS
by Marianne Willman

Bettany Howard was a young orphan traveling west searching for the father who left her years ago. Wolf Star was a Cheyenne brave who longed to know who abandoned him—a white child with a jeweled talisman. Fate decreed they'd meet and try to seize the passion promised. 0-06-104044-4

MIDNIGHT ROSE by Patricia Hagan

From the rolling plantations of Richmond to the underground slave movement of Philadelphia, Erin Sterling and Ryan Youngblood would pursue their wild, breathless passion and finally surrender to the promise of a bold and unexpected love. 0-06-104023-1

WINTER TAPESTRY
by Kathy Lynn Emerson

Cordell vows to revenge the murder of her father. Roger Allington is honor bound to protect his friend's daughter but has no liking for her reckless ways. Yet his heart tells him he must pursue this beauty through a maze of plots to win her love and ignite their smoldering passion.
0-06-100220-8